**Pra[illegible]**
**Allie Be[illegible]**
***Magic i[illegible]***

"Ms. Monk sweeps readers up in the drama and dangers of the heroine's life as it steadily changes and grows. *Magic in the Shadows* is an intriguing read with fascinating characters and new magical elements introduced to the mix." —Darque Reviews

"Delicious . . . action-packed, and full of magic, this series is really starting to hit the Kim Harrison and Kelley Armstrong level. Deep, dark, and addictive with a great leading lady. . . . Once you start reading, you won't be able to stop. Give Devon Monk a chance and try the Allie Beckstrom series. You will not be disappointed." —Amberkatze's Book Blog

"Mystery, romance, and magic cobbled together in what amounts to a solid page-turner." —SFFWorld

"[This] series is one of my favorites . . . a well-written story with likable and realistic characters. *Magic in the Shadows* is a fun urban fantasy with strong world building and characters readers can enjoy following." —BSCreview

***Magic in the Blood***

"Tight, fast, and vividly drawn . . . features fresh interpretations of the paranormal, strong characters dealing with their share of faults and flaws, and ghoulish plot twists. Fans of Patricia Briggs or Jim Butcher will want to check out this inventive new voice." —Monsters and Critics

"Ms. Monk weaves a unique tale of dark magic that will keep readers at the edge of their seat[s]. *Magic in the Blood* is so thoroughly described that the creepy bits will have you thinking of magic and ghosts long after you've finished the story. Fast moving and gripping, it will leave you wanting more." —Darque Reviews

"One heck of a ride through a magical, dangerous Portland . . . imaginative, gritty, sometimes darkly humorous. . . . An unputdownable book, *Magic in the Blood* is one fantastic read." —Romance Reviews Today

"[A] highly creative series about magic users in a world much like our own, filled with greed and avarice. I love the character of Allie and she is just getting better and stronger as the series continues. . . . If you love action, magic, intrigue, good-versus-evil battles, and pure entertainment, you will not want to miss this series." —Manic Readers

*continued . . .*

## *Magic to the Bone*

"Loved it. Fiendishly original and a stay-up-all-night read. We're going to be hearing a lot more of Devon Monk."

—Patricia Briggs, *New York Times* bestselling author of *Bone Crossed*

"Gritty setting, compelling, fully realized characters, and a frightening system of magic-with-a-price that left me awed."

—Rachel Vincent, *New York Times* bestselling author of *Shift*

"Highly original and compulsively readable. Don't pick this one up before going to bed unless you want to be up all night!"

—Jenna Black, author of *The Devil's Playground*

"An exciting new addition to the urban fantasy genre. It's got a truly fresh take on magic and Allie Beckstrom is one kick-ass protagonist!"

—Jeanne C. Stein, national bestselling author of *Retribution*

"The prose is gritty and urban, the characters mysterious and marvelous, and Monk creates a fantastic and original magic system that intrigues and excites. A promising beginning to a new series. I'm looking forward to more."

—Nina Kiriki Hoffman, Bram Stoker Award–winning author of *Thresholds*

"Monk's reimagined Portland is at once recognizable and exotic, suffused with her special take on magic, and her characters are vividly rendered. The plot pulled me in for a very enjoyable ride!"

—Lynn Flewelling, author of *The White Road*

"Clever and compulsively readable.... Allie's internal and external struggles are brilliantly and tightly written, creating a multifaceted character who will surprise, amuse, amaze, and absorb readers." —*Publishers Weekly* (starred review)

"Devon Monk has created a cool new heroine in Allie Beckstrom.... She has developed a system of magic that is intriguing and distinct from those filling urban fantasies by the score.... With a strong heroine, a great setting, and an interesting new system of magic, *Magic to the Bone* is likely to give urban fantasy readers more of what they want: a worthy read. Recommended." —SFRevu

"Devon Monk is casting a spell on the fantasy world.... Allie is a convincing, street-smart heroine.... Monk has done an outstanding job creating a gritty, authentic-feeling urban fantasy on par with Rob Thurman or John Levitt. It should be interesting to watch how this series develops." —Monsters and Critics

"With style and a magical world that is quite fresh, Monk explodes on the scene and makes a few waves. . . . For sheer guts, stubbornness, and determination, they don't come much feistier than Allie."
—*Romantic Times*

"Monk makes a grand entrance with her debut novel, captivating readers with a well-imagined tale of magic and suspense. *Magic to the Bone* delves into a dark-edged magic and adds a touch of romance that keeps the heroine more human than those around her. I'm looking forward to seeing where the next portion of Allie's journey takes her."
—Darque Reviews

"An intelligent, entertaining mystery. The kick-butt heroine is strong and independent. . . . Exciting fun, readers will look forward to more adventures of Allie."
—Genre Go Round Reviews

"The characters are anything but stereotypical. They defy expectations and truly come alive on the page. The use of magic in here is new and fantastically riveting. The plot is complex and wonderful, with excellent twists and turns. The not-particularly-explicit sex scenes are searingly hot in an unusually 'real' kind of way, and the emotions are incredibly poignant. Simply put, I can't do this book justice. You'll have to read it for yourself."
—Errant Dreams Reviews

"*Magic to the Bone* is a breath of fresh air in the urban fantasy genre, in much the same way that Ilona Andrews's Kate Daniels series is a breath of fresh air. Instead of the same tired werewolf/vampire soap opera that so many novels perpetuate, *Magic to the Bone* is more concerned with the ramifications of adding magic to modern society and exploring the realistic consequences . . . an exciting and often poignant story. . . . Devon Monk shows the potential to be a standout writer in the subgenre. Most importantly, I could not put this book down; I read it in two nights, with only work and sleep coming between me and the pages. Well done."
—Fantasy Literature

"A unique character, her interior quips are humorous. . . . The humor blends with the drama to make it stronger. Devon Monk has created some fantastic characters to inhabit her suspenseful story. The ending indicates this might be the beginning of a series, which is wonderful, because the story is as addictive as the use of magic, earning *Magic to the Bone* a perfect ten."
—Romance Reviews Today

Also by Devon Monk

*Magic to the Bone*
*Magic in the Blood*
*Magic in the Shadows*
*Magic on the Storm*

# Magic at the Gate

Devon Monk

A ROC BOOK

ROC
Published by New American Library, a division of
Penguin Group (USA) Inc., 375 Hudson Street,
New York, New York 10014, USA
Penguin Group (Canada), 90 Eglinton Avenue East, Suite 700, Toronto,
Ontario M4P 2Y3, Canada (a division of Pearson Penguin Canada Inc.)
Penguin Books Ltd., 80 Strand, London WC2R 0RL, England
Penguin Ireland, 25 St. Stephen's Green, Dublin 2,
Ireland (a division of Penguin Books Ltd.)
Penguin Group (Australia), 250 Camberwell Road, Camberwell, Victoria 3124,
Australia (a division of Pearson Australia Group Pty. Ltd.)
Penguin Books India Pvt. Ltd., 11 Community Centre, Panchsheel Park,
New Delhi - 110 017, India
Penguin Group (NZ), 67 Apollo Drive, Rosedale, North Shore 0632,
New Zealand (a division of Pearson New Zealand Ltd.)
Penguin Books (South Africa) (Pty.) Ltd., 24 Sturdee Avenue,
Rosebank, Johannesburg 2196, South Africa

Penguin Books Ltd., Registered Offices:
80 Strand, London WC2R 0RL, England

First published by Roc, an imprint of New American Library,
a division of Penguin Group (USA) Inc.

First Printing, November 2010
10 9 8 7 6 5 4 3 2 1



Printed in the United States of America

*For my family*

# Acknowledgments

Without the many people who have contributed time and energy along the way, this book would not have come to fruition. Thank you to my agent, Miriam Kriss, and my editor, Anne Sowards, two consummate professionals and awesome people who make my job easy.

All my love and gratitude to my fantastic first readers, Dean Woods, Dejsha Knight, and Dianna Rodgers, whose loving support and brilliant insights not only make the story stronger, but also make me a better writer. Thank you also to my family, one and all, who have been there for me every step of the way, offering unfailing encouragement and sharing in the joy. And to my husband, Russ, and sons, Kameron and Konner. You are the very best part of my life—I couldn't do this without you.

Lastly, thank you, dear readers, for letting me share this story and this world with you.

# Chapter One

Sure, love can make a person do crazy things. But not me. No, never me. Still, there was nothing else to explain the fact that I had ended up in a battle between magic users over the disks my father invented while a wild-magic storm tried to kill us all. There was nothing else but love that would make me turn away from my injured, possibly dying friends, and step through a gate into death with no one beside me but my undead father and my gargoyle. Nothing but love would make me leave this world to bring Zayvion Jones' soul back from death.

I suppose if I had never met Zayvion Jones, none of this would have happened. Man had a knack for messing up my life. Truth was, I liked it. He'd probably say the same about me, if he weren't in a coma.

As I took that first step off of the grass of Cathedral Park, and through the gate into death, I braced for pain. I'd never stepped into death before, but I figured it was going to sting a little.

No. A pause of breath, then cool, soothing numbness settled over me, whisking my pain away. I had never felt better.

As soon as I put my foot down into death, that sense of well-being was gone, replaced with a sense of foreboding.

Death itself had seen better days. Vacant, crumbling

buildings, and slick pools of black oil stretched out along the sidewalk of what I was pretty sure was supposed to be West Burnside Street. The city—and it was very clear we were in some twisted version of Portland—looked like a dump. If this was death, I wanted to meet the marketing team that had dreamed up both the fluffy-cloud, golden harp thing and the eternal fires of burning hell shtick.

This place was broken and empty. Achingly so.

"Allison?" my father, who had his hand on my arm, said.

He was fully solid, no longer ghostlike. A little taller than me, gray hair, wearing a business suit with a lavender handkerchief in the pocket. Death didn't seem to bother him one bit.

And it shouldn't. He belonged here.

He squeezed my arm, his eyes flicking back and forth, searching the details of my face. "Can you breathe?"

Of all the dumb questions. "Of course I can breathe. Let go of me."

His lips pressed together in a thin line and the familiar anger clouded his eyes. He pulled his hand away from my arm.

There was no air. No air in my lungs and none to breathe. I tried not to panic, but hey, this was death. I'd be lucky to get out of here alive. And I had to get out of here alive. Zayvion was here, pushed through a gate by his ex-girlfriend Chase, and her ex–Soul Complement, Greyson. Zay's body was in a coma, but his soul was here. Somewhere.

This was my one chance—my only chance—to save him. I didn't think anyone got to walk into and out of death twice. I was just praying that Zayvion and I got to do it once. The very real danger of never feeling his touch or hearing his voice while those dark, beautiful eyes looked into me, suddenly sank in. The possibility of never being able to find Zay's soul set off a sharp panic in my chest.

Well, that and not being able to breathe.

Dad put his left hand in his pocket, tucking something away. Then he crossed his arms over his chest and watched me gasp. Stone cold, that man.

I shut my mouth and glared. I would not reach out for his help. Yes, I was that stubborn. My vision darkened at the edges.

Could you pass out in death? I was about to find out.

Stone growled and stepped toward Dad, fangs bared. That's a good gargoyle. Take a bite out of Daddy for me.

Stone's normally dark gray body was now black, shot through with lightning flecks of blues and greens and pink, like obsidian with opal running beneath the glassy surface. He practically shone, his eyes glowing deep amber. Death didn't seem to be bothering him, which wasn't all that strange, since he was made out of rock and magic, and wasn't actually "alive" in the traditional sense.

"Touch the Animate," Dad said. "You should be able to breathe again."

It was beginning to dawn on me that passing out and leaving my dad conscious might be a really stupid idea. I put my hand on Stone's head. Air, good—well, if not good, serviceable—air filled my lungs. I hacked like a smoker on a three-day bender. My lungs *hurt.*

"You are in death." Dad hit lecture mode from word one. "A living being crossing into death. There is so little chance you could have survived that, Allison. No one can step into death if they are fully alive. And yet, here you stand." His gaze searched my face. "What part of you is dead, my daughter?"

I didn't know—my sense of humor maybe? My tolerance for his possession of me? Or maybe I could walk into death because my Soul Complement was in a coma and his soul was already here. Right now, I was too busy coughing and trying to breathe to get all philosophical.

He shook his head, dismissing the question as easily as he had always dismissed me. "To survive this place, you will need to stay in contact with something that is neither fully alive nor completely dead. Something that exists in a between state, like the Animate."

"Stone." I finally managed to exhale. "He has a name."

"Yes, Stone. He will act as a filter between life and death, and if you stay in contact with him, he will bear the brunt of the effects of death. But not for very long."

"You're dead," I said. "All dead. Why could I breathe when you touched me?"

"That answer is complicated. It involves choices I made years ago." He looked up and down the street, then at the building next to us as if getting his bearings. He started down the street.

I followed him, Stone somehow sensing the need to stay under my hand. There was no one on the streets with us, no wind, no rain. When I glanced up, it was nothing but terracotta sky and hard, white light.

"Tell me you're dead," I said.

"Very much so. That doesn't mean I'm not without resources in life."

Which meant part of him, some of him somewhere, was alive. Great. I did not trust my dad. I never had. For good reason. And that very calm, trustworthy face he was wearing made me twitchy.

"Where are you alive? Why?" I asked. "Who's helping you?"

He glanced back over his shoulder. "If I tell you those things, you will be at risk."

"I'm already at risk. I've been at risk from the moment I was accused of your murder. Probably before then. And now I'm in death. How can I be at more at risk than that?"

"If you walk away from this, out of death and into life

again with information you should not have, you will end up back here. Permanently. My plans are not your concern."

"Yes, they are. What is your angle in all this, Dad? I've lost track of whose side you're on."

"I am on magic's side. To see that it falls into the right hands. Magic was once whole—light and dark used equally through the disciplines of Life, Death, Faith, and Blood. But when Leander and Isabelle became Soul Complements, everything changed. Magic was too dangerous to be used in its full form, and magic was broken.

"Guardians of the gates, such as Zayvion, are trained to endure the strain of wielding light and dark magic for short periods of time. No one else. But separating light magic from dark magic hasn't made anything better. I've been trying to tell the Authority that for years. The separation has caused a rot in our world, and has given the Veiled and other creatures cause to seek out the living in search of the light magic they hunger for."

That was more than I'd gotten out of him in months, maybe years. Death made him talkative. Good. I planned to use that to my advantage. "So why are you getting involved? You're dead. Why worry about the living?"

He gave me a look that could melt rock. "My motives are not yours to question."

"I'll question your motives until the day I die. Again. For reals."

"This is real," he said quietly. "Very real. If you are to survive, you need to put your stubbornness aside and listen to me."

"Oh, I just love that idea."

"Love it or not, your options are limited. Living flesh does not travel well in the world of death. I believe if you stay in contact with the Animate, it will filter the . . . irritants of death long enough for you to accomplish your task."

He made it sound like he was teaching me the ABC's and knew there was no way I'd ever make it to Q.

He stopped, glanced back down the street the way we'd come. "Faster would be better." He grabbed my arm and propelled me down an alley. I shook free, my other hand still on Stone's head, and looked over my shoulder.

Watercolor people, about a dozen or so, mostly men, wearing clothing in the style of the recent century. The Veiled were the ghosts of powerful magic users—or at least pieces of powerful magic users—impressed on the flow of magic. Zay had once told me to think of them as a recording of a life caught on the film of magic.

I think he was wrong. These did not look like the nice kind of Veiled. Unlike the other Veiled I had seen in life, these ghostly beings barely resembled people. Twisted bodies, sagging faces—they looked like movie zombies more than ghosts. They also looked solid.

And hungry.

Stone growled.

The Veiled heard him and turned our way, sniffing, scenting, crooked hands tracing half-formed glyphs, as if they could use magic to find us.

"Veiled?" I asked, just in case the mutated watercolor people were something else.

"Quiet," Dad said.

Stone's ears flattened. He stopped making noise, but his lips were pulled back to expose a row of sharp teeth and fangs.

Dad traced a glyph in the air and magic followed in a solid gold line at his fingertips. I wasn't using Sight, yet magic was clearly visible. That wasn't how it worked in life. Magic was too fast to be visible. Here, it was slow and fluid and gorgeous.

I hadn't seen him set a Disbursement, nor a Proxy. He was bearing the price of pain for using this magic.

He finished the glyph. Camouflage glittered in the air like a filigreed screen. He whispered a word and the glyph stretched and widened, creating a swirling shell around us. I swallowed, but couldn't taste the butterscotch scent of the spell. That was different than in life too. Magic didn't smell or taste here.

Or maybe I just wasn't dead enough to sense it.

The Veiled were almost at the mouth of the alley.

"This way," Dad whispered. He rolled his fingers, catching up the lines of the Camouflage glyph and balancing it on his open palm. He pushed his palm outward like a waiter carrying a tray, and the spell moved with us, keeping us hidden.

Impressive.

Dad's mouth set in a hard line and his eyes narrowed. Clearly, casting magic in death and maintaining the spell cost pain. Well, at least something about magic was the same. Dad stormed down the alleyway—not once looking back—strong, confident.

And for a second, just a second, I saw my dad as a heroic figure. The epitome of what a magic user should be. The mythic wizard who knew the hidden strengths of magic, in life or death, and the power of his own soul. Even in death, my dad stood tall and kicked ass.

"Walk or be eaten," he said.

Okay, so much for the hero bit.

I picked up the pace and Stone padded along beside me. I didn't have a clue where we were going, but Dad seemed to know the place a lot better than I did.

The Veiled stepped into the alley behind us and shuffled over to where we'd been standing. They didn't follow any farther. Four dropped to their knees, patting the sidewalk as if they'd just lost something, while the other eight ran hands along the brick walls, mouths open. They leaned against the building and sucked at the walls, as if they were starving for even the slightest drop of magic they might contain. The dead were hungry for light magic. I didn't see how this could turn out well.

It creeped me out. I walked faster, holding tight to Stone's ear.

"I did not want to enter this way," Dad said, "but bringing you along has changed my approach. Why must you challenge me in every way, Allison?"

"I'd be happy to help," I said as pleasantly as I could muster, "if you'd tell me where Zayvion's soul is so I can take him, and me, the hell out of here."

He stopped. We were at the far end of the alley. A crowd of mutant Veiled blocked our passage—I gave up counting at twenty. A mix of men and women, they stared at us as if they could see right through the Camouflage my dad still held.

That wasn't good.

I put my hand on the hilt of Zayvion's katana, sheathed on my back.

"Don't draw the blade."

There wasn't a lot of room in the alley. I was behind Dad. I didn't know how he'd seen me reach for the sword.

"I'm not going to wait until they jump us."

And just like that, the Veiled rushed.

"Do you trust me?" Dad asked without looking back.

"No."

"That's unfortunate."

My dad broke the Camouflage spell, and I mean it shattered like glass exploding, gold ribbons and sharp edges falling *through* me, but not hurting, not drawing blood, then spreading out across the broken concrete at our feet to be sucked down into the cracks as if the magic had never been there.

The Veiled were almost on us. They were fast, fast, fast.

Dad spun, his back to the Veiled. He stuck his hands into my chest.

Wrist deep. Into. My. Chest.

It hurt. I inhaled. Exhaled. Yelled. Couldn't move to draw the sword, draw a spell, draw a breath.

Stone launched at him out from under my hand. Then I couldn't breathe even more.

Dad was fast. He yanked his hands free, pulling magic, pink and silver and black, out of my chest and pointing at Stone, who halted in his tracks and stepped on my foot with his back paw, so I had at least some contact. Dad carved a glyph out of the magic, my magic—a metallic sparking fireball—and threw it at the Veiled.

The explosion lit the street and slapped hard shadows across the alley.

The Veiled screamed. An unholy sound that echoed out and out and seemed to reflect off of the sky as if it were a low ceiling. It was too big of a sound, too much of a sound, in too small of a place.

Their scream vibrated somewhere deep inside of me where I couldn't get away from it, making their pain a part of me, as my magic was now a part of them.

No, no, no.

I reached for Stone, for my dad, for anyone, anything to hold on to to make this stop. Then Dad was in front of me, his hand over the old bullet scar just below my collarbone.

"Breathe, Allison, breathe."

I gasped. Got some air down. Tasted something sweet against my tongue, and the cool, rough bricks of the building against my back.

"What. The. Hell," I said.

"Light and dark magic, through Death magic," he said evenly, not moving away from me. "Death magic always takes a transference of energy. I took from the Life magic within you, and now I give you back the magic of death."

So that was the bluish glow coming from his hand.

"Wait. What? You are not putting dead magic in me." I pushed at his hands, but it didn't do much good. I was very, very tired and he didn't seem to have any problem keeping me pinned against the wall.

Why was I so tired?

Could it be because I was in death? And my father had just ripped magic out of my chest? And right before that, back in life, I'd Grounded a wild-magic storm and fought a bunch of crazy magic users, all the while killing nightmarish creatures while trying to save my friends' lives?

Yes. That was probably it. I'd had a hell of a day and the adrenaline of the battlefield was wearing off, leaving behind the very real horror of what had happened.

Zayvion was in a coma. Shame had almost died on the battlefield, trying to save his mother, Maeve. For all I knew, the crystal I gave to Terric to try to keep Shame from bleeding out had been only a temporary reprieve.

Jingo Jingo, who had been a trusted member of the Authority and a teacher of Death magic, had betrayed everyone, nearly killing Shame's mother. Jingo Jingo had kidnapped Sedra, the head of the Authority, and used my dad's disks to disappear with her.

Magic users had turned against magic users in a battle that had left several dead. The Authority wasn't cracking; it had broken. Sides had been taken. The war was on.

Whoever came out on top would rule how magic was used by the common citizen, and by the Authority. Whoever came out on top would control all the magic that the public knew about, and worse, all the ways magic could be used that they didn't know about.

The winners would have say over what technology was allowed to be developed to use with magic, how doctors could use magic, how politicians could use magic, how corporations could use magic. They would decide what every person could learn about magic. And they could kill anyone who stood in their way. There was a lot of power at stake here. Plenty enough to kill for.

And I was here, dead. With no one but my gargoylc and my Dad to help me find a soul for my lover, and the way home for me. Where were my ruby slippers when I needed them?

I had to find Zayvion soon. Yes, because I loved him. But also so we would have a fighting chance to stop the war. There was a city full of people who didn't deserve to die because a few secret magic users had suddenly become power hungry. I might not agree with everything the Authority did, but at least their tenet required that they keep magic safe and people unharmed from using it. That was worth fighting for.

"I'm not putting dead magic inside you." Dad's voice was gentle. He shifted so he wasn't pressing so hard on my collarbone. "I'm giving back the magic I used in a slightly different form. They won't be able to see you here now—or at least you won't stand out like a burning torch. It's the best protection I can give you."

"Don't," I said. But he ignored me like he always ignored me, and didn't move his hand. I was feeling better, stronger. Like I'd just taken a long crawl through the desert and he was tipping a cup of cool water to my lips.

That sort of kindness did not make sense coming from him. I couldn't look in his eyes, didn't want to see the concern there. He was a confusing man. I liked it better when I could just hate him and not have to think he was capable of compassion. So I gazed past him, toward the end of the alley.

The watercolor people walked past the mouth of the alley, smiling, and paying no attention to us.

Weird. They looked like normal men and women. No longer twisted and zombielike, they moved down the street as if they were out shopping, going to work, enjoying the first day of spring after a hard winter.

They looked like they had been healed.

"What did you do?" I whispered. "What did you do to them?"

Dad took a deep breath and finally pulled away. His hand, when he straightened his jacket, trembled a little.

Stone, who had been grumbling like a bag of rocks in a washing machine, stepped up to me and leaned against my leg. That was nice. Since my dad wasn't touching me, I needed Stone to breathe.

"I took an educated risk with magic and saved your life. Again."

Oh, he had not just used that tone of voice. I glared. "You took my magic and used it without my consent."

"*Your* magic?" He shook his head. "I thought you'd be pleased. The magic you carry healed them, restored them to a balance of light magic and dark magic together. It is how magic is meant to be. One. Whole. Not separated into two forms."

"You will never again take my magic. For anything or anyone," I said. "Understand?"

I pushed off the wall and strode past him to the edge of the alley. Stone paced me, a solid, breathable buddy. Not for a minute would I believe my dad was doing me favors. There was a reason he had agreed to let me step into death with him. There was a reason he hadn't let me get eaten by the Veiled. He wanted immortality. And I was pretty sure he wanted to be the one who came out on top of this war, with magic ending up in his hands and him having final say over how it was used.

Yeah, well, I wasn't going to let him use me in the process.

Except I had a problem. I had no idea how to find

Zayvion. Just because we were Soul Complements didn't mean I could find him in death. Right now, even the idea of touching the magic inside of me that Dad had messed with made me want to throw up. So Hounding was out.

My dad told me he knew where to find Zay. Which meant I had to cooperate with him.

I stepped up to the mouth of the alley. Watercolor people walked by, stopped to talk to one another, though I could not hear their words. They didn't seem to notice I was there. At all.

I waved my hand. Nothing. Not even a glance. I was a ghost to them just as they had been ghosts to me in life.

Dad stopped next to me. "You have always underestimated your natural ability," he said, with a tone I could not place. "Do you see what we have accomplished together? The healing of souls with the magic you carry. We have healed souls in death. With light and dark magic."

"We? No, you stuck your hands in my chest and stole my magic and threw it at them. If you try that again, you won't have hands. Where's Zayvion?"

Okay, maybe I was a little rusty on the whole cooperation thing.

"Where did I go wrong with you?"

"You never listened to me, to what I needed from a . . . from a father. You never once had time for me. Not even when Mom left and I thought my whole damn world was going to end."

He pulled back, surprised. I didn't bother to hope he felt something else, like regret or guilt or shame. No, those emotions were beyond my father. He wasn't built with that kind of heart.

"Allison, I have always cared for you and I have tried—"

"Where's Zayvion?" I repeated.

He held my gaze a moment, while we both decided if we were going to let my little emotional outburst slide.

"There is a man we must meet," he said, letting me win the unspoken argument. "He will take us to Zayvion's soul."

He started walking. I swallowed my anger until I didn't feel like yelling. After a few seconds, I followed him.

The street was black and white cobbles; the buildings rose above us like stone red castle walls, turrets at each corner.

No cars. The street wasn't wide enough for cars. I didn't see any functioning technology at all. Sure, there were streetlights, gothic iron-worked lanterns that blazed with multicolored flames behind thick glass shades. But no electricity, or motor-powered thing in sight.

We crossed the street, maybe east. I was pretty turned around. A building that resembled a medieval version of the Schnitzer Concert Hall was on our left. The Portland sign hung there, burning with flames of magic instead of electric lights.

I glanced at the sky. No sun. Just a hard white light that melted into brittle candy colors against the black shadows at the horizon. I hadn't expected death to look like this, to so closely resemble the living world and yet be so foreign. I wondered if the other souls here were happy, if maybe there were nice suburbs with heated pools and countrysides with ghost cows and ghost chickens and ghost people raising ghost crops.

"What man are we meeting? Is he one of the Veiled?"

"There are other beings in death than the Veiled. Souls who exist here."

"Like you?"

"Very much so."

Since he was being talkative again, I decided to try to get a little more information out of him.

"Aren't you a Veiled now?"

"Technically. Most Veiled are only a fraction of a living person—the part of them that paid the price for using magic, played out like a film with just a flicker of the soul to light it. An echo."

"Echoes don't attack people."

That got a tight smile out of him. "The Veiled have not always wandered the world attacking people. When light magic and dark magic were one, the Veiled were more like ghosts, and could be summoned and asked for specific knowledge. Our history is rich because of it."

"Why hasn't anyone put light and dark magic back together? It'd get rid of the Veiled, right?"

He shrugged. "Some of us have tried and failed. Some of us haven't given up trying."

The walk felt like an uphill chug. Even with my hand on Stone's head, I wasn't getting enough air to fill my lungs. "What has to be done to fix it?"

"Someone has to contain it."

"Come again?"

"There must be a Focal to contain both light and dark magic."

"And no one wants the job?"

"Anyone who's tried it has died."

"Zayvion can wield dark and light magic."

"For brief amounts of time, without going insane or losing control, yes. The Focal must hold magic, light and dark, together long enough for it to mend."

"How long does it take to mend?"

"No one's survived long enough for us to know."

I could see why people weren't rushing to volunteer.

"We're almost there." He pointed. "Just a little farther, by the river."

If we stepped through the gate in St. Johns, I wondered if he meant the Willamette River.

"Are we in St. Johns?"

"We're in death. The two worlds do not directly align.

That makes navigation . . . difficult. And there is a perceived misalignment in time."

"Time? What? How long have we been here?"

"That is not—" He glanced up suddenly.

I didn't hear anything, even with my good ears. Stone didn't react either. He just kept walking smooth and steady, growling so softly it was a comforting purr under my palm.

"I believe," Dad said, "we've arrived."

We were at the corner of the street. Gothic high-rises stacked to our right and left. A few more steps and the city opened up, revealing a river as wide as the Willamette, but filled with fast-flowing black water. Beneath the water flashed ribbons of magic, metallic rainbows and jagged lines, sparking and weaving glyphs that disappeared as soon as they were formed, like fish nipping the surface of the water.

"The Willamette?" I asked, because it didn't look like the river. "The Columbia?"

"The Rift between life and death, light and dark," my father said.

"Exactly," my father said.

Whoa.

I looked away from the river. My dad stood beside me. And standing beside him, was my dad.

That dad, the second version of him, looked younger than the dad who had crossed into death with me. New Dad had jet-black hair without a trace of gray, and instead of wearing a business suit, he wore black casual slacks and a black dress shirt.

"Daniel," New Dad said. "This is interesting."

"Daniel." Old Dad nodded. "Different than I imagined."

"Isn't it?" New Dad said.

Then they both smiled the exact same smile. Narcissism times two.

Oh, get a room already.

"It is good to see you, Allison," New Dad said.

I'd been standing there like an idiot. One dad was more than enough for me. Especially on a stroll through death when he'd already gotten grabby with my magic. Two dads? Worst. Day. Ever. And how the hell did that work anyway?

"Why?" I demanded. Not "how," because I didn't care how he had split himself in two. I just wanted to know his reason for doing it.

"It happened a long time ago," he said dismissively. "You were a little girl. It was a price I had to pay. A part of me died."

"That's crazy. What in the world is worth killing yourself for?"

Those green eyes of his caught my gaze. "You tell me, daughter."

I couldn't hold his gaze. I knew what I believed was worth walking into death and back again for—love. I didn't want to know if he felt that way too.

I looked away and saw dark, four-legged beasts, bigger than Stone, slinking along the edges of the street toward us. Silent as a starving wolf pack closing in on prey, they were the Hungers—creatures who crossed through the gates and fed on magic and magic users.

And right now, I was pretty sure we were their prey.

Magic eaters. Killers. I reached for the katana. I didn't know how I was going to wield the sword against a dozen of the beasts with one hand stuck to Stone, but I wasn't going to stand there and let the Hungers run us down. Well, run me down.

"Allison?" Old Dad said. "What do you see?"

A chill washed over my skin. There wasn't a lot of wind here, but the slight breeze dug beneath my clothes and made me feel stretched and cold.

"Hungers." I didn't turn, didn't take my eyes off the beasts.

"Do not provoke them."

Stone growled like a vacuum cleaner full of nails.

"I'm not going to provoke them." I drew Zayvion's sword. It sang free of its sheath. "I'm going to kill them."

The beasts paused as soon as light touched the edge of the sword. They tipped their heads skyward and howled, a warbling birdlike tone that was strange and beautiful. If I hadn't known what they were and what they could do, I would have been mesmerized.

"Put that away," Old Dad said. "Now."

Old Dad was not happy. So not happy that he grabbed my shoulder and squeezed. We were of a height, so this put his mouth right next to my ear.

"Put it away slowly. They scent the magic. The old magics of light and dark worked together into that blade. And they will tear you apart to get to it. Put it away slowly. Put it away now."

New Dad spoke. "Allie, that sword burns like a flame in the shadows of death. They see it, even if they don't see you. If you don't put it away, they will tear you apart. And I—we—can't stop them."

Did I trust him—either of him? No. Did I think he could be telling me the truth? Maybe.

The Hungers started toward us, heads hung low, scenting the magic. More Hungers poured out from the corners of the buildings, drawing up out of the slick pools of shadows on the street. Magic that had hung off them like leeches in life was multicolored ribbons here, draped across their bodies like woven harnesses that shifted against the roll of muscle.

Their ribbons glowed metallic, pastel rainbows, like the marks on my arm, like the magic in the river.

They were dangerous. Deadly. Hungry. Beautiful. And they were closing in. One of the beasts carried something in its jaws. I realized with a jolt that it was the shadow of

Zayvion's sword—the sword he'd taken with him when he was pushed into death—the shadow of the sword I carried.

Stone growled again.

I shifted my one-handed grip on the sword. The beasts lifted their heads, following that movement.

Okay, maybe the dads were right. Maybe I should put the sword away.

Breathing wasn't going so well. Holding the sword—just supporting the weight of it—was like holding up a mountain. My muscles shook so hard, the sword wavered with my heartbeat.

The beasts were a quarter of a block away now. If they attacked all at once, I wouldn't be able to hold them off one-handed. I tipped the sword back into the sheath, slid it home.

The Hungers paused, lifted snouts to the wind, and sniffed.

"I'd like to hear your plan," I said softly to the dads.

Stone growled.

The beasts growled back.

And I drew the dagger from my belt, ready to fight.

# Chapter Two

"Allison," the dads said.

I didn't care what they had to say about this.

"Come."

That last word was cast with so much Influence behind it, I fell to my knees.

I managed not to skewer myself on the dagger but lost contact with Stone, which meant I couldn't breathe. Maybe that was a good thing. I would have screamed if I'd had the air. Falling hurt.

Stone pressed against me and I could breathe again. I inhaled a long, ragged moan.

Pain stabbed my wrist. I looked down. Amber magic with sparks of red glinting through it, looped around my wrist and stretched back behind me, like a rope held taut. The magic was smooth and cool as marble or silk. And it was very, very solid.

I glared at the dads, at their identical expressions of anger. Old Dad held the other end of the amber rope in his fist.

"Fighting the Hungers in death will kill you," they said in tandem. Stereo creepy.

"Get this off me." I held up my bound hand, dagger and all.

The amber rope, the flecks of rubies, shone. Solid, real. I couldn't smell the honey sweetness, but it was Influence, the spell my father had most often cast on me—the spell I had never been able to fight against. Right here, before my eyes. And it wasn't just around my wrist. The Influence spell clasped my wrist like fine jewelry and followed the pattern of magic up my forearm, closing around my neck like a choker.

I'd always known my father was a powerful magic user. One of the most powerful I'd ever known. And I'd always known his magical signature was elegant and clean, defined by a grace and surety of the cast. But I did not know how beautifully he could use magic.

Yes, even though that magic was a chain, I was impressed by the skill behind it.

"Influence?" I asked rather stupidly, because, duh, what else would it be?

New Dad nodded. "Stand, and walk to us now. Quickly."

The rope around my wrist lifted my arm, tugged on my neck, and my body followed. I was on my feet and a dozen steps away from the Hungers, who were still sniffing the air for the scent they'd lost, before I remembered I didn't like doing what my father told me to do. Ever.

"Sheathe the dagger."

I did. We Beckstroms had a knack for Influence, and even though I was good at casting it, I was also vulnerable to it. Especially when my dad used it on me.

"Don't." I meant it as a threat. It came out like a plea. "They have Zay's sword. They know where he is. Let me go to him. Please."

I hated asking. Hated begging. But I would do anything to get Zayvion back home.

"It is too late." New Dad glanced over at Old Dad, who nodded.

"Turn and look, Allison."

I did. Well, I had to. Influence and all. The beasts were gone, and so was Zay's shadow sword.

Zayvion would never have let go of that blade. Even when he'd died, he hadn't lost it.

Fear gripped my throat and squeezed my chest.

"Where is he?" A shadow in the shape of a man detached from the steps of the building down the street. Not Zayvion—I would have recognized him even if all that was left of him was a shadow. I tried to make out details of who or what he might be, but he faded away.

"Come with us," Dads said.

I couldn't say no—the Influence made sure of that.

But just because I had to follow my dads like a puppet didn't mean I had to like it. Unless they told me I had to like it. I shuddered at that possibility.

"Where's Zay?" I asked again. My fear was strangely dull. Zay must be dead, really dead, but my mind couldn't figure out how to handle the pain of that yet.

"We're looking," New Dad said. Old Dad cast a Seek spell, the glyph as delicate as a white lace doily inset with bits of bluish magnifying glass. He tipped his finger, spinning the doily until it flushed bloodred.

"There," Old Dad said. "He has him."

A flood of relief poured over me. "Who?"

New Dad held his hand out for me, maybe to help me breathe or walk.

I glared and he pulled his hand away, surprised.

"You're angry?" he asked. Like he had to.

I held up my wrist. "I want this gone."

"You weren't listening. You would have killed yourself if we hadn't cast it. It is a gentle spell."

"Really? When was the last time you let a magic user wrap a spell around your throat and drag you around like a dog?"

He didn't answer.

We walked for a while—south, I thought, then down a side street. I was so turned around I didn't know which way we were going.

"Zay?" I said again. Just a wheeze this time. Air was quickly becoming my highest priority, even with Stone tucked up against me.

"Let me touch you," New Dad said. "It will help you breathe."

I shook my head.

"I don't know how much longer you'll be able to tolerate death." He rubbed his thumb over his fingertips in a circular motion. He used to do that when he was worried about something. I hadn't seen him show that "tell" in years.

"Allison." I had the faintest memory of him speaking like that, whispering, no, singing to me in that loving tone when I was very, very young. "One mistake will make this your place of rest for good. I want to help you get home."

The strangest thing? I believed him. And not because of the Influence.

But that didn't mean I would let him touch me. I still had air.

Old Dad hadn't said anything. Since casting that last spell, he looked gray, pale, sick. The price for casting magic was very, very high if just three spells—Camouflage, Influence, and Seek—could wear him down.

That worried me. I had to open a gate to get back to the living world, to get back to the living Zay. If one little Influence spell knocked my dad off his footing, I didn't know how I'd be able to throw around enough magic to open a gate before I passed out. Then who would haul me, and Zay's soul, home?

"How long do I have left?" I asked New Dad, since he seemed chattier than Old Dad.

"I don't know. There are legends of the living crossing and returning. Legends of magic users who have done so in the past. Leander and Isabelle." He glanced over at me. "Have you heard their story?"

I didn't waste my breath answering.

He looked over at Old Dad, who shook his head.

"Hundreds of years ago when all magic was one magic, there were two young lovers, Leander and Isabelle. Leander's father was a very powerful member of the Authority—a Voice of magic for all of Greece. Isabelle was the daughter of a strong line of magic users from England who had a knack for Blood magic.

"Isabelle's mother was in poor health, so they wintered in Greece, staying in Leander's father's home. That is where Leander and Isabelle met and fell in love. Leander's father was not pleased with his son's dalliance, thinking the girl no more than a distraction to his son's schooling.

"But when Leander's father forbade him to see Isabelle, she came to his defense. Together, she and Leander cast magic more beautifully and perfectly than he had ever seen.

"A gathering was called. They were tested as Soul Complements. And it was clear from the moment they stood across from each other on the testing floor that they were not only Soul Complements but perhaps two of the most powerful magic users ever known.

"They were young. Not even twenty. Magic came to them like bees to the flower, answering their every whim and asking no cost. Soon they used magic for every simple thing, casting together as one until they knew each other's thoughts, saw through each other's eyes, and even breathed in rhythm with each other. If one were cut or bruised, the other bore the wound; if one cried, the other shed the tears; if one spoke, the other whispered the words.

"At first, they were praised for their mastery of magic, and for using magic through each other, as each other. And then the insanity began. It is said they possessed the people around them and forced them to do their bidding."

I held up the bracelet and gave him a look.

"Not Influence," he said. "They crawled inside people's minds and bodies and forced them to do horrific things. Terrible things. People died.

"At first, the Authority thought they could teach them to resist using magic together. It was hoped that their insanity would pass if they were given enough time to be apart, to remember that they were two people, two minds, two souls. They were separated. Leander was made a prisoner in his father's manor and Isabelle was taken by a trusted advisor back to England."

"With her mother?" I asked.

"Her mother was found dead the day before they set sail. She had carved out her own heart with Isabelle's blood blade."

Why did I have a feeling this story wasn't going to end well?

"Five years passed. They underwent grueling training to learn control of their own minds, passions, and personalities again. But even that was not enough. They escaped their prisons on the same day, killing their keepers. Members of the Authority around the world were quickly found dead, triggering the most massive manhunt the Authority had ever undertaken.

"For three years they avoided capture. It was rumored they could walk in and out of death, as easily as walking through an open door. A world council was called. It was decided that the only way to separate Isabelle and Leander was to break magic into two, creating a Rift between light and dark, life and death, binding light magic to life, and dark magic to death, and each of the lovers to their own body."

"They can break Soul Complements?"

"It had never been tried before." He was quiet, and I didn't know if he was thinking about the legend or had just run out of things to say. I mean, seriously, my dad was in two places at once. I had no idea what that did to a brain.

"What happened?"

"Neither would let go of the other. Nor would they let go of magic. Leander died. Isabelle's mind shattered. She lived a long life, tended and guarded. She never smiled again, never cried, never spoke. When she finally passed away, the Authority set into place very strict tests for Soul Complements. Boundaries for how much magic they are allowed to wield together. The price of crossing that boundary is death.

"The Authority could not mend the Rift they had torn in magic. Still can't. Magic has been broken for five hundred years." He shook his head. "The man who finds a way to heal it will have his place in the history books. He will be immortal, crossing through life and death. A god among men, if magic doesn't destroy him."

We were walking downriver—I mean downrift. The neon slide and flicker of magic beneath the dark water was more sinister than soothing.

"Here." Old Dad stopped in front of a building and pressed his fingertips against the bricks. There was no door, no window, just a blank wall.

"Here?" I said. "This is where the Seek spell brought us? A dead end?"

"Be silent," Old Dad said with Influence.

I shut up. This was getting old fast.

New Dad and Old Dad stood near each other but did not touch, had not touched once since I'd been here. They moved in tandem and traced a spell, a glyph. Even though I'd never seen that exact glyph drawn by anyone before, I knew what it was. Gate and Death and Path.

Then they whispered something, the words fluid and fast, but not the same—more like two different prayers.

I kept my hand on Stone's head and he extended one wing up against my ribs. He had never touched me with his wings. The tip of his wing hooked like fingers and thumb into my shirt.

Such a smart gargoyle. If we got out of this, I was going to buy him a giant box of Tinkertoys. I took a deep breath and got a little more air.

Dads traced a circular motion around the glyph that hung in the air in front of them, then tugged on it.

I expected a gate to open.

I didn't expect a gate to pull free from the brick wall and literally slide out of the building. Old Dad was breathing hard. New Dad put both hands behind his back and took a step away from Old Dad. I wondered what would happen if they touched. Maybe they would become a whole soul—one person, as they should be. Maybe that would mean he would be dead for good.

Old Dad wiped his palm over his face. I stood behind and to the side of him—so that the rope of Influence between us stayed out of the way of his casting—but his exhaustion was clear.

New Dad walked to the gate, a single-wide cast-iron jobber gone cinnamon with rust, and pulled it open. It moved under his touch, silent. As soon as it opened, the temperature changed. It was colder in there. The kind of cold that got in your bones and didn't get out.

"I'll go through first," New Dad said. "Allie, you will follow with Stone at your side."

Where were we going? Why wouldn't they take this damn Influence off me so I could talk? Old Dad wasn't even looking at me. I pulled the rope a couple times to get his attention.

New Dad noticed. "Speak as you wish."

"I have to find Zayvion. Now."

Old Dad shook his head. "Don't you think I know that? This is the fastest and safest way to reach him. And we would be there more quickly if you would stop arguing every step of the way. Enter the gate. Now."

Influence made my feet move without me wanting them to. It was a nightmarish, out-of-control sensation too similar to when Lon Trager had used Blood magic to make me do his bidding.

Before I killed him. I did not like being stuck, bound, trapped, forced. As a matter of fact, I had impressive panic attacks over such things. And then I got angry and killed things.

It was good that Stone paced me, strong and solid, letting me breathe, while I worked on staying angry, which was better than going into a claustrophobic panic.

New Dad strode into the gate ahead of me, then took my right hand.

Old Dad, behind me, put his hand on my right shoulder. We paused, just inside the gate, in darkness broken only by the opalescent whorls of color beneath Stone's skin, his burning amber eyes, and the metallic colors that pulsed from my right fingertips up to the corner of my eye. My skin beneath the marks of magic glowed almost luminescent, shining between the bars of black on my left fingers, wrist, and elbow, and from between the whorls of colors on my right.

It was small in here, too small. I'd be in a cold sweat right now if I could sweat. I wanted out, wanted to run. But Influence held me button-tight.

"Pay attention," Old Dad said.

I looked back at him, paying very good attention, just as he commanded. The gate was closed, or at least there was no light beyond it, no glimpse of where we had been.

I could make out the cinnamon-colored bars, barely illuminated, and nothing but blackness beyond it and around us.

"Tell me what you see," he said.

"Blackness. The Gate. Stone. Myself."

New Dad made a sound like an exhale. "That's good. There is much more here with us. Things living souls should not see. The path is narrow. You do not want to step off of it."

Oh, didn't that sound wonderful?

"Can you breathe?" New Dad asked.

I nodded, then, since he might not be able to see me, said, "Yes."

"Good. Walk and don't lose contact with us, or the Animate. We will keep you on the path."

I walked. The ground beneath my feet felt strangely slippery, like it was moving at a different pace than I was. The gate we entered should be behind Old Dad, behind me, but I could see it ahead of us, ahead of New Dad in front of me. I couldn't tell if we were coming or going, or holding still.

And even though I knew I was walking and so were my dads, the gate, the darkness around us, moved too and nothing seemed to get nearer.

"You're doing fine," New Dad said. "We're almost there."

Weird. He'd never been so comforting. This New Dad was full of things Old Dad, the dad I knew, never spoke about, or maybe had given up years before my earliest memories. New Dad had a sort of hopefulness to him, an even demeanor, an easy smile. I wondered if I would have hated him less if I had known this younger dad. I wondered if I might have even liked him.

"Relax," Old Dad Influenced.

I felt like I'd just downed half a bottle of Merlot. If he did that again, there was no way I'd be walking.

Dad ahead and Dad behind cast magic. The gate ahead of us was solid, real, close.

The scenery behind it had changed, though it still looked like a city.

But the real kicker was that the light from the magic the dads cast revealed our surroundings.

Monsters faded in and out of my line of vision, people too. And magic, odd spells and glyphs that echoed with pain, with horrors that made me want to shut my eyes and click my heels.

"I see—" I started, my voice trembling.

Old Dad let go of my shoulder and gently pressed his hand over my eyes.

I knew I should fight him. I knew being blind to fears and danger doesn't make them go away. But this was too much. I could feel my sanity slipping like sand beneath an ocean wave.

"You're safe," Old Dad said. "I've got you. I won't let you fall."

And I believed him. Even without Influence. We walked like that for a while. I counted my breaths to keep track of time. I got to fifty.

Then a rush of warm air pushed over my skin. I gasped, which hurt, but I managed not to scream. Old Dad uncovered my eyes and stepped back. He let go of my shoulder too.

We stood in front of a castle.

I turned to make sure whatever had been in the dark wasn't about to jump us. Nothing there but a plain brick wall of a plain brick building.

I hoped it stayed that way.

There were no buildings other than the one behind us. A river flowed in the distance to my left. Three bridges spanned the water, none of them multileveled like Portland's real bridges. They twisted like tree branches reaching across the river to the fog-obscured bank on the other side.

Ahead of us was a single structure in the center of a clearing with grass around it. Made of stone and steel and hard shards of glass, tiles, and carvings, the massive structure was wide at the base, gnarled and knotted like a tree, or a stalagmite. It glowed faintly green-white, every edge softened as if wind or water ran over and through it, carving out doorways, windows, faces, and eye-catching, dreamlike creatures.

The building, tree, whatever it was, reached at least two hundred stories high. I squinted against the bright sky. Branches fanned out black skeletal umbrellalike framework, lace against the white-washed sky.

We were on a slight hill about two blocks away from the base of the tree. People were gathered around the structure. Watercolor people. The Veiled. Solid, mutated, broken people.

They faced the building but did not enter it. I didn't know what they were waiting for—the door was open. I could see it from here.

"Where are we?"

"At the pillar of Death magic," New Dad said.

"That's a pillar?" Could the tree somehow support this place? Give it not life but something else? Magic? Order? Vitality?

"It isn't an architectural pillar. There are no wells of magic in this realm, in death. Wells are a thing of light magic. Pillars are a thing of dark magic. It is where dark magic comes from, where dark magic is held, like the wells."

"I thought dark magic came from the Rift," I said recalling the dark water with glyphs sparking through it.

"No. That is the break between light and dark, life and death. No magic comes from there, though old spells often are caught by it before they fade."

Speaking of old spells. I held up my arm with my shiny shackle of Influence. "I want you to break this."

Old Dad spoke. "That will remain until we—until *you* return to life. I do not want to lose you in this place."

"We?" So that was his angle. He had no intention of staying behind, of staying dead. He planned to make me carry him—part of him, or all of him—back into life. Fat chance.

I'd been trying to get rid of him for months.

Well, only since he'd taken over my brain. Before that, when he was still alive, I'd just wanted him to leave me alone.

There was nothing that would make me take him back to life with me. This was a one-way ticket, and for once the odds were on my side.

"You." He stormed past me toward the pillar. "Come."

My feet, damn them, followed.

New Dad walked next to me and looked off after Old Dad as if he couldn't quite recognize himself in that man. "Zayvion is within the pillar," he said quietly. "Just a little longer now."

I needed a plan to get Zayvion home. I could feel the dark Death magic that made the pillar. I might be able to access it. That, along with the small magic I had always carried inside me, the little candle flame of magic that was all my own, should be enough to power at least one spell to open a gate to life.

I hoped.

Old Dad was a good twenty feet ahead of me, storming right toward the watercolor people like he was invisible. I scanned the people gathered, morbidly curious to see if I would recognize anyone.

There, to the left, I glimpsed the shadow of a man. The same shadow man I had seen on the street with the Hungers. I blinked, and he was gone.

Stone growled.

Yeah, that summed up my feelings too. I slowed my pace, watching to see what the watercolor people would do when Old Dad passed them.

He walked right by, not a pause, not a sideways glance. Walked like he owned the place—radiating that confidence he'd always had in life. Man could take on the world and come out on top. Take on both worlds and come out on top.

No wonder he was admired, even if only grudgingly. New Dad followed him past the Veiled and through the triple-wide, triple-tall door.

The Influence around my arm squeezed so hard it hurt.

"Let's go, big guy," I said to Stone. "Don't eat anybody, don't start a fight, and don't leave me alone." I took a breath, as deep as my struggling lungs would allow, and started walking.

We were almost parallel to the Veiled. They weren't just standing there. They were touching the walls, shaping them, a hundred palms pressing and pulling and guiding the magic in the walls to form the creatures, the dreamlike faces that flowed slowly, gently, ever upward, as naturally as glyphs in the air.

It was strange to see things—people who had tried to kill me in life—creating something this beautiful in death. Still, I held my right hand ready to cast a spell in case arts-and-craft hour suddenly ended and they went back to Killing 101.

The watercolor people were solid enough that I could see every strand of hair, stubble on chin, wrinkle in clothes. I passed through them so close I had to angle my shoulders not to brush against anyone. Just like my dads, I was invisible to them.

Only a dozen or so steps away from the open doorway. What had looked like a small opening from the hill was actually a huge arched doorway tall enough for two elephants, side by side, to march through and not bump their heads.

The dads were nowhere to be seen.

Nice of them to wait.

I stepped through the doorway into the dim interior.

Stone stopped on the threshold. And while I applauded his instincts, because—seriously?—we were strolling willingly into the pillar of Death magic, he did put me in the awkward position of one arm stretched back, fingertips caught on the big rock's forehead so I could breathe, the rest of me inside the building, pulled by the rope of Influence and unable to go forward.

"Come on, boy. Get in here. Let's go see if there's something you can stack, okay? Like blocks. Or maybe there are some Tinkertoys in there."

Stone crept forward, his ears flat against his skull, his lips pulled away from the arsenal of blades he called teeth.

He took exactly one step.

That did me exactly no good.

Fab.

I shifted to stand beside him. The watercolor people hadn't moved, hadn't seen us, were still busy being dead and artistic. Good. I glanced back at the interior.

Stunning.

From the outside, this had looked like a strange, twisted shell.

From here it was every shade of magic I had ever seen or imagined. It was the stuff of fairy tales, of dreams. Crystalline walls shone with gentle colors and gave hint to the levels that reached up and up until I could not see the top of the walls. A warm yellow light filtered down, catching gold and silver along the arched doorways and balconies. It was like standing in the center of a glyph.

The Influence squeezed my arm and neck. Ouch. The

dads weren't waiting. If they pulled any harder, I'd have to walk away from Stone and then I wouldn't be breathing.

"Come on, Stone. You can't hang half in and half out of the doorway. Zay's here. We have to find Zay."

Stone tipped his head and sneezed.

Nice. Dust poofed out of his nostrils and drifted lazily out the door.

I don't know why that caught the watercolor people's attention.

But the ones nearest the door stopped shaping magic and looked up.

Not at Stone. No, I just wasn't lucky that way.

They looked at me.

## Chapter Three

"Get moving." I grabbed one of Stone's ears and tugged.

Stone did not move. He did, however, sneeze again.

More of the Veiled stopped working and looked at me.

A few of them, maybe five, stepped toward the door and blinked as if they couldn't quite see it.

"Allison," Old Dad, from the disapproval in his tone, said. "Come. Now."

For cripes' sake.

I had to follow his command. And I was a little helpless in the whole breathing department. I took a deep breath before my feet jerked me forward and my hand slipped free of Stone's head.

Luckily, Old Dad was glaring at me and noticed: one, I wasn't breathing; two, Stone was sneezing again; and three, the watercolor people were waving their hands at the open doorway, trying to feel their way into the place.

Best of all? He decided to handle my breathing problem first.

Old Dad strode to me. "Must you always make things so difficult?"

Just because I couldn't breathe to tell him off didn't mean I couldn't lift my middle finger.

New Dad laughed.

That surprised me.

Old Dad did not laugh.

No surprise there.

"You are testing my resolve. As a parent *and* a magic user." His hand clamped over my wrist, over the Influence spell, and I gasped, inhaling like a swimmer who had been down too long. Everything went sparkly at the edges.

Dad waited while I tried to catch my breath. Some small kindness, considering.

Downright nice, even. That is, if I didn't already know that the only reason he was worried about me staying alive was because I was his ride back to life.

Stone growled. He didn't much like my dad touching me. That was because Stone was my buddy, my watch dog, my guardian, my pal. And pretty smart, even if he was a rock.

"Come, Stone," New Dad said. "Let's go home."

Weird. I didn't know he knew his name.

Oh, wait. If he shared a brain with Old Dad, he'd know a lot of things. About Stone. About me.

Stone knew the word *home*. He trotted up to me giving me those big round eyes that made him look pretty proud of himself for figuring this all out.

I stuck my left hand on Stone's head and glared at my father until he let go of my wrist.

"Just like your mother." He strode off to where the rest of him stood.

Hell of a thing to say. My father was my last and only link to my estranged mother. He knew her, had history with her, had shared his life with her, had shared my life with her. And since he was dead, and staying here—thank you very much—I was in a way losing both him and his memories of her.

I was, in a way, losing both my parents.

Again.

I stared at my father's back, then over at New Dad, who

watched me. He looked like he was apologizing. Like he knew I was missing my mother, my chance at having a father who knew how to do more than growl and command, my hope for a real and normal life.

"Are you ready, Angel?" he asked.

Angel. He used to call me that when I woke up with nightmares. Used to call me that when he held me on his lap and made my nightmares go away.

Memories I had forgotten years before I knew I should remember them rushed to the front of my mind. Of my dad, younger, kinder, brushing his fingers over my forehead, over my heart, his touch taking away my fears, my pain, my nightmares.

He had been there when I was little and terrified. He had made me believe I was safe. He had made me believe he loved me.

I swallowed the knot in my throat. I wasn't that little girl anymore. And that man, the man he used to be, was dead. Dead right there across the room from me, waiting patiently for me to take the next step forward. Waiting like he believed in me. Believed I was strong enough to do this, to bring Zayvion's soul home.

I took the next step. "Don't call me Angel." Because I couldn't love him. Couldn't hope for him to be my real father, my living father.

Stone walked with me, his head pushed up beneath my hand, his wing draped against my shoulder. We crossed the room, my footsteps muffled. It felt like I had cotton stuffed in my ears. A bell-tone ring echoed back from the walls, and from the floor beneath my feet. Pure and rolling like a chorus of angels, each tone rode the next, familiar, lovely, haunting, and made me ache to hear the next note.

I was halfway across the room before I realized I hadn't been paying any attention to where I was going.

Hypnotic, that song. Soothing, this place.

And the last thing I needed was to be distracted in death. To keep my head clear, I recited my mantra and took slow, even breaths. The air was a little easier to breathe in here. I didn't know if that was a good sign or a bad sign.

"In there," New Dad said.

We stood in front of an archway carved in flowered reliefs of gilded steel blue and metallic roses. As I watched, the flowers budded, blossomed into open blooms, then dropped their petals one by one to where another flower budded, and blossomed again in a tranquil cycle.

I lost track of where I was headed again. That was not good. I needed to pay attention. Needed to walk through this place and find Zay.

I bit the inside of my cheek. And I mean bit hard. I didn't feel a thing. Huh.

Both dads were watching me. "Look inside," Old Dad said.

I peered into the room and caught my breath. Zayvion was in there, seven feet tall, the black flame a hazy flicker over his glyph-marked skin. He stood in the center of the room, surrounded by Hungers. He had chains on his neck, waist, hands, and feet.

The glyphs worked into his skin were no longer silver but ash black. Threads of smoke spun off of him in colored threads, streams of magic that poured into the Hungers' mouths, filling the ribbons of magic around their bodies until those ribbons brightened and tightened like candy-colored bandages.

"Take this thing off me." I held my wrist out. I didn't care if all Dad planned to do was stand here and stare at Zayvion while the beasts ate at his magic.

I still had a katana, and I aimed to use it.

"Has it done any good?" Old Dad asked.

New Dad answered. "Some. There is still too little light magic. He is the guardian of the gates, but his connection to life is too tenuous. They can't pull enough magic through him. He's burning out."

I didn't know what they were talking about, but it didn't sound good.

"Break this," I said again.

Three of the Hungers in the other room whimpered, then moved slowly and heavily, as if bearing a huge weight. The ribbons wrapped around them were glossy and fat with magic—magic they had taken from Zayvion.

He wasn't burning out; he was being devoured.

Three more Hungers stepped up to take their place, entering from a wide door on the other side of the room. Ten beasts surrounded him, mouths hinged open to drink down the magic.

Old Dad was suddenly in front of me.

". . . Allison, hear me." He squeezed my shoulder.

I hadn't even seen him move.

I blinked. Got the prerequisite frown. But no anger this time. He placed his fingertips under my chin, tipped my face, and gazed into my eyes like a doctor checking to see if I had a concussion.

"She's drifting."

New Dad moved past us both and into the room with Zayvion and the beasts. "Now. It must be now."

"You are here to save Zayvion's soul," Old Dad said like maybe I had forgotten that already. "You are here to take it back with you into life so he may live. So that you may live. You must keep your hand on the Animate or myself to breathe. Do you understand me?"

"I understand that if I have to stand here while you tell me things I already know, I'm going to shove this Influence up your nose." I made a fist, to make my point clear.

He smiled. "That's my girl."

Then he stepped away and Stone was there, his big

warm shoulder against my knee and thigh, his wing up on my back, his head under my left hand.

Right. I had to hold on to him. I remembered that. And I had to go save Zay. I remembered that too.

Old Dad walked into the room where New Dad drew something in the air—a glyph? He held something in his other hand. I couldn't see since his back was turned to me. Whatever it was, that motion was a signal to the Hungers. They all backed away from Zayvion and lumbered toward the open door on the other side of the room.

Stone stepped forward.

Right. I was supposed to be walking.

I got busy doing that—walking—and pretty soon I was in the room. The ceiling was lower in here. It was warmer in here. I could breathe a little more here. And Zayvion was here. Things were finally looking up.

As soon as I was a few steps into the room, I could feel Zayvion's presence. Then I didn't need anything to remind me to walk. I ran.

I knew where I had to be. Knew where I belonged. With him. Even here. Even in death. Maybe especially here.

He stood in deep meditation, eyes closed, hands held low, palms up as if he were receiving, not giving away all of his magic. A glyph on the floor pulsed beneath his feet in rhythm to his heartbeat. The chains around his neck, waist, wrists, and feet anchored into the glyph and were made of the same blue-white substance of the walls.

How could I wake him, free him? The black flames that wrapped his body didn't give off any heat; the glyphs against his skin were concrete gray. If it hadn't been for the slow pulse of the glyph beneath his feet, I wouldn't have thought he was inside that silent, silent shell.

I pressed my fingertips against his bare chest, my palm over the fire of his heart. "Hey, lover," I breathed.

His emotions, his thoughts, filled me and I inhaled, wanting to make room for more of him, all of him.

*Allie,* he exhaled through my mind. *I couldn't find you.* Relief and fear. Then, anger. *You didn't follow. Tell me you didn't follow me into death. Tell me you're alive.*

"I'm alive," I said out loud. I remembered what New Dad had said about Leander and Isabelle getting too close and being unable to draw apart. Zayvion and I were Soul Complements too. If I started talking in his head, I might lose track of myself. I couldn't do that. I was counting on me to get us home.

But sweet hells, I wanted to lose myself in him.

*It isn't safe,* he said. *I told you not to come, not to find me. I told you not to risk yourself.* Then, almost in a panic, *You promised me you wouldn't be a hero.*

He was frightened. Angry. Tied down. Stuck. Dead. And I had thrown myself into the grave after him.

Yeah, well, maybe. But I'd been smart enough to bring a shovel and a ladder with me before I jumped in.

I pulled my hand away, breaking our connection. I didn't have enough brain to think my own thoughts, much less listen to his and deal with our combined fears. I was beyond tired and wanted to lie down on the floor and sleep. I didn't think I was going to last much longer in death.

We had to leave. Together. Now.

"How do I free him?"

"A Release, or Compulsion," Old Dad said. "You will need to find a vessel for him to inhabit. He cannot walk through the gate back into life in this form."

"What? Why? He came through the gate in this form without a vessel."

"Every living thing can pass into death. It's a door that swings one way."

"Hungers and other creatures come through gates into life all the time."

"The Hungers cross through but exist only briefly in life without magic to feed on and sustain them. When magic is gone, they are spirit form again. But a soul. . . . " He paused. "A soul is a very different matter. Once a soul crosses into death, it can never return to life. Always, the body follows into death."

"Not always," New Dad said.

Old Dad looked annoyed that he had brought that up. "True. There are exceptions. Rare circumstances. But Zayvion is not one of those exceptions. His soul will slip through your fingers and fall back into death before you can rejoin his soul to body—*if* you can rejoin his soul to body. That will take a mastery of Life and Death magic, which you do not possess."

"Won't you be surprised when I do it anyway?"

"Allie," New Dad said, "Zayvion carries the glyphs of light and dark magic on his soul. It is one of the prices of being a guardian of the gates and using both light and dark magic. It marks his soul. And that which gives him strength in life chains him in death."

"You said if I opened a gate, he could go back."

"I never promised it would be easy. The glyphs have taken root in death now," Old Dad said.

He was right. The ashy glyphs trailed down his body, long tendrils of silver and gray smoke that sank like the chains into the floor.

He was trapped here. Those chains on his ankles, wrists, waist, and neck weren't just magic—they were the magic burned into his soul.

No. Hells no. I knew how to break a chain. I was good at destroying things. And if Zayvion and I were really Soul Complements, then I was the perfect person to bring his soul home.

I reached for the katana over my shoulder.

"Do not draw the sword," Old Dad and New Dad said.

"If you won't break him free, I'll do it." Only problem? I couldn't pull the sword. I was still under their Influence.

"Without a vessel, you will kill him."

"Bullshit."

"You might free his soul here in death." Old Dad's voice rose. "But it will *not* survive returning to life. How many times must I say the same thing before you listen to me?"

Stone growled. And I knew why.

A man, easily eight feet tall, strode through the doorway and into the room with us. He carried himself with an air of command, and though he wore slacks and a button-down shirt rolled up at the sleeves, he really looked like the type who would be comfortable wearing a military uniform. His hair was short and black, his eyes iceberg blue in a face that might have been handsome if he hadn't looked so worn and sad.

The sadness surprised me. I had seen him only once before, when I was being tested as Zayvion's Soul Complement. He had been furious then. It was Mikhail. The man who used to be the head of the Authority before he tampered too much with dark magic and broke the rules. Before he had been killed and Sedra had taken his place as the head of the Authority.

Mikhail was the man who opened a gate in the middle of Zay's and my test and tried to kill all the magic users gathered, Sedra included. If Cody Miller, the broken-minded savant who pulled magic through me and gave me the marks on my body, hadn't jumped into the gate between life and death and sealed it, Mikhail and the Hungers at his command would have succeeded in killing us all.

He was not a man to fuck around with.

I pulled on the sword, but my muscles refused to respond. The dads had told me I couldn't use it. Well, that wasn't the only weapon I carried. I let go of the katana and drew the blood blade on my belt instead.

Problem One: I could wield it only at close range.

Problem Two: I could not let go of Stone's head and breathe at the same time.

Problem Three: I was in a very bad mood and felt the need to be killing something real quick if someone didn't get the hell out of my way and kick open a gate to life that I could drag Zayvion through.

"The blood blade will do you no good here," Mikhail said. His voice vibrated like a low bell through the walls and floor.

"Let's try it and find out," I said.

Mikhail looked at my dad—Old Dad. "Is this your daughter, Daniel?"

"Yes."

"Ah. As you said, she is rare. She carries magic in her body, and such magic in her soul. You have done well to bring her to me."

What? No. Hell, no.

"Then our agreement stands?" Old Dad asked.

"If she relinquishes her power to me."

They were in cahoots. All this time, my dad was on the bad guy's side. It shouldn't surprise me, but damn it, I thought there was a sliver of decency somewhere in his dark, calculating soul. I thought there was some good in him that made my newest stepmom, Violet, love him, grieve for him, have a baby for him.

But Violet was wrong and I was right. My dad was a lying rat bastard.

Old Dad walked forward and grasped Mikhail's hand in his own. It wasn't quite a handshake. It was more of a passing of something between them. Mikhail nodded. Old Dad stepped back.

Even though I was in a room full of things that could eat me, kill me, betray me, Stone, who usually had his hackles up in every dangerous situation, had been silent. Maybe I wasn't in as much danger as I thought I was.

Or maybe I shouldn't rely on a rock for my warning system.

"What power?" I finally asked. Just holding the blade was making me tired.

"Magic always demands a price." Mikhail's words thrummed through the room again. "This you know."

I raised an eyebrow. "That," I said, "any idiot knows."

My dad, Old Dad, shook his head and refused to make eye contact. Like I'd used the wrong spoon at a dinner with an important business client. He had something riding on this. Something important to him.

"For the right price," Mikhail went on with a little less thrum and a little more boom, "I will allow you to leave this realm of death, with the guardian's soul. I will open the doorway for you. Near enough the guardian's body that you may return his soul."

Why did I feel like I was making a deal with the devil?

Oh, right. Because I was.

"What's the price?"

"You will give up to me, willingly, the magic you hold within you."

I did not like that idea. Not at all. But carrying magic in my body was a new thing for me. I'd always had a small magic in me, just a candle-flame's worth in my soul that I could use for maybe one spell. Cody Miller had pulled more magic into me when he was dying and created lines and paths and channels so that magic filled me—sometimes too much. It might be a good thing not to have to worry about burning down the city every time I cast a spell.

"The magic in my body?" I asked, just to make sure I knew what kind of deal we were making.

"No," he said. "Not the magic in your body. I want the small magic in your soul."

# Chapter Four

Mikhail folded his hands. He didn't seem angry. He seemed resigned, as if he had seen too much pain and knew there would always be more pain to see.

He did not look like a world-crushing, magic-hungry maniac.

Then again, he was the first world-crushing, magic-hungry maniac I'd met.

"You can't take my small magic from me. It's mine. It's always been mine." It felt like my nightmare was having nightmares. Dad had stuck his hands in me and messed with my small magic already today. I never wanted to feel that again.

"That is true. I cannot take it from you. But you can give it to me. Willingly."

Yeah, give him my magic so he could break open the gates between life and death again and do what? Unleash those holy terrors upon my city and friends. He would use my magic to kill and destroy. I couldn't let him do that.

"No. A million times no." I wasn't going to put the entire world in danger.

Dad closed his eyes. "There are moments when I regret I allowed you to slip my control."

"If I have to pay a price, that's fine," I said. "Ask for

something else. I'll give you a two-for-one deal on my dad's soul."

"There is nothing else I want. If you wish to take the guardian's soul back to life, if you want to live, you will give me the magic in your soul. It is the only way you will leave this realm."

"No deal." I reached out for Zayvion again, my hand and blood dagger against his chest.

*Want to help me out with this?* I thought. My heart was racing. As soon as I touched him, his fear mixed with mine and only made things worse.

*Don't sacrifice yourself,* he said. *Don't give him your magic. Negotiate to open a gate and go home. I'll return to you.*

*You're chained down. They have you trapped, Zay. You can't get out of this. They're drinking you dry.* I couldn't say any more, couldn't tell him he was dying in death. But I knew he felt my fear.

He was quiet for a moment, sorting our fear, weighing our chances. Then, calmly, *Leave me here, Allie. I am already dead. You can still live.*

Great. Zay had turned martyr on me. Not helpful.

I didn't know what to do. I truly, truly didn't.

"I know you don't trust me," New Dad said. "And probably don't like me since you just tried to sell my soul. But let me say this: I don't want you to stay here. I've worked very hard. . . . " He glanced over at Old Dad. "I've worked very hard for a long time to make sure you would be safe if this day ever came. I never wanted this to happen, but life and death rarely go according to plan. This is the only way you can take Zayvion with you. To return to life you'll need to relinquish magic, Angel. This is the best I could do for you."

"Don't call me Angel. You haven't done anything for me. It's all been for you. You traded my magic without asking me. It's not yours—it's never been yours. And you expect me to honor your deal?"

"Yes. If you want to save Zayvion."

"I can't," I said. "If I give my magic away, what do you think Mikhail will do with it? Destroy the world? I can't pay that price. I can't make everyone else suffer so I can have Zay." I was angry and horrified that no one understood what was really going on here. They were making me choose between saving Zayvion and saving the world. I couldn't make that choice. I shouldn't put my love—my desperation—for Zay over the good of the whole world, and yet I wanted him alive with me so badly it hurt.

It was Mikhail who answered. "The magic you carry will not be used for destruction at my hands."

"I don't know that. I have no guarantee of that."

"The risk is yours to take," he said. "What do you want, Allison Angel Beckstrom?"

Zayvion. I wanted Zayvion. The whole world could go to hell for all I cared, as long as I could touch him again, hold him, be with him again. Alive.

It was selfish of me, greedy. But it was true.

"Don't," I said, torn between anger and need. If I'd had tears, I'd have been a sobbing mess. But there was no crying in death. Good thing. It forced me to keep thinking past the pain. And I knew what I had to do.

"I want the truth," I said. "If you want my magic, you'll let me cast a Truth spell and you'll answer my questions." Everything came with a price. That was how magic worked. It was time for the world-crushing, magic-hungry maniac to pay up.

He scowled, shoulders tensing. His hands, still clasped, went white at the knuckles. Not so much a sad guy now, he looked furious. I thought he was going to say no.

"Done." He held out his hand, palm tipped upward.

Old Dad inhaled. Even he hadn't thought Mikhail would agree.

I wasn't sure Truth would work in death. It took blood to cast it, and I hadn't seen a drop of blood since I'd been in death. I sure as hell didn't know if Mikhail would bleed. But it was the best I could do. Breathing was getting harder. Shadows closed in on my peripheral vision as I walked over to Mikhail. Stone was moving a little slower too, his head cool under my hand as if he was running down.

There wasn't any time left for second chances.

I stopped in front of Mikhail and worked on clearing my mind. It took me longer than I'd like to admit, but after a few verses of my "Miss Mary Mack," song, my thoughts finally slipped from fight or flight to something more meditative. I set a Disbursement out of habit—I decided on muscle aches.

Mikhail waited the entire time, his hand open.

When my mind was clear enough, when the panic was more than a breath away, I slashed my left palm and placed it back on Stone's head. Then I quickly drew the blade across Mikhail's palm.

No blood from either of us. Instead, a dim red light drifted from my hand, lifting like smoke, while a bright white-blue poured from his hand in an icy stream. I caught and mingled the ice and smoke along the blade of the dagger and used it to draw the Truth spell into the air between us.

The spell blazed to life; a geometric glyph burned in the air. The connection was made.

"Are you going to use my magic to harm those I love?"

"No." The word rolled through me, soft as a cat pressing and stretching. I knew he was telling the truth.

"Are you going to use my magic to harm or kill innocents?"

"No." Again, the truth.

"Are you going to use my magic to destroy the world?"

A slight hesitation this time, and a wash of possibilities rushed through my head like math equations I couldn't solve. "I have no desire to destroy the world."

True, if a not exactly what I had asked.

"Will you help me open a gate to life and let me take Zayvion's soul through with me if I give you my magic?"

"Yes." And that too was true.

Holding the concentration neccssary to support the spell was exhausting. No wonder my dad had looked so sick after casting only three spells.

That was all the truth I could endure. Literally four questions worth. Any more and I'd pass out. I drew a circle around the glyph with the tip of the blood blade, then slashed through the spell, breaking it. I did not pass out. Go, me.

I tipped my chin, stared straight into Mikhail's eyes, and forced myself to say it before I could change my mind. "I came here to bring Zayvion home. I know the price I have to pay. I'll give you my magic, but I don't know how."

Relief washed across his face as he closed his hand, dampening the light from his palm. It was strange to think that the devil might have been worried that I would say no. What did he have riding on my agreement? I hadn't thought to ask him what he planned to do with the magic. How stupid could I be?

Fear returned, thick, nightmarish. I had no idea if I was doing the right thing. I wanted to grab Zayvion and run. But there was nowhere to go.

"You will clear your mind and recite a mantra," Mikhail said. "You will reach into your chest and withdraw the flame that burns there."

I nodded calmly as I walked back over to Zay. A part of my mind was screaming.

"And the gate?" I asked without screaming at all.

"I will open the gate first. Once the gate is opened, I will break magic's hold on the guardian."

"No. That's not good enough. I want something more than your word on this."

He scowled at me. I scowled back. I was not going to back down. This was too important. I wasn't going to screw it up on a technicality.

Dad swore under his breath.

The corner of Mikhail's mouth quirked up. "You do not know what you ask." He strode to me, every footfall echoing through the room. It was as if he were made of heavier stuff than anything else in death. As if he was a part of the pillars that held the earth to the sky.

"I give you my seal." He caught my left hand in his own and pressed his thumb into the cut on my palm.

A sweet warmth filled me. Something bit deep beneath my skin and I tasted blood in the back of my throat. I gasped at the pain, and at the pleasure. I jerked my hand out of his hold.

My palm was just my palm. A slight shadow smudged the point where his thumb had been, but the wound was gone. I might not be able to see anything there, but I knew that magic, Death magic, curled there, planted like a seed beneath my skin.

It was more than a guarantee—it was a part of him. I knew he was telling the truth—that he would free Zayvion and open a gate, as if he had just worked a much stronger Truth spell on me.

And it was the only guarantee I was going to get.

I put my hand back on Stone, took a deep breath, and recited my "Miss Mary Mack, Mack, Mack," song again, trying to push aside the terror at what I was about to do.

I stared at Mikhail. He waited, didn't move, didn't send the Hungers that shifted at the edges of the room like shadows stirred by the wind to jump, to attack.

Okay, here was the part where it got tricky. I was supposed to reach into my own chest.

I sheathed the dagger so I didn't accidentally stab myself, and then pressed the fingertips of my right hand against my sternum. I pressed deeper. My fingers sank into my chest like they were sliding through soft sand.

Ew, ew, ew.

But I didn't let it break my concentration. Didn't look away from Mikhail's eyes. Blue, like Cody's. Filled with a curious intelligence, sorrow, and hope. Very human. Almost likable.

Yeah, well, if the devil went around looking like a monster, he'd never be able to pay his rent.

I continued pressing inward. I didn't know if I was doing this right, but Mikhail seemed calm, the weight of his seal on my palm somehow giving me the awareness of his approval.

I was up to the "elephant jump over a fence," part of the "Miss Mary Mack" jingle for a second time when my fingers brushed something soft and smooth and warm inside me.

Later, I was going to throw up. Right now, I gently got my fingers around that warmth.

My magic. My small magic. The one secret, sacred thing that made me me. The little bit of magic I knew was always there for me. The one thing no one could take away from me. The one thing magic had never harmed.

I felt like I was giving away the most precious part of me.

I drew it out of my chest—still no blood, no feeling of flesh and bones. Just the brush of warm sand falling away from my hand as I drew the magic out of me.

I couldn't help it. I looked down at the small magic.

It looked like a rose. A translucent pink rose that pulsed with a blush of magic. It glowed in my hand and sent a wave of light up the ribbons of magic that wrapped from my fingertips to the corner of my eye. Ebony thorns rode the stalk of the rose, each like a blade, curved and tipped with red. Beautiful. Strong. Fragile.

Me.

I didn't want to let it go. I didn't know what would be left of me once this was gone. I didn't know what I would become.

A single tear hit my palm. I had been wrong. You can grieve in death.

"It must be soon, Allison," Mikhail said. "There is no time left for you."

I nodded, or at least I thought I did. I was feeling strangely numb and drifty. It was hard to remember what I was supposed to be doing. I wasn't even sure how long I stood there, staring at the magic of my soul.

"Give the magic to Mikhail," Dad—one of him—said. "I'll help you get Zayvion safely home."

I looked up at Zay. Silent. And me with no strength to touch him and find out what he thought about all this. His eyes were closed as if he were sleeping, or dead. There was nothing he could do to help me make this decision. Or to change what I had done.

Pay the price. Was Zayvion worth giving up my small magic? Hells, I'd have given up more if Mikhail had asked. I loved him. And love could make a person do crazy things.

I held my hand, my magic, the single pink rose, out for Mikhail.

"I give it to you willingly in exchange for Zayvion Jones' soul returning with me to life, and into his living body there."

Something sparked in Mikhail's eyes. "You have taught her well, Daniel." Then, to me, "I accept this magic. In return I will open the gate into life, and do all within my power to help you return Zayvion Jones' soul to his living body and make all right again between our worlds."

I swallowed. Honey. I tasted honey. There had been a spell in those words. Something I could not focus on, because I was having a hard time deciding how many more breaths I got before I blacked out.

Mikhail's fingers brushed my palm over the seal beneath my skin. His hands were warm, which surprised me, and gentle. He lifted the rose from my hand.

I whimpered at the sudden loss, the absence, the raw hole that prickled and hurt deep inside me.

"Open the gate," I said.

Mikhail could not seem to take his gaze off the rose. He nodded, absently, which worried me, and he held the rose with reverence, which I tried to ignore.

"You will need a vessel to carry his soul," he said. "Time rides against you. Choose a vessel for him. Now."

I didn't even know what would work. The dagger? My pocket? No one had told me I'd need to bring a bottle to this genie party.

"He can enter your mind and soul," Old Dad told me.

My heart thrilled at that. A perfect solution. Exactly what I wanted. Zayvion would be close to me, really in my mind, not just talking to me there. We would be one.

And that was one of the most dangerous things that could happen. Just like Leander and Isabelle, we could lose ourselves, lose our individuality and go insane.

It wasn't something that happened only in legends. Chase, Zay's ex-girlfriend, and her Soul Complement, Greyson, weren't exactly sane anymore. A vision of Chase flashed behind my eyes—of her reaching out to give magic to the man-beast that Greyson had become as they fought magic users, fought my friends, killing them, killing the people they had once cared for.

I couldn't become that. Wouldn't lose who Zayvion and I were apart, just for us to be together. I was trying too hard to keep us alive.

"No. I can't let him in me."

"Then let Stone carry his soul," New Dad said.

"He can do that?"

"It is possible," New Dad said. "The Animate holds magic." He paused, stared at Stone as if he could see his inner workings. "There is magic in him. And room for more."

"Will it hurt him? Hurt Zayvion?"

"I do not think so. It will need to be a short transfer, though. The Animate wasn't made to carry the weight of a soul for long. Zayvion will need to be returned to his body within thirty minutes. Perhaps less."

"Has anyone ever tested this?" See? Even confused and worried, I could ask good questions.

"There are histories of experiments where Animates have held souls," he said, "albeit only briefly."

"Tell me Zayvion will survive. Tell me his soul will survive." I needed to hear it. Those words, from that man.

"If he has the willpower and stamina. Yes."

I didn't need to hear any more.

"Do it. Let's do it." My mind was swirling with questions. How close to his body could they open the gate? How much stamina did Zayvion have left after all this time in death? How many ways could this go wrong?

Thousands.

Dad—Old Dad—spoke. "I will need to be in your mind to free Zayvion."

Thousands plus one. I just couldn't catch a break.

I locked gazes with Old Dad. He wanted back in my head, wanted to possess me again. I knew he'd try to work this to his own benefit. He never did anything, not one single thing, without thinking it through and meticulously securing the avenues to his own success.

Giving up my magic wasn't enough for him. He wanted to ride me, force himself into me, use me.

"No." I didn't have a lot of air, but I had plenty enough for that word.

"Time," Mikhail said, "is nearly gone."

What, did the guy have an hourglass somewhere around here sifting out the last grains of my life or something?

Stone clacked, sounding more like a watch winding down than my happy singing vacuum cleaner. He nudged my hand, and I realize I'd been leaning pretty hard on him. Okay, maybe time was running out.

New Dad walked over, his hands extended and open, palms up.

"Once magic is finally put right, I will leave you and your mind forever. Until then, please do the right thing."

I opened my mouth to add *hell no* to my reply.

Too late. Surgeon-quick, he stuck his hand in my head and did something fiddly that felt like fingertips pressing a key code on the inside of my skull. I tried to step back, to jerk away, but was frozen. Not even Stone moved.

And then Old Dad was no longer standing across the room from me.

Old Dad was back in my head, a familiar, scratching weight I could not shove away.

I still had the katana. Almost got it through New Dad, but New Dad backed away fast.

I wasn't as good with the sword one-handed and half-dead.

"You bastard," I whispered. "Get the hell out of my head."

New Dad gave me a blank stare. "I can't." New or not, he was my father, through and through.

A moan, low, soft, turned me to Zayvion. Mikhail was near him finishing a spell that left a fine mist in the shape of a Canceling glyph hovering in the air around Zay. The silver glyphs against Zay's skin were no longer stretched and nailed to the floor. He was free.

Zay blinked, moved his hands, fingers posed in a Ward spell.

Got to love a man whose first instinct is to fight.

"Go to him," Mikhail said.

I was already on my way. I sheathed the sword, because with my current dexterity, I'd probably behead us both, then looped my arm around his waist to support his weight as he took a step forward.

The contact hit me like lightning.

Vertigo rushed over me. I fell. Into Zay. Or maybe Zay fell into me.

*Allie,* he breathed.

I inhaled, gorging myself on the luscious textures of him, filling my mind, my body, and my soul. He stretched through me and waves of pleasure followed. He was worried, joyful, sad.

*This is forbidden,* he whispered.

*I don't care.*

I wanted this, needed this, needed him to know I loved him. If I could just hold him closer, run to him faster, breathe in his breath, we could have everything, life, death, and all magic, at our fingertips. I knew it was true, reveled in the knowledge. Joined as one, we could make everything right in the world.

*Zayvion,* I called, my voice, my thoughts echoing through me, through him, through us.

Pain filled me, a hammer shattering the middle of my brain.

Inside my mind, my father's voice rang out like thunder. *Let go, or he will die.*

I couldn't let go. I wouldn't let go.

And I didn't.

Zayvion did. He pulled away, pulled back. Pushed me when I grasped at him, slipped between my fingers as I tried to hold him.

*No,* I whispered. *Don't leave me.*

*What have you done?* he growled, primal, angry, painful in my mind. *Do not touch me.*

He yanked, out of me, out of us. Yes, it hurt. Holy loves, it hurt.

I gasped, sucked air, sobbed out a moan. Opened my eyes, just my eyes.

I was on the ground. Stone stood above me. Stone was covered in black fire. And there was an angry intelligence shining out from those eyes that was not his.

I lifted my hand, amazed I could do that much, and touched Stone's snout.

"Zay?"

Stone growled and jerked his head away from me. He stepped back.

Which meant I couldn't breathe. Except I could. Enough to fill my lungs and roll onto one hip. I felt like every rib was bruised. Why could I breathe?

A moth-wing flutter snapped at the back of my eyes.

My dead dad was in my head—and having him there allowed me to breathe. I was now neither fully alive nor dead. And I had almost done the one thing I'd sworn I wouldn't do—become so much a part of Zay, I lost myself. Holy shit.

Mikhail did not seem to care about any of this.

He sang. I thought I'd heard glimpses of that song, in my dreams, in my fevers. It tugged at me. Made me sad and hopeful. But as soon as each note faded away, it was lost to me. The song brushed over me like a slow wind and left no echo behind.

He cast a glyph, and even though magic was visible, I could not follow the pattern he wove.

The rose in his hand, my rose, my magic, pulsed, sending tiny chains of ribbons into the spell he wove.

I ached inside.

The gate opened, a burning, beautiful filigree that pushed apart the reality of the room, creating a window. There was grass beyond it, trees, life.

Seeing life again, grass again, cleared my head.

I didn't know how close to Maeve's inn the gate was, but I did not care. I'd get Zayvion and Stone there somehow. I pushed up onto my feet.

Stone looked back at me, his ears pricked up. Not my happy lug. There was more Zen in that look. More intelligence.

It was really, really weird to see Zayvion looking out from that stone exterior.

"Go now," Mikhail said. "Stand strong."

New Dad raised his hand. "Good-bye, Angel."

The gate had almost burned open to its widest points, creating a hole big enough that I could get through it if I ducked and stepped up a little.

I walked as close to it as I could without stepping through, Stone-Zay at my side. I glanced once over my shoulder.

Saw Mikhail open another door, just a regular door, across the room. Caught the glimpse of a woman lying prone upon a bed draped in gossamer and white lace. He crossed to her, knelt beside the bed, and placed the rose, my magic, upon her chest. A bloom of ribbons poured out from the rose and sent threads, like roots seeking water, into the lace and then down to lock into the floor. She looked like Sedra.

But before I could think that through, a shadow in the faintest outline of a man sidled up behind me. I blinked, turned toward it, and it was gone.

Stone's head bumped the back of my thigh. We had to

go. Now, before the gate closed. No more time to think, to worry. There was only time to do.

I stepped up, ducked, and fell through the gateway.

Stepping into death had been easy. A pause of breath and then cool, heavy numbness spread through me, dulling all sensation.

Stepping into life hurt like hell.

Heat raked across my skin in a toe-to-head wave, stabbing down to my bones, catching fire in my veins. I screamed, my voice silent to ears that could not hear. All around me light burned, darkness froze, and I knew if I didn't push forward, push into the pain, I would end here.

I lifted my foot, forced it forward.

My skin was stripped away, the heat eating into my muscles, burning me up, digging deeper for my heart and making it beat—

—one heavy thump—

Making me inhale, shudder.

As I fell into life.

Alive.

Stone-Zay fell beside me.

Wet grass against my skin, cool, soothing, the rich loamy scent of soil and living things. The sharp oil of crushed grass filled my nose, so strong I could taste it in my mouth. It was raining—I could feel it across my back, my legs, hear the beetle-wing ticking of it against my boots and the hard leather of the sword sheath. I'd never thought rain would feel so good, as if the sky and earth were patting me down, assuring me I was indeed home again, alive, whole.

"Shit. Allie?" a man's voice, a familiar voice, said.

I looked up. Blinked. It was night, a thin layer of clouds against the sky lit by the lamps in Cathedral Park. I'd landed in St. Johns, in the park beneath the bridge. And standing above me was Detective Paul Stotts.

# Chapter Five

I tried to tell him I needed to get Stone to Maeve's, but nothing came out of my mouth. I swallowed, tried again. Just wheezy exhale.

Crap. I braced my hands under me and pushed. I felt, acutely, every blade of grass bend and then spring across my palm. Didn't manage to get anywhere, though.

Stotts bent and hooked my elbows, helping me sit. The heat of his touch made me suck in a breath, the grip of his hands against my elbows an overwhelming sensation. Real, living hands, touching the real, living me. My senses were blown open after being smothered in death. Any contact felt a thousand times stronger.

I wondered if this was how a prisoner released from solitary confinement felt.

The spices and orange of Stotts' cologne filled me with memories of flowers and food. My mouth watered, my stomach cramped. I was starving. For food, yes. But also for sensation, life, touch.

Stotts pulled away.

I managed to remain sitting. Sitting was good. The park spinning like a tequila roller coaster was less good. I felt numb almost everywhere, except my chest, which someone had carved a hole in and filled with ice. I pressed one hand against my sternum. No hole.

Then it hit me. My small magic was gone. I felt empty. Raw. Hollowed out. Death had changed me, and I had no idea what I'd become.

"Nice sword," Stotts said, drawing my thoughts away from that horror.

"I need . . . " Yay—I had a voice! I inhaled, coughed. Swore silently at the pain. I needed to get Zayvion to Zayvion. Needed to get Stone to Maeve's. Needed a car. Or a pair of legs that worked. He liked my sword?

A hand tapped my cheek. I blinked. Opened my eyes. Why had I closed them?

"Allie, keep your eyes open. That's good. Good. What is that thing?"

I looked at that thing. Stone. Who sat there like a big statue. Except his ears twitched and he blinked.

"Pet," I managed. "Good. Magic pet." I was getting better at this talking stuff. "Car."

Stotts frowned and tipped my face so he could better look in my eyes. He had squatted in front of me, cell phone or police walkie-talkie or whatever it was, in his other hand. He didn't look as wet as I felt. "Ambulance is more like it. You're burning up."

He was wrong. I was freezing. And an ambulance wasn't what I needed. I had to get Stone to Zayvion in less than a half hour. Dad had said I had only that much time before Stone wouldn't be able to carry Zay's soul.

I wondered if Dad was still in my head, but I couldn't clear my mind enough to find out.

"No. Please," I said. "I have to get Stone—the pet, to Vancouver. It's a magic spell. In less than half an hour. Or Zay dies."

Stotts frowned. Closed his cell. He hadn't talked to anyone. Hadn't gotten through to 911, or at least I didn't think he had.

"What's going on?"

"Zay's in a coma. His soul—it's in Stone. Magic. I found him. Just found him. Don't let me lose him."

He glanced over at Stone and squinted. "It's going to be okay. Stay there and rest. I'll take care of you." He stood.

I could tell by his tone of voice he thought I was delusional.

"Listen to me," I said clearly. "There is more magic going on in this city than even you know about. And that"—I pointed at Stone—"is a part of the magic. Someone bound Zayvion's soul to it, and if I don't get it back to Zayvion's living body, he will die."

He didn't look convinced. "Where have you been for the past week?"

Week? Holy shit.

"Looking for that." It came out almost all growl. "Help me get Zay's soul back to him, or I swear I will knock you out and steal your car."

"Can you even walk?" He looked back down at me. Didn't offer a hand. He was making a point.

Screw that.

I'd walk through death and back—again—to save Zayvion. One know-it-all detective wasn't going to stand in my way now.

I pushed up onto my knees and then somehow, out of sheer grit and stubbornness, stood.

Stotts' eyebrows notched up.

"You either help me, Detective Stotts, or get the hell out of my way." I took a step toward Stone. Just that one step made me want to weep in exhaustion. But I didn't stop.

"Come on, Stone. Let's find a cab."

Stotts breathed a curse. I smelled the ashy afterburn of a spell—probably Sight. He'd gotten a look at Stone through magical eyes. Using a spell like that made it obvious that magic fueled him.

Stotts took the time to rattle off a few more swear words. I didn't think they were in English.

My ears were ringing now. The magic in my soul was gone, but the magic that flowed beneath the city could still follow the lines and paths Cody had painted in my bones, my blood, my body. Since I was in St. Johns where there was no natural magic, I wasn't suffering from overload yet. As soon as we passed the railroad tracks out of town, I'd be screwed.

Stone was under my hand again, the subtle textures of his head like fur beneath my fingers. He supported me in life as he had supported me in death, which was good. I was pretty sure I was about to pass out.

An arm wrapped around my waist, strong, warm, and I moaned a little. I wanted him to hold me, so I would know skin-to-skin and heartbeat-to-heartbeat that I was alive.

My logical mind knew that need for contact had to be a reaction to being dead. To being so devoid of sensation. I was starving for touch. Any kind of touch.

"Think you can make it to the car?" he asked.

I pressed my lips together, glanced across the park. The parking lot was maybe a block away. I could do that. I hoped. I took another step.

Stone grumbled like a bag of rocks, then cooed louder, like he had just figured out how to make that sound. He swiveled his head to look up at Stotts and me, and pulled his lips back from his fangs.

"Is it dangerous?" Stotts asked.

"No."

"It's not alive?"

"It's magic."

"No magic I've ever seen."

That was a problem. Stone was one of those things that the Authority didn't like common magic users knowing about. Hells, the Authority didn't even like common magic users knowing about the Authority. I'd just exposed Stotts, a man of the law and my best friend Nola's boyfriend, to something he should not have seen.

Which put him in danger of having his memories wiped out by the Authority. And put the Authority in danger of being discovered by the justice system.

I tried to think up a solution as we slogged through the damp grass, with only the lap of the river to our left and the hiss of car tires on the distant street to our right breaking the silence of the night.

"It might be better if you don't come with me," I said. We were almost at the parking lot. If this was what Mikhail called opening the gate close to Zayvion's body, I was going to kill a compass and a slide rule and send them through the gates of death to him.

"I've been looking for you for a week. Nola hasn't heard from you in a week either." He grunted as we made it up a small incline to the pavement. "You are in no shape to drive."

I wanted to argue, but the man was right. I was beyond exhausted. My vision was still closing in. I watched as Stotts' car approached us with jerky steps—or rather, as we approached it.

Stone trotted ahead of us and crouched near the passenger's side, out of sight of the rest of the parking lot. I was glad it was dark.

"It's coming with us, right?" Stotts asked. He was breathing a little hard. I wondered why.

He leaned me against the car, let go of my hand over his shoulder, but kept his arm around my waist. The sword sheath on my back clunked against the car, and then wet metal soaked through the back of my shirt. Oh yeah. He was hauling around a stupid, almost unconscious person. Me. No wonder he was out of breath.

"Don't move."

Like I could.

Stotts reached across me and opened the front door. He smelled good, his body lean and heavy against mine. I savored the heat and movement of a real living body touching me and was absolutely no help getting myself in the car.

"Duck." He braced with his knees, and somehow got a hand on my shoulder to push me into the seat.

It was enough to clear my head. A little.

The interior of a car had never felt so much like a luxury hotel. I managed not to fall asleep as Stotts leaned in and buckled my seat belt for me.

"Will the gargoyle get in the car?" he asked. He look prepared to Tase it, cuff it, and read it its rights if necessary.

"Backseat."

Stotts shut the door, and opened the back. The car dipped under Stone's weight as he got in. I stared out the window working hard to stay awake. I watched the yellow streetlights of St. Johns that were stair-stepped up the hill away from the park as I waited for Stotts to come around to the driver's side. Ahead and to the left, a stand of trees filtered the light of the park lamps through bare spring limbs.

A shadow moved near the tree line. There was enough light that I should have been able to make out the features. No features. Just a shadow in the shape of a man, blackness against blackness.

Watching me.

I hadn't smelled anyone else in the park, and with my senses so high, I know I would have smelled him. I hadn't heard him either.

What might have been a few minutes or a few hours later, Stotts slid behind the wheel and started the car.

"Where does it need to be?"

"What?" I looked away from the shadow man.

"The gargoyle."

"Maeve Flynn's place. We need to take him to her. At her inn. Vancouver."

"Why Maeve?"

I hated a man who knew how to ask questions. I glanced back toward the shadow. It was gone. Hells. Could I be seeing things? "Maeve's very good at magic. As good as my dad was."

Stotts knew how powerful my father had been.

"You need a doctor," he said.

"She has one on staff."

His mouth pressed tight as he drove out of the parking lot. I looked, but didn't see the shadow anywhere in the trees.

"I don't like this," Stotts said.

"If I need a hospital, we can call an ambulance from there. I have to undo this . . . this. Paul, if you don't take me to Maeve's, I will shove you out of this car."

"That's how you convince me you're of sound mind and body?"

It was tempting to use Influence on him, but I didn't trust my control with magic. We were just over the railroad tracks and I was trying very hard to hold magic down, while it was trying very hard to press up into me like hot fingers digging for purchase, stinging against my bones. I didn't have the brain cells for anything else.

"You know this isn't about normal magic," I said. "You know there's something more going on in this city. You've probably suspected that for a long time."

A sharp pain shot through my mind. Ah, so my dad was still along for the ride. Well, I didn't care if he didn't want me to spill the Authority's secrets.

"I trust Maeve. She knows what's going on—enough to help me save Zayvion. I'll tell you anything you want to know if you just get me there. Fast."

No Influence. Still, that got through. Stotts was no dummy. He must have suspected for a while now that there was more back alley, black market magic going down in this town than he could account for.

And he was right.

"How long does he have?" He glanced in the rearview mirror at Stone, who sat uncharacteristically silent and still on the floor, looking more like a statue than Stone ever did.

"Less than thirty minutes."

I looked at where we were headed for the first time. Multitasking was way out of my reach right now. Even monotasking was stretching it.

It was dark and a light drizzle, not even enough for windshield wipers, spattered the window. The city was wet in the aftermath of a storm. Stotts drove toward Vancouver, making good time in the relatively light traffic. I was surprised he hadn't turned on the police lights at the top of the windshield.

"I'll get you there in fifteen or less," he said.

I closed my eyes. I didn't want to sleep. Too many nightmares waiting for me there, but holy hells I was exhausted.

Stotts shook my arm gently. "Come on, Allie. Time to go."

The engine was off, my door was open. Stotts was outside my door, tugging at me.

"We're there?" I wasn't tracking very well. The world skipped in a jerky half circle to my right. "Where's Zay? How long was I asleep?"

"Not long. Walk, Allie. If you really need to get to Zay, you'd better do it now." He dragged me out of the car, while I did what I could to help. We bumped into the back door, which was hinged open.

"Zay?"

"Right ahead of us."

I'd have to take his word on that. I couldn't see my own feet, much less three steps in front of me.

We made it across the gravel, then climbed a mountain of stairs, which was weird, because I'd thought the inn had only a couple stairs leading up to the porch. By the time we hit the front door, I didn't care about the stairs; I was blacking in and out and everything sounded like it was underwater. Good thing Stotts was strong.

I remember the door opening. I remember voices, too many, too burbly to distinguish one from the other. The smell of food engulfed me and made me hungry and sick at the same time. This was not the hospital, which I'd worried Stotts might have dragged me to. I knew by the familiar scents, this was Maeve's inn.

If this worked out, I was so going to give that man a big kiss. In a sisterly sort of way.

Then there was a brush of fingertips across my forehead. Cool, soothing.

"Allie?"

I opened my eyes. I was lying down, on a bed, I thought. And the man frowning above me wasn't Stotts.

"Shame." The word carried all my worry and relief to see him alive.

Shame was Zayvion's best friend, and a hell of a Death magic user. He'd blamed himself for Zayvion's being thrown into death and had pretty much made himself my bodyguard. The last time I'd seen him he was wounded on the battlefield, begging me not to step through the gate into death. It was great to see him alive.

He did not smile. He didn't look like he'd smiled in the last year. His usually fair skin was still a weird greenish shade, the circles under his eyes taking away all the laughter that sparkled in those green depths. No, not green anymore. His eyes were black. It looked strange on him, like his eyes were one big pupil.

"Here you are now, love," he said. "Good of you to wake up for us. Detective Paul Stotts, who is standing in the room with us, told me he found you delirious in St. Johns. Want to fill me in on how you got there?"

"Zay . . . " My breath gave out. I was getting seriously fed up with this. I took a deep breath. The room smelled of honeysuckle and antibacterial soap. "Zay's soul is in Stone. I brought it back with me. He needs to get back in his body. They said he can only stay in Stone for half an hour before it kills him. Can your mom help?"

"Me," he said flatly. He moved out of my vision, leaving me to stare at brown wood rafters against a white ceiling. The inn. Maybe even the room Zayvion, the Zayvion who was in a coma, was in.

I had never felt so tired in my life. I blinked. Opened my eyes when I realized someone was talking. I think some time had passed. My eyes felt hot, sticky. The voices were coming from the left.

I turned my head, the feather pillow cool beneath my cheek. The voices belonged to two people standing at the foot of Zayvion's bed. Shamus wore his usual black T-shirt and black jeans, his hair long enough that he had to brush his bangs out of his eyes. He wasn't wearing his fingerless gloves. Terric, who used to be Shame and Zayvion's close friend before he moved up to Seattle, was taller and thinner than Shame, with more of a fencer's build and a hunter's eyes. He'd cut his silvery white hair to a shoulder-length shag that sharpened his jaw and cheek. It was so good to see him alive too.

They were, of course, arguing about something.

They did not get along, even though everyone except Shame knew they should be Soul Complements.

Zayvion was still sleeping—well, still in a coma—in the bed I'd last seen him in. Between the beds stood Stone. He tipped his head side to side and stared at Zayvion, as if he couldn't quite figure out something.

On the other side of the bed was the doctor who had cared for Zay and me the last time we'd been here. Dr. Gina Fisher was stocky, confident, and blended both magic and medicine with such casual elegance she made it look easy.

Over in the corner of the room, watching every move we made, was Detective Stotts. Who should not be here, and who certainly should not find out what we were about to do with magic.

"Allison," Dr. Fisher said, "I'll need your help."

"How long?"

"It won't take too long."

That wasn't what I was asking. "How long have I been here?" I pushed at the covers, managed to shove the comforter down to my waist. Wished the room wasn't spinning.

"Five minutes is all," Shame said.

Terric helped me sit. His hands were strong and cool, and he gave me a brief smile. But there were lines of pain across his forehead and bruised purple circles beneath his eyes.

He looked as tired as I felt.

"What do I need to do?" I asked.

Shame answered. "You are the link, the bridge between life and death for him. You'll need to be in contact with Stone and Zay's body. Touch them both. Then I'll trigger the transfer."

"As for you, Detective Stotts, I'd say you could come over a mite closer." Shame sounded like a professor inviting a star student to step up to the blackboard. "This isn't something that's done round here every day."

Stotts stepped forward, but kept enough space between himself and the bed that Shame and the doctor had plenty of room to work. For the life of me, I did not know why Shame wanted to show Stotts this kind of thing. The Authority had worked very hard not to let the police, especially the police who specifically dealt with magical crime, like Stotts, catch any hint that other magic, darker magic, and simply undiscovered magic were happening every day in the city.

The doctor was already tracing a glyph in the air. She whispered a few words, then placed her fingertips on Zayvion's forehead. She turned her head to watch the monitor next to her. I didn't know what kind of equipment they had him on, but it showed his heartbeat and other numbers and lines.

I pushed my hair back behind my ears and took a breath. I needed to do this right.

"Now would be a good time to begin," Dr. Fisher said.

Terric helped me to my feet, both of which felt like overfull water balloons. He propped me up around my waist, and I took the three steps to Zay's bed.

"Touch Stone," Terric said, quietly, calmly. I glanced over at Shame. His head was bent, black bangs covering his face. He was singing, both palms flat toward the floor. I'd seen him like this before, when he'd pulled in magic and energy for the transfer of Death magic. What was he pulling on in the floor? Oh, right. The well of magic beneath the inn. If he could access magic on the other side of the railroad tracks in St. Johns, then I was pretty sure he could get through four or five stories of the inn and tap the well, even with the wards blocking it.

Something glowed beneath Shame's T-shirt, right in the center of his chest. Maybe a necklace? I didn't know; I'd never seen him wear anything that glowed.

I put my palm on Stone's head.

He rumbled, a deep purr that Stone never made. He lifted up on his back legs, and placed his hands on the bed, shifting until he was balanced on one and could place the other, lightly, on Zayvion's chest.

My hand slid down from Stone's head to the top of his shoulder.

Magic poured up through me, as it had been trying to since I belly flopped back into life. I felt like I was standing out in the sun with a day-old sunburn heating me everywhere except the cold dead pit where my small magic used to be. I was too sensitive, too aware of both the magic I had and the magic I was missing.

It hurt.

"Do I need to do something?" I asked. "Cast something?"

"No," Terric said. "Don't draw on magic at all. You're just the guide wire for his soul. The lightning rod." He paused. I didn't know what he was waiting for. I didn't know how my hand on Stone was doing Zayvion any good.

"When I tell you, touch Zayvion's body." Terric shifted, his left arm still around my waist, holding me up, and his right hand on my right wrist, so he could guide my hand.

Like I didn't have any motor skills or something.

Stone-Zay purred again.

Shame stopped singing. He lifted his hands, traced a glyph, and spoke one hard word.

"Now." Terric held my hand as I placed it gently on Zay's stomach.

Shame's spell hit.

It was like someone had pulled back the curtains on my exhaustion and let the sunlight and oxygen in. I felt awake, alive. I tasted mint and pine, and felt the warm wind of Zayvion around me, as if his arms instead of Terric's circled me, felt his lips brush my own, ghostly and soft, heard his whisper: "Allie . . . "

"Don't leave me," I thought, or maybe said.

My eyes were open. Without casting Sight, all I saw was Stone exhaling over Zayvion and Zayvion inhaling deeply. Dr. Fisher watched the screen and Zayvion. Shame chanted, a singsong this time that reminded me of a jump rope song sung in a minor key.

Stotts' body language was wire-tight.

Terric, behind me, was Grounding me. I could taste the cool spring-water scent of his magic at the back of my throat.

What did he think? I was going to lose control of my magic?

I wasn't even using magic.

"Enough," Shame said.

Terric tugged me back so that my hands fell off of both Zayvion and Stone at the same time.

"No." I didn't want to let go, didn't want to lose the ghostly awareness of Zayvion against my skin, inside my mind, close enough that it would just take a focused thought to hear what he was thinking, to feel what he was feeling.

To be us, instead of just me. Alone.

Wow. Déjà vu.

Terric had broken the connection between us. I tasted the separation from Zay as a sharp bite of heat, like sun-baked rocks on the roof of my mouth.

Stone dropped down off of the bed and sneezed. Several times, sending out little clouds of dust. He clacked and gurgled, then scrubbed the top of his head on the side of Zayvion's bed, shaking the whole thing. Poor thing looked like his brain itched.

"You okay, boy?" I asked.

Stone just rubbed his head and made bag-of-rock mumbly sounds.

Shame had one hand on Zayvion's foot. The doctor still had her hand on his forehead. She traced a glyph there, and for a moment it glowed silver against his skin.

Stotts shifted to better see what was happening. He didn't look happy about what was going down, but there was a sort of impressed curiosity in his expression too.

Seeing magic used like this was pretty amazing.

"His soul is returned," Dr. Fisher said. She nodded at Shamus. "Do you agree?"

Shame blinked, slowly. Traced a glyph with his left hand. I noted his hand was shaking, and Terric, who still had his arm around my waist, grunted very quietly. Probably Proxying for Shame's magic use.

That, I realized, was what the argument had been about.

I couldn't tell what glyph Shame cast. Maybe Sight. Whatever it was, it seemed to take far more effort than it should.

Shame stared. For a long time. For what felt like forever. Then, "Yes. His soul is there. Faint. But there. You—" He turned and stared at me with his dark, dark eyes. I'm not sure what he was going to say. But his eyebrows shot up. I could only guess that he also saw my dad in my head. Or maybe the hole where my magic used to be.

"Oh, Allie, what did you do?"

"I brought him back," I said. I didn't need him to tell me how screwed up I was. I didn't need him to remind me of everything I had lost, of the prices I was still paying. I brought Zayvion back. That was all that mattered. Wasn't it?

I tipped my chin up, daring him to call me out on the stupidity of my choices.

"Terric," he said softly, "help her back to bed. She needs rest."

Terric stepped back, but I pushed out of his arms. "I need to see." I braced both hands on the side of Zay's bed and looked down at him.

Dr. Fisher was applying nonmagical medical care, making notes on a clipboard chart, checking the IV hooked up to his left arm—the arm farthest away from me—and doing other doctorly things.

Zayvion was very still. Just like I'd last seen him. Coma-still.

"Zayvion?" This wasn't right. This wasn't how it was supposed to work. I brought his soul back from death, for cripes' sake. Walked into death, fought things, bargained with my father, with Mikhail, gave up parts of myself, and brought Zay's soul back just how they told me I had to. He couldn't be so still. Couldn't be so deathlike.

"Something's wrong," I said. "You did it wrong, Shame. He's not waking up. Why isn't he waking up?" My voice climbed an octave or so. Terric put a hand on my arm, but I shook him off. Anger, and maybe panic, was doing plenty to keep me on my feet.

"He's in a coma," Shame said.

"No. That's not good enough. Wake him up."

"Don't you think I would if I could?" Shame snapped.

Stotts stepped forward. "Take it easy," he said to Shame.

Shame didn't look at Stotts. He was too busy glaring at me.

"You are hurt, and you need to get in bed so the doctor can take care of you." At least his tone was back to normal.

The doctor calmly drew a glyph in the air.

"Do not," I said to her. "Do not cast magic on me." I was having a severe inclination to start screaming at people. I'd had too many people doing things to me, taking things from me, sticking their hands and magic where they didn't belong into me, changing me, to be reasonable anymore.

"Leave me the hell alone."

Terric put his hand on my arm again. Stone, who was done sneezing, growled at him.

Terric removed his hand and stepped back.

I needed to leave, leave the room and take Zayvion with me. I needed to find someone who would really help us. Someone who would really make him well. Thoughts rushed through my head so fast, they were a storm raining through me whipped by bitter fear. I needed to go somewhere safe. Somewhere nonmagical.

I needed Nola. She was my best friend. She always took me in when things went wrong, always let me stay on her farm in Burns that was miles away from any natural magic. I needed away from all this. From magic and everyone who used it. I needed Zay to be alive.

"I need to take Zay away now," I said in a voice so stilted it didn't even sound like my own.

A small, logical part of my mind was pretty sure I was going into a full-blown panic attack.

"It's okay," Dr. Fisher said in a reasonable tone. "I think Shamus is trying to help. You do need to rest and let me take a look at you. We have time for that. Zayvion's soul is back in his body. He's breathing well, his vitals signs are stable, he needs to rest before he goes anywhere with you. Now's a good time for us to make sure you aren't hurt."

She walked past Detective Stotts, giving him a reassuring nod as she passed. Then, to me, "I think Zayvion just needs a little more rest. His soul has gone through so much. As have you."

"He needs to wake up," I repeated. "I need to keep him safe. Nola. I need Nola."

Shame, smart man that he was, stepped away from Zay and leaned against the wall, his head back. He crossed his arms over his chest, watching me.

Terric, had oh-so-casually walked over to block the door. What did he think? That I was going to grab Zay and make a run for it?

Oh. Right. That was exactly what I'd said I wanted to do.

"Shame?" I said, looking for his reassurance.

He smiled. A little crooked, a little mocking. Thoroughly familiar. It did wonders to take my heartbeat down a notch. "Darlin', I know you've had a fucked-up time of it, but you are speeding down the fast lane to crazyville with no brakes. Listen to the nice doctor."

"I'm crazy?" Sad thing was, that would not surprise me.

"No, love. You're downright sane for someone who's been dead for a week."

Stotts shot a look at Shame. "Would you like to explain that to me, Mr. Flynn?"

"Sure. There was a huge magical fight out in St. Johns. Right when the wild-magic storm hit—you remember the storm, yes?"

"Yes."

The doctor had made her way over to me and she gently took both of my hands in hers. "You're okay. Let's get you in bed."

I let her lead me to the bed, too tired to fight, too tired to panic anymore.

She pulled the covers up over me and placed her hand on my forehead. "Any pain?"

"No. Wait. My chest. And my skin. And my head."

"That's a lot of no pain," she observed.

I nodded, not really listening to her. I was listening to Shame tell Stotts all the secrets the Authority had worked very hard to keep away from police like him.

"So we created a storm rod using the disks—you do know about those? The disks Allie's da and his wife, Violet, developed? They hold magic in them, and then let you use that magic for no price."

"I know about them," Stotts said. "They were recently stolen."

"Right. They were brought to us. And we used the disks to channel the wild magic of the storm, so it wouldn't blow out the city's networks. Problem is, a few of the people in on this little maneuver decided the time was ripe to push their own agendas."

"What agendas?"

"It'd take a while for me to go through them all, but to sum up: some magic users got angry and started a fight."

Oh, that was the understatement of the year.

I checked to see if Terric was aware of Shame blabbing all the Authority's secrets to the police. He caught me looking and lifted his eyebrows in a tolerant expression. Apparently, Shame doing this wasn't that big of a surprise.

What the hell? Had the Authority suddenly decided to let the cops in on their secret—and if not illegal, certainly unregulated—use of magic? And all this time they'd been telling me that if I let one little secret slip, they'd take my memories away. Totally unfair.

"In the middle of that fight," Shame continued, "a gate into death was opened, which brings me to the reason I'm going into this round-a-ways explanation. Allie went through that gate into death"—he turned and looked at me—"because she is a crazy, lovely fool."

He looked back at Stotts. "And today you were there to catch her when she fell out of death. Then you brought her here instead of to a hospital or a mental ward. I can only guess because whatever she told you, you believed. I have to admit I'm more than a bit curious what she said to you."

Stotts didn't say anything. I was surprised he didn't just laugh at Shame. It all sounded ridiculous when rattled off like that.

But Stotts had seen enough, dealing with magical crimes in this city, to know the truth—no matter how far-fetched—when he heard it.

"What are you planning to do with her now?"

"Let her get some shut-eye, and some medical care. She and Zay both, for that matter. As for the rest of us sorry souls, we have coffee and pie two floors down. Let's say we get out of the doctor's way and get in the way of some apple pie à la mode."

"That would be fine, Shamus," Dr. Fisher said. "If you have further questions, Detective Stotts, I'll join you for coffee in just a few minutes."

Stotts hesitated. He looked over at me.

"I'm fine. Tired." And just in case he didn't believe me, I

added, "Dr. Fisher has taken care of me before and I trust her. Everything sort of hit me at once."

He glanced again at Zayvion and at the doctor, who was currently taking my blood pressure. "I wouldn't mind a cup of coffee," he said. "Mr. Flynn?"

"Shame," Shame said. "All my friends call me Shame. Coffee it is. You're not coming are you, Terric?"

"Someone has to make you pay the bill."

Shame snorted. "I'll put it on my tab."

They walked out, Shame in the lead, talking to Stotts about his mum being out of town. Terric paused at the door, watching the two men walk down the hall.

"Is he okay?" I asked.

"Shame?" I couldn't read his expression, but his body language was tight with exhaustion. The way family members look when a loved one is fighting a disease and the outcome is grim. "He's very stubborn and focused." He turned enough I could see his eyes. Tired, but with that hunter's glint.

"Don't worry about that right now. Just rest. You did a hell of a thing, Allie." He stopped, as if searching for words, and finally just shook his head. "An impossible thing. It's no wonder you're Zayvion's Soul Complement. Get some sleep. You're safe here."

I was going to ask him what I was safe from, but by the time I thought to ask, he had shut the door behind him.

# Chapter Six

I didn't dream and I didn't have nightmares. I did wake up in the middle of what may have been night or morning, having thought I heard Zayvion calling my name. But when I whispered his name in return, nothing but his deep breathing in the bed next to mine answered. I thought I felt a hand press on my forehead once and had a foggy recollection of finding my way to the bathroom, but mostly it was just deep, deep sleep.

The inn was usually such a noisy place I always slept fitfully. Now it was quiet, as if someone had wrapped the room in wool. I reveled in it.

When I finally woke, I savored the soft, warm blankets, the steady rhythm of Zayvion's breathing, and tried to imagine I was at home, in my bed, with Zayvion's arms around me.

I wasn't ready to open my eyes. Because I knew as soon as I did, all the things that were going wrong, all the pain and fear and disasters would crowd in, and I'd have to take care of them.

What I wanted was a cup of coffee, something to eat, because damn, I was hungry, and a quiet place to catch my breath, even if for only a few minutes.

"Mornin', darlin'," Shame said from somewhere on the other side of Zay's bed. "Want coffee or a shower first?"

I was sure I was going to say coffee, but the idea, the memory of warm water on my skin got a soft moan out of me.

"I'd kill for a shower," I mumbled into my pillow.

"That sounded like shower." I heard him shift and walk to the bathroom.

The squeak of a handle and the rush of water against tile was enough for me to pull my head out from under the covers. I rested there, eyes still closed, wondering if I had the energy to make it all the way across the room.

"Need a hand?" Shame asked from right next to me. Boy could be a quiet thing when he tried.

I opened my eyes.

Shame must have recently taken a shower; his dark hair was still wet, dripping down on the shoulders of his gray T-shirt. I don't think I'd ever seen him in anything but black. Gray looked good on him, and so did the faded blue jeans. It helped to relieve the sallow green of his skin, and the engulfing blackness of his eyes. Sure, he still looked like the winner of a yearlong insomniac marathon, but Terric was right—stubborn and focused.

"Hand?" he repeated. "Or do you think you can wander along on your own?"

Right. Conversation. I might want to try some of that. "Maybe some help."

Turned out it took more than some help to get me to the shower. Sitting made me dizzy, but it passed quickly. Still, Shame didn't take any chances. He tucked his arm around my waist and did most of the heavy lifting as I walked across the floor.

Once in the bathroom, though, I had gotten the walking thing down. Plus, I really needed to pee, and did not want Shame's help with that.

"I'm good," I said as I sat on the small bench along the wall.

"Are you sure?"

I patted the fluffy towel folded on the bench next to me. "I got it from here."

"I wouldn't want you to get in the shower and then pass out or some such. How about if I help you get out of your clothes? I'm an expert in platonic undressings." He gave me that wicked smile.

"Give it a rest. I'm not going to strip naked in front of you, and I'd rather pee in private."

"Half the injuries in a home happen in the bathroom. What kind of friend would I be to let you face that kind of danger alone? I mean, sure, you walked out of death, but this is a *shower*."

"Shame. Get out of my bathroom."

He chuckled. "Oh, so that's the way you show gratitude—and me the person who's loaning you a bed, I might add."

"It's your mom's place. She's loaning me the bed."

"Details," he said, waving his hand. "I'll be outside the door if you need anything."

"You mean so you can laugh at me if I fall."

"That too."

He finally left the room, shut the door, and left me to my business. I used the toilet, then got out of my shirt and sweatpants. I wasn't wearing a bra, and didn't recognize my panties.

That, let me tell you, is a strange feeling. But since Maeve had a knack for attracting wounded magic users—or maybe just me—I had to assume she kept some basic supplies on hand.

I shivered in pleasure as the water caressed my skin and washed away the sweat, dirt, and stink that clung to me. My thoughts drifted to death, to my time there, which felt like a foggy dream, but clear enough I remembered what had happened and what I had done. With the cold emptiness in my chest, how could I forget?

I opened my left hand and tipped my palm so the light could catch it, looking for the mark Mikhail had left in me.

A smudge, like the slightest silver against my palm, formed a circle. The lines of my hand cut a perfect X through it. It didn't hurt, didn't impede movement. Without the silver sheen, it might not even have been noticeable.

But I knew it was dark magic. A part of Mikhail. A guarantee. Maybe more than that. I'd have to ask one of my teachers—Maeve or Victor or Jingo Jingo—what they thought about it.

Jingo.

Like a car kicking from neutral to fourth gear, all the events of the last few days, weeks, rushed through me. We had been in the middle of a battle, in the middle of a wild-magic storm, when I stepped through the gate to death. I had a lot of catching up to do.

I made quick work of washing. I didn't look for new scars, didn't care that the black bars on my left elbow, wrist, and knuckles looked sort of silvery-gray. Didn't take the time to see if the ribbons of color on my hand and arm had changed.

Getting Zayvion's soul out of death was the only thing I'd been thinking about. But there was so much more going on. So much more going wrong.

I turned off the water, toweled, and found a soft white terry-cloth robe on the back of the door to shrug into. I rubbed my head with the towel one more time, then had to sit to catch my breath.

I wasn't all well yet, but I was getting better. Food would do me wonders.

I heard a knock at the main room's door, and Shame answering it. Then clacking sounds like dishes on a cart.

Food.

I brushed my hair, used a toothbrush, and opened the door.

Shame sat in the chair on the far side of Zay's bed, near the curtained window. In the shadowy corner, there was a strange pinkish glow on Shame's shirt—right in the middle of his chest. I'd seen that same glow when he was drawing on magic. I stopped in the doorway to the bathroom, one hand on the doorjamb to keep me steady.

"Ready to eat something?" he asked.

"Why are you glowing?"

"I'm happy?"

I stopped staring at his chest and met his gaze. "Your chest is glowing."

"Did death completely kill your appreciation for sarcasm?" He shoved up onto his feet, pressing both palms against his knees to do so. "Because you used to get my jokes."

The glow moved with him. It definitely wasn't from an outside source. Something was glowing under his shirt.

He sighed and stared up at the ceiling, his hands slack beside him. "Would you just stop with the deer-in-the-headlights thing and sit already?" He tipped his head down. "I promised my mum I'd see that you ate before she came by to see you."

I heard what Shame was saying, but my mind was stuck on what I suspected that glow to be.

"Lift up your shirt," I whispered.

"Here? In front of your boyfriend? Naughty."

"I need to see."

Shame tucked his fingers under the edge of his shirt and lifted.

His skin was pale, freckled, his stomach flat and muscular, with a couple scars, one that looked like he'd had his appendix out, others that were from knives, or broken glass or maybe teeth.

In the center of his chest dead-square in his sternum was a rose-colored crystal. It was as if someone had implanted a jewel the size of a quarter into his skin. And that jewel was glowing.

"What is that?" I asked.

Shame dropped the T-shirt back in place and walked over to me. "That is the crystal Terric used to save my life. The spell he cast clashed with the wild-magic storm. We think."

He took my elbow and got me moving, across the room to the bed, where a tray was set with food for me. "The crystal sort of melted until a thumb-sized disk was left and when Terric completed the spell, the crystal grafted itself into me. I fucking sparkle."

"You hate that, don't you?"

"You have no idea."

I climbed into the bed and Shame waited while I pulled the covers back over my feet before swiveling the tray over my lap.

"Do you remember much about the fight?" He strolled across the room and brought the chair around between the two beds.

"I think so." My tray had breakfast on it. Oatmeal, eggs, apple juice, toast, and a cup of coffee.

"Terric told me you threw him that crystal—the one you found at the labs when you were Hounding for Stotts to find out who stole all the disks."

I nodded. I remembered that too. I took a sip of coffee. Rich, black, hot, it burned all the way down to my stomach. I followed that up with a scoop of oatmeal—cut oats sweetened with a little brown sugar and orange marmalade. Best. Oatmeal. Ever. If someone told me it was poisoned, I'd still eat it.

"Terric," Shame said, "has apparently been doing a hell of a lot of studying since he and I used to be on talking terms. Took up some of the medical side of spell casting, trying to build his ability to endure Blood magic and Death magic. He's a Closer, right? So his specialty should be Faith magic, but no, he's still studying them all. Crazy git.

"Whatever. The outcome is he bound the crystal to me and got Blood magic mixed up in it too. It's not supposed to work that way. I mean, I've never seen a crystal like this, and I don't know what your da did to it, but it connected to me. Maybe because I was pulling Death magic like a freakin' fiend and was starving for a transfer of energy—any energy." He rubbed his hand over his hair, dragging his ring finger and thumb through his bangs to pull them back from his face.

"I don't know. Neither do the doctors. Right now we know it worked—it kept me from dying. And the side effects aren't more than I can handle, so . . . " He shrugged.

It was a lot to take in. I moved on to my toast and eggs and demolished the eggs in short order. "Side effects?"

"Like the wrist cuffs we use, but stronger."

"The crystal tells you where people are?"

"Just Terric. I know where Terric is. Always where Terric is. And I know what he's feeling."

He watched me, waiting. Shame told me once that he had nearly killed Terric with magic. Most people in the Authority believed Shame had been under the control of a Hunger—one of the creatures from death—when it happened. Shame believed that he alone had nearly killed his friend. And the only reason Terric had survived that attack was that Shame's and Terric's magic blended. Like Soul Complements.

But Shame refused the test to find out if he and Terric were meant to be Soul Complements, meant to use magic together, were meant to spend a lifetime together. He told me he owed Terric that much—the certainty that Shame wouldn't try to kill him again.

Now that I knew about Leander and Isabelle, I understood his hesitation better.

The damage to Terric had been severe enough that he lost the chance of ever becoming a guardian of the gate. He'd moved to Seattle and, if I had the story right, hadn't been back here to see Shame, or Zay, until a few weeks ago.

So I understood that being connected to Terric wasn't Shame's idea of a good thing.

"Does Terric feel you too?" I asked.

"Yep."

"Huh."

"I tell you I have a magic stone *implanted* in my *chest* that ties me to the one man I most want to be untied from and all you give me is a 'huh'? Where's the love, Beckstrom?"

I drank the last of my coffee, then frowned at my empty cup. "Here's the love: I'm glad you're alive."

"Well, that's something at least."

"Dad told me he grew glyphs into the crystal," I said, digging back into my memory. "He was pretty proud about that. Maybe whatever spell he grew in it is part of what made the crystal connect to you. I don't know anything else about it, except he said he found the crystal in St. Johns."

"I'm sure the doctor will be happy to hear that. Or a geologist." He wove his fingers together and propped them against his mouth, elbows resting on his thighs. "So. Want to tell me why your soul magic's gone?"

I swallowed the last of the toast. What was it about Shame? When he looked at me like that, like he could see all the way into my soul and find it lacking, which apparently, he just had, all I wanted to do was cry.

"I had to pay a price," I said, my voice steady, flat. There were so many emotions crowding my heart that none of them could rise to the surface. "I had to get Zay's soul back."

"And your magic was the price, then?"

I nodded. "How long have you known?"

"That you had a small magic in you? Since the first day

you tested with Mum and me. The thing with you carrying magic in your body is unheard of, but when Mum pushed you past using that, you drew on the small flame inside you. That's crazy-rare."

"And now it's extinct."

I pushed the tray away but held on to my cup. "Could I have more coffee?" I really didn't want to talk about it. Didn't want someone else looking at my wounds, my lack, my deformity.

"It's amazing, what you do, what you endure. Have I told you that?"

I shook my head and my hair swung forward to hide the right side of my face. I didn't think it was amazing when you had no choice but to endure the consequences of your own stupid decisions. "Is Zay really going to wake up?"

Shame rocked forward and took my coffee cup and hand.

I lifted my gaze.

"Yes. His soul is back. He's strong. And he has someone to wake up for. You. Z's a smart man. He isn't about to give up on what the two of you have. Now"—he pulled the cup out of my hand and strolled over to a carafe I hadn't noticed on the dresser—"I'm going to fill you in on a few things. Mum wanted to be the one to talk to you, but she's not here right now, and I'm not the patient sort."

"Is she okay?" The memories of the fight flashed behind my eyes again. "I don't know who was badly hurt, I don't know how the fight ended." Memories tumbled faster and faster and my mouth couldn't keep up.

Sweet hells, what was wrong with me? I felt so out of step with myself, with everything.

My hands shook, and tears hovered just behind my eyes again. "I don't even know what day it is. How long have I been . . . "

"Dead?" He turned, the coffee in his hand, a smile on

his lips. "Let's start there. We didn't think you were going to come out of that, you know. There's not a single historical footnote indicating survival. People can't just stroll over into death, easy as you please. Those who do never come strolling home again.

"You, my dear lass, are either very lucky or very strong. And if you ever try to do that again, I will break your damn legs."

He handed me the coffee and sat in the chair.

"You were in death, Allie. The real deal. You were dead. And now you're alive. That's a bloody miracle."

"Yay?" I said. It came out kind of small and breathy and Shame just shook his head.

"The storm," he continued, "hit eleven days ago. Detective Stotts brought you here three days ago. You've been sleeping most of that time. Despite the fact that there's no logical reason you should be alive, you are healthy. With enough rest, the doctor thinks you'll be making a full recovery. Not that any of us know how you did it."

I took a sip of coffee, trying to get my head around losing a week of my life. Unfortunately, it wasn't all that hard. I'd had a lot of practice with such things.

"My dad," I said. "He was there, with me. Told me how I could breathe, how I could survive." I stared at the wall, remembering the mutated Veiled, and the city of death, the pillar and Mikhail.

"Do you remember it?" he asked.

I nodded. "Is my notebook around here somewhere?" I asked. "I want to write it down in case I forget."

"Don't know where your book is. But I can get you something to write in." He walked over to the dresser again, dug in the top drawer, and pulled out a pen and scratch pad. "Good enough?" he asked, holding up both.

"Yes. Thanks." The coffee was doing me some good, or maybe it was the food. Whatever it was, I felt a little better.

I took a solid five minutes writing down everything I could remember in my quick shorthand.

"What was it like?" Shame finally asked when I stopped writing.

"It was a city. A broken city that looked a little like Portland. But no angels, no flames. It wasn't what I thought death would be." I picked up an orange slice on the tray and ate it.

"We ended up at a massive treelike structure. Only it wasn't a tree. Dad said it was the pillar of Death magic. He said it's like the wells and holds the magic in death. Inside that was where we found Zayvion. The details are sort of fuzzy."

"Through the eyes of the living, only death's mask can be seen."

"Poetry?" I asked, going for a second slice of orange.

"It's from the old texts. Death magic. Means only the dead can see death for what it really is. The living mind can't interpret what it's seeing, so it supplies its own images."

"I can tell you there were no angels there."

He shrugged. "Have you ever met an angel? For all you know they might look like toaster ovens."

"Not a lot of toaster ovens either." But I was smiling, and some of the intensity in Shame's gaze softened as he leaned back.

"So who else was hurt from the fight?" I asked.

"No one got out of that mess without some kind of injury. Everyone who didn't run is recovering. Mum's doing some physical therapy. The hit she took, the fall . . . " He stopped and I could almost taste the anger pouring through him. "She has some nerve damage. Doctors don't know how extensive the damage will be. She still needs more time to heal."

"Jingo Jingo?" I asked, knowing he was the one who had hurt Maeve.

So much for the intensity going down a notch. "He's free, gone, disappeared. Took Sedra with him, and fuck all if we can catch a sniff of where they are. Fucking backstabbing bastard."

"He tried to kill us all, didn't he?" I asked. I was there, I'd seen it, but I needed to hear it from Shame, needed to know that what had happened before I stepped into death had been real, and not just a bad dream.

"Fucking sold us out. We don't know why he's holding Sedra—haven't gotten a ransom note, demands, or any contact from him at all. Think he took most of the disks with him too, though we took a few dozen and locked them up down in the vaults. He's not the only one who's turned against the Authority.

"Liddy's dead." His voice cracked. She had been his teacher a lot longer than she had been mine. Taught Death magic, the discipline Shame used. For all I knew, she had been his teacher since he was a kid.

He pulled his hair back off his face again. "There wasn't anything left of her to bury."

"Chase and Greyson?"

"Locked up."

"Downstairs by the well?"

"No. They're locked away in a place where people who really piss off the Authority are taken."

"Are you going to tell me where that is?" Seemed to me they were our best link to finding Jingo Jingo and Sedra, and whoever else was involved in this mess since they had turned on us all and sided with Jingo Jingo.

"I don't know where it is. Only the Voices get that information."

Voices of the Authority were members who spoke for a certain discipline of magic. Maeve was the voice for Blood magic, Victor for Faith, Liddy had been for Death, and Sedra was both the voice for Life magic, and also the Head of the Authority. I guess my father had been the voice for Flux magic—the newest, and technologically integrated, form of magic use.

I wondered who would be the new Voice for Death magic now that Liddy was dead and Jingo Jingo had betrayed the Authority. I wondered if they were planning on Closing Jingo Jingo when they found him, or if they were going to lock him away too.

If I had any say about it, he'd be dead.

Because if I was right, he was the one behind Greyson and Chase shoving Zayvion into death. He had tried to kill Maeve, betrayed the Authority, kidnapped Sedra, and Chase and Greyson had fought right alongside him. He was quickly acquiring a long list of crimes. And those were only the things we knew about. What else was he involved in that we didn't know?

"Do you think Jingo Jingo's behind it all?" I asked. Flat, emotionless. That strange disconnect again, where too many emotions made me feel like I had none.

Shame nodded. "Even if he's not the mind behind it all, his hands are so dirty there's not enough water in the world to wash his soul clean."

"Has anyone gotten into Chase's and Greyson's heads to see what they know?"

"Victor's been working on it. But there's not a lot left for him to work with."

"What do you mean?"

"They broke. Their minds broke. Chase and Greyson aren't much more than vegetables. Empty, drooling husks." His voice dropped into a growl, and his hands were fists.

"Soul Complements," he said. "Ain't no happily ever after."

I looked over at Zayvion. He was still breathing, still, to all outward appearances, sleeping.

Shame said his soul was safely back in his body. But

there were no guarantees. There were never any guarantees for Soul Complements. I was beginning to wonder why they let anyone find out they were meant for each other in that way. What good ever came of it?

For an organization that stole people's memories and magic, it didn't seem like it would take much to simply forbid Soul Complements to ever be together or to ever remember that they had been together.

Shame looked at Zayvion too. "Not you and Zayvion. That story's not done being told."

"You really think we're going to have a happily ever after?"

"Maybe not bubblegum and roses, but yes. I think you two are going to be the exception to the rule."

"Why not you and Terric?"

"First, we'd have to test to see if we really are Soul Complements. Don't look at me like that. And second, he and I are better off if we stay out of grenade-throwing distance."

"He saved your life."

"I know."

"You could have killed him when he was trying to save you during the fight. He held you for a long time on that battlefield. Fought off the Hungers and other beasts. Protected you. There was plenty of life and magic in him. You could have drained him to save yourself."

"I know."

"And you didn't."

"I know."

He didn't say anything else.

I knew a brick wall when I saw one. I wasn't going to get any more out of Shame about the state of his relationship with Terric. At least he wasn't arguing. He might not want to think about it, but he knew something had changed between him and the silver-haired Closer. Something more than just a strange magic crystal beating in his chest.

"So Jingo Jingo is missing with Sedra, Chase and Greyson are in jail. Who else decided to pick a fight in the middle of the storm? Mike Barham?" I thought I remembered the Closer who had come down from Seattle to help with the storm, and whom Shame had tried to stab with a cheese knife, fighting against us but I wasn't sure.

"Mike's as gone as Jingo. Dane Lannister's missing too. It's a mess. That's what I wanted to tell you before Mum showed up. The Authority is falling down. No one trusts anyone—for good reason."

"I trust you." Yes, I was surprised that came out of my mouth. I wasn't the trusting type. But it was the truth. I did trust him. He had done everything in his power to try to save Zayvion, his mother, and me. I knew where his heart was, even if he didn't.

"Yes, well. You should know better than that," he said with a smile.

"So who are the good guys?"

He took a deep breath and stood again, stretching. Even though he looked really tired, there was a restlessness in him that I hadn't seen before. Like he knew the time for running was long gone but the danger hadn't hit yet, and all that was left to do was wait.

He moved back over to the carafe and poured some coffee into the other cup.

"Good guys. Well, in the most general terms, me, you, Zay, Terric, Victor, and Mum. Most of the Seattle crew—Hayden, the Georgia sisters, Nik, and Joshua, though I don't think Joshua is well enough to fight. The twins, Carl and La, and of course Sunny." He poured a generous share of cream into his coffee, then spooned in three heaps of sugar.

"There are other people who weren't at the storm, who aren't causing trouble. And many, many more throughout Portland who say they're all for one for the Authority but don't see the need to get involved in the fight.

"Fine by me, I say. That way I don't have to trust anyone outside the small circle I just mentioned." He took a drink of his coffee, poured in a little more cream, then stood at the foot of my bed.

"The Authority in Portland isn't the only governing body over magic. Every district has one. But we are unique because we have four wells in such a small space. Most cities have one well, and need only one Voice to govern for the Authority's rules. We have four wells, four Voices, and of course your da's idea of magic—the networks and storage cisterns that are a man-made well of magic that we have to take care of. So four natural and one technological well means there's a lot of strong magic here and a lot of strong people with strong opinions.

"Districts outside Portland are waiting and watching what happens here. Other cities, other members of the Authority are waiting to see if we implode, break down, break up. They want to see how we fail, and who loses, so they can learn from our mistakes."

"They won't let us die just so they can learn a lesson, will they?"

"It's an old, old business, magic," he said. "Rules aren't as neat and pretty as the modern world likes to make them. So yes, they'd watch us die if it meant they learned something about magic and governing it. But it's not just our deaths they want—they want to see if this grand experiment has failed."

"What grand experiment? The disks?"

"No, magic being ruled by the few, in five different disciplines. In the old days, there was just one discipline of magic. And then that was broken into light and dark magic."

"Because of Leander and Isabelle," I said.

He gave me a curious look. "That's right. Because of Leander and Isabelle. Over the centuries it became clear that magic was being used in four basic forms—Life, Death,

Blood, and Faith—and none of the disciplines was considered stronger than the others. That's the question now: what magic discipline should rule, and how? I'd say Jingo Jingo has aligned himself on the side of Death magic. It's just a matter of time before someone champions Faith magic, Blood magic, Life magic."

"What are we championing?"

"That all magic is equal. More than that: all magic should be used equally. Including light and dark magic. Ever since the break, using dark magic almost always leads to insanity. It's a heated argument as to whether or not blending dark magic into light magic will fix that problem. And there isn't an answer to be found.

"So that leaves us with light magic in its four disciplines. It was going all right for a while. For years. Then your da had to go and give magic to the public and invent technology that can pipe it through a city. It polarized the Authority—and not just here in Portland. Very few people thought it was a good idea to put magic in the common man's hands. Treating all disciplines as equal, and giving magic and technology a Voice was our shot at showing that the right way to rule magic, safe for us, safe for the common man, was to treat *all* disciplines equally, including magic used through technology.

"If we fail at keeping all disciplines equal, it will be one more nail in the coffin for the modernization of magic."

"But doctors use magic," I said. "Teachers use magic. Scientists use magic. There's a lot of good that's come out of giving it to the common man."

He gave me half a nod. "Listen, this war, this fight over how magic should be used, as one discipline of light by a handful of people, or five disciplines known by a few people, or allowing the study and use of dark magic—these things have been brewing and clashing and churning for a couple thousand years. We're just late to the game is all."

"Well, crap," I said. That was about all I had left in me. "So if everyone is interested and worried, we'll have lots of people coming in to help, right? Magic users?"

"No. We're on our own."

"Because . . . ?"

"Territory rules forbid it."

"Oh, come on." I rubbed my forehead. I think I was getting a headache.

"Ancient stuff, remember. Territory is very important to the Authority. Portland is our problem. No other Voice can have a vote or sway in what we do. And dragging more people into this will just mean there are more people fighting on all sides. We've been over this the last couple weeks—and so far the one thing most of us agree on is we need to take care of this ourselves, and quickly."

"So how do I help?"

"Come back from death alive, that's a good start. Oh, and maybe bring back the living soul of Jones over there."

"And then what, Shame? What's our plan? Who are we fighting? Where do we hunt?"

"That's all stuff Mum's going to go over with you. The basics? We're screwed. That bastard Jingo Jingo is holed up somewhere so tight there isn't room for him to exhale. But he'll have to come out eventually. So we're waiting. Sounds familiar, doesn't it?"

I nodded. Waiting had pretty much been Sedra's plan for when the wild-magic storm was going to hit too. And look how that had turned out.

"Have you heard anything about Violet?" Last I'd seen my dad's widow, she was in the hospital, injured from the break-in at her labs where the disks were stolen.

"She's back at Kevin's place. With Kevin. Bed rest, I think. She hasn't had the baby yet."

"But she's okay?"

"As far as I know. Kevin's got the place locked down like

it's fucking Armageddon out here. He takes 'bodyguard' to a whole new level of obsession."

"I'll need to talk to her. And Stone, where's Stone?"

A coo came from the shadowy corner of the room and the curtains moved. Stone walked over, giving Zayvion's bed a wide berth as he passed. He propped his big head on my thigh and rumbled.

"You okay, boy?" I rubbed his head. He was smooth, warm, and seemed to be moving well, if a little slowly. I wondered if death, and holding Zayvion's soul had hurt him.

"Is he all right?" I asked Shame.

"Think so. He is moving a little slower since you came back."

"It's because you followed me into death, you big lug. Stupid rock." I scratched behind his ears and he made a happy gurgle.

"Maybe," Shame hedged.

I looked up at him. "Maybe?"

"We don't know that much about Animates. And now that he's gone into death, and also carried a living soul—" He lifted one hand. "Who knows?"

"He's going to be fine," I said, giving him one last pat.

"Oh, one more thing," Shame said. "After the wild-magic storm, gates have been opening up all over town. We've been hauling ass to Close them and hunt down the things that got through. You weren't the only one having a good time for the last few days.

"But ever since you fell back from death, ever since you brought Zayvion's soul back and returned it to his body, the gates are harder and harder to close. I think things might be slipping through, though none of the Closers agrees on that."

"And we have a plan for that too?"

"Same as the other one, except this plan involves lots of

us out there sweating and casting and muscling the gates closed."

"Don't you have any good news?"

"It's not going to rain today."

I laughed. "Hells." I rubbed my face, then let my hands fall in my lap. I was suddenly really tired again. "Dying sucks."

"Not if you do it right. Need some sleep?"

"I don't want to. We don't have time."

"There's time enough for you to sleep. You might as well while you can. I'll tell Mum you're resting." He walked to the door.

"Shame?"

"Yes?"

"Why did you tell Stotts everything? I thought the Authority doesn't want the police knowing that kind of stuff."

"I didn't think you were paying attention."

"That wasn't an answer."

"How about this? It's okay. We took care of it."

"That's worse. What did you do to Paul?"

"I didn't do anything."

"Shame, tell me they didn't hurt him." I went back over all the things Shame had just told me. Had I forgotten anything? Had he told me something about Stotts? Had I gotten him hurt, put him in danger by having him bring me here?

"I don't know what's going through that head of yours, but you just went pale as plaster. I'll go get the doctor."

"Wait. No. Tell me. Tell me what they did to Stotts." I wanted to pull on magic and force him to tell me the truth, but magic cannot be cast in a high state of emotion, and I could not get my head or heart to calm down.

"We Closed him."

"No."

"Pretty much, yes. He can't know the things he's seen—

you falling out of death with a living gargoyle carrying Zayvion's soul? Please. You think we'd let him remember that?"

"I think you'd keep your hands off him. He's not a part of this."

Shame smiled a tight smile. "We're all a part of this. One big stage and he's a player too. Just a bit part right now, since he can't remember coming out here. Still."

I pushed the covers off my legs. "Who?" I said. "Who did it? Terric? Victor? Who Closed him, Shame?" I stood. Me and anger went way back. It kept me steady and strong even though the room swayed a little to the left. I marched across the floor and grabbed hold of the door to keep Shame from closing it.

Shame didn't look at all threatened. Well, he wouldn't be the first person to underestimate me.

"I could just cast a Sleep spell on you and not have to tell you," he said with such a soft hunger, I knew that was exactly what he wanted to do.

"Try it, Flynn, and you'll be choking on your own blood."

The corners of his eyes tightened. I waited, ready to block whatever he was going to throw at me. Instead, he stepped aside, and opened the door.

"Victor," he said. "He's downstairs right now, talking to Mum."

I didn't have any shoes on, no bra. Just the robe. I couldn't remember if I'd brushed my hair after the shower. Didn't matter. I knew that whoever Closed someone had the ability to un-Close them. And I would not let them screw around with Stotts' head just because he had helped me.

My left hand was strangely warm. The heat came from my palm, like a coal lay beneath the skin there, heavy and hot. Zay moaned in his sleep. I looked over at him, but he was silent. If not for my Hound ears, I wouldn't have heard him. His breathing returned to normal, and my heartbeat calmed. I wanted him to wake up. I wanted to be there when he regained consciousness.

But right now I had a friend's brain to get back.

"Stay with him," I told Shame. He opened and closed his hands like he was itching to strangle someone. Probably me.

"You don't get it, do you, Beckstrom? I stay with you." He caught my left hand. "Listen—" His eyebrows shot up and he turned my hand over. "Fuck me, what's this?"

I glanced down. The silver-black circle smudged my palm, the mark Mikhail had left on me. It was darker now, bigger, the lines of my hand still crossing it square through the center.

I pulled my hand away from him. "A bruise."

"Okay, don't tell me the truth. I don't care. But you are punching at the wrong wall. I stay with you because Zayvion would want me to look after you."

"Like I need—"

"Not listening. Old, stupid argument. You know going down there won't be worth the effort to fight over a few non-life threatening memories."

"You wouldn't understand," I said as I started down the hall. "You've never had your life taken away from you, bit by bit."

He shut the door, then followed behind me. "He can't know about this stuff."

"He deserves to keep his life and experiences. He's a police officer. He's out there every damn day trying to make the city a better place for people who use magic. Isn't that what the Authority says it's all about? Making sure magic is safe for those who use it? Or is it just about the power now? Who gets to control magic?"

"Dying makes you cranky, you know that?"

I was at the top of the stairs, and trying to brace myself for getting all the way to the main floor.

Shame leaned against the wall, crossed his arms over his chest. "You could do this tomorrow."

"I'm doing it now." I started down the stairs, and instantly broke a sweat. That didn't stop me. After the first flight, Shame caught up and walked next to me. By the last flight, his arm was around my waist, and I hated how much I needed that to stay on my feet.

We were in the hall that led to the dining room, and it was fairly noisy, like most nights. The smell of steak, onions, and rosemary hit me hard, and I wanted to stand there and absorb the flavors through my skin.

Then Shame cast a very subtle Illusion.

"What are you doing?"

"Making it so people don't see you. You look like an escapee from a mental ward. And while I personally think it's a turn-on, most people would speed-dial 911 if they caught a glimpse of you."

"Do you always talk this nice to girls?"

"Only the crazy ones."

He started down the hall, stopped at a door, knocked, then opened it.

It was one of the several sitting rooms on this floor. Like the sitting room I had taken classes from Maeve in, this one was dripping in wards, tastefully decorated, and arranged for conversation and magic casting, if the need arrived.

"Dead girl walking," Shame announced.

We stepped in and Shame closed the door behind us, activating the privacy wards.

Three people in the room: Maeve, Victor, and the mountain of a man, Hayden.

"Allie, why are you out of bed?" Maeve sat on a love seat, a blanket over her lap, her feet up on the seat cushions and a pillow behind her back. Her hair was pulled away from her face in a loose bun, tendrils falling onto pale cheeks. I noted, with a twinge of dread, the cane propped within hand's reach.

"I need to talk to Victor. About Stotts."

Victor, sitting in a leather armchair, wore slacks and a dark shirt, his shirt unbuttoned at the collar. His sleeves were rolled up, to allow for the bulk of a bandage over his right hand and wrist. He gave me a long look. "The answer is no."

"I wasn't asking. Give him back his memories."

Hayden, sitting on the couch with his legs stretched out, boots propped on the coffee table, chuckled.

"Allison, take a seat, please," Victor said. When I didn't move, he glanced at Shame. "Shame, please help her sit."

I didn't want to admit how much I wanted to sit down, didn't want to lose the anger that kept me standing, but I didn't want Shame helping me either. So I sat next to Hayden, who moved his arm down from the back of the couch to make room for me.

I hadn't spent very much time around Hayden. He had come down from Alaska to help us deal with the wild-magic storm that hit the city. Last I remember, Shame was hoping Hayden and Maeve would date. But it didn't look like there had been any time for that sort of thing since the storm.

I didn't see any injuries on the big man, though he smelled faintly of cloves and eucalyptus—like a heated rub for muscle pain.

"Good to see you're back," he said.

"Thanks."

"How was it?"

I frowned.

"Death," he supplied.

"Strange and painful."

He grunted. "Here I thought it'd be different than life."

"Trust me, it was. Victor, I want you to un-Close Stotts."

Victor pressed his fingertips together gently and didn't flex the right-hand fingers at all. Unless he could cast left-handed, which I wasn't sure about, he was in no shape to be drawing glyphs.

"I understand your concern—"

"Anger. Not concern. You can't do this to him. He's a police officer and he is my friend."

"We are well aware of that. It is the reason we removed his memories. For him to continue to do his job, a vital function for magic to work well in this city, and for people to stay safe, he can't know about the Authority."

"He saved Zayvion's life and you punished him for it."

Victor simply held my gaze. Zen, calm. Just like Zay. Except I hated him for it.

"There is no negotiation on this matter," Victor said in his teacher voice. "I understand it offends you."

"Fix it, or I'll fix it." I pushed up onto my feet. No, I wasn't a Closer and I didn't know how to retrieve someone's memories. But I'd find a way.

Looked like Victor could tell I was serious. He was a smart man.

"That would be a grave mistake," he said. "You could do far more harm to him."

"I bet if I told him he'd had memories taken away, he'd be more than happy to let me try to get them back."

He didn't say anything, but there was a smile at the corner of his mouth. It was the look he gave me when I'd done a spell or a sword routine particularly well.

He leaned back into his chair. "We can't un-Close him now. It is too soon. Closing someone is delicate, and the last thing I wish out of this is for our haste to harm Detective Stotts."

Reason. Like that would stop me. "There has to be a way."

"There is. And in the next two weeks, I will discuss it with you again. We may be coming to a point in time where it behooves us to have a man such as Detective Stotts on our side."

I swear, he was the only guy I knew who used *behoove* in a sentence.

"That sounded like a yes."

"It was a positive maybe. But until we take care of other matters first—the disappearance of Sedra and Jingo Jingo and others, the gates, the unrest—we should best let Detective Stotts' mind alone. If we do give his memories back to him, it will be done safely, and according to the rules, laws, and strictures of the Authority."

"I want your word on that."

"You have my word."

"And your blood."

"Allie," Maeve said, shocked. Like I'd just asked him to strip naked or something.

I looked over at her. "I won't believe him any other way." Plus, I didn't know why she was so shocked. She was my Blood magic teacher. She was the one who had taught me these spells. Oh, maybe that was exactly why. Victor was my teacher too. I shouldn't have to question his word.

And Liddy, who had turned against us all, had been my teacher. I had reasons to be suspicious.

"It's fine, Maeve," Victor said. He produced a straight pin from his cuff and stood.

The pin was gold—just like the pin my father had given me when he let me use Truth on him. Back when he was alive.

The room spun a little, and I felt tears at the back of my eyes. My throat hurt. Oh, of all the times for me to get teary-eyed over my dad's death. He wasn't even dead. He was renting out a corner of my mind.

I blinked a couple times and waited for Victor.

"Your hand." He held his left hand out, the straight pin in his right, bandaged fingers.

I held out one finger, tipped up, and he placed his bandaged right hand in support under mine, pricked my index finger, which hurt, and then pricked his thumb. He whispered a spell and pressed his thumb against my finger.

Blood magic was intimate. I could feel Victor's emotions; he was angry, frustrated, and not nearly as Zen as he looked. He was also tired.

And I knew he could feel my emotions.

That was the downside to this deal.

Still, if he noticed how angry I was, and how pass-out exhausted, he didn't say anything.

"You have my word I will reconsider the state of Detective Paul Stotts' memories, once matters have settled."

I felt his promise as if it were my own, tasted it in my mouth like the warm sweetness of Earl Grey tea. He meant it.

That was good.

"Thank you." I pulled my finger away, breaking the spell.

He looked past me to Shame. "She needs to get some sleep."

"I'm fine," I said, or at least I think I said it. All of a sudden my ears weren't working too good.

"Allie?" That was Maeve.

"Fine," I repeated. The room was getting black at the edges, like someone was slowly turning down the lights. Had Victor cast something more than just a promise in that spell? Had he knocked me out?

"What did you—" I mouthed, but no sound came out. The room rushed up around me as I fell. I was swallowed in darkness. Before I hit the ground, I felt Hayden's arms catch me. Then . . . nothing.

# Chapter Seven

I woke next to Zayvion, feeling too good to be mad at Victor for knocking me out. The pine scent of Zay's cologne was muted by soap and sweat. His breathing was even, almost mechanical. I knew he was still in the coma, still in bed, still at Maeve's.

And I was apparently still at Maeve's too.

I scooted closer to Zay, checking first to make sure I wasn't going to foul up any tubes or wires on him. I was on his right side, his arm tucked under the covers with me. I ran my fingertips gently down his arm. Muscle and smooth skin. No wires.

I pressed up against him, his arm between my breasts and down my belly so I could rest my head on his shoulder. "Morning," I said. "How about a nice cup of coffee and scones? I could go out to Get Mugged and see what fantastic concoction Grant has baked up today. Then maybe we could catch a movie, or drive to the coast. Bet it's a nice day for some sand and rain."

I rubbed my hand over his chest. He was wearing a thin T-shirt, and through the soft material I could feel more of his bones than I should. It was a grim reminder of how long he'd been here.

Math was not my strong suit. I frowned, trying to calculate how many days he'd been in bed.

It would help if I knew what day today was. "You have any idea was day it is, babe?" I asked.

"Saturday."

I lifted up, peered over Zayvion at the man sitting in the corner. Silver hair, dark button-down shirt tucked into jeans: Terric.

"So how long since I've been back?"

He put down the book he was reading, a Bradbury, I think, on the table next to him. "You came back four days ago. It's the morning after you talked with Victor. You've been asleep ten hours or so."

Wow. From how much better I felt, I was surprised I'd only been asleep that long. "It's morning again?"

"Eleven o'clock. Hungry?"

I shifted in the bed, made sure I had on a shirt and pants. Check and check. "I could eat something. Got any scones?"

"The kitchen might. I'll go down with you."

"What, no breakfast in bed?"

Terric stood. "The doctor said you should get up today. You are feeling better, aren't you?"

The way he said it made me suspicious. "Yes? Why?"

"Victor worked a small healing spell on you. Something to encourage your body to rest and recuperate. He didn't expect it to knock you out. You must have been running on empty."

I ran my fingers down Zay's arm one more time, then slipped out of the covers as carefully as I could and tucked them back around him.

"Still on empty." The room didn't sway, but I could eat a pachyderm twice dipped and deep-fried in batter. "Let me use the bathroom. I'll be right out."

Terric pointed over at the empty bed. "We raided your apartment. Shoes and clothes if you want them."

"How'd you get in my apartment?"

"Zay's key."

Oh. I hadn't thought of that.

Terric picked up the book—definitely Bradbury—as I grabbed some of the clothes they'd brought, then walked to the bathroom. I used the facilities, washed my hands, and splashed some warm water over my face.

I was surprised my dad had been so quiet since I returned. I hadn't heard or felt him more than once. I wondered if I'd dreamed that he had come back to life with me.

One way to find out. I could always see the shadow of his presence in my eyes.

I looked up into the mirror and jerked in surprise. Not because of my eyes—my eyes were mine, pale glass green, with the multicolored ribbons of magic at the corner of my right eye swirling down my jawline. My eyes and face were the same.

The difference was the strands of white that streaked my normally dark brown hair. Not gray. Not silver. White.

Death couture. Funky.

It didn't look bad. Kinda edgy. It gave my face a harder angle, and made my green eyes shine like a predator's. I decided I liked it. A lot.

Might have to buy myself a leather jacket and some stiletto boots to go with the new look. I tucked my hair back behind both ears. Yep, with the marks of magic down one side of my face, and the shock of lightning-white tattering my hair, I had cornered the market on tough.

Zay was going to love it. As soon as he woke up.

I brushed my hair and teeth, put on my own underclothes, black jeans, and a heavy slate gray sweater. Wished I had my gloves and boots, but at least they'd brought my running shoes.

I walked out of that bathroom feeling hungry, human, and ready to kick ass.

"Breakfast?" I asked.

Terric put the book down and stood. "You look a lot better."

"Than what?"

He grinned. "You look like you're *feeling* better."

"I am. Good enough that I'm going to go home and take care of a few things today."

"Hmmm."

"I'm not forbidden to leave, am I?"

"No. But I doubt you'll be going alone."

"You can't put me under guard, Terric. I'm a big girl. I can handle myself."

"Not me."

I took my coat off the back of the door as we stepped out of the room and strolled down the hall, our feet making hollow *thunks* on the old hardwood floor.

"Who?"

"Shame."

"Wish he'd give it a rest. Would you talk to him for me?"

"I don't think you want me in your corner. He's . . . uncomfortable with our current arrangement."

I headed down the stairs, happy that my knees were holding up. I didn't know what kind of healing spell Victor had cast, but it had really done the trick. I'd have to thank him for it. But first, breakfast.

"What exactly is your current arrangement?" I asked. "I saw the crystal."

He exhaled loudly behind me. "It had side effects I didn't imagine."

"The connection."

"Mmm," he agreed. "It's been difficult. We're both used to privacy. I've tried to ignore him. But you know Flynn. He doesn't make anything easy—he is one of the most difficult people to ignore."

We made it to the bottom of the stairs. I smelled bacon and sausage, fried potatoes and fresh coffee. I was starving.

"This way." Terric stepped past me with a smooth movement that reminded me of someone who knew how to dance. Or who knew swordplay. The room was filled with the breakfast crowd: families, couples, friends, going out on a Saturday morning for a good hot, home-cooked meal. A small table by the window was open, and that was where Terric was headed. I followed.

It was strange to look at those normal people with normal faces and normal lives and realize I didn't feel like I was a part of them anymore. Somewhere in the last few months I had begun to see myself as a person living on the edges of normal—more so than I used to be when I was a Hound doing questionable jobs for questionable people in questionable parts of town. Somehow I had started thinking of myself as a magic user caught up in so many important, dangerous things that a normal morning out for breakfast sounded as foreign and strange as walking through a gate into hell.

When had I changed?

Or maybe I'd always been this, and trying to be normal, trying to blend into the crowd and want the same things everyone wanted—a house, a job, a lover—hadn't been enough for me. Maybe I'd always needed more. Or if not more, different.

Wanting different was a lot of what had driven me to become a Hound.

Speaking of Hounding, I was surprised Davy wasn't around. Davy Silvers was a good kid, and a good Hound. He was my right-hand man when it came to providing basic support for Hounds in the city, and he did a hell of a job at it too. But he had some crazy idea that it was his job to follow me. Everywhere.

Terric stopped at the table near the windows. Sunlight, real, beautiful, buttercream sunlight, splashed in through the old watery glass and drew copper and honey tones out of the tabletop.

"This okay?" he asked.

"So good." I pulled a chair out and sat in the sunlight.

Terric sat across from me, facing the length of the room, while I had a view of the lunch counter and the few tables and windows beyond it.

The waitress, Jenny, showed up with a carafe of coffee and two cups.

"Black, right?" she asked me. "Love the hair by the way."

"Thanks," I said. She poured coffee for Terric, and plunked menus down in front of us.

"I don't need a menu," I said. "Two eggs over easy, bacon, sourdough toast, and hash browns. Oh, and grapefruit juice if you have it."

"We have it fresh. And you?" she asked Terric.

"Just the coffee."

"There's apple-ginger coffee cake fresh out of the oven."

He smiled, and I could tell Jenny liked the look of him. "I think I'll stick to coffee for now, thanks."

She picked up the menus, and looked back over at me. "I'll have that out to you in a minute."

I was too busy sipping coffee to answer. Terric seemed content to drink in silence. I stared out at the trees that lined the Willamette, at the spring sky with patchy clouds padding the blue. The murmur of people talking, of laughter, of normal, wonderful, boring, beautiful living, filled me. I closed my eyes, savoring it, lonely for it. Lonely for normal.

When I looked back at Terric, he was frowning slightly, cup halfway to his mouth, as if he heard a far-off voice.

"Problem?" I asked.

"No."

"Have you seen Davy Silvers?"

He shook his head and put his cup down. "Should I have?"

"It's just that he's always following me around. I thought he might have stopped in while I was sleeping."

"No. And I'd know. We've been holding meetings here every night. For members," he added. "If someone had been by looking for you, we would have seen him."

It wasn't like Davy to keep his nose out of my business. I'd been telling him for months not to follow me around—ever since our friend Martin Pike died, actually—and he never listened to me. I wondered what he was up to. Another thing to add to my To Do list: check in on Davy.

"Do you have a pen?" I asked.

Terric pulled an expensive pen out of his pocket. It was the kind of thing I'd expect an architect to use.

"Nice pen."

"Thanks," he said distractedly.

I flattened my paper napkin and jotted down a list of people to check on: Davy, Violet, and Stotts. I wanted to look in on them quickly and then be back here to stay with Zayvion for the evening. And since Terric still looked like he was trying to listen to a radio station through static, I opened the napkin and jotted down everything else that came to mind: *find notebook, transfer notes, and ask about Mikhail's history.*

Mikhail might be the best place to start.

"Do you know anything about Mikhail?" I asked.

"Some," he said. "What have you been told?"

"Not a lot. I met him in death."

Terric's eyebrows shot up. He leaned his elbows on the table and kept his voice low. "Want to tell me about that?"

"I'd like to know a little background on him first."

"Mikhail was the head of the Authority for fifteen years. He and Sedra were lovers. They had a son."

"Cody?" I asked.

"Yes. That's when things started to go wrong. Sedra almost died in childbirth. When she finally recovered, Mikhail said she had changed. They became more and more distant. Soon that distance turned into anger.

"Some people thought they might have been Soul Complements, but they never tested. The rumor is they were fighting over how to raise their son, who was obviously magically gifted at a very young age. Sedra wanted him raised outside the Authority, and Mikhail wanted him to be a part of it.

"They had a fight. Mikhail opened a gate to death and tried to push Sedra through it. If Dane Lannister hadn't been there, she would be dead. Instead, Mikhail walked through the gate—willingly—vowing revenge on Sedra and the Authority.

"He never came back, though he has tried. So far, we've been able to keep him on that side of death."

"And Sedra took over as Head of the Authority?"

He nodded. "It was a political move, mostly. Mikhail was also the voice for Death magic. It made sense to have the voice for Life magic replace him. A yin-yang kind of thing."

"So Jingo Jingo kidnapped her because he wants Death magic to be the head of the Authority again?"

"Probably more than that. It's possible he wants to open a gate to death and bring Mikhail through. You making the crossing has all of us worried." He smiled. "Don't get me wrong. We're happy to have you back, safe. But if you can do it, why can't Mikhail?"

Why not, indeed? Because he didn't have a gargoyle for his soul? No, Terric had said he walked through the gate. If that was true, maybe all he needed was enough magic to open the gate. I'd given him my magic, but he hadn't used it to open the gate for me. He'd taken it back to the woman in the room. He opened the gate, but didn't step through. If he really was looking for revenge and a way back to life, he'd lost a prime opportunity. This was not adding up.

"Maybe he doesn't want to," I said.

Three people—a man and two women I didn't recognize—stared at us as they walked past the window. They headed to the door. I took a drink of coffee, expecting to hear the door behind me open. The door didn't open. That was odd.

From where I was sitting I had a good view of the parking lot. The people weren't there. I looked back down the porch. Nothing. Maybe they had walked farther up the road.

"What are you looking for?" Terric asked.

"I was trying to figure out where those people went."

"What people?"

The waitress strolled over and put my plate down in front of me. It looked like fried heaven. "Here you go," she said. "Need anything else? Ketchup? Hot sauce?"

"I'm good. Thanks."

"And you're sure I can't talk you into some coffee cake? It's sweet with a little kick." She batted her eyes at Terric.

"No, I don't have the time," he said. "Thanks, though."

She left, and Terric waited for me to get a few bites in. Then, "People?"

"Man and two women who walked past our window? Looked in at us? I thought they knew you and were coming in." The eggs were amazing. Who was I kidding? It was all amazing.

"No one walked by our window."

"Yes they did. You weren't paying attention."

He looked at me for a minute. "No one walked past, Allie. I was paying attention. Very closely."

I drank some of the grapefruit juice. Tart. Wonderful.

"So what, I'm seeing ghosts?" I grinned, picked up the bacon and took a bite.

Terric leaned back and watched me eat. "Shame told me you've seen the Veiled. Ghosts are simply the spirits of the dead. Much like Veiled are spirits of dead magic users. If you can see one, why couldn't you see the other?"

"I think it's more likely you just didn't see them walk by."

He smiled, and it made him look younger, softer. "I'm naturally observant. But you could be right." He flipped open his phone, made a call. "Are you on perimeter? Keep an eye out for a man and two women wandering around on foot. They might also be ghosts. Yes. Thanks."

He hung up. "Never hurts to be careful. Do you see anyone out there now?"

I looked out. "Nope."

"Tell me if you do see someone."

I nodded, but mostly paid attention to my plate. Once my stomach was full, I slowed down and picked at the last bits of potato and onion. I sat back, drank coffee, and looked at Terric. Really looked at him.

Okay, I don't know how I missed it, but he wasn't kidding he was observant. He was keeping an eye on the dining area, the window, the sounds behind him—

"What are you thinking?" he asked.

—and me.

"I'm thinking you'd make a good Hound."

"Low pay, bad hours—I'm thinking I like the job I have."

"What job?" Come to think of it, I didn't even know his last name. I knew he lived in Seattle, but that was about all I knew about his regular life.

"Other than the obvious?" he said. "I'm a graphic designer. Freelance."

"Nice way to keep your own hours."

"It works for me so far." He glanced up, watching without looking like he was watching the arch that led to the hallway and stairs beyond.

Shame came striding out of the shadows. He was back in black again, jeans, heavy black fisherman's sweater with a hood, fingerless gloves.

Terric didn't move, but everything about him changed. As soon as he saw, or maybe felt, Shame coming, he vibrated like a plucked string. I watched as he very carefully slouched, relaxing shoulders, arms, hands, and fingers. He even schooled eyes, mouth, and forehead to be blank, easy.

For someone who looked like he was just kicking back drinking a cup of coffee, he sure had to work hard at it.

Shame was flicking his cigarette lighter, the metal lid snicking up and clicking back as he made his way over to us.

"Mornin'." He pulled a spare chair away from a table that had just emptied and set it between Terric and me.

"Get some sleep?" Terric asked.

Shame's eyes narrowed. "You know I did, you arse."

Terric smiled behind his coffee cup.

"So you know when Shame is sleeping too?" I asked.

"I do when I cast a Sleep spell on him."

"May you toil in hell's basement among the devil's dirty socks," Shame said.

"And have to see you there every day? Not on your life."

They glared at each other. I knew they wouldn't get into a fight here in the middle of Maeve's restaurant. But the longer they stared, the more I worried. Maybe they really did want to break a few chairs over each other's heads.

"It has strained my ability to trust you," Shame said.

"Nothing new there. Allie might be seeing ghosts."

Shame pulled out a pack of cigarettes and tapped one free. "That's newish." He stuck the unlit cigarette in his mouth. "Anyone I know?"

"I don't think they were ghosts. They were people."

"People who disappeared before they got to the door," Terric said.

I glanced over at him. "I think you're reading a lot into this."

"Plus, she said she met Mikhail in death."

"Aren't you the celebrity? You still have your da in your attic?" Shame asked.

"I'm not sure."

Both men leaned back in tandem and waited, obviously not believing me.

"Don't want to let us in on your little secret? I thought we were your friends," Shame said. "Well, me anyway. I don't blame you for hating Terric. He's a bastard through and through."

"The sleep did wonders for your mood." Terric rubbed at the bridge of his nose with his middle finger.

"Oh, grow up," Shame said.

"Grow up? Good God, Flynn, have you looked in a mirror lately? Most men get over the punk rocker look in their teens. And move out of their mother's house."

"It's her inn, not her house," Shame said archly. "And most men don't have the rank and title I have."

Terric chuckled. "True. You are one of the rankest"—he made the air-quote gesture—"men I know."

That got a genuine smile out of Shame. "You are a bastard. Funny, but still a bastard."

The conversation had a lot of hope wedged between the insults. Maybe these two would find a way to get over the pain they'd caused each other and rebuild their friendship again.

Shame turned his shoulder toward Terric, ignoring him.

Or maybe not.

"Smuggled your rock out," he said.

"Rock?"

"Rock, stone, you know." Shame waved one hand in front of him like the details didn't matter.

"Stone?" I'd wondered where he'd gotten off to. "Where did you take . . . it?"

"Back to your place. Thought it'd be better than Victor taking it apart."

"What?"

Terric hummed, a sort of keep-it-down noise.

"What is Victor doing with Stone?" I whispered.

"Nothing. Yet. And you're welcome. The most recent *thing* you did with him? It was making Victor and Mum curious. Once they started talking about deep sea exploration and space, I knew it was only going to get worse from there."

"I am so not following you."

Terric rearranged the salt and pepper shakers on the table and cast a Mute spell to dampen the sound of our conversation from any curious ears.

"Stone was used as a carrier," Terric said. "A vehicle." He waited to see if I understood. Got the idea that I didn't.

He tried again. "Stone carried Zayvion's soul back from death. It brings up some interesting ideas about what can be done if one was willing to take the risk."

"Pretend like I have no idea what you're talking about, and explain it slowly," I said.

"It's the first hard evidence we've ever seen that a soul can be contained in an unliving, magical object—an Animate. And that a soul can pass into or out of death in such a way, and still be returned to the living body. Stone showed us that the possibility exists to use Animates to hold living souls. If things weren't going to hell around here, this would be the biggest breakthrough in magic use since your dad came up with the network lines, cisterns, and storm rods."

"And disks," Shame added.

Terric nodded. "Those too."

"Stone isn't an experiment," I said.

"Which is why I took him back to your place," Shame said. "Were you not paying attention?"

"Will Victor want him back?"

Shame shrugged. "Our hands are full trying to keep the gates closed. Plus there are rogue Authority members on the loose, other members kidnapped, a bunch of stolen disks out there—I bet he won't worry about one little gargoyle for a while."

The weight of what Shame was saying finally sunk in. "Do you need me to help with any of that right now?"

"You, darlin', aren't a Closer. Short answer—no. There is a meeting tonight you'll want to be at. Why? You in a hurry to get somewhere?"

"I need to go home. Pack some clothes so I can stay here with Zay—I can stay, right?"

"I should hope so," Shame said. "But we brought you clothes."

"Not the ones I want to wear. Also, I want to check in with Violet and the Hounds—you haven't seen Davy, have you?"

"No."

"Then I'll be back soon. I think I'll be gone three or four hours."

"And how, exactly are you going to get home?"

"Cab. Unless you want to drop me off at a bus or MAX station over the river."

Shame shook his head. "Unbe-fucking-lievable. No, you will not go home, or anywhere else on your own in a city at war, with magic users out to kill each other."

"Yes, I will. You know why? Because I am more than qualified to take care of myself for an hour or two."

"No. Absolutely no. It's not safe." He did a fair impression of his mother.

"One, you can't tell me what to do, and I know how to

swing a sword and cast a spell. And two, I just walked into death and back. That proves I can deal with anything life throws at me."

He pointed to his face. "See how much I don't care? You're just wasting time. Let's go."

"Someone should be here if Zay wakes up," I said.

"Terric's going to stay with him," Shame said.

Terric shrugged. "I'm not due for gate patrol for a few hours. Nik and Sunny are on it right now."

I didn't want Shame to come with me. I really did want some space, some room to breathe, and a break from all the magic users who were out to kill each other.

"Is there any way to get rid of you?" I asked.

He raised an eyebrow. "Not unless one of us is dead. And probably not even then."

Terric broke the Mute spell and the conversations of other diners in the room rose to a normal volume again. He and Shame stood, in perfect, fluid unison. Unconscious of each other, they carried a sort of connection I'd seen only in brothers, or twins.

"Be careful," Terric said. "I'll call if there's any change with Zay."

Phones. Why did I always forget my cell? "Either of you know where my phone is?"

"It died on the battlefield." Shame started off toward the door, and Terric strolled over to a very happy Jenny to settle the bill.

"I liked that phone," I said.

Shame flipped the hood of his sweater up over his head, hiding his face in shadow. "We'll get you another one. Remind me when we come back. I'm pretty sure Mum keeps a spare."

He opened the door, hunched deeper into his sweater, and stepped out.

It was early afternoon, cool, damp, and clean, with only a promise of spring's warmth. I took a deep breath and loved it.

Shame lit his cig while we crossed the gravel to his car. "Zay's sword came back through with you, though." He exhaled smoke with each word. "Probably the wards protecting it, the dagger too. Good thing phones are easier to replace."

"Speaking of which, I feel a little naked not carrying a sword right now."

"Happens when you hang out with Z too long. Think the best way to take care of yourself is with steel. You do have other protections at your disposal. Things you were just convincing me would keep you safe."

Magic.

"I know," I said.

"That was the most halfhearted agreement I've ever heard." He stopped on the driver's side of his car and looked over the roof at me. "You can use magic, right?"

"Do you even know me?" I held up my right hand, which was wrapped in magic's colors.

"The real answer." He waited.

This was something new about Shame. For all he liked to make jokes and poke fun at people, there was a seriousness, a deadly seriousness, about him now. Ever since the battle, or maybe ever since Zayvion had been almost killed, he had changed.

"I haven't tried it yet and I don't want to." He wanted honesty. He got it.

"You should."

"Not now." I pulled the door open and got in the car.

Shame got in too, and started the engine. He rolled down the window halfway and tapped his cigarette over the edge.

"How about now?" he asked.

"Shame, I didn't even want you to come with me. Don't

make it miserable, or I'll try out more than just my magic on you."

"You talk tough." He blew smoke out the window but didn't put the car in gear. "I'm not joking around. Cast something small. It's better to find out now than when you might need it the most."

I realized I was rubbing my fingers with my thumb, uncomfortable, stressed. On a scale of one to ten for how much I did not want to cast magic I'd give it a hundred.

The hollowness inside hurt. The comforting candle flame of magic that had always filled me was gone. I felt like I'd lost a limb, or had just woken up to find life was the dream and my nightmares were real all along.

There was a little part of me—okay, a big part of me—that wondered if leaving my magic in death in Mikhail's hands might have been a really bad idea. What if he was connected to me?

If I cast magic, would he know it? Would he try to use me to get through the gates into this world? There was still magic in my body—the magic from the cisterns and rivers that flowed deep beneath the earth. I just didn't have my soul magic.

"I'll spot you," Shame said after I had been quiet for too long. "Let's face this and move forward."

"Since when has it ever been a good idea to listen to you?"

"Since there is the very real possibility that the little slap fight we got into back in St. Johns is just the beginning of magic users trying to kill magic users. You walked into death. But that doesn't mean you can't be killed. Cast."

He sounded way too much like a teacher right now.

He sucked the rest of his cigarette down, then tamped it out in the ashtray.

Arguing was getting me nowhere. "I don't like you," I said without any heat.

"Get in line." Cast. I'd been using magic for almost all my life. My dad started teaching me young—easy things like making a spark of light or changing the color of flower petals. I was good at magic. I'd always been good at it.

Then why was I sweating at the thought of doing it?

I took a deep breath to calm myself. Magic can't be cast in high states of emotion.

My heart was pounding so hard, I bet Shame could hear it.

"I got you," he said. "Go ahead now."

Something easy. Something I did all the time. Something that wouldn't hurt. I recited a mantra—the "Miss Mary Mack" song, and set a Disbursement—headache, because I was used to that.

I traced the glyph for Sight with my right hand. My hand shook so hard the glyph did not fully form, and I knew magic would not take hold in it.

Holy shit, I hadn't been this scared since my first semester in college, learning magic basics.

Shame didn't say anything, even though I had just failed spectacularly at drawing a glyph I knew as well as my own name.

I focused on the distance between myself and the windshield and tried again.

Almost got it. Lost my concentration. Swore.

"It's fine," Shame said, low and soft, like maybe he'd talked people through this kind of thing before. "We have time."

I licked my lips, tasted the salt of my fear. And tried tracing the spell again.

Got it this time, a nice clean glyph for Sight. It was a Hounding glyph and one I used most often. I hooked the glyph with my pinky, then poured magic out through my bones, my body, into the spell.

Magic filled me—everywhere but the cold hole in my

chest. Magic lifted, wove with warm pressure down my arm, into my finger, and into the spell.

My vision sharpened. The world opened up like fog had just burned away.

Shame's car was just a car. I sensed something receptive to magic in his glove box—maybe a void stone or some other Authority trinket.

"What do you see?" he asked.

I glanced out the window. "Nothing particularly magical. Not a lot of spells out here in the parking lot." My heart was still pounding, but I'd had a lot of practice being scared out of my wits and still using magic. All in a day's work for a Hound.

"The inn?" Shame asked.

I twisted so I could look back at it.

A shadow, black, thick, solid, a man, near the door, then gone, slipped the edge of my vision as I tried to track his passage, and almost slipped my mind. I felt a paper-dry brush at the back of my skull—my dad—pushing the image forward to me again.

The shadow man.

I shivered. It was same shadow I'd seen in death. And in St. Johns.

"What?" Shame asked.

"It's . . . I saw a shadow. It's gone now, but I saw it in St. Johns too. It's a man, a manish shape, with no features, no . . . details. Like a man-shaped black hole. But it moves. Fast. I think it's following me."

"When did you first see it?"

I turned, looked at him. I still had Sight, and Shame looked completely different. Without Sight, Shame looked like he was nursing a three-month flu. With Sight, he looked thin, pale, but burning hard, light pouring from him to make his black eyes not strange but hypnotizing. He was sharp, his skin silky-pale, a contrast of light and shadow and something more, something powerful, sexual. I felt my pulse quicken.

Shame looked like someone who could make you want more of anything he did to you.

If Zay, when seen through Sight, was a silver-glyph, black fire warrior, Shame was a blade edged with liquid heat and blood.

I'd never seen him like that before, not even when he'd cast magic and I was watching him with Sight.

"You changed," I breathed.

He gave me a smile and I could feel it like a thumb dragging down the marks of magic on my arm. The palm of my left hand warmed, like someone had just poured heated oil over my skin.

"Do you like it?"

I nodded, my left hand reaching up for my collar. It was suddenly really hot in here. Stifling.

"It's. . . . it's . . . " I turned my head, looked away from him. What was wrong with me? I knew Shame. He was Zayvion's brother in everything but blood. He had always been very brotherly toward me and I wanted it to stay that way.

"It's fine," I finally spit out. "What did you do? I mean, why are you all . . . " I almost said *sexy*, but caught myself in time to say, ". . . Death magic powerful and Blood magic hypnotic?"

"Is that how you see me?" He actually sounded a little surprised.

I nodded. I stared out the window, still holding Sight, and keeping my left hand in a fist. Having to concentrate on the spell helped me not think about other things. Things like the power Shame was radiating.

"Since Mum's been hurt, and both Jingo Jingo—may he burn in hell's Dumpster—and Liddy are gone, I've shouldered more of the responsibilities for Death magic, some for Blood too. Don't worry. As soon as Mum is herself and the gates stay closed, and we find Sedra, and take down Jingo Jingo and whoever else is trying to screw with the Authority, I'll go back to my do-nothing, magical slouch-boy self."

*He's a master*, my dad whispered in the back of my mind. *He's finally showing what he truly can do. Greater than I believe Jingo Jingo ever was. Such a waste.*

*I like it better when you don't talk,* I thought to him.

"So how long?" Shame asked.

"Since?"

"Since you've been seeing the shadow?"

I let go of Sight. Turned back to him. Without Sight, Shame looked like a man in deep need of rehab. Strange how that broken exterior hid such pure burning power and ability. I'd never expected him to be filled with such fierce strength. Or maybe it wasn't all that strange. People, like magic, are rarely what they seem to be.

"I first saw it in death," I said. "I think it followed me here."

# Chapter Eight

Shame shook his head slowly. "You're a bloody lot of trouble, you know that, Beckstrom?"

"Define 'a lot.' "

He pulled out his cell, dialed, then backed out of the parking space, the tires of the car crunching on gravel. "Terric?" he said as he drove up the access road. "What? No. Listen. Beckstrom says a shadow followed her through the gate. Here. Well, at St. Johns and now here. About two minutes ago. Man shape. That's what she said. I don't know. I'm not a Closer. That's your job." He paused. "Bite me." He thumbed off his phone and scowled at the road.

"Terric going to take care of it?" I asked.

"Terric's going to look into it. He'll call if he knows anything."

We were headed to the bridge back to Portland.

"There are wards around the inn, right? Around Zayvion?" I asked.

"Yes. Since the well is there, we have a lot of protections in place. Old spells that we can trigger when we need to. It's the safest place he could be."

I bit at my bottom lip, wanting to believe that. I didn't know of a safer place. Certainly not my apartment, not my dad's old place, and not the police department. When you didn't know the danger you might face, *safe* was hard to achieve.

"Does Terric know what it might be?"

"There are a lot of things that can get through gates. Hungers, the Veiled, creatures, and fragments of once-living things that stumble through. Not every gate leads to death. Some lead between countries."

"Seriously? Why don't more people use those?"

"It takes a hell of a lot of magical output to open a gate. There's a lot of pain behind that—more than one person can bear. You don't get enough people to Proxy, and you end up dead. It's a last-ditch kind of thing, and even then, the gates aren't reliable. You might end up in the country you want to go to. Or you might end up in the middle of the ocean. Fun, huh?"

"Thrill a minute," I said. "They train all Closers in this stuff?"

"Yes. But not all Closers can open gates. Guardians, like Zay, can. You have to use light and dark magic. And down that road is crazy. Chase," he said. "But gates opened from the other side, from death, happen way too much. Oh, bloody hell." We were across the bridge and making our way toward my apartment. Shame slowed the car, took a tight right turn.

"What?"

"A gate." He dug for his phone, dialed, and forgot to use his blinker around the next corner.

"Victor, there's a gate on Southwest Thirteenth Avenue and Southwest Washington. Don't know. I'm getting there."

Another turn and we had made the full circle. Instead of easing out into traffic, Shame parked in a loading zone.

"Stay here." He got out, his hood covering his face as he stormed up the sidewalk. The people on the street gave him a wide berth.

Oh, like that would work on me. I got out of the car too,

checked it for keys—which Shame had taken—then locked the door and started after him.

It was cool enough in the shade of the high-rises that the wind still carried winter's teeth. But it wasn't raining, and the sky, between the restless clouds, was a shock of blue. I tucked both hands in my pockets and tipped my chin down into the collar of my coat. I wished I'd had a hat.

No rain meant more people were out on the street. Other than giving Shame space as he passed, no one paid particular attention to him.

I closed the distance between us, trailing him to a parking lot with gutted, uneven pavement gone to weed at the edges. The dilapidated red, white, and blue pay booth creaked a little in the wind. There were no attendants. The lot was full of cars except for one space against the brick wall of the neighboring building.

That was Shame's destination. Even though I kept a good pace, he made it up the street before I did. He stopped a car's length away from the parking space and lit a cigarette.

I traced the glyph for Sight. Yes, I set a Disbursement first. Yes, I was going to be sucking on a double dose of headache tonight.

But at least my hand was steady enough I drew the gylph right the first time. It was weird to pull magic up through me, to have it wrap hot tendrils around the cold hollowness inside me. I tried not to think about it.

The world brightened. Old spells and new spells hung on cars, the side of buildings, skittered along with traffic. Someone had even taken the time, energy, and pain to cast a spell on the dilapidated pay booth. The spell created a hat with a propeller on top sitting at a jaunty angle on the roof of the booth. The propeller spun lazily in the wind.

That spell did nothing more than look good if someone

cast Sight. I had heard there were walking tours, and other treasure-hunt-type trips you could take to see what magic art was hidden around town. It was the latest rage. The very temporary nature of magical art—spells just didn't last that long unless they were refreshed constantly—drew a lot of enthusiasts.

Which meant there either had been or would soon be people walking through here to see the pay-booth beanie.

Great.

To the unmagical eye, Shame was just a guy in a sweater, pacing, smoking, and talking on his cell phone. His pacing route blocked the parking space and made it look like he was saving the spot for a buddy, or calling the cops to report a stolen car.

Either way worked. No one seemed interested in trying to park there.

And I knew why Shame wouldn't let them.

A gate, about ten feet tall, pulsed in deep blue, black, and a strange lime green against the brick wall. I didn't see anything coming out of the gate. I did a quick look around to see if any lines of magic trailed off. If there were Hungers loose in the city, those beasts from death would hunt down the first magic user they could find and drink the life out of him. They were deadly, ruthless, and, I sincerely hoped, not on the streets.

I wondered who Shame was calling, and hoped they'd get here soon.

Shame closed his cell and took one last drag off of his cigarette before flicking it to the wet ground. He looked over at me and threw his hands up in frustration.

"This is how you stay in the car?"

"I'm not going to let you deal with this on your own."

"Allie, you're not a Closer."

"Neither are you. Deal. Who's coming?" I strode over to him. I was glad they had picked one of my heavy sweaters from my closet, but it was windy enough that I was still chilly.

"Nik and Sunny are busy shutting down a gate in the southeast."

"Terric is still staying with Zay, isn't he?"

"Yep."

"So?"

"Victor or Hayden, I'd guess. But they just pulled the graveyard shift and I don't know who Mum's going to be able to wake up."

"Anything we can do while we wait?"

"Not you, no. But I thought I'd throw an Illusion or two around."

"I don't think that's a good idea."

He drew a glyph in the air—definitely an Illusion of some sort. Then lit another cigarette. When he drew his fingers away from his mouth, he flicked them. Magic is fast—you can't see it with bare eyes. But I could feel magic lift out of the ground, sticky and slow, like coagulated glue. It filled the glyph, and then there was a pickup truck in the parking space and a very convincing, very solid-looking wall of bricks covering where the gate had been—where the gate still was.

"See how I don't listen to you and everything turns out?"

"There's an art tour coming."

"What?"

"Do you see the beanie on the tollbooth?"

He glanced over. "No."

"Sight," I suggested.

He pulled a quick glyph for Sight in the air. "Oh, for fuck's sake. When?"

"I have no idea. But that spell doesn't have more than a day left and today's Saturday."

He squinted at it. "Are you sure?"

"Stinks like old milk. And here they come now."

Shame looked up the street and swore. There was nothing we could do to further hide the gate. The pickup Illusion was solid, strong, the brick wall clear. I set a Disbursement and drew Sight, not intending to hold it for long. With Sight, the pickup was outlined in a chalky blue neon, like someone had found a way to make crayon glow under black light. That was a dead giveaway that the truck was an Illusion. So too the rosy glow of the bricks. That didn't worry me.

No, what worried me was the gate pulsing black behind the fake rosy bricks and slowly eating through the Illusion. A wisp of ghostly green pushed through the bricks and attached to the pickup, swirling along it like a wave of tentacles trying to catch hold.

Something was pushing its way through from the other side. And that something wasn't human.

Shame swore again, then drew a glyph with the ring finger of his right hand. He was burning hot, strong, and yes, sexy, hooking the glyph with his thumb, and drawing more, shifting the glyph, and shifting how the magic filled it. He was finger painting with magic.

I had never seen anyone make magic shift from glyph to glyph, fluid, mobile, alive like that. That was going to cost him a hell of a lot of pain.

Magic responded like a paint-filled brush, drawing the glyph with the turns and angles of Death magic. The longer Shame used that magic, the more the mark on my palm warmed, sending sweet, slow heat through my body. I opened my mouth and inhaled spring air to try to cool down.

Death magic had never affected me like this before. I looked away from Shame and dropped Sight. It helped a little.

The crowd of art enthusiasts was really more like

a dozen people. Two men near the back of the group in matching red rain jackets with an art gallery logo across the chest had that migraine-sufferer look of professional Proxies. The rest of the people were young, maybe art students. They all held their hands in front of them with fingers of both right and left hand pinched together. It was the most simple, and least pain-inducing version of Sight. Didn't do a lot to reveal the nuances of a spell, or the burned-out aftermath of casting like the Sight I used when Hounding. It was like having a good pair of glasses, or binoculars at your disposal that let you see spells.

They were looking at Shame and me, and past us to the Illusion.

Shame lit a cigarette, blowing smoke away from me, but there was enough wind that I tasted the butane bite of it.

The crowd let go of their Sight spells, and clapped politely. Ten people, a few more women than men, walked over to us, excited smiles on their faces.

"I don't see you on the program," a pretty young thing said, holding out her brochure.

Shame nodded, sucking on his cig. "I'm not an official part of the tour. Just happened to be in the neighborhood." He exhaled, looking neither impressed with his work nor with their reaction to it.

Which got me curious. Just what had Shame done with the magic he'd used?

No one seemed the least bit interested in me, except for the two Proxies over with the crowd who were still staring at the beanie on the tollbooth. They both nodded to me, a sort of professional-to-professional thing. They thought I was Shame's Proxy.

Well, it could be worse.

I backed away from Shame's adoring crowd, who asked him where he showed, and how long he'd been doing this kind of thing. I cast a quick and simple Sight spell, the same spell the tour had used, fingers of my right hand curved into a circle that I pulled up to my eye so I could see through it.

The pickup truck and wall had become something else—something more. Instead of the bricks hiding the gate, just enough of the bricks were broken out, the gate behind it showing through like a star-filled void. Tendrils of magic floated from the gate, and seemed to create the pickup, which was only half formed. Internal bits of the engine glinted through the holes where chunks of the hood and front half were ripped away and hovering, as if caught in the gravitational pull of the starry void.

Inside the car, a man pressed down on the accelerator as he kissed the woman next to him, a woman who was dying, her body so faded that glimpses of her bones showed through.

Illusion on top of Illusion, on top of Illusion. His art was raw, angry, sad, and blazing with magic. Shame had obviously missed his calling.

What surprised me the most was that through all those layers of magic and Illusion, the emotion was real. The art spoke of destruction, fear, hope, death. And love.

I felt like I was staring into a Shame I hadn't met before. A Shame who believed love was possible, even if it was fleeting.

I let go of Sight, and watched him handle the crowd like he'd done this before. A smile, brush his hair out of his eyes, quick laughter. Then the tour leader called for the group to move on. There was an exchange of business cards, and I think a few phone numbers; then everyone headed up the street.

Once they were up the block a ways, Shame rubbed his hand over his face, the cigarette smoke trembling in the air.

"How long can you hold this?" This was no garden-variety Illusion. It was fluid, like the glyph he had cast, and was changing, re-forming, remaking itself as the gate—the real gate into death—ate away at the spells.

Maintaining that kind of decay rate was crazy. I didn't see the Refresh, but knew he was paying the price, right here, right now, for the spell to stay in the air.

"Not long," Shame said, conversationally. "An espresso—or whatever other stimulant you can score in this neighborhood—might help."

I wanted to ask him if he was going to be okay. Dumb question. No one who used magic like that came out of it unscathed.

"Got any money?" I asked.

"You're the rich girl."

"Who just came back from death and hasn't been home to get her credit card yet. Pay up, Flynn."

He swore, dug in the pocket of his jeans, and held out a ten.

"Looks like it's gonna be coffee," I said.

He lit another cigarette off the last one. "Now would be nice."

He'd need a lot more than coffee if he had to hold this spell for too much longer. He'd need a doctor.

I got moving. Crossed the street. No coffee shops here, but there was a fancy import chocolate shop in the building just down the street. I hurried without looking like I was running from or to anything. Traffic was picking up, several bikes zipped past. I kept an eye on the people around me. The fact that Shame had asked me to go alone when he'd just lectured me about magic users bent on destroying the Authority made me a very vigilant woman.

The chocolate shop was a part of a bigger building. Luckily it was all glass in the front. I pulled open the door, glanced back at Shame, who was pacing, much slower, and stepped into the shop. My left hand suddenly went cold as ice, and I shoved it in my pocket to try to warm it up.

I could still see Shame through the front window, so I took my place in line. Only then did I actually inhale.

I'd gone to heaven. The sweet, rich scent of chocolate filled me with thoughts of happier times when a chocolate bar was all I needed to end my troubles. The shop decor ran toward the understated metro European, with deep wall colors and wood and black accents. Chocolates in all shapes and colors perched on tables, heavy wooden shelves, and glass cases, like gifts from angels, wrapped in twine and gold and lace.

The low tables tucked along one wall had enough space to hold two cups, but that was about it. Still, ten or so people sat at tables, drinking out of tiny cups, or nibbling bars and other decadent delights, while maybe another five were in line with me.

Everything seemed normal in the shop. Except for one person. A woman stood near one of the heavy shelves on the other side of the room. I might have thought she was looking through the selection of treats, but she was facing the store instead of the chocolates.

She wore a long heavy coat, leather with lamb's wool at the seams and collar, hiking boots, and loose slacks. A thick, knobby brown scarf wrapped around her neck so many times it was as wide as her shoulders and made her face look fine and fragile, brown eyes too wide beneath her boy-short hair.

Even though she held a cup in one hand, something about her set off warning bells. She looked normal. She acted normalish. But if she was so normal, then why were all the hairs on the back of my neck pricking up? I rubbed my hands over my arms, scrubbing away goose bumps.

"What can I get you?" The girl behind the counter asked.

Right, Shame needed a buzz.

"Hot chocolate, no, wait—your drinking chocolate, dark, as much as I can get to go for ten bucks." I put the money on the counter and moved to the side so the person behind me could look at the goodies in the glass case.

Also, so I could spy on that woman.

I took some time staring at truffles, which gave me a good peripheral on her.

She walked to the door, staring at people—even when they met her gaze—as if they couldn't see her. She still had her cup in her hand, but held it in such a wooden way I didn't think she'd even taken a drink out of it. She didn't go out the door, just stood there to one side of it, staring. Was she looking for someone? Couldn't she tell she was making people nervous?

It was like she thought she was invisible or something.

Instinct told me to stay far, far away from her. But there was something not human about her. As if she was something else entirely, trying to get used to wearing a woman's body. That was a very creepy thought. And with the gate open just half a block away, a thought I should follow up on.

The girl behind the counter handed me Shame's drink. I turned and couldn't avoid meeting the woman's gaze. As soon as I did, the mark on my left palm bit down so cold I sucked in a hard breath.

The woman's eyes widened and her mouth opened. The cup slipped her grip enough that a little chocolate spilled out over her fingers. "You can't be both. Alive. Dead." Her voice was rough, as if she hadn't used it in a while. She skittered away from the door—and was down the narrow walkway to the restroom in the back before I could even say anything.

She smelled like burned blackberries. She smelled like the disks. Disks Jingo Jingo had stolen.

The ice in my palm warmed again.

It didn't take a genius to guess she was probably one of the Death magic users working against the Authority.

I glanced out the window. Hayden, a hulking figure in a bomber jacket and flannel shirt, stood next to Shame. Shame pointed toward the shop and Hayden looked over, but couldn't see me through the glare on the window. If I'd had my cell, I would have called and let him know there was a crazy lady who might have a disk, and therefore a lead to find Jingo Jingo and the kidnapped Sedra. For all I knew she'd already found a back door out of this place. If I were quick and careful, I could at least make sure she was in the restroom, maybe even get a Tracking spell on her, before bringing in the big guns.

I strode to the back of the shop. No obvious exit. The only door led to the restroom. Just to be sure, I nudged open the door.

She stood at the sink, facing the mirror, her cup still perched in her hand like she was expecting someone to put money in it.

But here's where weird high-dived into a big ol' pail of impossible.

There was no reflection in the mirror. She was only a few feet in front of me. I could see my own reflection in the mirror—I looked surprised and angry, the white streaks in my hair wind-mussed into jagged lines, my skin too pale, my eyes too pale. I set a small Disbursement, quickly drew Sight. All the mirror showed was a light greenish glow in front of me.

The mark on my palm went so cold I felt like I'd stuck it up a frozen mastodon. I dropped the spell and tucked my left hand to my chest, which my reflection mimicked. I wanted to throw a Tracking spell on her. But what could I throw at someone who didn't even show up in a mirror? I didn't even know what she was. Vampires weren't real. But that was the only explanation I could come up with. What else couldn't be seen in a mirror?

*The dead,* my dead father said from inside my head.

The woman turned. "Yes," she said, answering my father, which added a nice extra screamy scoop of holy shit to the whole thing. "That's right. The dead." She no longer looked surprised. She looked hungry. "What sort of thing are you? Magic fills you and empties you. Alive with a dead soul." She squinted, wrinkling her nose. "You carry the dead. I could make use of you."

She held out her hand, and I had a sudden need for a sword, a machete, or hell, a gun. I calculated the collateral damage of a ten-dollar cup of drinking chocolate and eliminated it from my go-to weapons list.

"Who gave you the disk?" I asked, stepping into the room. At this point, I didn't want to let her out of here. I didn't know what she'd try to do, and I was pretty sure I had a better chance of stopping her than the chocolate shop employees did. I set Shame's drink on top of the paper towel dispenser because, hey, that stuff's expensive. Plus if I had to do a hand-to-hand bathroom grapple with a dead chick, I planned to keep her talking until I found an advantage.

"Your father, of course," she said.

*Dad?* I thought.

*No,* he said. *I created the disks, but I have not given them to her.*

"Yes," she said at the same time. "Oh, yes, you have."

"Are you a ghost?"

"Not anymore. I am *alive*." She darted forward, way too fast. My brain did a full and total disconnect. The Veiled. She was a Veiled. I pivoted on my feet, threw up my left hand to block.

Black flame poured out of my hand, so dark it hurt my eyes, and wrapped her from head to foot. She stopped cold and screamed, though I could not hear her. The flame swallowed all sound, swallowed all light, covered her face, her head, until she was a woman-shaped column of flame. I didn't know how to control it—didn't know how I had cast it. Using it felt like I'd just opened a vein. The room spun and went dark at the edges. I couldn't feel my arm.

I stuck my right hand out for support. Found the wall. Yay.

My left arm dropped, numb, useless. I fumbled for the door. I needed out. Needed help.

Late. Too late. As soon as my hand was down, the flames extinguished.

She was on me, fast, pushing me against the wall and shoving her thumb into the mark on my palm.

A shock of cold froze me, froze my blood. I should be shivering, screaming in pain, but I couldn't move.

"This dark magic token will do you no good. Mikhail's time has passed. He will remain in death while we retake life. You were wrong about the histories, Daniel Beckstrom, but oh, so right about your technology. It will change the world. It will give us immortality."

Holy shit. She knew my dad.

Dad reached forward in my head. He put his arms around me and pushed me back into the shadows of my mind.

No. Absolutely no. I was done with him using me like a doll.

*Let go of me,* I yelled. *Get your hands off me and get out of my head!* I shoved back at him, but he held strong.

"Truance," Dad said with my mouth, "this is not the way to immortality. You bear a body, but for how long? When the disk drains, you will have no way to recharge it. You cannot break the laws of magic at no cost."

She laughed, a sound like she was hacking up dust. "You, of all people, know there is no cost too high for immortality. There is a way recharge the disk. You would not make something so valuable disposable. All I need is your knowledge."

I couldn't see what was going on, but I felt the build of

magic in the room. She was going to cast a spell. She was going to suck my dad out of me just like Greyson had tried to suck him out of me.

Fine. If she wanted him, she could have him.

*Get out of my head*, I yelled again.

Dad wasn't listening. He pulled magic through my body. Too hot on the right and too freaking cold on the left. I pushed at Dad again, but he wasn't giving up control. He was chanting.

*No, no, no.*

Dad stopped chanting—for just a slip of a second.

Long enough for me to push free, push forward in my mind, push him out of the way.

I was away from the wall, my body in motion, right hand finishing a glyph I did not recognize, left hand cold and covered in black fire licking like cool silk between my fingers.

Magic can't be cast unless you are calm and focused. Even though this wasn't my spell, and I still didn't know what the black fire was all about, I had no problem calmly focusing both at Truance's head.

The spell hit her in the neck. She grabbed at her throat like she'd just swallowed acid, and stumbled. I was already casting Impact. She croaked out one word that made my ears pop. A rush of wind and magic and voices, too much, too big, too similar to a wild-magic storm, exploded in the tiny room.

And I mean *boom.*

I fell backward, hit the wall. So much for my Impact. I scrabbled up onto my feet, tracing Shield.

Truance was gone. Nothing left but a ring of black ash, glossy as crow feathers, circling the floor where she had been standing.

Shit.

*Dad?* I thought.

No answer. Good. Maybe she'd taken him with her.

I grabbed two handfuls of paper towels and dropped them on the ash. I used my shoe to muss up the ring. I didn't want anyone seeing this. Didn't want anyone calling the police, like Stotts, to check on it. Didn't want a Hound tracking it down. I used another paper towel to pick up the rest, and shoved the wadded ball to the bottom of the trash can. The rest would either fade, or get mopped up at closing.

I glanced at my watch. I'd lost five minutes. I needed to get back to Shame.

*Dad?* I washed my hands, taking time to make sure none of the residue from the spell was on my skin. Then I picked up the cup of chocolate and headed out. Truance was nowhere to be seen. Furthermore, no one looked the least bit bothered, which meant they hadn't heard the explosion. Magic can be weird like that.

I crossed the street, letting the walk, the speed, the wind cleanse me, cool me, remind me that my body was mine. Mine. And no one could use me, take me, hurt me again. Halfway to the parking lot, I felt a faint brush in the corner of my mind.

*Dad?*

Feather-soft flicker behind my eyes.

Sweet hells. He was still with me.

Shame sat on the bumper of a car—a real car, smoking a cigarette. Hayden stood in front of him, his back to the wall where I knew the gate was, his arms crossed over his chest. Hayden was big enough, he was hard to miss, even from a block away. He wiped his hand down his mouth and beard, squinting against the afternoon light as I neared.

"Here's your drink." I handed the paper cup to Shame.

He took it, sipped, then gulped it down.

"What's going on?" I asked.

Hayden unfolded his arms and stuck his hands in the front pocket of his jeans. "Art," he said, a little distastefully. "Art is going on."

"The gate?"

He nodded. "Victor." It was weird to get such short, quiet answers out of him. I looked a little closer. He had dark circles under his eyes, like maybe he hadn't slept in a few weeks, but otherwise was himself. Still, something seemed off. Either that or I was just feeling a little jumpy.

"Illusion," Shame said.

I glanced at the wall. The pickup was still there, and the plain brick wall. But without drawing on Sight, I couldn't see the magic that was going on.

"What happened to you?" Shame asked.

"Nothing."

"You have never known how to lie. What took you fifteen minutes to get a chocolate that is cold enough I can gulp it? Did the Oompa-Loompas go on strike?"

"There was a woman in the shop." I stopped talking as a man strolled past to a nearby car, unlocked the door, and got in. "Maybe I'll tell you later."

Shame nodded. I didn't know why he or Hayden didn't just cast Mute. For that matter, I could probably cast it, but every inch of me cringed at the idea of using magic right now.

Magic had never felt safe, but right now it didn't even feel predictable. I mean, black flames? Seriously?

And holy shit, an undead, reanimated Veiled woman-thing who knew my dad had just kicked my ass. So I stood there, hands in my pockets, trying to get my blood pressure and breathing under control.

Hayden buzzed on about a construction job he'd done up in Juneau that involved wrestling grizzly bears, riding moose, and living in an igloo.

Most of Shame's comments were "bullshit" and most of Hayden's were disbelief that Shame would question his story.

Hayden spread his hands out and up, like he was done trying to talk to him, and in that motion, dropped the Illusion he was holding.

Victor walked up next to us. I bit back a yelp. I hadn't seen him coming. It looked like he had walked out of the wall itself. Just as soon as I thought that, the memory skittered away, replaced with a general memory of shadows against the wall, and a man—Victor—walking from the sidewalk to the front of the parked cars.

Which I know I had not seen. Which I knew most people wouldn't think twice to question if that memory was really their own. Or if it were placed there, in their head, by a masterful Closer who could take memories away, and give you new ones.

I didn't like it.

"Don't do that to me," I growled.

Victor shook his head. "It's not just you, Allie. It's for anyone within a half-block radius. You know what you really saw. Simply choose to disbelieve what you think you saw and the true memory will remain."

He was so calm about it. As if messing with people's minds was a philosophy to discuss instead of being hurtful and wrong.

He was Zayvion's teacher, and mine too. I knew he had the Authority's best interest in mind, and had done everything in his power to keep me safe in the past. But I was so done with this stuff, so done with people messing with me.

"That it?" Shame asked. "'Cause I'm freezing my arse off."

"That's it," Victor said.

"Hold on." Hayden pointed up the street. "I think you've got an audience waiting on you, boy."

Sure enough, another small crowd of art enthusiasts was coming down the sidewalk. When they caught sight of Shame, several smiled and started talking and pointing excitedly.

"Better make it fast," I said to Shame. "You're about to be mobbed."

He exhaled smoke and pushed up onto his feet, shivering hard enough I could see him shake. He wasn't kidding he was cold. I don't know how he did it with such shaky hands, but he drew a Cancel spell.

A few people in the crowd were fast enough to cast Sight and hold fingers and thumb together toward Shame's Illusion. He slashed his right hand from left to right, waist-high, ending the Illusion. The crowd, gasped, smiled, and clapped.

"They're clapping because?" Hayden asked.

"Because I gave them what they were looking for."

The pickup was gone. The brick wall looked like a brick wall. And it was. Which meant Victor had Closed the gate. Since I didn't see any dead magical creatures on the ground, I assumed he had been able to close it before anything got through.

Well, anything other than Truance.

"Fireworks?" Hayden asked.

"Art," Shame said. "I am so out of here. Victor, Hayden. See you tonight."

"Be careful, Shamus. See that you get some food soon," Victor said.

"Planning on it. Allie's going to cook for me."

"Like hell."

Shame pressed his fingertips against his chest. "Must you crush my delicate soul?"

Hayden chuckled. "Boy, devil came calling for your soul before you could walk."

"How would you know?"

"Maybe I'm that devil."

"Maybe you are full of shit."

Victor rubbed at the bridge of his nose with his left, unbandaged hand. "I think it's time we all get some rest. Allie, why were you and Shame going to your apartment?"

"I need to pack a few things and call Violet. Do you know someone named Truance?"

His shoulders tightened like I'd just swung a cricket bat at his spine. "I used to."

"Was she a part of . . . " I almost said the Authority, then remembered there was a crowd of people at the other end of the parking lot. The average person wouldn't be able to hear us, but there could be a Hound in the crowd.

Victor walked over to me and smiled. It looked genuine. Unless I looked in his eyes. He was worried. Still, I knew how to play along.

He raised his hands to hug me, and I let him do that. No, I hugged him back. If any of the people in the crowd were looking, they'd think we were saying good-bye.

"Where did you hear her name?" Victor whispered in my ear. He smelled like Earl Grey tea and something deep and earthy.

"I think I saw her. Alive. Dead. Today. Just now. I don't know where she is now. She's a Veiled, right?"

Victor patted my back. "Pack your things quickly. Come back to Maeve's. Do not use magic in the meantime."

That was so not the answer I wanted.

He let me go and was on his way before I realized what had just happened. He thought I'd seen the Veiled because I was using magic—a reasonable deduction since that was usually how I saw the Veiled. But Truance hadn't been an insubstantial Veiled, or at least she hadn't been one of the watercolor people who tried to eat my magic every time I cast. She was solid. And a lot more real than the other Veiled I'd seen.

I opened my mouth to tell him he had misunderstood me, then gave up because I'd have to yell, or cast Mute and then yell. I just didn't have the energy to do either. Besides, I would see him soon. I could fill him in then. I mean, what more could go wrong in an hour or two?

# Chapter Nine

"Walk, Beckstrom," Shame said. "Let's go see if my car's been towed."

I fell into step behind him. Even though he obviously felt like shit, he moved like a man who owned the city. As a matter of fact, he'd treated Hayden and Victor a lot more like equals than like elders or teachers. Maybe his standing in the Authority had changed.

Which made some sense. Liddy had been the head of Death magic, Jingo Jingo next in line below her. Shame might be next in line. Or at least the most powerful Death magic user still on the right side of the war.

He took another drag off his cigarette, then held it low and at his side. Smoke curled off it, the cigarette burning down faster than it should, the smoke forming a glyph for Transference—a wee bit of Death magic there—before it was broken apart by the slight breeze.

That boy was throwing around a lot of magic for just smoking a cigarette. I wanted to use Sight on him, to make sure he was okay, and well . . . not possessed or anything. But just the idea of pulling on magic made me want to barf. I'd already done too much too soon with too many people sticking their fingers in my business.

"Fuckin' A. Finally, good luck." Shame turned around and walked backward, his arms extended, the cigarette already gone to ash in his fingers. "The car, she is untowed, and naren't a ticket upon her." He grinned, the wind pushing his hair into his eyes. I couldn't help it. I grinned back at him. He was a good-looking guy, my friend. I'd seen him go through a lot of hell lately. It was good to see him smile, really smile.

"You know what they say about good things," I said as I caught up with him.

"What do they say about good things?"

"Good things come in threes." I opened the car door and got in. Shame walked around and was in the driver's seat in short order.

"I think you have your superstitions on the wrong foot." He started the engine, then pulled out into traffic.

"Nope. My mom used to tell me that when I was little." I suddenly felt a little shocky.

"What?"

"I remembered that."

"Yeah?"

"I remembered something my mother said."

"Things you hear in therapy," he guessed. "Threats at family reunions, boring beginnings to old-people conversations. Can I buy a vowel?"

"Shut up. I haven't thought about that, about her telling me that, for years. It's a memory, Shame. A memory I thought I'd lost. No, I know I'd lost. Holy shit." I tried to remember my birthdays, her face, school, anything. Nothing came to me, but that memory of her, holding my hand because I had done something good, or maybe gotten a good grade or something, was clear and sweet.

"This a memory you've lost before?"

"I think so. Yes."

"You don't ever get them back once magic takes them from you?"

"No. Never." I was smiling—I couldn't stop smiling. If

I were more of a girly girl, I might even get a little weepy over this. Instead I patted my pocket, looking for my book. I did not want to forget that I had remembered.

Yes, my life is confusing.

No book, but I found the napkin. "Pen?" I asked.

"Glove box."

I opened the glove box, and pulled my hand back like there was a cobra curled up in there. A small, plain black box gave off enough magical vibes, I didn't want to be in the same car with it, much less accidentally touch it. I quickly snagged a pen and shut the compartment. I wiped my left palm over my jeans, trying to ease the itch there.

"Do I want to know what's in the box?" I asked.

"A good girl like you? No."

Usually I'd fight him for it. But right now I didn't want to know what magical nasty Shame kept hidden and handy.

I pulled the cap of the pen off with my teeth and wrote down a quick note about my mom and the memory.

"Anything else?" Shame asked.

"No, just that one thing. Why?"

"Because I hear good things happen in threes." He slid a quick smile my way. "And we're almost there. Do you have your key?"

"I don't have anything. We can talk to the manager, though."

"I got it." He parked the car, and pulled a key, my key, off the key chain. I noticed his hands were no longer shaking.

"Anyone else have the key to my place?"

"Nope, just me." Shame got out of the car and I did too. We didn't say much until we were in the building, and up three floors at my apartment door. I paused at my door—a habit I had yet to shake—and heard a shuffling inside. Stone. Probably. Just in case, I cleared my mind to cast magic if I needed it.

I unlocked the door and stepped in.

Stone trotted out of the living room, one of my shoes in his mouth, the other perched at an angle over his ear.

"Oh you have not been rummaging through my closet again," I said.

Stone whuffled at my hand, then moved over to Shame as I caught the shoe off his head.

"Hey, rock dude, are you destroying the house? Causing mayhem? Who's a ferocious gargoyle? Stoney's a ferocious gargoyle."

Stone's ears pricked up at his name, then he trotted back toward the living room. I turned to make sure my door was shut and locked. Stone waited for me, looking back over his shoulder, his wing pressed down tight against his torso.

"Looks like he wants to show you something." Shame was no longer joking around.

He stalked off after Stone into my living room, then I heard his footsteps going toward to my bedroom.

"Seriously, Shame?" I called out. "You think anything dangerous would still be breathing in my house with Stone around?"

I wandered into the living room. There wasn't anyone in the house, or anything out of place. Well, except every one of my shoes was stacked up in a pretty good replica of an Aztec step pyramid in the middle of the floor.

Where did he get the ideas for this stuff? Did he watch TV while I was gone?

Shame strolled out of my bedroom. "No one there. The windows are locked."

"Thanks." I was too tired to tell him even I could have figured that out on my own.

"Not a problem." He tapped out a cigarette.

"Please. Not in the apartment."

"Right. Sorry. So you're going to pack?"

I wanted to say no. Wanted to spend the next hour or so alone, to think things out and maybe take a nap in my own bed. But even more, I needed to get back to Zay. Back to Victor and Maeve. So I could tell them about Truance. And Mikhail. "Yes."

Shame parked it on my couch and exhaled a caught breath. He clunked his boots up on the coffee table. "Don't let me get in the way."

He closed his eyes and leaned his head back.

"Have a nice nap." I flipped him off, even though he couldn't see me.

"Back atcha," he mumbled. What, could he see through his eyelids?

I took the phone into the bedroom and shut the door. I dialed Nola, and dug around for a suitcase or duffel I could use while the phone rang.

She picked up the phone on the fifth ring.

"Allie! How are you, honey?"

Nola's voice was soft and warm, and it made me feel a hundred times better.

"I'm good. I know I'm the one who said I'd call every day to keep you up on things. I haven't called in a while."

"That's just fine. Shame called me a few times. I'm so sorry you caught the flu. Are you feeling better now?"

Flu. So Shame had decided it was better to lie to my best friend than tell her what had really happened. Of course if Nola knew what had really happened—that I'd gotten into a magical war and then walked into death to save Zay's soul, she would either not believe me or be furious that I'd almost killed myself.

But lie to my best friend? I never lied to Nola. I tried to keep her safe from the really bad magic stuff, but our whole relationship was based on me being able to tell her anything. Anything. She was the only person in this world that I told everything to. She was my memory when I lost it, and had more than once read back to me things I still can't remember doing.

"So was it really a flu?" she asked. I heard water running in the sink, then the sound of a peeler over a carrot or potato.

"It wasn't a flu. It was magic. But I'm better now. Well, a few things have changed. You're going to love what I did with my hair."

"What did you do?"

"Streaked it with white."

"Sexy. Not the best way for a Hound to blend in, though."

"No, but I wanted something.... Okay, fine. Magic did that to my hair. I'm hoping it grows out normal. You know how impossible it is to lie to you?"

"Yes. So why did you call?"

"Two things, mostly. Well, three. One, to see how you are doing."

"Well, thank you. Busy with the fields, but Cody's been a big help to me and the hands."

"That was two. How's Cody doing?"

"He's had some nightmares lately. He's talking to himself a little more. But if he's out working on the farm, he's happy. You should see his cat. She's queen of the farm. Even Jupe bows to her now." Nola laughed, and I laughed too.

I'd give anything to be out there on her farm, peeling vegetables, knitting, and not worrying about the end of the world. "Wish I were there."

"Me too. So why not come out and visit?"

"I can't. Zay's still in a coma. The doctors think he's showing signs of waking up. Maybe soon. I want to be here for him."

"What? What happened to Zayvion?"

Crap. I really hadn't kept up with her since everything had fallen apart.

"He was using magic—a lot of magic. And it sort of fell apart on him. Knocked him into a coma. It's been . . . " I paused to count on my fingers, gave up. "It's been a couple weeks at least. I'm so sorry I didn't call. Things have been crazy."

"There's more you aren't saying, isn't there?"

"Probably. A lot has happened since I saw you."

"I was just there a month ago. How much trouble can you get into in a month?"

"Too much. I'm good at it. Listen, the third thing is, I think Stotts got mixed up in some weird magic stuff."

"Paul?" The sound of the vegetable peeler stopped. "Is he okay? What kind of weird magic?"

"He's okay, but I haven't seen him yet. I thought I'd try to talk to him today or tomorrow. Just, if he seems a little strange, or . . . or I don't know—call me, okay? There are . . . things I know—and no, I can't talk to you about them right now—things that might help him if you think he needs help."

Wow, could I be any more vague?

"That's a little vague."

"It's a lot vague. I'll tell you all about it. Not over the phone. Sometime when we can have a glass of wine without worrying about if the world's going to end."

"The world's going to end?"

"Figure of speech."

Nola paused. "Maybe I should come to visit. I'm sure Cody would like the trip. There are plenty of hands here to take care of the farm and Jupe for a few days."

"No. Very no. This is what I didn't want you to do. Please. Don't come to town. Give me a few days to see if Zay wakes up, and handle some other stuff."

"You're in trouble, aren't you?"

"I'm not. I mean, yes, there are some problems I'm trying to work out. But I'm not alone. Shame's here, and you know, Violet. Plus, Shame's mother has been very supportive. I'm okay. I've finally made a few new friends."

"I know," she sighed. "It makes me miss you more, somehow."

"Aw, you'll always be my best friend."

She laughed. "Oh, please. So is there anything else? Your one, two, three list?"

"I remembered something about my mom."

"Awesome!" I could tell she was moving around, heard a pen click and a notepad open. "Spill it."

See, this was why I loved her. She knew just how precious memories—any memories—were to me.

"I was little. I think I'd just brought home a good report card, or a good grade on a project from school. And Mom . . . she was really pretty . . . she knelt down and hugged me. She smelled like apples. And she told me, 'You know what they say about good things? Good things come in threes.' That's it. That's all I remember, but it's still really clear. I know I didn't know this a while ago."

"Got it. I'll add it to your files. What brought it back?"

"I don't know. I think I got lucky."

I stared down at the empty duffel on my bed. I was supposed to be packing. Instead I'd just stood there, talking to Nola and not doing anything else.

I got busy with my dresser and closet. "I'm going to be staying with Zayvion for a while. My cell phone broke, but I'll be getting a new one soon. It should be the same number. And let me give you the number out at Shame's mom's place."

"The restaurant?"

"Well, it's an inn too. Lots of rooms upstairs, more room than my apartment. And Maeve knows good doctors who do house calls. So he's getting medical care, and it still feels pretty homey. Nicer than staying at a hospital, anyway."

"Are you sure I shouldn't come out?"

"I'm sure. I'll try to call again soon. Here's the number." I read it off; then we said our good-bye.

I waited until she hung up before I disconnected the call.

Even though I wanted to see her, it really was better she stayed away for a while. I did not want my very nice, very sweet, very un-magical best friend to wander into the middle of a magical war zone.

I finished shoving clothes in the duffel, looked for my spare pair of boots, and remembered seeing them in Stone's pyramid contraption. I'd get those on the way out.

All packed, I had one more call to make. Violet.

I dialed her cell, waited.

"Mrs. Beckstrom's phone, may I help you?" a male voice asked.

"Uh . . . can I speak to Violet?"

"Whom may I say is calling?"

"Allie. Beckstrom. Who is this?"

"Kevin. I'll see if she's available."

And then he hung up on me. What the hell?

I waited a couple seconds, stared at the phone in my hand. Dialed again.

"Mrs. Beckstrom's phone, may I help you?"

"Don't hang up on me, Kevin."

"Sorry about that." He didn't sound sorry. "I'll see if Violet's available."

This time I heard the phone set down. Kevin's footsteps across hardwood floors, then a hush of voices in the background. More footsteps. "Just a moment."

"Allie?"

Violet sounded happy.

"Yes, it's me. What's up with Kevin?"

"He's been . . . Kevin, would you please let me take this call in private? Thank you." She waited. I heard a door close. "He's been horrible!" She laughed. "You'd think ninjas were going to jump out of my underwear drawer or something. I swear, I love that he's my bodyguard, and ever since that . . . problem in the lab, he's been extra careful about everything, including phone calls, but oh, my lord, I could use a rest from the man."

"I'm sorry I haven't been by."

"Don't worry. Maeve told me you were dealing with . . . business. Are things worked out?"

I didn't know how much Violet knew about what had happened. Dad let her in on a lot of the workings of the Authority. Kevin was a part of the Authority, and Violet knew that. But I wasn't sure how much she had been told since the storm hit. Last I saw her, she'd been in the hospital, Kevin had been in the ICU, and they were worried she might have the baby too soon.

"The baby!" I suddenly remembered. "Is everything okay? Are you okay? Did you have him or her?"

"Everything is good. No baby yet. I'm on bed rest for the next couple weeks. Then I should be able to deliver just fine."

"And Kevin? I mean, I heard him on the phone, so I'm assuming he's back on his feet. Last I heard, he was in ICU."

"He's . . . " She thought a moment. "He's physically well, or so he tells me. But I think he's still in pain from the break-in. His mood has changed. He's angry all the time—not toward me. He's civil and just as thoughtful as he's always been to me. But the break-in changed him. I think it's because he wasn't able to do his job and keep me safe, so now he needs to prove just how safe he can keep me."

Yeah, that or maybe it was because people from the Authority, people that he probably trusted, had tried to kill him and Violet for the disks.

Which made me wonder. "Have the police come up with any leads on that case?"

"I haven't heard much. I think it's being taken care of by the detectives who specialize in such things."

She meant Stotts and his Magical Enforcement Response Corps, the MERCs. "Do you remember what happened?"

"Only some of it, which is strange. I am usually very clear under stress. Have an almost photographic memory. But all I can remember is someone breaking in, a fight or struggle of some sort, then waking up in the hospital. It's not like me, but it's true."

I had a pretty good idea of why she didn't remember it. Probably someone had Closed her. Sweet hells, was the Authority going to take everyone's memories away?

"Allie?"

I'd paused for too long.

"Huh. Well, that is weird. Think it's because you're pregnant?"

"That's all the doctors can attribute it to. I tell you, I don't regret being pregnant for a second, but I am so ready for this to be over. I want to see my feet again." She giggled. "But, until then, and since I'm on bed rest, it would be great if you could stop by when you have the chance. I've been taking care of the business via e-mail and videoconferencing. I need your signature on a couple documents. Nothing life-threatening, but I'd like to get them taken care of. When can you come over?"

"Are you at the condo?"

"No, I'm still staying with Kevin. Do you have time today?"

Violet had switched out of her girlfriend mode and was all no-nonsense business now. There was a reason I wanted her to take over the job of running my father's business. She was very good at it.

"Today's not good. Maybe tomorrow?"

"Let's make it Monday. I'll call you in the morning."

"I better call you," I said. "My phone's broken. I'm getting another one today, I think."

"All right, that works fine." I heard her tapping on a keyboard. "Call me anytime. I'll probably be right here." She sounded resigned.

"Tired of the bed?"

"And the couch. And the recliner."

"Well, once the baby arrives, you might not get any rest at all. So enjoy it while you can."

"I suppose. Bye, Allie."

"Bye."

I waited for her to hang up. The line still sounded open even though I'd heard her phone click.

"Good-bye, Kevin," I said.

"Good-bye, Allie," he said.

We both hung up. I patted my pocket for my book, remembered I didn't have it on me, and took a new blank book out of my nightstand drawer. I transferred my notes from the napkin into the book, added a quick rundown on my conversation with Nola and Violet, and made a note to check in with Kevin later to see what his angle was on all this.

I thought about calling Stotts. But what would I say? *Gee, sorry to tell you someone took your memories away because there is even more illegal magic going on in the city than you know about?* Or maybe, *Hey, so there's a magical war going on, gates into death are opening and not closing, which means all sorts of nasties are getting through, and by the way, we shredded your memory.*

No, when I talked to Stotts about this, and I very much intended to do so, it would be face-to-face so I could explain everything necessary.

So that meant I needed to give Stone a pat and take my bags back to the inn, where I could tell Victor and everyone else about Truance.

Maybe find out what Terric had done about that shadow man I kept seeing.

I shrugged the duffel over my shoulder. One of Zay's sweaters, a deep green cashmere that I'd bought him, hung on the back of the door. I walked over to it and held the sleeve against my cheek, inhaling the familiar pine scent of him. A lump caught in the middle of my chest and I leaned my head against the door, wishing it were Zayvion and not his sweater I was holding.

Sweet hells, I missed him. I rubbed at my eyes, trying to brush away the itch of tears. But the tears wouldn't stop. I pulled the sweater off the hook and slid down until I was sitting on the floor, holding the sweater against my chest like it could somehow fill the hole inside me. Like it could somehow erase the taint of my father's hands digging in my heart, giving away pieces of me, using my mouth, my mind, my body. Like the sweater could somehow restore my magic and my body, and make me me again.

I cried silently. I didn't want Shame to hear me. Didn't want Stone to hear me. I didn't want anyone to ask if I was okay. I just wanted to be alone, with enough time to pick up all my broken pieces and put me back together again, a stronger me, a better me. But I couldn't even be alone anymore. Not even in my own mind.

It might be easier to tell Victor, yes. Take my memories. Let me live my own life again. But it would mean leaving Zayvion forever. The idea of that hurt even more.

When I could control the tears again, I pushed myself back up onto my feet and used an old T-shirt to wipe my face and nose. That was it. That was all the time I got for myself. And even though the pain of losing my magic was right there—a lump I couldn't think around, couldn't swallow around—I was done with it. That pain might be a part of me, but I refused to let it be the only thing I was.

I was not a broken doll.

I pulled on Zay's sweater and walked out into the living room. Shame, on the couch, didn't move. His head was still back, his eyes closed. He was breathing heavily enough, I knew he was asleep. Stone had crawled up onto the couch next to him, his head on Shame's thigh. Shame's hand was on top of the big lug's nose. Stone's eyes were open—he slept that way—and I was pretty sure he was asleep too.

I quietly put the phone back on the hook, then went into the bathroom and splashed some cool water on my face. Maybe I did get a little more time. If not to myself, at least for myself. Terric and Victor had both said Shame needed to get some rest. And after all the magic he'd thrown around, I figured we could afford to stay here a half hour longer.

What was I going to do with a half hour? Not sleep. I'd never get up again. Not cry. I'd never stop.

When all else failed, make coffee.

Back out in the living room, I managed to tug my boots out of the pyramid and not send the other shoes tumbling. The rock had a good eye for architecture. I put the boots in my duffel, then prowled into the kitchen to brew coffee. I tried to do it quietly, but it was impossible to make coffee in absolute silence. No movement from the living room—that told me Shame was more than tired.

I deconstructed the stack of spice jars and cans on my countertop that looked a lot like Mount Hood, including parsley that had been poured out at the foot of the mountain like little trees. Seriously? Did the beast have to express his artistic side in my kitchen?

Then I filled a mug with hot black coffee and wandered back into the living room.

I sat at the little round table by the window, and tugged the curtain to the side so I could look out at the city below me. Portland looked like Portland. In the back of my mind I half expected it to look like the warped version of the city in death. But even though a wild-magic storm had almost shut the city down, people on the street walked by, unconcerned, going about their daily business as if nothing had happened. It was weird to think that not so long ago I could have been one of them. And even though I was no longer as carefree, I felt a little pride for what I'd done. I had been a part of keeping thousands of people safe. The Authority had been a part of keeping people safe.

I wondered if this was what a superhero felt like.

Halfway through my cup of coffee, and just as Shame moved on from heavy breathing to light snoring, I noticed a man on the street below. He stood in the middle of the sidewalk, his arms extended slightly out to the side, taking up so much room that the other pedestrians had to make an effort to walk around him.

There was something wrong with this picture. The same crawling creepiness I felt around Truance slithered down my spine and one slow, cold pulse spread out from my left palm. I glanced at Shame—still sleeping. Stone too. I calmed my mind, set a Disbursement—I was going to have a migraine tonight if I kept this up—and cast Sight.

Magic drew up through me, sluggish, and aching. I gritted my teeth against the dull pain in my chest, and kept my concentration on the glyph for Sight.

Magic heightened my vision, revealing all the burned-out and still active spells in the city. None in my house, except my door where Zay had set a Ward so strong I hadn't found how he kept it powered. I suspected he had tied it into the network in some sort of sleight-of-hand way. I'd refused to let him set Wards on my windows. Stone used them to come in and out of the place and I didn't want a Ward going wrong on him, or hurting him in some way.

Which meant I had a nice clear view of the street.

And where the man should be standing—where I knew he was standing—was nothing but a luminescent green glow.

Just like Truance.

Holy shit.

I dropped Sight. Yep, he was still there. And yep, he was looking up at my window now. "Shame?"

"Just resting my eyes."

"I need you to see this."

It must have been my tone of voice. Shame was on his feet and next to me so quickly I didn't even have time to blink.

"See that man down there looking up at us?"

"Yes."

"Look at him with Sight."

Shame cast magic—he was behind me so I didn't see it, but I felt it.

"Balls. What is it?"

"A Veiled?"

"Not like any I've seen. Pale things, ghostly. This thing's solid. At least to the outward eye. How long's he been down there?"

"A few minutes. Do you recognize him?"

"No. Do you?"

I hesitated. *Dad, do you know him?* Only silence in my mind.

"No. But I saw a woman like that, like him. When I went to get you chocolate. Her name was Truance. I tried to tell Victor, but we were in public."

"Not a lot of Truances around," Shame said. "One used to work for the Authority. Back in the day. Like when your da was young and killing his way up the ladder. She's dead, by the way."

"She might be dead, but it hasn't stopped her from walking around Portland's chocolate shops. We fought. She has a disk."

"And you tell me this now?"

"Do not," I warned him.

He gave me a surprised look. "Okay then. Let's go see if that fellow downstairs happens to be a friend of Truance."

Stone had lumbered over and pressed his forehead against the glass. He growled.

"You see him too, huh?" I got up. "Stay here. Don't go out there. It's too light. Someone will see you." Stone listened with his head cocked to one side as he trotted behind us to the door.

"Stay," I said, opening the door.

Stone lowered his head, his butt up in the air.

"I said stay, not play. It's sleep time. Don't you want to get some sleep?"

He grumbled a reply, then shoved past me and was out in the hall before I could stop him. Luckily, no one was on the floor right now. "Bad gargoyle," I whispered. "Get back inside."

Stone trotted down the hall to the window at the side of the building that overlooked the alley. He stood on his back legs, and used his very humanlike fingers to unlock the window, push it open, then pull himself up into a crouch on the sill. He fanned his wings and leaped.

I jogged down the hall, caught the window. Stone was already on the building next door, stuck to it with hand and claw like a big gray gecko the size of a Saint Bernard. He muscled up another story or so, then slipped silently over the roofline.

"Fantastic. Now there's a gargoyle on the loose."

Shame was already heading down the stairs. I shut the window and jogged to the stairs, then down, catching up with him by the time we hit the bottom floor.

"Back door?" I asked.

"Straight out front." Shame cast something with his left hand and shoved the door open with his right.

I thought it might be some kind of Illusion or Camouflage, but when I stepped out into the fresh air and smelled the sweet scent of cherries, I realized it was Blood magic.

Shame muttered something, then bent his arm like he was pushing his sleeve aside to look at his watch. The spell cast across the street.

The man hadn't run. Not at all. Instead, he walked across the street toward us, paying no mind to cars that slammed brakes and horns as he cut across traffic. I shifted the grip on my duffel and drew a Shield with my left hand, holding it pinched between my fingers, empty of magic but ready to cast. Shame's left hand was at his hip, clenched in a fist, as if he had a rope there he was pulling.

And he did. Blood magic worked that way. A drop of blood fell to Shame's boot and was immediately absorbed. That would be Death magic.

The man was shorter than I expected, dark skin, wide smile. Not a nice smile. He had a scar down one cheek. I noticed what he was wearing—not because it was all that unusual—dark slacks and a leather jacket, but because he had a thick black scarf wrapped several times around his neck. Just like Truance.

Shame placed his right hand over his heart and tipped his head down. He was humming a soft song, pulling on Death magic. I'd seen him do this when we hunted down the Hungers out in St. Johns.

The man either didn't notice or didn't care. He bulled straight at Shame, his right hand out, palm forward, chin high.

Shame stopped singing. Looked up, and opened his arms to the man.

The man tried to stop. I could see it in his face. But Shame pulled him in, left fist clenched, blood pooling in the spaces between his fingers, but not losing even one drop. They embraced. Shame muttered a long list of syllables, and suddenly the guy was all smiles, patting Shame on the back, talking to him like an old friend.

It was an Illusion.

I set another headache Disbursement and cast Sight, ready to cast a lot more.

Shamus-burning-bright still had the man in his grip, his right hand over the man's throat, staring straight into the guy's horrified eyes as he drank down every last scrap of magic inside him. The man convulsed, but Shame's hand squeezed his throat and kept him standing. Shame tipped his face up, his mouth open, and moaned as the man faded and faded. He was no longer solid. I could see the traffic through him, the buildings through him; then he was nothing but a green fog that fell to the ground like a waterfall. And was gone.

Shame didn't move, even after the man was gone. His face was both fierce and serene. Ecstasy. Finally, he licked his lips, and looked back down from the sky.

I dropped Sight. The Illusion of the man was still standing in front of Shame. He laughed, said good-bye. Shame, or the Illusion of him, did the same. The man walked away down the sidewalk. Shame turned to watch him take the corner into the alley, then dropped the Illusion.

Holy crap. I'd never seen someone use Illusion while they killed someone in broad daylight in the middle of the sidewalk.

"What the hell was that?"

"Mostly Death magic with a dash of Blood." He gave me a lazy smile, and his eyes were far too black. He looked a little drunk. "Come on, now. You walked through death. You must have seen lots worse than that." He started down the street toward the back of the building where his car was parked.

"The things in death were dead. They had every right to be scary," I said.

"You aren't scared of little ol' me are you?"

"Did you just kill that guy?"

"Oh, yes. Yes, I did indeed." He fished in his pocket, but kept walking. " 'Course, he was already dead. Still, that kind of performance deserves a smoke, don't you think? Hold this for me."

He dropped something into my hand.

Not something. A disk. It was flat, and cast-iron gray. Not a spark of magic left within it, but it was clearly one of the disks my father and Violet had made.

"Where did you get this?"

"Out of that Veiled's throat." He lit up, sucked down a lungful. "That, Beckstrom, is something we can both be afraid of."

# Chapter Ten

"Who the hell is giving Veiled disks? And bodies?" I asked.

"I have a feeling we're going to be real busy finding out," Shame said. "Let's see if Victor has any ideas. So tell me about Truance."

I switched the disk to my left hand, where it made my palm hurt, so I unzipped my duffel and dropped it in there.

Shame's car was in sight. A man stood next to it.

Sid Westerling, one of the Hounds, leaned against the front bumper, hands stuck in his jacket pockets. He wore business casual and a Windbreaker, his glasses catching a spark of light as he turned to watch our approach.

"Sid," I said.

"Good to see you, Allie." He pushed away from the car. "Shamus, isn't it? Flynn?"

"It is."

Sid didn't offer to shake hands and neither did Shame. Hounds don't like leaving their scent or picking up someone else's scent unless necessary. I used to be that careful. Now being tracked by my scent was the least of my worries. My, how things change.

"Are you looking for me?" I asked.

"Some business you should know about. The Pack."

"Can it wait?"

"It's Davy."

"I'll be in the car," Shame said. "Give you two a minute to talk."

I waited until Shame shut the door. "What's wrong?"

"He's at the warehouse. He won't talk. Except to say he wants to talk to you. And you've been a hard person to find." He pressed his glasses up on the bridge of his nose. "Very hard. Almost like you dropped off the face of the earth." His gaze searched my eyes, looking for a reaction there.

"Maybe I did."

"I'd love to know your hidey-hole."

"Wouldn't be a hidey-hole if I told you where it was. I can't see Davy right now, Sid. I have too many things on my plate."

He pursed his lips and nodded. "Heard that your boyfriend was hurt. How exactly did that happen?"

"Oh, give me a break. If you don't know, then it's none of your damn business," I said. "We work together, Sid. We're not married."

That got a quick smile out of him. "Good thing. You'd be a shock to the wife."

He was married? When was I going to get that personnel questionnaire worked up for the Hounds? It would be nice to know this stuff.

"Can you take care of Davy for a couple more days?"

"Already been doing it for a couple weeks. Think it might be your turn now."

"Weeks?"

Sid stepped up into my personal space. With his hands still in his pockets, he leaned close. "Davy's hurting. He's asking for *you*. Maybe when you're done running around doing . . . whatever sorts of things you're doing, you can give the poor kid five minutes of your time. Isn't that what this Pack is supposed to be all about? Looking out for each other even when it's inconvenient?"

He stepped away. Waited.

Hells.

"I'll come by now. Let me tell Shame." I opened the passenger's-side door, and held my breath for a second while the smoke escaped the car. "I need to go see Davy."

"You're joking."

"I'll come by after I get this straightened out." I tossed my duffel into the backseat. "See you there."

"I can't believe I have to tell you this again." He pointed at his chest. "Me." He made walking motions with two fingers. "Follow." He pointed at me. "You. Get in."

I made a face at him, then straightened and leaned on the top of the door. Sid had heard all that. He was a Hound—good hearing came with the job.

"I'll meet you there," I said, not lying because Sid would smell it on me. A good nose was another sign of a Hound. "Shamus here has an awkward sense of loyalty, but at least it means I don't have to walk."

"You should get a car."

"I've been thinking about it, but paying for parking sucks." I gave him a smile. "See you."

Sid moved out of the way. He didn't go immediately toward his car, just stood there and watched us, waiting to see if we turned in the direction of the warehouse. Suspicious. Hound. Most of the time those two things were synonymous.

"Are we really going to check in on the kid?" Shame asked.

"I am. You can stay in the car if you want."

He shook his head, then pulled out his cell phone and dialed a number with his thumb. "Mum? Listen, we've run into a bit of a problem. Allie needs to check on one of her puppies."

I slapped his arm.

"Ow. We'll be maybe an hour or so. Also, we ran into an undead Veiled with a disk. It made him solid and capable of using magic. Took care of him, have the empty disk with us." He paused. "Nothing. Looks just like anyone else, except he was acting a little strange. I wouldn't have thought twice. Allie. I dunno." He glanced over at me. "How did you know he was a Veiled?"

"When I cast Sight, he looked like green fog. Truance looked like that too."

"Before Sight. What tipped you off?"

"The mark in my left hand got really cold."

His eyebrows shot up. "You catch that?" She hadn't, so he repeated it. "She just told me about Truance. Yes, I'll get it out of her. About an hour, I think. As if you wouldn't. Bye." He hung up. "Truance. Let's have it."

"She was in the chocolate shop, staring at people like she was surprised they could see her. When she saw me, she ran to the back. I followed her to the restroom."

"For fuck's sake, Allie. We were right down the block, and you went into that alone?"

"Deal with it." I was tired of being told I couldn't take care of myself.

He got the hint and pushed his bangs out of his eyes. "Go on."

"I smelled the disk on her. Since Jingo Jingo is the only person I know who has disks—other than the ones locked up at your mom's inn—I thought I might be able to put a Tracking spell on her. But when I looked in, she had no reflection in the mirror. I cast Sight and saw the green glow. My dad spoke to me—in my head—and she answered him.

"She said Mikhail's time is over and Dad's disks will give

her immortality. When he told her she wouldn't be able to recharge the disk, she tried to suck him out of my brain. That's when I got control of my body again and hit her with whatever spell Dad had been casting. Plus, my hand was covered in black flame. I threw that at her too."

"Hold up. Is your da still in your noggin?"

"Yes."

"And the black flame?"

"Left hand. That mark of magic in my palm—that's the only thing I can think it might be from." I hoped that was the reason I had suddenly gone pyrotechnic. "I don't know how to control it, and it makes my arm goes numb pretty fast."

Shame tugged his hair back again, nervous. "Not to spook you or anything, but I don't think your hand catching on fire is a good thing. We'll have Victor and Mum check you when we get back. Think you could flame on demand if you had to?"

"I could try."

"Did you kill her?"

"No. She disappeared. She said a word and set off a magical explosion. The only thing left was a black circle of ash on the floor."

"Lovely. Bloody fucking lovely. There could be dozens of things like her on the street."

"Solid Veiled with disks?"

"If Jingo Jingo is making them—though I don't know what kind of good comes out of raising dead magic users—yes."

"How many of the disks did Jingo take? What happened after the storm?"

"I wasn't entirely conscious," he said. "I saw you step through the gate." He paused. Took a long time before he started talking again. "Don't ever do that again. It about killed me to see you throw yourself into that hell."

"I did it for Zayvion."

"Who would kick your ass if he saw you do something that stupid. Understand?"

"Yes." Maybe even more than he did. He was right. Zay had been really angry at me for walking into death to save him. I'd lost my small magic. I hadn't gotten rid of my dad. Zay hadn't woken from his coma. Right now, it really did seem like a stupid thing that hadn't done much good for anyone.

But I am nothing if not stubborn. "I couldn't let him die."

Shame didn't say anything.

"You would have done the same thing."

"No, I would have done it better."

"And I would have gone in after you."

"I tried. Terric—"

"Terric saved your life. You were already too close to being dead, Shame. Coming back from death would have been impossible. Death wouldn't have let you go."

"You know Victor tried to keep the gate open," he said. "I think he was going to go in after you." He glanced at me. "Did you really use Influence on him?"

"Um . . . yes?"

Shame hooted. "He was furious about that. I'm surprised the only thing he did to you when you pulled that little blood promise yesterday was put you to sleep. Anyway, when the gate collapsed, we had about five minutes to gather our wounded, pick up our dead, and grab all the disks that were left before the MERCs showed up."

"Stotts was there?"

"We were gone before then."

"And you took all of the disks?"

"All that were left. Most went with Jingo, we think, and some burned into slag from channeling the wild-magic storm. We took those with us too. It's possible some of the other magic users grabbed them before they ran."

"We had at least a hundred disks there. We recovered most of them, right?"

"No."

"How many do we have?"

"Maybe a quarter of them."

"And the rest are in the hands of our enemies?"

"We think so. I'm sure we'll go over all this tonight, especially with the new development in your duffel bag. And Truance. And your flaming hand trick." I stuck my hand in my pocket, feeling self-conscious about it. I mean, really? Did I need another strange thing about me? Wasn't I strange enough?

"So you do think Jingo Jingo is making the Veiled solid? He knows how to do that kind of thing?"

"Maybe. If it's done the same way Greyson was made half-dead, then it's a mix of Life magic, Death magic, and light and dark. Lots of forbidden stuff all stirred together. Living people don't survive that combination. Maybe the dead tolerate it fine and dandy. It's a brilliant idea to try it on the dead. Twisted, but brilliant. Still, the old necromancy spells have been locked away and forbidden for hundreds of years."

"Looks like somebody found them."

"Or experimented until they fell on the right combination of magic and disks to make it work," he said.

We had made it to the broken part of town where Get Mugged stood strong on the corner. The old warehouse next to it, owned by the coffee shop's owner, Grant, wasn't looking too bad either. In front of the warehouse was the paranormal investigator's van—they rented the bottom floor. I leased the top two floors. One was empty, one was the sanctuary and landing place for Hounds, the gathering place that Pike, one of the best Hounds in the city, had hoped he could make happen. But Pike had died and left the Hounds in my care. Not too fancy, not too noticeable,

I liked to think Pike would have been happy with the den we'd made.

Shame found a place to park about a block away. We got out and headed down the street. I kept my eyes open, looking for anyone who set off my creepy radar, or made my hand cold, but the few people who walked past were creepless, at least in a magical sort of way.

We passed Get Mugged and I didn't even glance in. I hadn't been by for more than a week, and I knew if Grant caught sight of me walking by without stopping in for a cuppa and a chat, he'd have a fit.

Luckily, Grant didn't see me, and we opened the warehouse's heavy wood and glass door and walked through the carpeted lobby to the staircase beyond.

"Elevator, right?" Shame asked.

"Stairs." I didn't say any more. The Hound floor was only one story up, an easy walk for me, though I was a little more out of breath than usual by the time we reached the top. Dying had eaten away at my resources, and even though I'd felt really good this morning, the run-in with Truance and everything else made me wish I'd taken a nap back in my apartment with Shame.

The entire floor was one big open space. I'd managed to set up an office area on the side nearest Get Mugged, and put in a couple bunks, sets of couches, and TVs on the other side, where there was also a small, open kitchen and a couple of bathrooms that had four solid walls built around them. There was a meeting table that doubled as a dining room table and a scattering of chairs.

The advantage to the open floor space was I could see everything and everyone, pretty much at once. Necessary when dealing with Hounds.

"Doesn't anyone have a job to do?" I didn't raise my voice. Didn't have to. They all probably heard me coming up the stairs.

The only Hounds in the rec room were Jack and Bea, sitting on the couch, watching TV. Bea looked a lot better than when I'd last seen her after she'd been hit in the park and taken to the hospital. Jack looked the same, tough as leather and functionally drunk.

Jamar, who usually handled jobs for the police in neighborhoods dealing with gang crime, was cooking something that had a lot of garlic in it—he waved as I walked in. And then there was Davy.

Davy, who paced in front of the windows and didn't even look up. He had his gaze on his feet, or occasionally glanced out the window before going back to looking at his shoes. Hands tucked up under his armpits, he looked like he was cold or hurting.

Heat wasn't broken. Which meant he was in pain.

"People, this is Shamus Flynn. He's my friend, and not a Hound."

Jack lifted a couple fingers in salute, and Bea said it was nice to meet him. Then they all watched me, watched for what I was going to do about Davy.

I crossed the room, stood just out of arm's reach, at midpoint of his pacing route. "Sid said you wanted to talk to me," I said. "What's up?"

He walked past me without looking, walked back, almost passed me again.

"Davy. What's wrong?"

He stopped. "In private."

"All right." I thought about it. Where could I take him that a bunch of hypersensitive ears wouldn't be able to hear us? "Where do you want to go?"

He looked around, and I swear it was the first time he realized how many people were in the room. Something was seriously wrong with the kid. He was a good Hound, maybe on his way to being really good. Details didn't get past him. He should know how many people were in the room by counting the exhales.

"Come on." I turned and walked toward the doors. Davy followed behind me, and so did Shame.

"I said private," Davy said to Shame.

"He's cool, Davy. I trust him to hear any kind of thing you're dealing with. Plus, I think you and I could take him."

"Hey, now," Shame said. "That stings."

Davy didn't fight me on it. Also not like him.

"Do you need a doctor?" I asked as I opened the door to the stairs.

"No."

I started up the stairs, Davy behind me, Shame behind him.

"Is it Tomi?"

"No. I don't think so. No."

And that was all we said until we made it to the next level.

The floor plan was identical to the floor downstairs, only this didn't have a scrap of furniture in it unless you counted the mattress I'd put in the corner. I wasn't kidding when I said I didn't know what I was going to do with it yet. I mean, I didn't want to live here—not this close to the Hounds—but I loved the idea of having all this space to myself. It was like my latent rich-girl tendencies had taken over when Grant had offered me the killer deal if I'd lease out both floors.

I thought maybe I could sublease it to another business or something, but I just hadn't gotten around to doing anything about it.

"Okay, if we keep it quiet, I think there's enough brick and plaster between us and the ears." I strolled over to the curtained window and leaned my hip against the sill. Davy walked with me, and Shame, bless his little black heart, stayed over by the door, giving us some privacy.

Davy stopped in front of me, still not looking at me.

"You're making me worry. What's wrong?"

He shrugged. "I think I'm losing it."

"Losing what?"

"My mind, you know?" He looked up. His eyes were bloodshot and he was so pale I wondered if he'd been sleeping at all. I resisted the urge to tell him to sit down.

"What makes you think so?"

Mental breaks weren't all that uncommon among Hounds. It was another reason why I was setting up some kind of insurance coverage for the group. Hounds used magic a lot, and they had a tendency of never hiring a Proxy to bear their price of pain. Therefore, they were lousy at pain management, and usually ended up taking their own lives in a bad combination of sheer agony and stupidity.

"You know how I can feel it when Hounds are hurt?"

I nodded. What Davy didn't know was the reason he could feel pain inflicted on us was because of how Greyson had made Tomi, Davy's ex-girlfriend, use magic on him. Blood magic and Death magic. I kept hoping it would wear off, but just like Davy carried a thin scar down his left temple, he still carried that Blood magic awareness too.

"I felt you. Hurt. I couldn't find you. I mean it was like you had died or something. You were more than gone. I even checked the morgues, followed police reports. And now, here you are." He swallowed. Waited for me to come up with an explanation.

Then he reached over with one finger and poked my arm.

That was weird.

"I was hurt—you weren't wrong about that," I said. "I'm okay now, though. So is that it? You felt my pain—and got worried?"

I was trying to keep it light, but I was responsible for the state he was in. If he could sense Hounds in magical distress, I could imagine what it must have been like for him when I stepped through a magical gate into death.

"That's not it," he said. "Not all of it. I've been seeing stuff. Hallucinating. Hearing voices."

"What are the voices saying?"

"He—I mean, they told me to find you."

"He?"

Davy stared at me, as if all the air had left him and emptied him of words.

"Who, Davy? Who are you hearing? What are you seeing?"

"Pike," he said. "I've been seeing Pike."

# Chapter Eleven

"Pike's dead," I said. Mouth in gear, brain stuck in neutral.

"I know. I know." Davy pressed his hands over his face, fingers pulling at his forehead. "I know he's dead. I . . . I saw him die. But, I swear, it's so real. He—" His laugh had a manic edge to it. "He talks to me. Not things he used to say, but full conversations. He keeps telling me I need to find you. He keeps telling me he needs to talk to you. He keeps telling me I have to tell you." He dragged his hands down his face and stared at the curtained window behind me. "God, this is crazy. It's crazy. I'm crazy."

It wasn't crazy to think Pike might be trying to contact him. Shame had just sucked the life out of a Veiled. I was possessed by my dad. There was a flying statue loose in the city. Weird stuff happened around here. But Davy didn't know about any of those things.

And if I told him, I risked him getting Closed, just like Stotts.

Davy needed to know something, or he'd check himself into the psych ward. Or do something worse.

"It's not crazy. Do you remember at the first Hound meeting I asked if anyone had ever seen ghosts? And then I made up some story about Hounding for someone who had seen ghosts? It wasn't a client. It was me. I saw ghosts. Still do."

He stared at me like I'd just turned into a hallucination.

"Pike talked to me about it. Said he'd seen a lot of weird things in this city. Plus, you know, there are paranormal investigators downstairs. They treat this kind of thing as scientifically as possible. We could talk to them about it. Is there a place or time that he, uh, that Pike shows up?"

"No. Well, the first couple times it was when I was looking for you—using magic searching for you."

"What did he say to you?"

"Same thing. He wants you. Wants to talk to you."

"I see." I glanced over at Shame, who was pretending not to hear us.

"Don't try to tell me this is normal."

"It's not. Not normal. But weird shit happens, you know? When was the last time you ate or got any sleep?"

He shrugged a shoulder and chewed on his thumbnail. "I don't know. Yesterday maybe."

I looked at Shame again. He tapped his wrist, like there was a watch there.

"Here's what I think you should do. One, get some sleep. Eat something. Then make an appointment with the investigators downstairs. And call me if you see Pike again. Maybe tell him to come find me. I'll be in town."

"I've told him to find you. He said it's damn hard to navigate in the living world. Maybe I should use magic right now and see if he shows up."

"No," I said, clenching my left hand around the mark there. "I don't think using magic is a good idea."

"Listen, if it would get him out of my space, back at rest or whatever, then I'll do anything. He won't leave me alone, and every time I see him, it just reminds me that he's gone.

"And if Pike wants to talk to you about something he thinks is so important that he rose from the grave, then I think you should give me a damn minute to try to call him." Davy wasn't quite yelling. He was freaked out by this, yes. But he was also angry.

I tucked my hair back behind my ears. I wasn't sure I wanted Davy around if Pike did show up and start talking. I did not want to get Davy Closed.

I'd deal with that if it came to it.

"All right. See if you can get him to show." I held my hands to either side, ready to block, or cast, or hell, catch Davy if he passed out from the effort.

For the first time since we'd come up here, he looked over at Shame. "I know you heard us."

Shame held his hands palm up. "Hey, man. It's none of my business."

Davy gave me a do-you-trust-him look. I nodded.

He took a step away from me and cast a Light spell. A strange choice, or maybe not. If the idea was to illuminate himself so that Pike could find him, then the big flaming ball of white fire that reached from floor to ceiling ought to do it. I was glad the curtains were closed.

"Pike?" Davy said quietly. "I found her. Found Allie. She's here. Now's your chance to talk to her."

Nothing.

After a minute or so, I said, "Is he here?"

"Do you see him?" Davy snapped. "No, he's not here."

Touchy. Tired. I knew how he felt. I didn't like talking to dead guys either.

"I'm going to cast Sight," I told Davy. "If he shows up, you tell me."

I cleared my mind with a jingle, took a couple deep breaths, because, really, just the idea of pulling on magic right now made my skin hurt. Sight hadn't seemed to make my left hand go up in flames, but I was not going to rule out the possibility. I set a Disbursement and worked on not setting myself or the nice kid on fire.

I traced the glyph, pressed my lips together so I wouldn't embarrass myself and groan or something, then pulled magic up through the networked pipes and conduits that caged the building.

Magic hesitated, seemed to pull away from me, and I had to grab for it mentally before it slipped my fingers. I almost lost my concentration, then magic flooded up the underground conduits and into me, filling me, following the marks and trails that magic had carved through me, and then sliding out of me and into the glyph.

Tired. Maybe too tired to be using magic.

Sight caught hold and my vision sharpened. There wasn't much magic in the room. Except Shame, who smoldered like a shadow in moonlight, and Davy, who glowed like a neon sign.

And Pike, who was striding across the floor toward me, his footsteps making no sound.

"He's here," Davy said.

"I see him," I said.

"So do I," Shame said.

I didn't drop Sight, but I hadn't felt Shame draw on any magic. Which meant Pike could be seen without Sight.

"Hi, Pike," I said. "It's good to see you."

Pike didn't look happy. Of course, he never looked all that happy in life either. He nodded. "You can stop casting," he said. "You too, Davy."

Davy and I let go of magic at the same time. Pike did not disappear.

I released the breath I'd caught, and felt the headache I'd hoped would hold off until tonight creep up the back of my skull. Great. With how much magic I'd been using, it was going to be a doozie.

"You needed to talk to me?" It came out little more

than a whisper. Yes, my dad's ghost was in my head. And I'd recently tussled with some dead chick in a bathroom, and I'd taken a tour of death and seen lots of dead people.

But this wasn't a stranger's ghost. And though I was related to my dad, he was a more a stranger to me than Pike. Pike had been my friend. And now I was looking at my dead friend's ghost.

Now I understood why Davy was practically crazy about this. It hurt to see Pike standing there, frowning, his hair still military short, his eyes still sharp, just like in life. Except he was translucent. If I focused too hard, I'd be able to see the other side of the room through him.

I worked on not focusing too hard.

"I know I'm dead," Pike said, "but I don't feel dead. I sleep, get hungry, hell, even my feet itch. But I remember dying."

"You're pretty much dead," I said.

"I'm a ghost?"

"I think so."

"Doesn't that beat all? Then I'll make this fast. I've been called, Allie. I'm going to war."

He paused, like maybe he expected me to understand what he was saying. I was having a hard time not asking him if he was all right, if he was hurting, if I could help him.

"Who called you?" Shamus asked, which was good because I still couldn't get past wanting to tell him how sorry I was that I hadn't gotten to him in time, hadn't saved him in time, hadn't killed Trager in time.

"Allie," Shame said, "ask him who called him. Ask him what war."

Oh, maybe Pike couldn't hear him.

"Who called you, Pike? What war?"

"I don't know. Don't know who, but I can't fight it any longer. Seems like I've been trying not to answer that call for a lifetime. As for the war, all I know is there are more,

more like me, alive through magic, who are answering the call. There's a hunger gnawing at my gut, and that call promises I'm not going to be hungry anymore.

"I don't trust it. Ain't no free lunch in life. Don't figure there's one in death either."

"Do you know where you're going? What you're going to do?"

"For Christsakes, Beckstrom, I'm a ghost. You figure out the details, I can barely remember how to find Davy. The whole damn world is nothing but streams and lines, and rivers of damn magic, with sucking black holes catching at me every time I turn around. If I didn't know this city—and I mean really know this city—I'd be lost for good. It's no wonder most people only haunt their homes. Life's messy."

"I'm sorry," I said. "I'm sorry I didn't get there faster to save you, Pike. I'm sorry I didn't keep you from going alone to kill Trager. I'm so sorry you died."

He took a step toward me, lifted his hand as if he could touch me, then let it drop. "Listen. It's fine, just fine. I don't regret where I am, what I am. We all die. I just thought there'd be a little more rest in my eternal rest.

"I remember the end. You were there, on your knees, pouring magic and your own blood into me to try to heal me. Death came easy. That magic you used on me made some difference, I think. Maybe even helped me come back here and find you, find Davy."

"I wish I could have saved you."

He shook his head and looked annoyed again. "Move on, Beckstrom. The past is the past. It's today that's gonna kill you. I don't know what the war's about, but I'll try to get inside, find out what I can and get back to you, though I don't think Silvers likes me around much."

"That's not it," Davy said. "I thought I was going crazy. You can stay. As long as you like." It sounded like he really wanted Pike to never leave him.

Pike nodded at Davy. "You," he said to me, "used to have a shine of magic to you, Beckstrom. All those marks and colors. Thought you'd be easy to see. You look different now."

"I've had a hard day."

He grunted. "Show me your hand."

I lifted my right hand.

"The other one."

I lifted my left hand. And swore. My palm glowed green. Just like the green from the Veiled. Just like the slight green hue around Pike.

"That I can see. Very clearly. I just didn't think it was you. It's . . . it's a piece of death, isn't it?"

"Yes."

"I'll be able to see that. Can't miss it, if I need to find you. You still stand out, Beckstrom, just not in the same way you used to. Davy too. When he works magic, there's a taint of death in it. Your half-dead friend over there is pretty clear to me too. But that mark on your hand is a goddamn lighthouse beacon. You can't hide from me. I'll always be able to find you."

"That's good?" I said.

"That's bad. If I can see you that well, so can anyone and anything else like me. Ghosts," he added in case I hadn't been paying attention. I had.

He looked over his shoulder, not at Shame or Davy, or anything I could see. I closed my hand and stuck it in my pocket, hoping that something else like Pike wasn't headed our way.

"That's the call," he said. "Hear it?"

I held my breath, listened. "No."

Pike smiled. "Good. I'm guessing that means you're not dead enough to hear it. See that you keep it that way."

"I will."

He started fading. "Beckstrom?"

"Yes?"

"Nice place you put together."

And then he was gone.

I exhaled. My ears were ringing. I felt dizzy, a little nauseous. The headache had crawled behind my eyes and was stabbing at my forehead.

Nobody said anything. I rubbed at my eyes with my right hand, which only made my headache worse.

"Did any of that make sense to you?" Davy asked.

"Kind of. There are people better at this whole ghost thing than I am. I'll go talk to them. See if they think what he said made sense."

"He could be crazy."

"What?"

"He just sounds, I don't know, like he's reliving his war days, in a warped kind of way."

That was a good explanation. I could agree and then Davy would stop asking me questions that would lead to him losing his memory. But ignorance, if Pike was right, might just kill the kid. I liked Davy. I didn't want to see him get mixed up in this and be bleeding and half-dead again.

Once was more than enough for me.

"Davy, there's some crazy magic shit going on around town right now."

Shame huffed, then stared at the ceiling.

"The storm?"

"More than just the storm, but yes, that's part of it. You being attacked by Tomi in the park is part of it too, and me disappearing for a few days. I don't think Pike is crazy. I think he's trying to warn us that there might be a lot of trouble. So I need you to take care of a few things."

He tucked his hands back under his arms again. "What?"

"Contact all the Hounds on the list and tell them to stay sharp. Remind them not to go into any dicey situation alone. I trust Pike too much to ignore his warning. If they hear anything, see anything, weird—weirder than usual—tell them to report it to you. Keep a record, okay?"

"So basically, you want me to do your job for you." He sighed, shook his head. "Too bad you're not paying me enough for that."

That was the kid I knew and hadn't killed yet.

"Think of it as on-the-job training. I pay you, *if* you keep it together for the next couple weeks at least, and do my job. That means sleep, food, and no booze."

"It's cute how you think you're my mother." Some of the sparkle was back in his eyes. "Where are you going, and why haven't you answered your phone? I called you. A lot."

"I'm going to track down anything about the ghost and magic stuff. And my phone broke—yes, again. I should have a new one this afternoon. Call me if you need me."

"Will do, boss."

I wanted to pat him on the shoulder, or something. Tell him he had held up pretty good considering he thought he was going insane and had been haunted by a ghost. But intimacy between Hounds, even just casual friendships, was rarely acknowledged.

"You did good," I said.

"Mm." He shrugged.

"Have you heard from Tomi?" I asked. Tomi was an ex-Hound. She'd had the bad luck of getting mixed up in Greyson's attempt to tear the world apart.

Davy didn't know Greyson was behind what had happened. The Authority had Closed Tomi before I could fight for her to keep the memories. But with how badly she'd been used by Greyson, I wondered now if maybe taking those memories away had been a kindness.

"No. Her grandma called me once, just to see how I was doing. It was . . . I don't know. Okay."

"Let me know if you need anything."

"No offense, but I'd rather you stayed far far away from my relationships."

I shook my head and the whole room spun. Hells, I needed some painkillers. And a bed. "Tell the Hounds." I started across the room.

"Hey," Davy said, walking slower behind me. "You did hear what Pike sounded like? Toward the end of the . . . haunting, séance, whatever we just did?"

"No. What did he sound like?"

"Proud." Davy still looked like last-week's garbage on a slow cooker, but a little of the pain? anger? something, was gone.

"Well, he better be. We're working our butts off for this little dream of his." I gave him a scowl, didn't really mean it. "See you. Be safe and smart."

"One or the other, anyway."

I headed to the stairs and straight down before Shame could complain about the elevator again.

"Nice enough kid," Shame said.

"Who we leave out of the line of fire, right?"

"What do you mean?"

I kept walking, didn't answer until we were in the lobby and safe, I hoped, from Hound ears. "I don't want anyone in the Authority messing with his head. No questioning, no manipulation, no fake memories, and no Closing."

"You're pretty soft for him, aren't you?"

"He's my friend. And it would be just really damn great if at least one of my friends doesn't get screwed over because of me."

The wind picked up as we walking toward the car. Late afternoon, and the temperature was dropping into the cellar. It was going to be a cold night.

"Promise," I said.

"Or what, you'll stab me?"

"If that's what it takes to get a promise out of you."

"I don't know what's happened to you. You used to be such a nice girl. Now you've gone all stabby and whatnot."

"Shame."

"I promise." He slapped his palm over his chest. "From the bottom of my soulless heart, I won't do anything that would cause your little teen crush harm. Including"—he held up his hand and counted on his fingers—"Blood magic, Death magic, Closing, or any of the other memory manipulations, which *I* don't do anyway." He stuck his hand in his back pocket. "Go bark up another tree. I don't do the nasty. Well, not that kind of nasty."

"And don't talk to Victor, or your mom about it—about anything that will get Davy Closed."

Shame paused by his car. "You can't catch smoke, Allie."

"What does that mean?"

He grinned. "I don't know, but it made me seem mysterious, didn't it?"

"It would be even more mind-boggling if you gave me a straight answer."

"All right. Straight. Davy's too close. He's also a curious, cynical kid, and he's a Hound who's been hurt by Blood magic and Death magic. That means he's going to start snooping around as soon as he gets on his feet. He's already almost landed himself on the Authority's Close list, and if he hadn't been so hurt from the crap that went down in St. Johns with Greyson and Tomi, I know he would have been brain-wiped whistle-clean.

"Since that didn't happen, and since, as far as I can tell, he's not trying to kick trouble in our face, there isn't a single reason why I'd even want to mention him to my mum or Victor. There are bigger things at stake here, bigger problems than your Hound friends. That storm started a damn war—a silent war right now—which is almost worse, because we don't know where the next hit is coming from.

"Chase tried to kill Zay—kill him—and she used to love him. You never saw them together. I did. They had passion, they cared and trusted and fought side by side to make the world a better place, all that crap. And she turned on him. For Greyson. Because someone screwed him up so bad, he isn't even human anymore. And now both of them are drooling, brainless casualties.

"We're being mutated, broken, killed. That's what you should be worrying about, not if I'm going to rat out your little Davy. But I will tell you, if it comes down to it, and Davy losing his memory is the only thing that will turn this war in our favor so more people don't die? I will be the first one in line with a dull screwdriver to give that kid a lobotomy."

He pulled his door open and got in the car, leaving me standing there.

# Chapter Twelve

I took a minute to breathe my anger away so I didn't just slap Shame upside his head once I got in the car. He was right. Zay had almost died. So had Shame's mom. And Shame hadn't exactly come through the last few weeks unscathed. He sported a crystal in the middle of his chest, and I didn't know if it kept him alive or pushed him closer to death.

I got in the car, wincing a little as my headache surged. "I said straight." I buckled my seat belt. "You didn't have to sharpen the point and shove it through my heart."

He was smoking again, tapping his fingers on the steering wheel, restless, angry.

"You are impossible to please." He pulled out into traffic and kept his eyes on the road.

"Just tired," I said. "I didn't get a nap." I closed my eyes, hoping the short drive to Maeve's would be enough time for my headache to let off its vise grip. While I rested, my headache got busy.

By the time he pulled into the inn's parking lot, the headache was in full force. I'd stashed some painkillers in my duffel. But the very idea of twisting around in the seat to drag it out of the backseat made me nauseous.

Shame parked and I unbuckled, then risked cracking open my eyes. Ow. I pressed the heel of my hand against my forehead to keep my head from exploding while I carefully turned in my seat and stretched back for my duffel.

I dug in the bag, avoided the disk, fumbled with the bottle, and shook two pills in my hand. I took a second to really stare at them and make sure they were one: painkiller, and two: the correct dosage. Old Hound habits really do come in handy. Two pills. Good to go. I recapped the bottle and dropped it back in the bag.

There was no way I could swallow these without water. Just thinking about pills stuck and burning in my throat made me want to gag.

"Coming?" Shame said from about seven miles away.

I got out of the car and shut the door as quietly as I could without making it look like I cared. I knew how to hide pain. Hounds did a lot of work under Proxy pain and really, most people didn't notice.

"You sick?" Shame asked.

Shame wasn't most people.

"Headache. I could use a glass of water." It took a lot to push those words out and to make them sound normal. But like I said, I was a pro at this.

I started off to the porch, the gravel under my feet sounding like I was in the middle of a blasting zone in a rock quarry. Why did they even have gravel here? Surely the inn did enough business to afford nice quiet concrete. Or carpet. I'd really like to be walking across a nice, quiet carpeted parking lot right now.

Shame caught my elbow. "This way."

He led me around the back of the building, which meant more gravel, but less climbing up the porch. I'd come out this door once. Wooden, plain, original to the building, and probably where the help used to enter back when the inn serviced railroad passengers.

"Why?" I asked.

"Less noise."

Oh, I liked how he was thinking.

He opened the door and the cool, dark interior of the hall was like a deep, soothing river. I stepped in, wanting to drink the darkness down until it filled my belly, my body, my mind. I stood there, wishing my brain would stop barfing in my head.

Shame walked away. I was going to follow him, I swear I was. But by the time I pushed myself away from the wall I was leaning on, he was in front of me again holding out a glass of water.

Behind him towered Hayden, both men watching me, as if I was going to do a circus trick.

"Thanks." I took the water, and swallowed the pills. Tada! For my next trick: trapeze!

I finished the water so I'd have something in my stomach if I ended up on my knees in the bathroom.

The headache was a lot worse than I expected. I tried to remember how many times I'd used magic. Besides in death? Once, when trying to put Zay's soul back in his body, but I was pretty sure I'd slept that off in my forty-eight-hour nap. So, once when forcing Victor to promise he'd fix Stotts, another time when casting Sight at the gate Shame was throwing Illusion over. Maybe a half a dozen Sight spells in the last few hours. Then there was the fight with Truance.

Dad had taken over. I was pretty sure he hadn't set a Proxy. Or maybe he had. Maybe he was using me for his Proxy.

"Thanks just a hell of a lot," I thought at my dad.

"You're a hell of a lot welcome," Shame yelled at me. Okay, maybe he wasn't yelling, but his voice was full of claws-on-chalkboard and tinfoil fillings on fire.

"Not you," I whispered. "Dad."

Hayden grunted, then wrapped one big arm around my waist. "Let's get you in bed."

"Do not," I pushed at him. Wonder of wonders, he let go of me. "Do not haul me around like a doll. It's just a headache. I can walk."

I proved it by making it over to the stairs. Took a step up, broke out in a full-body sweat. Okay, there are times when my big stubborn mouth puts the rest of me through a world of hurt.

The worst part? Hayden walked up right behind me. I mean, I could hold still for an extra second or two and the big guy would probably pick me up and carry me over his shoulder. I'd be upside down, which meant I'd probably yark, then pass out from the blood rushing to my head.

That would be one way to shut my big stubborn mouth.

"Allie, can you take another step?"

I didn't know who was talking. I think it was Maeve, which was odd. Then she was beside me, her hand on my arm. "Let me see your eyes."

I turned, tried to get my eyes to open. Must have done well enough. She brushed her fingertips over my forehead and the rusty hook stabbing my brain backed off a little.

I loved her fingers. I was going to knit them little hats and send them thank-you cards on the holidays.

"Shame, see what she took. Hayden, could you get Dr. Fisher, please? Allie, if you can't walk, I will have Hayden pick you up and carry you to bed."

Oh, I was so not a wilting flower. I'd let a man pick me up and carry me because I couldn't handle the price of using magic when I was dead. Again.

I lifted my foot and kept walking. I didn't count the steps, couldn't see them, didn't think. I just kept moving. My world narrowed until it was me, my pain, and my will.

I knew I made it to the bed when my knees touched the frame.

I also knew I was in the room with Zayvion again. Not because I could hear his breathing. Not because of his pine scent. But the presence of him, calm, Zen, a little worried, was so strong, I looked up, expecting him to be standing in front of me.

He was in bed still, sleeping still. I knew, without a doubt, that he was there, really there. Really alive.

Maeve got around the other side of the bed and moved the covers aside. Shame, I think, helped me crawl onto the bed. The pillow was heaven feathers in six-hundred-count cotton joy.

I wanted to tell them I was okay, but instead I held very still and waited for the medication to kick in.

Luckily, Dr. Fisher showed up, played maracas with my painkiller bottle, then stuck something in my arm.

Wow, like magic, I had my body back.

"Tell me that comes in a six-pack," I mumbled.

She pressed her lips together—not quite a smile. "Afraid not. But it should take care of that headache. How are you feeling?"

"Like Superman. Woman. Super Someone." Okay, maybe a little loopy. Someone snickered. That would be Shame.

"You should get some rest," the doctor said.

I wasn't all that tired. Now that the pain was gone, I could mostly think again.

"I'm good. How's Zay?"

"Why don't you ask him?" Maeve said quietly.

I looked over at her. Okay, moving my head was stupid. The room fuzzed out at the edges and got sparkly in the middle.

Maeve was a little too thin, and too much shadow carved her cheek and lips. She really hadn't recovered from the damage Jingo Jingo had done to her. No wonder Shame was worried.

But her eyes were fierce, and her smile soft.

"He's awake?" I asked.

"He was. Just a bit ago."

I had never heard sweeter words.

I sat, got my feet over on the side of the bed nearer Maeve. She moved off to one side of the room, to where Shame was standing by the window. It took me a minute, but I finally noticed her gait was off. She was walking with that cane. It didn't look like the left side of her body was moving in concert with the right.

Shame helped her sit in a soft chair and I put another log of hate on my Jingo Jingo fire.

I stood. The doctor hovered. Nice, but unnecessary.

Then I sat down on Zay's bed. He had moved since I last saw him.

"Could I be alone with him for a minute?"

Shame, Maeve, Dr. Fisher, and Hayden, whom I hadn't noticed by the door, all left the room.

I touched Zay's cheek. My fingers shook. It was hard to hold my arm out like that for very long. Even though the pain meds pushed my migraine far enough away that I couldn't feel it, my body was still experiencing the pain. I pressed my hand on his chest.

"Zay? Are you awake, love?"

His breathing didn't change. His eyes didn't open. I thought about shaking him. Decided it was a bad idea. Not only was I not up for it, I didn't know how much physical damage he'd suffered from Chase and Greyson's attack and with his soul chained in death. It was safe to say he could probably use some TLC.

"Zay, it's Allie. I'm here now. Maeve told me you were awake. Can you wake up again for me?" I waited. Nothing.

"Sweet hells." I hated that I had missed out on seeing him wake up. I wonder if he had said anything. Wondered if he understood where he was and what had happened.

They say people in a coma can hear the people around them. I couldn't remember if I had heard Nola or Zay when I was in a coma, but I had a fleeting memory of not feeling alone.

Sitting wasn't doing me any favors. I settled down next to him, moved his arm and rested my head on his shoulder, my leg tucked up over his. He'd shifted and there wasn't a lot of room on this side of the bed, but I made it work.

"Fine," I said. "Be that way. But I'm going to talk until you wake up and tell me to shut up. Do you remember the fight with Chase and Greyson? We were trying to find them, and they attacked you. They dragged your soul out of your body and shoved you through a gate into death. I was there. I was trying to get to you, but I couldn't. I couldn't.

"I never seem to get to anyone in time. First Pike, then Davy, then you. Hells." I was quiet for a bit. His breathing changed a little. Was he waking up?

"We brought you back here. You've been sleeping for a while. No, not sleeping. You've been in a coma. Missed the wild-magic storm and the fight. The Authority fractured, like you've been telling me it would. People were hurt, damaged, changed by magic. Shame. I don't even know what to think about Shame. I'm worried for him. I'm worried for Maeve too.

"I went through a gate to try to get you back. I went into death. Just for a little bit. Dad was there with me, and Stone too. Do you remember that? Mikhail trapped you and was draining your magic."

I frowned. I probably should go over everything for Victor or Maeve. Especially since Truance had mentioned Mikhail too. I couldn't remember if I'd told that part to Shame.

"Shame says there's a meeting tonight. The gates keep opening and they're getting harder to close. There are ghosts running around. Pike's a ghost. I talked to him. And the Veiled are somehow using disks to give them real bodies. They want my dad. They want immortality. We don't know where Jingo Jingo is or if he's the one making the Veiled solid. He kidnapped Sedra."

I tucked my head closer to his chest. "It feels like I stepped out of death into the wrong world. Everything's going to hell.

"I wish things could just be normal for just five minutes. Is that too much to ask?"

"Probably," he breathed.

I lifted up. His eyes were closed.

"Zay?"

"Mmm?"

"Open your eyes. Please, please open your eyes."

He took a deeper breath, let it out. I worried he hadn't heard me.

"I'm right here." I shifted so I could touch his face. "Right here. Please open your eyes."

He frowned, a line creasing between his brows. Then, finally, opened his eyes. His eyes were yellowed, fever-glossy, but the corner of his mouth lifted when he saw me. "Hey, beautiful."

I grinned like a fool and worked on not crying. If I fell apart, I'd miss the chance to tell him everything was going to be okay.

"Hey, handsome. Don't you look sharp? How are you feeling?"

"Like Super Someone." The smile got a little stronger.

I laughed, even though it made my head hurt. A rush of relief filled me.

"Maeve said you were awake already. Do you remember that?"

"I remember you. You came in a dream?" He frowned. "Did I dream you?"

"No, I'm real."

"Mikhail? He trapped me. Your dad . . . "

"That all happened, but not here. You were pushed

through a gate by Chase and Greyson. Your soul was pushed, your body stayed here. And I found you, and brought you home." I waited to see if he would be angry. He had certainly been angry at me in death when I wouldn't let him go. Not until this very moment had I considered that there was a very good chance this could be a problem in our relationship.

"You didn't. No. Allie. No." His voice was soft as a worry stone.

"I did, and it worked out okay. You're fine. Stone's fine. I'm fine. Everything's fine." The way it came out, rushed, overly happy, I wasn't doing a very good job of convincing anyone everything was fine.

"Your magic." Zay stared at me. No more frown. He'd reverted into Zen mode. Which meant either he was feeling better or he was really angry. "What did you do?"

"It was the price I paid to get your soul back. But it's okay. I'm okay. I'd do it again."

"You said you wouldn't"—he swallowed—"be a hero."

"Don't like getting saved by a girl?" I teased.

"I told you to go home."

"I did go home. We both went home. I brought you with me."

He stared at me, then turned his head away. "I can't. Allie, too dangerous. I wish you wouldn't. Have. So foolish."

My chest clenched like a fist. Was he angry about me saving him? So much that he didn't even want to see me? I sat there, stunned. I didn't know if I should be mad or hurt, or understanding. He had just turned away from me when I'd risked everything—everything—to save him.

His breathing was already deeper, even. He was asleep again.

Had I just screwed that up? Screwed us up?

I got out of the bed, numb. Confused as hell. My head followed above the rest of my body as if filled with helium.

Pain hovered there, barely buoyed by the helium, heavy as a concrete hat that could fall and crush my brain at any minute.

I crawled back into the other bed and pulled the covers around me. I didn't fall asleep.

I felt bad about what I'd done for about thirty seconds. Then I remembered what it was like to pull up out of a coma. I remembered how vulnerable and confused and less than myself I felt. I remembered how much of my life I had lost, how much control over who I was I had lost.

It had scared the hell out of me. Made me feel angry and helpless. I had a lot of practice pulling myself together when I lost control of my life, my memories, and my mind, and lately, my body and magic. Still, coming out of that coma had been one of the hardest things I'd done.

Zayvion had sat with me for two weeks, patiently waiting for me to come back.

This was probably the first time Zayvion Jones hadn't strode out of the flames and wreckage of a battle as the shiny unscathed hero. This was probably the first time he'd failed, the first time he'd had to lie there and come to grips with the fact that his life had been torn apart and put back together by someone else's hands.

It was tough to swallow. Some people never got over it. The people who did knew it took time and patience to glue a broken soul, a broken life back together. I could give him that time. I could give him that patience.

A soft knock at the door was followed by it opening. From the three-point footstep, two feet and a cane, I knew it was Maeve. Someone strolled behind her, heavier, longer stride. I caught the scent of muscle rub. Hayden.

"Allie," Maeve said, "I brought you some soup."

I wanted to tell her to go away, but I was starving.

I sat and leaned against the headboard. "Thank you."

Maeve pulled the lap tray over and Hayden handed her

a bowl of soup and a glass of orange juice. "I wasn't sure if you'd had a chance to eat lunch." She went through the motions of setting up the food, cutlery, napkin, slower, but with grace even though she leaned on the cane. She handled pain and injury like it was a familiar inconvenience.

"When's the meeting?" I asked.

Hayden brought a chair in from the hallway and placed it at the foot of my bed. Maeve sat and Hayden leaned against the door, cleaning his nails with a knife.

"As soon as you're ready. Everyone's here. Shame briefed us on most of what happened—the gate he handled, you running into two Veiled. The trouble with Davy Silvers and Martin Pike's ghost. He also said you've been marked." She rested the cane against one arm of the chair and folded her hands in her lap.

"How are you doing with seeing Martin Pike?"

I scooped another spoonful of soup—mushroom with bay leaf and onion and something else sweet I couldn't quite place—to give myself time to think.

"He said he wasn't in pain. He wasn't exactly happy. It was . . . it was good to talk to him again. Shame told you what he said?"

"Yes. I'd like to hear your version too, but let's do that downstairs." Maeve glanced at Zay. "Did he wake?"

I finished off the soup. I'd practically inhaled it. "He did. It was really good to talk to him too."

Maeve stood and walked to the door. Hayden took her elbow and helped support her out into the hall.

I stepped up to Zay's bed and put my hand on his shoulder. It used to be when I touched him I could feel his emotions, hear his thoughts. Since the coma, I hadn't felt anything. Now I could tell he was sleeping, fitfully, probably dreaming, tired, agitated.

"You're going to be okay," I said quietly. "It won't be easy. Nothing's easy. But you are strong enough to get through this, to get back on your feet again, to be the guardian of the gates again. I know you're going to be fine. Don't give up."

Even though he was asleep, I knew he heard me. A slow burn of anger and helpless fury rolled through him. I wished I could say something to ease his mind. Instead, I bent and kissed his forehead.

"Love you," I whispered. Not that it made him any less angry. But that was okay. Like Shame said, it was better to be angry than dead.

# Chapter Thirteen

By the time I found my shoes, got them on, and made it to the hallway, Maeve and Hayden were just descending the stairs. They'd either waited outside the door or taken their time walking.

I followed them down two flights, and through the halls to one of the sitting rooms I hadn't been in before, about three times the size of the other sitting rooms. The ceiling was a grid of cream-painted beams squared across maple tiles with subtle plant-themed molding. The walls were sage, and wood-and-cream chairs and couches cupped the corners, nearly hidden beneath liberal piles of decorative pillows.

A rug centered the wooden floor, ending just shy of the fireplace in the corner that gave off the cherry and ash smell of recent use. Low maple bookcases squared the walls, and a map of Portland hung over a desk with a computer on it. There were enough side tables and footstools, chairs and couches, to accommodate thirty people.

Only a dozen or so people were present. Were we really down to just that few?

Me, Maeve, and Hayden. On opposite sides of the room, Shame and Terric, and the rest of the familiar faces, the twins Carl and La, Victor, Nik, Joshua, the three Georgia sisters, and Sunny.

They each glanced over as we entered. I got a lot of

strange looks. Might be my new hairdo. More likely it was respect or barely concealed fear. I picked out an empty armchair, sank down into it with a sigh. Maeve knew how to keep comfort in her decor.

Victor, who wore a long-sleeved crew neck sweater—the most casual I'd ever seen him—and still had his right hand and wrist wrapped, started things off as soon as Hayden shut the door and activated the wards.

"Thank you all for coming here. Let's get down to business. The gates are still opening at a steady rate. About four a day. They are not opening in any pattern we can see. I've updated the map with today's gates. At this time, there are no open gates as reported by our scouts. Still, I hope to keep this meeting short.

"Allie, you're late to the discussion. I assume Shamus has filled you in on the current standing of events?"

"Basically, yes."

"Is there any information we should know?"

"A couple things," I said. "One, when I was on the other side of the gate, Zayvion's soul was bound and Hungers were draining the magic out of him. To free him, I made a deal with Mikhail."

You could have dropped a speck of dust and heard it hit the carpet.

"He was the only one who could release the spells on Zay and open a gate into life. I gave up a part of my . . . magic. . . ." Wow, that was hard to say. I bulled on. "A part of my magic in exchange for his help. He took that, the, my magic to a woman who was sleeping, I think. She looked a little like Sedra, but I probably couldn't pick her out in a lineup. The whole thing is a little fuzzy, and I was busy trying to get Zay home, so I didn't ask questions."

I took a shaky breath. "Okay, in exchange for taking my magic, he marked my left palm." I held it up for everyone to see. They all looked; no one moved.

"It's hard to see in this light, but there's a little smudge there." Doubtful faces. Yeah, it didn't sound like a big deal.

"It's easier to see if you cast Sight."

A dozen hands traced the glyph for Sight.

I kept my palm steady. "Pike, um . . . he used to be a Hound and now he's a ghost—said he could see this mark on me like a beacon. He said any of the dead, or Veiled, could see it because it's a piece of death. Also, it makes my hand catch on fire. But only sometimes."

Someone swore. Several people canceled their spells. I tucked my hand back into my lap and did not let on how much it freaked me out too.

"So the good part of this is the mark hurts and gets cold when I am around the Veiled. The bad thing is they can see me too. As for the flame . . . " I shrugged. "I don't know how to control it. It does seem to hurt the Veiled. I met one, a Veiled, in a chocolate shop this afternoon when Shame was dealing with the gate. Her name was Truance, and she was solid. She was using a disk to stay alive and said Mikhail's time was over. She said she was going to be immortal thanks to Dad's technology—well, as soon as she figured out how to recharge the disk.

"We fought. I can't remember what spell I used on her, but my hand was on fire, and that was what stopped her. But then she said a word—I don't remember the word—and disappeared in a storm of magic."

Victor pinched the bridge of his nose like he had a headache too. "You didn't mention this when I saw you earlier."

"You told me to fill you in tonight."

"Yes, I did. Is there anything else?"

"Pike thinks he's being called into some kind of war, and that more of the dead are being called. I don't know why. Neither did he."

More silence. I looked at Shame. He just gave me a slow shake of his head.

"Shame pulled the disk out of the man—the Veiled—who rushed us on the sidewalk. It was in my duffel. You gave it to them, right?"

"Yep."

"That's it," I said. "That's what I got. Do you know who's giving the disks to the Veiled?"

"What we know," Victor said, "is the disks taken from the battlefield have been changed by the wild-magic storm. Either the Veiled can see the disks or someone is, indeed, supplying them to the Veiled. Of all the people at the scene, Jingo Jingo is under the most suspicion since he was seen taking most of the disks with him.

"There's a slight chance no one is behind it. A short time ago, the Veiled became more . . . agitated." He frowned, thinking. "As for Truance." He wove his fingers together gingerly, and pressed the tips of his index fingers against his mouth. "She's been gone a long time now."

"Was she from around here?" I asked.

"Oregon City. Why?"

"Pike said life is confusing for the dead to navigate. He said it's all rivers of magic and black holes that pull you off the path. If the Veiled are coming back to life, and the Veiled are powerful magic users, or at least people who used magic a lot, it would be good to know if they are going to be locals. I mean, I don't know the history, but I'm assuming there have been powerfully dangerous magic users throughout the world, not just in Portland."

"We've thought of that," Maeve said. "And from what we know about death, and passing over"—here she gave me a slight nod—"those who died nearest this place should be the ones who would naturally find it again. We cannot, however, rule out the possibility that other powerful dead members of the Authority may have the disks."

"And there's the problem with Closed Veiled," Shame said.

Maeve frowned. "There are no Closed Veiled."

"My point. People who have been Closed because they did something bad, something in direct opposition to the Authority's rules, are Veiled now too. And becoming the walking undead. Was Truance ever Closed? Because if there was something someone didn't want her to remember, she remembers it now. And she knows who took that memory away."

Maeve pressed her fingers against her eyes. "Ah, Shamus. That's true."

The mood in the room took a dive.

"We know more than we did," Victor said. "It's grim, but useful information. If anyone else sees another angle on this, don't be shy." He waited, then went on. "Are you sure you didn't recognize the male Veiled, Shame?"

"Positive."

"Allie, have you ever seen him before?"

I thought about it. Just because I hadn't been a part of the Authority for long didn't mean I hadn't been alive. I'd worked as a Hound for years in the city. Before that, I lived here. I'd crossed paths with a lot of people.

Problem with the Veiled, though, was that other than the smell of burned blackberries from the disks, they didn't carry their own scent. I couldn't remember his face, and he had no smell for me to correlate it to.

I could always ask my dad. I didn't want to. But if he had a lead, I'd take it.

*Dad?* I thought. *Do you know who he was?*

A slight shuffling, like a shoe scuffing dust in the back of my head was all the answer I got.

He had been quiet since the fight. I wondered if Truance had permanently shut him up. Maybe I owed the old girl a bit of thanks.

"No," I said.

"So," Victor said, "do we all understand we are up

against the unliving Veiled, and must deal with the gates opening?" He was up now, pacing with the thoughtful, controlled movements of a professional swordsman. "And we understand there are magic users who have not weighed in on either side of the fight?" He turned and made eye contact with me.

"Those persons shall be seen as neutral in this struggle, until they throw in their lot."

"Is there a list?" I asked. "Are they wearing a DON'T HIT ME. I'M NEUTRAL sign? Maybe a secret neutral handshake?"

Terric chuckled. Victor didn't think it was funny.

He gave me a look and continued pacing. "Those in this room are adhering to the Authority's rules. Those we fought in St. Johns: Jingo Jingo and Mike Barham are known defectors. Others have not made their decision or will not fight at all."

"Wait, they can do that? Just stand back and let a few of us fight it out?"

"It is the way."

"Well, the way sucks. I think anyone who isn't against the way the Authority has been running things should have to pitch in to keep things going. No sitting back and letting other people bleed for your privileges. This isn't politics."

Victor stopped pacing. His hands were behind his back, I'd guess clenched, his elbows rested outward. I'd seen him take that stance a hundred times when he was teaching me the basics of Faith magic. Not that I'd ever been any good at Closing. But the general style of Faith magic usage, I liked.

He took that stance when he was waiting for my outbursts to wind down.

I leaned forward in my chair, not willing to back down on this. "If we're fighting, we're all fighting. There is a strength in numbers, and having neutral parties standing around eating popcorn while we decide the fate of . . . of the world, is insanity."

"I agree," he said quietly.

You could have knocked me over with a marshmallow. He never agreed with me on these kinds of things.

"But we have no sway over those who abstain from the fight. The fractures run deeper than just those of us in this room and those who fought us during the wild-magic storm. At least we know where the neutral stand."

I didn't see how that was good news. What was keeping the neutral from throwing in their lot, as he pointed out, with the bad guys?

"So it's just a handful of powerful, disk-carrying magic users we're fighting." Hey, I was doing my best to shove sunshine into this bag of coal.

"Perhaps. We are bound by the rules. That does not mean that they are."

I laughed. I mean, I really laughed. This was ridiculous. When I focused on him again, on his reaction, I didn't see annoyance or anger. I saw calm. Zen calm. And suddenly his words took on a different meaning. If they weren't bound by the rules, that meant they were breaking all the things the Authority stood for—for keeping magic safe for those who used it. If they were breaking the rules, they were fair game to be hunted down and killed.

No regrets.

No mercy.

No remorse.

That was what his words meant. It meant we were to do everything in our power to bring these people to their knees. Everything.

That, I approved of.

"If the Veiled are looking to recharge the disks, and if they are ex-members of the Authority, they know of the wells," Victor went on calmly. He had gotten his pace on again. "Four wells. Life, Death, Faith, and of course, Blood here, beneath the inn."

"We have monitored their levels, checked the wards. I want a team of at least two out again. Look in on the wells. Search for any sign of change. Call back to Hayden, who will be coordinating tonight.

"I've mapped out the next sectors of Portland to investigate for signs of Jingo Jingo or Sedra. Once again we'll work in a sweep formation, cross over and cross back before returning and reporting. Teams of three.

"Watch for changes in the networks and conduits. Report spikes or drains. There still hasn't been any contact from Jingo Jingo or anyone else in the last twenty-four hours. No threats. No ransom. Nothing."

The muscle at the edge of his jaw tightened. He was angry. Worried. He knew—we all knew—that the longer a kidnapper wasn't in contact with someone, the more likely we'd need to start looking for Sedra's grave.

"We have not heard from any other branch of the Authority. This is still our problem to take care of. Let's keep it that way, shall we?"

The mood in the room released in a shared exhale. They hadn't been hoping the cavalry was on its way. They just wanted to be sure the cavalry wasn't coming to wipe out their memories and take away their power.

"Who wants to travel with whom?" Victor strolled over to the desk and retrieved a leather ledger.

People paired up. I glanced around the room. Knew Shame would follow me no matter what. I got up.

"You and me, Flynn?" I asked.

He nodded and looked past me to where Terric stood next to Victor.

Terric shifted his stance, camping back on one foot. He knew Shame was looking at him, thinking about him. Even in the short time I'd been back, I could tell they were having a harder time ignoring each other.

Terric walked our way. He smiled, a sad lift to his lips that clashed with the challenge in his eyes.

Shame actually sighed.

"Looks like the three of us will be a team tonight. How does that sound?" He was talking to me, not Shame.

"Good."

"We don't have to have three," Shame muttered.

Terric didn't look at him, but clamped the smile between his teeth and said to me, "Yes, we do. One of us has to Proxy and cover our tracks. That's me. Two of us will hunt. That's Shame and you. That's the way it works. That's the way it's always worked."

"Well, then, that makes a lot of sense," I said before Shame could open his mouth and start a fistfight. "When are we going? And where?"

"We're handling the East side of town," Terric said.

"Death magic," Shame said. "Winter well."

"Wait. Winter?" I asked.

"Way back, they were given names of the seasons. Four wells. Four seasons. Four disciplines of magic: Winter for Death, Spring for Faith, Summer for Life, Autumn for Blood."

Very cool. And it was one more reminder that I had a lot to learn.

"Winter well is a plum assignment," Shame said. "Victor must like you, Terric."

"Reasonable people always like me, Shame," he said with a straight face.

Shame flashed a smile and the tension between them let up a bit.

These two ran hot and cold so fast, they were going to wear me out. Maybe it wasn't too late to trade up for new hunting partners.

"After we check the well," Terric said, "we'll sweep Laurelhurst to Forty-seventh, then up to Grant Park. It'll be nice to have you along, Allie. Hounding could make this a hell of a lot easier. You feeling up to this?"

"Dr. Fisher gave me some painkiller. I'm fine. But I need to get into some warmer clothes first. And my coat. Give me a minute, okay?"

They nodded in unison.

"Shame's car?" I was already walking.

"Yes," they said together. Shame swore. Terric laughed.

I didn't stop to talk with anyone else. Everyone was busy going over maps and working out who would bear Proxy for the night. From the snippets of conversations I heard, this had been a nightly event for the past two weeks or so. No wonder everyone looked so tired.

I really did want to change into warm clothes. Unfortunately, my duffel was in the room with Zayvion.

I crept in, not wanting to wake him. Not wanting to have to deal with him being angry at me, at himself, at life. I simply did not have the bandwidth to deal with that right now. It made me feel a little guilty. I mean, I'd said if we were going to be in a relationship with each other, we needed to be honest and present for each other no matter what.

And here I was sneaking around, hoping I didn't have to deal with him, deal with us.

I dug in my duffel, pulled out a long-sleeved T-shirt. I shrugged out of Zay's sweater and my own, put on the T-shirt and my sweater, then pulled Zay's sweater back over my head.

"Going?" Soft. Just more than a whisper. Zay.

I tucked my hair behind my ear. "Yes." I walked over, sat on his bed. I put my hand on his chest, and he lifted his arm—which looked like it took some effort—and placed his hand over mine. Warm, wide. It felt so right to be touched by him again.

"Where?"

What should I tell him? That I was leaving, going out?

To rescue the world. Without him. He'd be angry. Angrier. But it was the truth.

"Out. Hunting with Shame and Terric."

Anger. Worry. Frustration. Yep, we could definitely feel each other's emotions.

"Don't," he said. "You don't know . . . can't. You won't be safe. I can't keep you safe."

He didn't think I could do this. Didn't think I was strong enough without him. I took a deep breath. Time and patience. Time and patience. He'd sat with me for two weeks when I was in a coma.

Then he'd dumped me.

Thinking about that did not help.

"I'm sorry," I said, keeping my tone even. "There just aren't enough of us for me to stay here. I know how to keep myself safe. And I'll be careful." I stood. Watched as his gold-brown eyes studied me.

"Take my sword."

That was my man. I nodded. "I will." I took his sword from where it rested in the corner of the room and pulled it over my shoulder. The weight of it was beginning to feel familiar, comforting. It made me feel safe. Safer.

But just in case, I also tucked the blood blade into my belt. I picked up my coat and looked over at him. He was watching me, his dark gaze begging me not to go, even though he said no more.

"I'll see you soon," I said. "Promise."

"Allie, I—"

And just like magic, there was a soft knock at the door. Not Shame or Terric. Dr. Fisher.

"I thought you were awake," she said. "It's good to see you up, Zayvion. How are you feeling? Think you could eat something?"

I slipped out through the door before I heard his reply.

# Chapter Fourteen

I took the stairs down, my journal open, and scribbled updates as I went. Not my best work or handwriting, and as vague as I could make it in case it ever fell into the wrong hands. I noted that Zay was awake and recovering. Then, in smaller letters, I noted I had seen Shame's art out in the town, and that Davy told me he had seen a ghost, just like Pike. Good enough for me to know what happened, not so blatant that anyone would suspect the sorts of people I was currently running with.

I tucked the book back in my pocket and exited through the side door Shame and I had used earlier.

Cold—it'd gone dark early. The sky was clear, stars catching moonlight against the darkness. Very little wind stirred the night, which was odd considering how close to the river we were. I wished I was wearing gloves and a hat, not that I'd thought to pack either when I was back at my place. Too busy worrying about Nola, about Violet, about Shame, about Zay.

My friends were going to give me gray hairs.

I didn't see Shame's car. Which meant it was over in the main parking lot, around the front of the building. I thought about calling him to make sure he was out here, and patted my pocket. Journal, but no phone. And I'd forgotten to ask Maeve for a new one.

Should I go back in to get a phone?

I glanced at the inn. No, Shame and Terric were probably out front trying to kill each other. It'd be better if I got moving.

This side of the building was mostly unused, though a couple industrial-sized garbage Dumpsters squatted against the wall, giving off a strong old-vegetable stink. A couple cars could park back here, or continue on the mostly gravel road that led around the full length of the building, quite a lot of it to my right, or east, and then curve in toward the river. The inn was built when the railroad functioned. Even in those days someone may have wanted to get a horse and cart, or even a full wagon, around the building to load and unload supplies.

Beyond the open space on my right was a stand of trees that stretched all the way up to the main road.

I inhaled the clean, cool air and sharp green and earth scents of the river. There was another scent on the wind. Licorice, and a slightly chemical tang. I knew that scent.

Jingo Jingo.

I stepped away from the light pouring through the windows and covered myself in shadow. I was already halfway through a Shield spell.

Too late. Much too late.

Shadows pulled away, flowed like a silk scarf over my skin, wrapped tight around my wrist, tangling in my fingers, locking my hands, stiffening my joints, my muscles. I could not move, could not swallow, could not blink, could not breathe except for careful, shallow breaths.

"Ain't no hiding from me, girl," a low voice purred.

Trapped, stuck, chained. I'd be screaming if I could find that much air. I had to get out, had to get free, had to get air and space.

Jingo Jingo walked up from behind me. I didn't hear his footsteps in the gravel over the panicked screaming in my head, didn't hear the shush of fabric rubbing over his massive bulk. I could not smell the magic I knew he must be using on me. Only the stench of licorice, his scent, clogged my nostrils.

He stopped in front of me. Wore a pin-striped suit under a nice rain jacket—like he was headed to Sunday service.

"Oh, I know you don't like being tied up. Don't like little spaces either. I apologize for that, Allison. Least I didn't bring a box to put you in. No one likes that. No, sir, no one likes the boxes." He stepped closer to me, drug one thick, hot finger down my cheek, along my jaw, and tucked the tip of it in the corner of my mouth.

If I could have moved, I would have bitten his finger off.

Anger. Best way to clear my head.

"You know how pretty a child you were? Oh, so pretty. I could have brought you home. Fed you candy, made you my little secret. But your daddy had plans for you. Even then."

I tried to move anything, a finger, a muscle. Nothing.

Jingo Jingo's fingernail rubbed along the edge of my mouth, and he licked his own lips. "So pretty."

If thoughts of hatred could kill, he'd be bleeding out his eyes right now.

"Where's your daddy now, Beckstrom? He still in that pretty head of yours?" He pushed the rest of his fingers along my jaw, thumb on my chin, and clamped tight against bone, like someone who was used to holding skulls. Even if I could have moved my head, I wouldn't have been able to budge in that grip.

He stared into my eyes. "We need to talk, Beckstrom. Now."

He wasn't speaking to me.

"I know you're using her. Always known. And what you do with her, I don't care. But if you don't come forward, I'm going to come in there and find you."

Nothing moved in my mind; nothing scraped, fluttered, or shifted. If Dad was still there, he was being incredibly still.

Jingo's bloodshot eyes flicked back and forth, as if he could look through the windows of my soul and find my dad on the other side.

"Didn't think you'd want me to tear into this child's mind to find you. Might not do it in a way she'll like. Might even do it in a way she won't recover from. Always did want to get my hands on your pretty little daughter. Teach her how to be a good girl. Empty out her head."

He pushed his big, meaty finger into my mouth, drew it along the inside of my lip, then pulled it out and sucked it.

"She's delicious, you know."

I wanted to vomit.

I tried thinking to my dad, not to ask him for help—okay, maybe to ask him for help—but mostly for information. I needed to break Jingo's hold on me. Dad broke Truance's hold. It felt, as much as I could let myself think about it, the same. I didn't know if Death magic was involved—Death magic is hard to track, and seriously, I just wasn't at my cognitive best now—when Truance had me pinned. But whatever trick worked on Truance might just work on Jingo Jingo.

I didn't have to think to Dad. Because all of a sudden he rushed forward, was around me, and did that same thing he did back when I was fighting Truance. He picked me up, turned his back, and stuck me somewhere in a corner of my mind where I could hear but not see what was going on.

I hated it as much now as I did then.

*Don't,* I thought.

"You forget yourself, Jingo." It was my voice, but my dad's words. And it made me want to gargle with gasoline.

"So you are still in there. I'd been told you might have flown this little nest."

Told? How? Was someone spying on me? Was Truance checking back in with him? I pushed at Dad. No luck.

"Do you have her?" Dad asked.

"Of course. And she's been . . . prepared. I've done my part, just as I said I would. Now you pay me."

"Pay?" Dad laughed, a short scoff that sounded strange coming out of my mouth. "Until I have witnessed the results with my own eyes, you receive nothing. That was our arrangement."

"You underestimate who is in power here," Jingo Jingo said. "Oh, you were something once, but you're dead now. And keeping you that way would be as easy as squeezing her throat. Tell me where you've hidden the simulacrum."

"Do not push me." Dad put enough Influence behind it, I could taste the honey-coated hatred. "I, and those who walk with me, are more powerful than you can imagine. Magic will be restored. Mikhail will have his revenge on those who betrayed him. But not until the wells are closed. That is your responsibility. See that it is done. Soon. And then you will receive your payment."

Jingo Jingo clicked his tongue against his teeth. "Now, how I see it, I've done more than my fair share on nothing but promises. On nothing but your good word. That good word of yours is wearing down to a whisper with every passing day. Pretty soon, I just won't hear it no more. I saw what you did to Greyson. Getting in his mind like that, and making him crazy." Jingo Jingo chuckled. "And you said I was a monster who should be Closed."

"I was not responsible for turning him into a Necromorph. I would never waste my technology on a man determined to leave the Authority. But times are changing. The war is changing. Those who survive, change. I have never doubted your loyalty to the cause that most benefits you."

"That's as much respect as you've ever given me," Jingo

said. "Too bad I'm not a man who needs to be respected. I follow my own cause—and maybe that isn't your cause."

Dad pulled on the magic in my bones and blood. Twisted it, molded it, cast it. Without ever moving my hands. Without ever chanting a word.

But when he spoke, there was a dread softness that stitched each word down in my head and made them hurt. I didn't know what magic was behind that. I didn't know what it would feel like to have that . . . whatever that was . . . cast at you. Maybe like broken glass dipped in acid. "Tell me. What cause still benefits you? Jingo Jingo?"

Jingo Jingo took a deep, hard breath. And when he exhaled, I knew every word hurt. "Your cause, Daniel Beckstrom."

"Of course it does," Dad said. "Never forget that. See that the wells are closed. Leave, and do not be followed."

*That* was Influence.

Jingo grunted and then I heard his shoes scrape across gravel. "You've let something through, Daniel Beckstrom," he said quietly. "You've come back from death and let something through that gate. There ain't no power against it. Mikhail can't stand against it. Someone's making living Veiled with those damn disks of yours. Even you can't win against the monsters that are walking this city."

I felt Dad hesitate, not quite panic but a quick calculation. Jingo Jingo kept walking and Dad let him. Maybe three footsteps later, Dad turned around in my mind.

*I never intended for you to hear that. Never intended for you to become this involved, this at risk. But I cannot let you remember.*

Before he even got to that last bit, I was bracing for his attack. I reached for my small magic, the magic that had always been there, the magic that had always kept me if not safe, safer than I would have been without it.

It was gone.

Given away.

By me.

When I was dead.

So Zay could live.

I reached for what I could, trying to hold anything, everything, pieces of me I didn't want to lose, memory I didn't want erased, didn't want him to touch, didn't want him to have, own, use.

*Get away from me!* I yelled.

But there was nothing I could do to stop my dad from Closing my memories.

# Chapter Fifteen

"Allie?" Hayden said. "You looking for something?"

"Water," I said without thinking. Or rather, I said to buy myself some time to figure out where I was and what the hell I was doing. Didn't take me all that long to get my bearings. I was standing in the hall of the inn. Hadn't I just been on my way out? Going to meet Shame and Terric? Right, and then I'd remembered I needed to come get a phone from Maeve.

"I mean a phone," I said.

Hayden tucked his chin and looked down at me. And I do mean down. I clocked in at six foot even. Hayden had at least six inches on me.

"Lost your phone?"

"Yes. Shame said maybe Maeve had another one that was warded." Even as I said it, I knew that sounded wrong. Hadn't I decided I was going to wait? Go around front and meet up with Terric and Shame?

"Could have brought that up at the meeting." He turned and motioned for me to follow him. "She's gone now, but I think I know where she keeps them."

"Didn't think about it at the meeting." I tucked my hair back behind my ear and stopped. I smelled something sweet on my skin. I licked my lips. Tasted licorice and sweat in my mouth.

That was weird. Last thing I ate was the soup Maeve brought me.

The moth wing flutter of my dad scraped against the back of my eyes, then went very, very still.

*Dad?* I thought.

Silence. No, more than silence. Super silence and super stillness. Almost like he was afraid for me to see him, to notice him. Wasn't that interesting?

I pulled my hand back from my hair. My jaw hurt. I pressed fingertips there. It felt like I had a bruise along the bone. Had it been bothering me before I went to the meeting? I had a vague memory that it had been troubling me. Nothing to worry about.

Which was exactly why I was worrying about it.

"What time is it?" I asked Hayden.

He checked his watch. "Ten 'til."

"Are you sure?"

He held his wrist in front of my nose so I could see his watch.

I went through the math. "I was just upstairs with Zay," I said. "It only took me a minute to get downstairs, maybe another to step outside and then turn back around."

Hayden stopped in front of the door to Maeve's office. "Uh-huh."

"It's been five minutes since I left Zay's room. Maybe ten."

He looked over his shoulder. "What?"

"Something's wrong."

"A damn lot of things are wrong," he said distractedly, sliding a key in the lock. "Victor thinks he's the king of the world, and Maeve won't stand up and tell him otherwise. I know I'm not a part of this local squabble among the voices, but there's more than a war going on. They don't start working on the same page, there's nothing going to hold this side of the fight together. Come on in; I think she has a phone in the drawer."

I started after him, but stopped at the door. The smell on my skin was more than licorice. It was licorice mixed with chemicals. And that mix belonged to only one man. Jingo Jingo.

"Jingo," I whispered.

That got Hayden's attention. He stopped, gave me a hard look. I suddenly realized Hayden was a man I did not want to fight. Not in a physical battle. I might be able to take him magic-to-magic. If there were enough magic to fight with. If I were feeling normal, instead of feeling like I'd just woken up to find myself sleepwalking along the edge of a cliff.

*Dad?* I thought again. *What's going on?*

Nothing.

"What about him?" Hayden asked.

Took me a second. He meant Jingo Jingo, not Dad.

"I think I smell him. Maybe smelled him outside." I didn't like the look in Hayden's eyes.

"That so?"

I still hadn't stepped into the room. Wasn't going to either. Alarm bells were rattling through my head. Something was wrong. Wrong with this whole thing. And I didn't know if Hayden was a part of it or not.

"You hear that?" Hayden asked someone behind me.

I pivoted to see who had snuck up on me so quietly, and to put a little more wall at my back.

"We're already looking." Shame pocketed his phone. "Wondered where you got off to and came looking for you. You missing time or memories?"

"Both. I think both."

Shame cast a variation on Sight. "Well, well. You've been working dark magic, girl. What's that all about?"

Okay, there were two ways I could handle this. I could

either freak the hell out and have a nice cozy breakdown. Go upstairs, curl up with Zayvion, and wait for the world to sort itself out. Or I could get angry and get even.

Angry and even every time, baby.

"Did someone Close me?" I asked nice and calmlike—thank you very much.

"Let's find out." He pointed toward the room and I walked in.

Hayden was still giving me that look. As soon as Shame shut the door and the wards automatically engaged, Hayden cast a spell.

"Wasn't Victor," he said, walking over to me, his wide hand held thumb and ring finger tucked, palm outward in front of him. "Not his signature."

"I didn't know you were a Hound," I said.

"I'm not," he said, still distracted. He let go of whatever form of Sight he'd been using and cast another with his left hand. Looked like he knew tai chi. "But I know how most of the Closers around here use magic. It's easy to see their mark if you know what you're looking for. But this . . . "

Shame pulled out his lighter, and flicked the metal lid, open, shut, open, shut. Waiting.

Hayden's eyes narrowed. "Allie, I'm going to put my finger on your forehead."

"Why?"

"I just need a physical connection. I'm a forehead guy."

"Don't mess with my head. At all."

"I'm not going to touch your mind."

"Running out of time here," Shame said.

"Hold your panties, Flynn," Hayden said.

"Go ahead," I said.

Hayden placed his fingertip on my forehead, then just as quickly pulled it away. He cast one more spell, and I felt a pressure on my ears, like I'd just climbed a very tall hill. The pressure eased, and my ears popped.

"No Closer I know," Hayden said. "But Allie, it looks like you did it. You used magic to Close yourself, push your memories away. I've never seen anyone use magic like that and I think it's a bad idea. You should never Close yourself. Too easy to screw up and end up brain-dead."

"I didn't—"

"You did. And you wouldn't remember that you did." He walked over to the desk. "I'm not your teacher, but my god, woman, don't ever do that again. It could kill you." He tugged open a drawer, paused, then moved things around and pulled out a phone.

"I didn't do it," I said to Shame.

"I know. You're a little anal about your memories. I can't think of a reason why you'd wipe your own mind."

"Thanks." It meant a lot to have someone believe me. Especially after Zayvion's vote of nonconfidence earlier.

"She wiped her own mind," Hayden repeated.

"That doesn't line up for me," Shame said. "We don't know who might be working with Jingo Jingo. Maybe someone from outside the area came in and hit her."

"Terric looking?" Hayden asked, dialing his phone.

"Around the inn," Shame said. "Allie, you should stay here."

"What?"

"You were attacked, and it wasn't just some random thing. They were aiming for you, darlin'. With all the magic users coming and going, they hit you. You knew something they didn't want you to know. It'd be stupid for you to go out there until we have a better idea who's behind it."

"Like hell. I'm going." Yes, I said it with a little more heat than he probably deserved. Intellectually, I understood his concern. But I was angry, and sitting around while someone else fought my battles wasn't going to do any good for anyone.

"I am going to check the well, and I am sure as hell not

going to sit here when I could be out there looking for Jingo Jingo. Terric said my Hounding skills would come in handy. I might have been Closed, but I am still the best Hound in the city." I strode across the room and held my hand out for the extra phone. Hayden dropped it in my palm.

I think he was talking to Victor on the other line.

"You just had your brain hacked," Shame said. "By yourself, or by someone else. That makes anything you do, or say, or *want*, a little suspect, don't you think? You could be a danger to us."

I thumbed the phone on, stuck it in my pocket, and turned on Shame. He lounged against the wall, snicking the lighter open and closed. He didn't look nearly as concerned as he sounded. His gaze measured me.

"I think it's not the worst thing that's happened to me lately. I can handle it. If I'm dangerous to you, you have my permission to take me down. But I know I smelled Jingo Jingo's scent on my skin. I know he's part of it."

"Jingo Jingo's not a Closer," Hayden said, done with the phone call.

"I don't care. Jingo Jingo is the only person I smell on me. On my skin. He was there, here. He touched me." I swallowed hard to keep the terror at bay. Anger. Anger made me strong.

Shame stopped clicking his lighter. "You don't think—"

"What?"

"Could it be your da?" He pointed at his head. "Inside job?"

The alarm bells went into high mode. "Son of a bitch."

"Shame told us he thought your dad possessed you," Hayden said. "Gotta say you Portland people take weird to a new level."

"My dad isn't a Closer," I said.

"Your dad's dead," Shame said. "Who knows what he can do?"

"Think he did it?" Hayden asked.

*Dad?* I thought. *Did you do this? Did you take my memory?* Nothing. Not even the slightest sense that he was in my mind.

"I hate this!" I yelled at the ceiling. Counted down from ten. Twice. Didn't help.

"Shame," I said through my teeth, "can you look in my head and see if my dad is there? And if you find him, let me know, 'cause I'm going to tear him apart."

He gave me a crooked smile. "I can. It will take time and finesse. Two things I'm short on right now. He was in your head when you ran into Truance, right?"

"Yes."

"And he used magic through you, took over your body, right?"

"Yes."

"How did he take over? Did he knock you out or something?"

"Truance used magic to freeze me. I couldn't move. I couldn't pull on magic much, or cast a spell. Dad picked me up and put me back somewhere in my head where I could hear what was going on but I couldn't see it. And he used magic."

"If he's got that kind of understanding of your brain, then there'll be no chance of finding him the easy way," Shame said. "Nothing personal, love, but I don't feel like taking on your da right now. If he's quiet, and you think you're in your right mind, I can go with that."

"Someone should watch you," Hayden said. "Shamus?"

"I'm still coming," I said.

"I know," Shame said. "Being possessed never stopped me from taking a girl out on the town. But it's best we take a little precaution."

"Garlic?" Hayden asked.

Shame grinned. "Only if it comes with pizza and a beer."

He pushed off the wall and dug around on the bookshelf. "Void stone."

"That's huge," I said.

He nodded like a kid who'd just found X-ray glasses at the bottom of the cereal box. "If you, or your da, tries to pull on magic, you'll have to get around this beast. Pretty, isn't it?"

"Um, no."

It wasn't. The last void stone I'd worn was a beautiful black stone caught in vines of copper and silver. It looked like a necklace, a piece of art, really. This thing was spud-ugly. The size of a tennis ball, green as river slime, and pocked with splotches of white like it was rotting, or being taken over by fungus. A plain leather cord looped through it.

"What's the matter, suddenly develop a fashion sense?"

"Give me that." I grabbed the thing out of his hand and dropped it over my head. Hello, relaxation. The headache that had been creeping back up my neck was gone. I must have been too angry to pay attention to how much magic had been pushing at me, filling me. The void stone lifted a weight off my head, off my shoulders. I took a deep breath, savoring the respite from pain and magic.

"I have always had fashion sense," I said.

"Tank tops and jeans every day isn't fashion."

"This is a sweater. And like the goth look is something original?"

"Goth? Who's goth?"

"You, Mr. Nothing-but-black-from-head-to-boot."

"I like black. It makes me look dangerous."

"Oh, yeah, that's what it does," Hayden said. "Get going, danger man. There's work to do."

"That hurts right in the soul." Shame pounded a fist on his chest.

"We all know you don't have no soul, boy," Hayden said. "Go."

Out in the hall, Hayden locked the door and tried the handle to make sure it was set.

"I'll see you two dark and early. Be careful. Call if anything goes sideways." He strode toward the dining area, phone in his hand again.

"Who's he going out with tonight?" I asked.

"He's not. Pulled shift here. Making sure nothing gets in, or"—he paused to stick a cigarette in his mouth—"gets out. Holds the fort, keeps in contact with all of us, reports on gates, critters, and such. Backup Proxy if anyone gets in over their heads." He pushed the outside door open—the same door I'd exited before—and was lighting his cigarette before his boot hit gravel. Exhaled smoke. "I hate doing it, 'cause you can't leave the place no matter if it's burning to the ground."

"Why not?"

"The well. Can't ever be unguarded. Ever."

The sound of an approaching car filled the night, and Terric pulled up in Shame's car. Terric swung out, strode around the car. "Evening. You driving?" He tossed Shame the keys. Shame snatched them out of the air without looking.

He took a step, which would have put him in rhythm with Terric. He paused, a subtle hesitation to purposely walk in a different stride. I could tell he wanted to relax and fall into pace with Terric. I could see he fought that instinct. Constantly.

And I thought I was stubborn.

"Any sign of Jingo?"

Terric shook his head. "We searched. Thoroughly. Nothing. Are you sure, Allie?"

"I'm sure he was around me. I'm sure I smelled him. I'm sure I'm missing five minutes. After that, I'm not sure of anything."

Terric opened the front door for me. "Well, I'm sure he's

not here now. Nice rock. You should know better than to let Shame dress you."

"I needed a void stone. He gave me a void stone."

"You just can't keep your hands off that ugly thing, can you, Flynn?"

Shame grinned. "This is a magical emergency. It was the closest stone I could find." He ducked into the car.

"There are at least a dozen void stones in any private room of that place," Terric said as he got in the backseat. "You're just torturing the girl."

"I don't care what it looks like so long as it works."

"See?" Shame said. "She appreciates my thoughtfulness."

"Plus paybacks are hell," I said.

Terric smiled. "You said you lost five minutes?"

"Someone Closed her," Shame said.

Terric had stretched out to lean on the driver's-side door, one long leg across the seat, his arm up over the back.

"That's interesting," he said.

"Hayden couldn't suss who. Said she did it to herself."

"Did you?"

I glanced back at him. "I'm horrible at Closing. I'd never try it on someone else, much less myself."

"Plus, she has that whole, 'I-keep-losing-my-memory' thing she whines about," Shame said. "Gets all prickly and whatnot when anyone so much as glances at her past."

"Payback, Flynn," I said. "Hell."

"So who?" Terric asked.

Shame took a breath to answer.

"Holy shit, you're kidding? Her father?"

"I hate when you do that," Shame growled.

"Read your mind? You think like you're yelling into a bullhorn. It's hard to ignore you, Flynn. Trust me, I try."

"To hell with you," Shame said.

Terric motioned to include the interior of the car. "Already there. Your dad Closed you, from inside your head?"

"Probably." It sounded as angry as I felt.

"We should make sure we write this down. Whatever you remember of it. I've never heard of a Closer doing that—of conceiving of the way to do that. How does he Proxy his magic use? Are you bearing his cost of pain? How does he use magic without you knowing exactly what he's doing before he does it? He must be blocking you in some manner."

"If I knew any of that, I'd stop him and get him the hell out of my head."

"So you have no control over what he does?"

I thought about it. I had some control. I'd found my own ways to block him, to construct walls between us, to push him away and push him down. But it hadn't gotten easier. Every day, Dad seemed to grow stronger. Sometimes he'd do something and falter—like when Greyson had tried to eat his soul, or when he fought with Truance—but he always recovered. And came back stronger.

He was like an undead boomerang. A zomberang.

"Not enough control," I said. "I can hold him back. That's about it."

"What have you tried on him?"

Terric was way too interested in this. I didn't know if it was because he was a Closer and had once been up for the job as guardian of the gates, or if he just wanted a conversation that had nothing to do with Shame.

"I haven't really thought about it. Mostly block spells. Influence, I think."

"You have your father—one of the strongest magic users of modern times—possessing your mind and you've used Magic 101 on him? Allie, I'm disappointed. Shame?"

"Give her a break, Terric. You don't know what it's like for her."

"I don't know what *what* is like? Being steamrolled by

magic and death? I actually think I have a pretty good bead on that."

"Fuck it all," Shame muttered.

"Don't." I lowered my voice, softening it. "It's been a hard day. We're all tired. Let's not make it worse. I'm used to my dad screwing with me. I don't like it, but I can deal. I just don't know how Jingo Jingo got so close and no one noticed. How can that happen?"

They were silent. We were already on the Portland side of the river. Soon Shame was navigating city streets toward Belmont, where two-story houses of questionable color palettes with barbecue grills up on their porch roofs sat side by side with brick plumbing shops, spray-painted coffeehouses, and solid historical buildings teetering on the edge of disrepair.

"He was a part of us," Terric said.

"Terric," Shame warned quietly.

"I'm not out for a fight," Terric said. "But that's why he could get through, Allie. Jingo Jingo was a part of us, of the Authority, of the people who swore to see that magic would always be in the right hands and used correctly. Safely. He knows us. Knows our ways. It's . . . worrisome."

"Haven't things been swapped out since he left? Different wards? Different shield and protection spells? Different locks on the doors?"

"Casting a new ward doesn't make it different," Shame said. "Not in a substantial way. It's not like changing locks. Magic is magic. It only follows certain paths, glyphs, spells."

I shook my head. "I don't know about that."

"No," Terric said. "He's right."

"Maybe."

"Maybe?" Shame said. "You doubt?"

"I doubt any of us knows what, if push came to shove, magic could really do. Face it, there's a hell of a lot left undiscovered. Like Animates can be maintained on a scale as large as Stone. That an Animate can store a living soul. That a woman can survive walking to death and back. We just found that all out within the last month. Today, we discovered the disks can be used to make the unliving Veiled alive again."

"Is there a point to this?" Shame asked.

"My point is we haven't yet begun to scratch the surface of what we can make magic do."

Silence again. The huge brick Catholic school passed by on our left. On our right was a concrete wall that appeared to be held together by ivy and moss.

Finally, Terric spoke. "That's exactly what your father used to say."

I clunked my head on my window and swore quietly. Now I was talking like him. How fan-damn-tastic was that?

# Chapter Sixteen

Shame slowed the car and made his way along the road, taking the first left.

"You've got to be kidding me," I said.

"About?"

"Is this where we're going?"

"We not only know people in low places—we are people in low places."

Terric chuckled.

I didn't know what else to say. It was so expected. So obvious. So cliché.

"A graveyard? The Death magic well is in a graveyard?"

This was one of the oldest graveyards in the city. About three city blocks long and two wide, it was crammed between the Catholic school, a modern apartment building made of wood and metal, and an assortment of houses and squat repair garages and small shops. Inside the cemetery were so many trees, my claustrophobia tickled the back of my throat.

Graves slid by to our right and left, tall carved pillars, concrete tree trunks, and shiny black marble with ghostly white faces laser-etched into the surface.

"What's got your knickers in a bunch?" Shame asked.

"The wells correspond to the disciplines of magic, right?"

"Yes," Shame said. "And the Winter well represents Death magic. So what? Where did you want us to put it? Under a hospital? Powell's?"

"As if we could put it anywhere," Terric said. "The wells were here long before there were bones to bury."

"A lot of bones buried here," Shame said. "Magic doesn't care."

"Magic doesn't have to. People care," Terric said.

I wondered why Terric's answer had sounded like an apology. Then it came to me: Shame's father was dead. I had never asked where he was buried. Maybe here.

Which brought another worry to mind. What if people like Shame's dad were some of the Veiled, or ghosts being called to whatever war Pike was talking about?

I wondered if Shame had thought about that.

He didn't drive all the way to the end, but instead stopped about halfway, just before the intersection to the right.

"This?" I asked, looking out at the gravestones settled between a tall steepled crypt surrounded by a black metal fence and a smaller brick crypt surrounded by garbage cans.

"This," Shame agreed. "Can't you sense it?"

I tugged the void stone away from my chest. "No."

"And you thought that rock was just ugly," Shame said. "It's ugly and powerful."

"No wonder you like it so much. Birds of a feather . . . " Terric mumbled as he wiped his hand over his mouth.

"When are you going back to Seattle?" Shame asked.

We got out of the car, walked toward the crypt. Cold. Nice night, even for a graveyard. Recent rain had left the slight grassy rise where the crypt sat among cedar, holly, oak, and maple squishy with mud that obscured the row of flat headstones sunk in the ground.

Shame cast Sight. Terric cast something too. They were both looking at the back of the crypt.

"Holy shit," Shame said.

All I saw were rows of gravestones, trees, crypts, and garbage cans.

I inhaled, tasted the wet soil, moss, concrete, and the hint of teriyaki from a local kitchen. Didn't taste magic. Didn't feel magic. Wearing the void stone was like putting blinders over a blindfold.

The train hooted softly in the distance, carrying over the hush of traffic.

"Talk, Shame," Terric said. He was looking at the crypt too. "I see a crypt above the well, and magic flowing up into it. What do you see?"

Okay, no way I was going to let the boys have all the fun. I set a Disbursement. I was done with headaches and chose a head cold instead. I hated head colds, but I wasn't planning on using enough magic to do more than give me the sniffles. I drew Sight and pulled magic up through my bones. Magic rose, pushed against my skin, pressed outward until I felt stretched and stingy. Then magic collapsed inward, like a gum bubble sucked in by the stone around my neck.

I couldn't cast magic with this thing on. "I'm taking the void stone off," I said.

Terric glanced at me.

"Don't worry. I'll let you know if my dad is trying to take over."

"Did we make a hand signal for that?" he said.

"If I'm acting like a bastard, it's him."

I yanked the void stone off and hooked the leather strap with my pinky, keeping the ugly thing as far from my body as I could.

"Veiled," Shame said. "You can't see them?"

"No," Terric said. "Hold on." He canceled one spell with

a slash of his hand and cast another. "There's a gate. Holy fuck. There's a gate open in the crypt. Right over the well. I still don't see any Veiled."

"They can see us. Pretty sure they can see us." Shame took a step back.

I drew Zayvion's katana, and cast Sight with my left hand, the void stone swinging in counter rhythm to the spell, but as far as I could tell not affecting it. The graveyard caught fire in pastel light.

Veiled were everywhere, in the trees, between the graves, moving like a slow river of eyes and open mouths. They pulled out of the ground, out of the graves, out of the smaller crypt. Ghostly, like Pike, pressing closer and closer to the crypt, surrounding it, burying it with their bodies, their needy hands, their hungry mouths.

The Veiled, men and women, clung to the crypt and pulled the well's magic out of the stones with skeletal fingers, gulping it down with huge, body-arching shudders.

Magic burbled out of the ground beneath the crypt like a fountain. It filled the stones of the crypt until they glowed, pulsed dark, and grew bright again.

"There's a gate?" I asked, not seeing it.

"In the crypt," Terric said again.

Didn't matter if I couldn't see it. That was bad. Real bad.

"Anything coming through?" I asked.

"Nothing solid," Terric said. "Doesn't mean something hasn't already come through. And there's movement on the other side. A hell of a lot of movement. Shame," he said, "the gate is being fed by the well. It's hardwired in."

"Plum assignment, my ass," Shame said. "What'd you do to piss off Victor?" He broke the Sight and cast a spell a little like the one he'd used hunting Hungers—no Blood magic involved, just Death magic.

And the more the Veiled drank, the clearer, stronger, and more solid they became.

"Does this rate 'unusual' enough for us to call Hayden?" I asked. "Or is this standard procedure?"

"It's not standard," Terric said. "I've never seen a gate tied in to a well. Do you still see the Veiled?"

"Yes. They're all around us. Maybe a hundred. Most of them sucking magic out of the crypt, the rest of them coming up out of graves to join the party."

"Do you see anything else? Hungers? The horrors?" He sounded calm as he canceled another spell and cast again. I wondered how much pain Hayden was Proxying for all this magic use.

I did a three-sixty. Trees, graves, Veiled, road, trees, graves. A shadow, a man-shaped shadow in the trees, gone before I could be sure I saw it.

"Maybe that shadow man. Too fast for me to track. All the way out there in the trees. Can't see it now." I recast Smell and Taste. "I don't smell anyone but us. Don't smell any other magic being used. Don't smell the disks. Shame?"

"Back away slowly," he said. "We're going to have to Close this thing down, and that's not going to make them happy."

"We?" Terric said. "I'm the only Closer here, Flynn."

"You can't Close it on your own. Not with the well feeding it."

"You know I love a challenge," Terric said. "One of us could be getting the capstone he has stowed in his glove box."

"Can we cut the feed?" I asked. "Disconnect the gate from the well?"

"*We* can do nothing." Terric turned, looked at me. "*I* will take care of it." His eyes were dark, clear. He didn't look nervous, didn't look frightened. He looked like he faced down this kind of dragon every day. Reminded me of Zay. As it should. Terric had almost been the guardian of the gates.

Terric strode off toward the back of the crypt.

"Horseshit hero fucking martyr," Shame swore, striding off after him.

The Veiled who had been attached to the crypt turned. Stepped away, stepped through their companions.

And absorbed them.

Two sets of eyes in one face, like a shadow behind a screen. Two sets of mouths, two bodies filled the same space. Twice as solid as they had just been. Stepping through yet another Veiled, and absorbing them.

Dead magic users possessing dead magic users.

Two, now three deep in the space of one body.

Holy shit.

A dozen of them, more—headed straight for us.

"The Veiled are possessing the Veiled and getting stronger," I said, catching up with them in the slick grass. "They see us, Terric."

"Shame. Capstone would be good."

"Not leaving you out here alone."

"The Veiled." I pointed with my left hand. A beacon, a green fricking glowing floodlight poured out of my palm.

And then the Veiled weren't just walking anymore. They were running. Straight for us. Well, me.

Shame cursed, turned it into a chant, a song. Terric chanted too—their voices pulling perfect damn harmony. Shame a tenor, Terric a bass, like they did this all the time, like they were meant to use magic together.

Shame pulled magic up out of the soil, the graves, from the bones of the dead, the crypt itself. He turned his back on the crypt and cast a Shield around us like a dome, his hands pointing downward at the soil, not upward at the sky.

Terric cast too, pulling on the magic from the well and the gate and the crypt, moving more like Hayden moved, like Zay moved, wide, smooth motions, hands, wrists, arms.

He braced and pushed magic into a Containment glyph, flowing rhythms weaving a net. He twisted and threw the net. It flew free of the Shield, sparking as it passed through. It grappled around the crypt and sank through the Veiled gathered around it.

The spell was still attached to Terric's hands, which he held about shoulder high, fingers cupped and busy as he pulled and pushed the magic in the spell.

His eyes? Closed. He manipulated magic blind, guiding it, moving it around the gate inside the crypt by feel alone.

The Veiled hit Shame's Shield so hard my ears popped. Neither man so much as twitched. Veiled skittered, clawed, too many eyes in those eyes, too many voices in those throats, too many dead people in those dead people. They screamed out at us, and attached to the Shield like eels, wide, sharp-toothed mouths scraping, throats drinking down the magic.

Sure, they were alive once, but right now, they were not sane and not human.

Terric was inside the Shield, casting magic out. Time I did the same.

Shame and I had used magic together before once. We were Contrasts. Somtimes our magic worked when it crossed, and sometimes it went up in flames.

Now was a good time to risk an inferno.

Safety first. I set a Disbursement—head cold again. If I survived.

I cast Impact around the katana's blade. My left hand suddenly went cold as hell and black flame tracked down the hilt to the blade, where it mingled with Impact. I didn't know what that would do, but I didn't wait to find out. Sword burning with magic and flames, I swung the blade through the Shield.

A dozen Veiled exploded at the touch of the blade. Watercolor flames flashed to pastel smoke. The spell hadn't broken the Shield and hadn't given Shame a concussion. Go, me.

"Back, back, back," Shame sang. He might have been singing to the Veiled, but it sounded like a good idea to me. I wanted the car and about a hundred miles between me and anything that couldn't fog a mirror.

"Down," Terric sang. "Down and down."

It was great they were all singy and seemed to know what the hell they were doing, but all I had going for me was killing the freaks.

I cast Impact again, swung again, took out a dozen more. There were too many Veiled taking their place. My left arm was going numb. I couldn't keep this up.

New plan. I needed a bomb, a grenade, something that would do massive damage on a three-sixty instead of at sword's reach. Why hadn't anyone taught me how to make a magic bomb?

Time to improvise.

Shame grabbed my sleeve and tugged me toward the car.

"Out of here. All of us," he panted. His other hand was still fingers to the earth, his words clipped as if he were working hard to do three things at once.

"Terric?" I said.

"Coming," both Terric and Shame said at the same time. He was walking with us, backward, while Shame walked forward. Terric's eyes were still closed, his hands still manipulating magic as we slipped and slid toward the car. I didn't think he was singing anymore. He was swearing.

Since Shame was also being Terric's eyes, that meant he was concentrating on four things.

"Call Hayden." Shame let go of my shirt.

I dug out my phone, dialed Hayden.

"Allie," his familiar deep voice said.

"We're at the graveyard. By the crypt. A gate opened over the well. Terric is working to Close it."

"Alone?"

"Shame's Shielding us from the Veiled."

"How many?"

"They're pouring out of the gate. Hundreds."

"Tell them to cap it. Cap the well."

"He said to cap the well," I said to Shame.

"Getting there. Tell him to check in with the other teams."

"I heard him," Hayden said. Good ears. I knew he'd make a good Hound.

"Shut it down before any more get loose in the city," he said. "Don't worry how messy it is. We'll clean up. I'll check in as soon as I get someone to send out to you. Don't let them do anything stupid."

He hung up before I could point out that I was pretty sure everything they were doing right now was stupid.

"Ready?" Shame asked.

"Can't read your mind," I reminded him.

"Don't have to. We're going to break for the car. You, me. Then Terric."

Terric was still manipulating magic, sweat glistening over his pale, pale skin, his silver hair brushing his shoulders like spun silk in the moonlight. He was breathing hard. Shaking. He chanted a low litany of the same few words in a string, over and over. A language I did not know, knotted and twisted, tugging magic to do his bidding.

Shame cast another spell. "Take the keys." Both his hands were holding spells, holding the Shield, holding the Veiled off of us. His head was down, bangs covering his eyes. He was breathing hard in the same rhythm as Terric.

"Pocket," he said.

I sheathed the sword and rushed around in front of him. I patted his back pockets, then front, and slid my hand into his front pocket. He tipped his head up, his eyes slits of pain through the dark swing of bangs. "Lower. Slower."

I scowled. Really? He was joking around about sex at a time like this? If that Shield fell, we were going to get eaten alive. Well, at least I was. The Veiled liked to tear me apart.

I pushed my fingers a little deeper in his pocket, caught the keys and a lot of thigh.

"Oh, baby," he cooed.

"I don't want to hear it," I said.

He gave me a flash of teeth, then whispered, picking up the chant Terric was intoning.

These two worked together blind better than any magic users I'd seen work together with years of training.

They say Complements can cast magic together. They say Soul Complements can cast magic as if they were one person. It didn't take a test to tell me Terric and Shame were very much Soul Complements.

"Ready for the car?" Shame inhaled, exhaled, then, "On three. You're closer to the driver's side. Get in, but don't start the engine yet. Terric?"

"Three," Terric repeated. "On three."

Shame swallowed, lifted his hands to either side, shoulder high, head still tucked down. "And one, and two, and three." He drew his hands together, clapping.

The Shield shattered, blowing outward in a concussion of sound and force. Veiled shattered with it, not every Veiled, not those who were possessed and possessing. But a whole hell of a lot of undead magic users screamed and exploded into pastel smoke around us.

Hayden wanted messy. That was messy. I was pretty sure it was visible for miles.

We sprinted for the car.

The Veiled howled. Their chilling, curdled screech made me want to run, run, run. And run I did. To the car, around the car, keys in hand.

The Veiled are nightmarishly fast. Faster than any living thing.

Except me when my life was on the line.

I opened the door, got inside.

Terric was half a breath behind me, and threw himself into the front seat, digging for the glove box. Shame was still out there, arms spread wide, face up to the dark sky. He was smiling.

"They're on the car," I said a little too loudly.

"Wards in the paint. They'll hold for a minute."

"There aren't any wards on the car," I said.

"I know." He fumbled a stone jar out of the glove box, the black box it had been in falling away. "I just thought it might make you feel better."

"Oh fuck this." I drew a glyph for Hold.

Terric snatched my hand in mid-cast. Something sharp licked hot across my thumb.

"Ow!"

He tipped my hand, recited something, and squeezed my thumb until a drop of blood fell into the jar. He had a small blade in his hand.

"What the hells do you think you're doing?"

"Saving our asses. I'm not about to let him kill himself. I won't give him the damn satisfaction. Suicidal bastard."

Terric let go of my thumb, slammed a lid on the jar, and rubbed his own bloody thumb around the edge to seal the lid.

And then he ran out of the car. Ran. Out. Of. The. Car.

What the hells?

I pushed on the door. It wouldn't open.

I'll be damned. There *were* wards on the car. Wards that locked me in.

Hated this. Officially.

Terric ran to Shame, the jar tucked tight against his chest. That had definitely been Blood magic Terric used. I thought he couldn't use any of the other disciplines since Shame got possessed by a Hunger a few years ago and tried to kill Terric. That had broken Terric, made permanent scars in him. My thumb throbbed. I pinched it to keep it from bleeding all over the place. As soon as Terric was beside Shame, Shame fell into step with him. Shame chanted; Terric, from what I could see, held the jar. Then they both strode to the crypt, Shame's arms still open. Terric worked a spell with his left hand, and held it there, uncast, his blood tracing a black line down his arm, the jar pressed against his heart.

The Veiled backed away step by step with them, hovering, stalking. Every time one came too close, Shame flicked his fingers and drank them down to screams and smoke. Death magic was a transference of energy. And Shame was very good at Death magic. But even he had to have a limit.

The two men walked through an ocean of Veiled straight to the crypt. Terric walked up the two concrete, moss-covered steps, got up on the low stone wall, then grabbed the top of the fence that surrounded the crypt. He heaved and jumped the fence. He jogged to the crypt's tall arched door. Shame, still outside the fence, flicked the Veiled around Terric to dust.

They couldn't keep this up much longer.

I tried the door again. Nothing. Wondered if the car would go up in a ball of fire if I hit it with magic.

Terric grabbed hold of one of the pillars carved into the stone beside the door and hoisted himself up on the stone wall. The carved faceless angel with its single wing glowed a soft blue just to one side of him. He pushed the jar onto the small ledge atop the pillar.

The window above the door had been replaced by a wooden board painted to look like glass. As soon as the jar touched the pillar, the window flared, green, red, and blue, shifting, changing places like a lock tumbling to a close.

I felt more than heard a *thunk* at the base of my spine. Something very heavy had just fallen, hit the ground. The gate was closed. And so was the well.

The Veiled stopped moving. Froze, as if they'd just been unplugged.

And then they turned away from the crypt, away from Terric. Faced the trees where I had seen the shadow man. I didn't hear anything. I didn't see anything there. But they did. I was sure of it.

My left hand went painfully cold. Something more than just the Veiled was out there.

The Veiled ran. A blur of eyes, faces, shadow, light, and screams melting into the night air.

Gone. Into the city. Shit.

Terric hopped down, missed his footing and staggered back, falling.

Only, he hadn't missed his footing. A woman straddled his chest, one hand against his throat, the other pulling a knife out of his side.

Truance. She must have been hiding in the shadow of the doorway.

"No!" I slammed my hand against the car window. That wasn't going to do any good. I calmed my mind, recited a mantra, cast a Shield. I didn't know if I could get it past the wards and around Terric in time.

Shame was way ahead of me. He didn't jump the fence. He blew it apart. He ran the short distance to Terric, already throwing another spell at Truance. She flew off of Terric like she'd been hit by a battering ram and was slammed into the door of the crypt.

He threw another spell at her, and she disappeared. Again.

Bitch.

Shame knelt, waved a hand in my direction and released whatever ward had been holding me tight in the car.

Which was good. I felt a yelling coming on and I preferred my yellings in open air rather than in cramped quarters.

Shame pressed his hand to Terric's side, then helped him up. They turned back toward the car, Shame's arm around Terric to keep him on his feet.

"Fuck this," I started. "You do not lock me in a car. Ever. I don't care what boogeyman is out here."

Terric swallowed. Twice. He looked like he was trying not to barf. "Didn't know they'd kick in. Must be because of the jar."

"Blood magic," Shame said a lot gentler than I expected. "I modded the wards for Blood magic. Since Chase screwed me, I set the car to close down if Blood magic was used inside it. You know that, Terric," he chided gently. "It was your idea."

"Oh, yah," Terric said. "Forgot."

I met them halfway and got my arm around the other side of Terric. It had seemed like low-level magic—stick a jar on a pillar—but they had just done something huge. Plus, they'd had to do it while fighting the Veiled.

Terric was bleeding pretty badly. I glanced over at Shame, but he seemed calm and collected.

"Help me get him in the car," he said with that measured gentleness. "And hand me the void stone."

I opened the back door. Shame eased Terric into the car and convinced him to lie down as much as space would allow.

Terric did not look good at all.

"How bad?" I asked.

"The knife wound isn't too deep. She wasn't trying to kill him. The bitch used Blood magic to tie him to her. She's drinking down his life. Where's the stone?"

I handed him the ugly spud.

He took it in one hand, and transferred it to the other as

if it were too hot to hold. "I'm going to put a void stone on your chest, Terric," Shame said. "It might sting a little. Or you might want to fall asleep. Sleep would be good."

Terric started to say something, but never got to the end of it. As soon as the void stone pressed against his stomach, he was unconscious, his arm falling toward the floor, his chin tucked down. He exhaled, one shivering breath. I held my breath waiting for him to inhale.

Nearly passed out before he did.

A switchblade flicked to life in Shame's hand, the blade a slice of steel and glass and glyphs. "You might not want to watch this."

I watched.

He opened the hole in Terric's coat and shirt, revealing the wound. Just like the Blood magic that had been used on me, the wound looked like a glyph made out of blue twine had been implanted beneath his skin.

Shame traced the glyph with one finger, his head tipped to the side as if he could hear what the glyph sounded like. Then he quickly sliced across the beginning of the glyph. I'd done that to myself. I remembered how much it hurt. But Terric didn't twitch. Shame must know how to keep the area numb.

He whispered, the crystal glowing in his chest through his coat as he pulled on magic. Even without Sight, I could see the glyph unspooling, rising up and away from Terric like a dense smoke and re-forming in the air between them. Shame nicked his own finger, caught the blood on the blade, then slashed through the glyph, ending the spell.

It broke with an audible crack, and left the scent of sweet cherries behind.

Truance's connection was broken.

Shame's shoulders slumped, and he braced one hand on the side of the seat to keep from falling on top of Terric.

"Shame?"

"Drive."

I didn't argue. I ducked into the front seat and so did he, but he turned so he could put one hand on Terric's wrist, keeping track of his heartbeat.

"Get us back to Mum's."

I started the car, put it in gear, and stomped on the gas. "Is he going to be okay?"

"If we get him to a doctor."

"Did he close the gate?"

"Yes."

"Did the Veiled get loose in the city?"

"Yes."

"Did you kill Truance?"

"No."

"Son of a bitch," I said.

I followed the road as fast as I could, and was in sight of the gate when I saw him.

Detective Stotts, standing next to his car. And all around him, though he couldn't see them, the Veiled were closing in.

# Chapter Seventeen

I stopped the car.

"What the hell?" Shame said.

"He's going to be eaten alive."

"They'll walk right past him. Drive."

I drew a spell for Sight. Forgot a Disbursement, which meant I was going to be hurting soon, and looked more closely at the Veiled.

Two deep, three deep possessing the same space, somehow stronger even though they were not solid.

Stotts carried something in his hand that drew them.

It took me a second. Then I knew what it was. A disk. A disk filled with magic.

Holy shit.

They would shred him to get that.

"He has a disk," I said. "Charged."

"Allie—"

I got out, slammed the door.

"This is why I don't let people drive my car," he yelled.

"Paul, don't use the disk."

He camped back on one foot, his hand with the disk still in his pocket. "How do you know I have a disk?"

"I can see it, smell it. You need to give it to me. Now."

His thick eyebrows rose. "Allie, I've been looking for

you for over a week. And Nola tells me you called her and talked to her this afternoon. About me."

Shit. I had forgotten they'd Closed him and he wouldn't remember he'd found me in St. Johns.

The Veiled approached him slowly. I wondered if the disk was warded. Because I was pretty sure if it wasn't, they would be on top of him, devouring the magic it held.

"And now," he said into my silence, "I find you in a graveyard while on my way to investigate a hot spot in the network. A hot spot that flashed, then went cold just about the time you came driving over the hill. What's in your hand, Allie?"

"What?" I stupidly, instinctively, opened my hands. The Veiled saw the mark on my left, the burning green beacon.

They howled, and rushed me.

Two choices came to mind: do nothing and get clobbered by the Veiled or cast a Shield—the kind that people like Detective Paul Stotts did not know about—to save our asses.

"Don't move." I ran to him, stopped about three feet away, turned my back on him, even though I was pretty sure he was reaching for either a spell or a gun. Probably both.

Turning my back on someone about to pull a gun on me was as much trust as I'd ever extended to anyone. He'd better treat Nola right.

"That disk attracts creatures. Echoes of old magic, like ghosts, but mean and hungry for magic."

"I don't see anything."

"You won't have to. You'll feel them real quick and real bad."

I set a Disbursement and cast Shield, pulling the magic up out of the ground and into my body, my bones, then out of my fingers and into the spell I traced in the air. No black flame this time.

The Veiled hit the Shield like a wall of bricks. Holy shit. I felt the impact in my skull. How had Shame maintained a Shield against them for so long?

"Give me the disk," I said.

There is one thing I like about cops. They have great instincts when it comes to if and when they should believe a crazy person isn't talking crazy.

And there is one thing about cops that is troublesome. That they are hella good at fact-checking.

Stotts drew Sight. He cast right-handed, keeping his left, unmagical hand around the disk in his pocket.

"I don't see anything."

"Regular magic users can't. The marks you wanted to know if they were left on me by magic? Yes. And they make it so I can see magic in ways most people can't."

It was true. I'd never seen Zayvion in his black-flame and silver-glyph warrior glory until I had magic pounding through me. And I'd never seen the Veiled before Cody had pulled magic through me. Well, actually, I first started seeing the Veiled when my dead dad touched me, opening me, I think, to a sensitivity to the dead. But that would take a lot more time, and sound a lot more crazy to explain.

"The Shield?" He was not as impressed as I'd thought he would be.

"Is keeping them from attacking us. You. The disk. Paul, I am not screwing with you. You know there's a lot more going on with magic than most people know about."

He made a *huh* sound.

The Veiled pressed their mouths against the Shield and sucked on the magic. It felt like I'd just been covered in leeches. My skin stung as blood was drawn out through my pores.

Damn it.

"I can't hold this for long." Honestly, I was pretty surprised I could keep my head clear and calm enough to continue Refreshing the spell to keep it whole. And I knew Shame wasn't coming to my rescue, because he was in the car trying to keep Terric alive.

"Give me the disk or throw it as far as you can."

Stotts took the disk out of his pocket.

The Veiled broke through my Shield. Clawed at me, bit, tore. Did the same to Paul, from the sound of it.

I stumbled back into Paul, who stumbled back into the bed of rosebushes, but didn't fall. I furiously cast Camouflage. The butterscotchy spell closed in around us.

The hands, the mouths, the pain, stopped. Camouflage was officially my newest favorite Shield spell.

"Shit," Stotts whispered. "You doing this?"

"It's a variation of Shield," I said. "Can you drain the disk?"

"Why?"

"They want the magic in it."

I felt him shifting behind me, just his arms. Another thing I liked about cops. They knew when being quiet and holding still was a good idea. We were pressed together, my back against his chest. I could feel his heart beating fast. Camouflage might be good, but it wasn't unbreakable.

"How much magic does it hold?" he asked.

I'd never asked Violet for the specs. "Enough for one spell, I think."

"Something big?"

"Don't leave a drop of magic in it."

I could tell he was thinking, his breath caught. "I'm going to step back on three. You drop the Shield. One . . . "

I felt the fingers of his left hand slide across my shoulders as he began drawing a glyph.

"Two . . . "

I braced for it.

"Three." He shoved away. I broke Camouflage and it pelted down around us in slow-motion butterscotch drops.

I threw my hands over my face to ward off the Veiled.

Stotts closed the last line of the glyph and threw the disk into the trees like a seasoned quarterback. An explosion of light poured out in midair. Then darkness swallowed us.

And the Veiled were gone.

I heard the distant thud of the disk hitting the ground.

"Anything?" Stotts asked.

I cast Sight to be sure, keeping my left hand closed so the mark did not shine. "No. They're gone. Are you okay?"

He walked over to me. Even in the patchy light of the moon through the heavy tree limbs, I could see the blood on his forehead and cheek.

"I'm fine. You?"

I nodded. "Bruised." And I was. Everywhere the Veiled had stuck their fingers, a burning bruise was left behind. I'd been here, done this. I knew the bruises would heal.

"We need to get the disk," I said.

"Who's in the car?"

God. Terric. He needed a doctor. The fight with the Veiled had only taken a minute. Maybe two. I had to get him to Maeve's fast.

"Allie?"

I could use Influence on him and make him go away so I didn't have to deal with this. But he was my friend, and Nola's boyfriend. He had already lost his memories because of me. There must be a way to explain this without endangering him or the Authority.

"Shame and a friend of his. I'm Hounding a case for them." Lie. When the truth just isn't good enough.

"In the graveyard at night?"

"People do weird magic things in lots of places. Especially at night. I need to get going. Good luck with the disk."

He gave me a hard look. Might have believed me and let me go. If Stone hadn't picked that minute to come trotting up with the disk between his fangs.

Stotts pulled his gun. I would have too. Stone was a brute.

"Don't," I said. "He's friendly."

"Now that I know what mood he's in, would you mind telling me what he is?" He didn't put the gun down.

Shame got out of the car, cupped his hand, and lit a cigarette as he strolled over to us.

"Hey, Detective. Nice night."

"Mr. Flynn."

"What do you think of the art?" Shame exhaled toward Stone.

"This is yours?" He did not sound convinced.

I worked on an isn't-that-interesting look, because I had no idea where he was going with this.

"I've been doing a little art on the streets lately. Crashed the sidewalk art and magic tour a little while ago, and thought I'd bring Stone out here to see how he worked. What do you think?"

"What is he?"

"Stone mostly. Some gears in there. I modded a couple storm rods, have a small storage basin in his belly. He can keep a magic charge for over an hour. But that's about all the pain I want to pay to keep him going." He gave a wicked grin. "Unless I get picked up for a showing at a good gallery. Then maybe I'll bring a few hot Proxies who are into that kind of thing onto payroll."

Stotts looked at me, looked for Shame's truth to be reflected in my face.

"I just found out yesterday that he was into art. He told me he wanted me to Hound the gargoyle to see what kind of a magical signature he left behind. That's probably the flare you saw."

"Don't quite have it down," Shame said, "but the idea is when he's off, people think he's a statue. When he's on, he looks real."

"He does look real," Stotts agreed. "Just like the statues outside the Gargoyle."

Oh, shit. More than just like the statues at the Gargoyle. Stone used to be one of the statues at that restaurant. And I'd set him free, woke him up, whatever. But what I hadn't done was pay for him.

"They have statues up there?" Shame asked.

"One less since a couple months ago." Stotts holstered his gun. "Reported stolen. Mr. Flynn, I'm suddenly very curious as to where you got your hands on him, why you're in a graveyard, and what you have to do with the magic spike."

"You can't be serious." Shame smiled, but it was tight, angry.

"I am. You're coming into the station to answer those questions."

Shame's hand twitched. I didn't know what kind of spell he was going to throw at Stotts, but I didn't want to see the nice policeman go up in smoke.

"Can't it wait?" I stepped in front of Shame to foul his aim. "We have a meeting at his mom's inn to discuss her interest in Beckstrom Enterprises, and Shame and I were both supposed to be there."

"This late?"

Crap.

Stone, meanwhile, dropped the disk at my feet, then sniffed at Stotts, tipping his big head to one side and rumbling at him.

"He won't bite," I said. Adding, "Right, Shame?"

"Sure. Let's go with that."

Stotts motioned toward his car. "You're coming with us too, Allie."

"Me? Why me? What did I do?"

"I want to hear your side of the story about what happened tonight. Get in."

Stone, ever a good rock, trotted over to Stotts' car and lifted up on his hind legs to look in the windows and try the door handle.

"Son of a bitch," Stotts said. Yeah, Stone was easily six foot when he stood up. Plus he was curious, liked car rides, and knew how to open doors.

"I'm not coming with you," Shame said.

Stotts shifted to keep an eye on both Shame and Stone. "Probable cause, Mr. Flynn. You don't want to go down that road."

"We have a friend," I said. "He's in the car. Injured."

"What kind of injury?"

"I might have miscalculated the charge on the gargoyle," Shame said. "He Proxied the charge."

Well, now I knew Shame could lie as smooth as satin over Teflon. I didn't even smell the lie on him. I was impressed and worried. Once Stotts got Shame and me in two different rooms, our stories were not going to match up.

Hells.

It would be easiest to Influence him, to cast Sleep on him. Yes, to make him forget.

But I refused to take someone else's memories away. Shame did not have the same qualms.

"I'll call 911," Stotts said.

"There is no way I am getting arrested," Shame said.

"We'll come with you and explain it all," I said.

"We?" Shame laughed, and it was not a pretty sound. "Have you lost your mind? *We* don't have time for this. There are important things *we* should be taking care of. For Christsakes, Allie, get your priorities straight."

He was talking like that in front of Stotts because he had just decided Stotts was going to be Closed. Again.

Not on my watch.

"The art can wait," I said, keeping my calm and keeping

our cover. "We could call your mom and let her know we'll be late. You don't mind if we make a phone call, do you?" I flashed Stotts my innocent eyes.

"Phone calls can wait until we get to the station. Let's walk. I want to see your friend."

We strode over to Shame's car. Shame radiated anger. He wasn't a Closer, and therefore shouldn't be taking anyone's memories away, but I didn't think that was going to stop him.

My phone rang. I answered before Stotts could tell me not to.

"This is Allie. Hi, Nola."

Hayden, on the other end, caught on quickly.

"Who's there with you?" he asked.

"I'm sorry. I know I didn't check in. I'm out with Stotts right now, as a matter of fact."

"The MERC cop?"

"Yes, I'm fine. I'm Hounding a job for a friend of mine, Shame. You remember Shame? Yes. It's an art thing here in the graveyard. Shame's into making these gargoyles look like they're alive. We kind of hit a magical snag. Shame's friend Terric pulled a hard Proxy. No, I think he'll be okay. Stotts is calling 911 right now." I raised my eyebrows at Stotts, who had already looked in the car and seen Terric passed out in the backseat. He gave me a curt nod and thumbed his phone.

"Did you close the well?"

"Yes. Now we're going to go down to the station and talk to Stotts about the legalities of Shame's art."

"I'll send someone to get you. We'll take care of Stotts."

"No, that's fine. I don't need you to check in on me later. I'll call you once it all gets straightened out."

"I don't care what you want. We'll be there. We'll take care of Stotts."

He hung up on me. The bastard. To keep from swearing, I laughed. "I know. Guess that's just the way it goes when you date a cop. Okay. Talk to you later. Bye."

Ass.

Shame was smoking, and throwing me angry looks. I know. Terric was hurt. The Veiled were loose. And Hayden hadn't sounded nearly as relaxed as the last time I'd called. I was pretty sure this wasn't the biggest problem on his hands right now.

The ambulance pulled up in literally a minute—lights, no siren. It helped that there was a station just a few streets away.

The EMTs asked a few questions, which Shame had all the answers to, including that Terric was allergic to penicillin, and that this was a Proxy problem, and that he probably needed a night's sleep and an aspirin and maybe a doctor who knew how to set a magical syphon.

They dragged the barely conscious Terric out of the car. He looked worse than when we'd put him in there. Shame wasn't kidding that Terric couldn't do Death and Blood magic. His color was off, he was shaking, and fever-incoherent.

The void stone wasn't on him. Shane had probably stashed it before he got out of the car. Boy was smart that way.

And angry. At me. He glared at me, still as a snake before a strike. If Terric was permanently hurt because of me trying to protect Stotts, he would never forgive me.

"Let's go," Stotts said.

Shame watched the ambulance drive off. Lights, no siren, which I took as a good sign. He flicked the cigarette to the ground, where it sputtered and died. Didn't move until the calliope slide of red and yellow lights coating gravestones, tree limbs, and angels was replaced by darkness again.

Stotts gave him a minute. I liked that about him. He really was a decent guy. Which was why I wasn't going to let him be used.

"Mr. Flynn." He opened the back door. "We'll retrieve your car later."

Shame stared up at the sky, took a deep breath, then shot me a look of pure hatred. "Maybe you should have stayed home." He got into the car, Stone tromping happily after him.

I walked around to the other door. I wasn't feeling all that well—a stomachache and fever, I thought. Fever was the beginning of that cold I'd given myself for the magic I'd been throwing around. Stomachache was the fear that I had just made a huge mistake.

# Chapter Eighteen

Stotts drove out of the graveyard. He didn't say anything. Neither did I. Shame was a broody shadow with dark, burning eyes that even the streetlights seemed to slide away from. I sat as far away from him as I could, my shoulder against the cold window.

Stone sat backward, his head against the rear window, clacking at the city.

It was late. The rush of adrenaline was gone, replaced by the sticky feeling of an oncoming flu. As soon as Stotts parked, I got out of the car. If I was going to throw up, I'd rather do it where there was lots of fresh air.

Shame and Stone got out and Stone trotted over next to me, pressing against my thigh and extending his wing up along my back like he had in death. Guess he could tell I wasn't feeling very well.

"Let's go," Stotts said. Half a dozen steps toward the station and Stone's ears pricked up. He growled toward a break between buildings, then took off at a gallop.

"Son of a bitch." Stotts jogged a few steps after him, but Stone was too fast and too quiet. Plus, he had functional wings that tipped the odds in his favor.

Stotts stormed back.

Rock, one. Angry cop, zero.

"Did you tell it to do that?" he asked Shame.

"No." He stood there, hunkered in his sweater like he was cold. Hurting was probably more like it. He'd pulled on a shitload of magic tonight too, and even if he'd sucked some of it down, and Proxied most of it to Hayden, what he'd done to keep Terric breathing and break Truance's spell had come at a price.

Stotts didn't seem to be in pain. The force had legal Proxies to bear their approved limit of magic usage.

"It will wind down soon," Shame said. "I'm sure someone will stumble across it."

I wanted to thank Shame for going along with this, for keeping our story straight, for helping me keep Stotts safe. But I was pretty sure he'd just flip me off.

Stotts pulled out his cell again, and told one of his crew—Garnet, I think—that he needed him to look into a magicked gargoyle on the loose. Took him a while to convince Garnet he wasn't joking. During this, he followed us up the stairs and through the doors into the station.

The lobby was empty except for a man pushing a soft, shaggy broom over the floor. Beyond the lobby people moved and phones rang.

Stotts didn't take us back to the normal offices. He opened a door to our left and started down the stairs. I expected to stop a flight down, at the wall that was really a door hidden by a powerful Illusion spell. I'd been through that door exactly once, the first time I'd met Detective Stotts.

"Keep going. Next landing," he said.

We clomped down another flight of stairs and stopped at a normal-looking door. I didn't touch it. I wasn't that stupid.

Stotts swiped a card and threw a nice little Trip spell that further unlocked or deactivated the mechanical, electrical, or maybe magical behind the door.

"Come in and shut the door behind you."

I walked in. Shame shut the door. The room was an office. Not fancy, but enough space for a desk, a couch that looked like it had been used as a bed more often than a couch, a small refrigerator, a few chairs, and shelves of file boxes. No windows. Wards so strong they stung my nose like I'd been snorting rubbing alcohol.

Shame's mood shifted from broody to carefully interested in the place.

"Have a seat." Stotts shrugged out of his coat and threw it over the back of a chair with a practiced aim. "Coffee?" He was across the room and in the corner where a coffeepot, microwave, sink, and refrigerator made up a small kitchenette.

"No," Shame said.

"Not me," I said.

He poured himself a cup. I picked a chair—vinyl, but padded and deep enough I could sink in it and lean my head on the back—which is exactly what I did.

Shame took the couch. Stuck his feet up on the coffee table between a couple empty Chinese food cartons and a stack of file folders. "Nice place," he said.

"Thank you. Used to be a storage room." He looked around the room, gesturing with the coffeepot at the rows of metal shelves and dust-covered boxes. "I think the upgrade is pretty nice." He clunked the pot back on its burner and drank as he walked over to his desk.

His chair squeaked when he sat. And I mean loudly. Squalled when he swiveled to face Shame and me.

"So. What were you three really doing in the graveyard?" He took another gulp of his coffee, shifted. Squealed.

Shame just gave him a slacker-boy stare.

"I was Hounding."

"Looking for the statue he stole?"

"He didn't steal it." That was true. I did. "Would you give the statue a rest? We were out there checking the signature of magic it threw. And then those other things, the ghost things, showed up. I thought there might be a leak in the network or something."

Thank you Magics History class. Leaks in the network was one of the old problems when copper lines were used instead of the superior lead, iron, and glass that now networked the city. The leaks had caused widespread hallucinations. Now that I knew about the Authority, I'd say what people had been seeing were not hallucinations.

"And you didn't call me?"

Oh, he was not going to use that tone of voice. "I'm a Hound. My job is to investigate magic being misused, *then* contact the police. You were second in line, Stotts. If there had been a crime behind the magic being used, I would have called."

He drank coffee, tried a different tack. "What did you find?"

Shame had his eyes closed, ignoring the entire conversation. No help there.

"I found those ghost things. There were a lot of them. I don't know how else to describe them."

"Uh-huh. And how did you know they were attracted to the disk?"

Shit.

"It was in the report Violet gave me."

Stotts leaned back, pulled a manila file off the shelf behind him. "This report?" He tossed it on his desk.

The tab said BECKSTROM ENTERPRISES.

"From your tone of voice, I'm going to say no. Not that report."

"Funny, she said she gave us a full disclosure on the disks. I don't recall her mentioning ghosts."

"I know what she told me. If you have a question about it, maybe you should ask her."

"Good idea." He screeched forward and pressed speed dial on his cell. "Anything you want to add, Mr. Flynn?"

"I didn't steal the gargoyle." He didn't open his eyes. "May I go now?"

"No."

"Then tell me what charge I'm being held on."

"Shame." I rubbed at my eyes. My hands trembled, my fingers felt like icicles. I was rocking a fever. And the burns from the Veiled were starting to sting.

"Listen, Allie," Shame said. "I get he's a friend of yours. But *your* friend just dragged me to the feckin' police station while *my* friend is in the hospital. I want to know what I'm being held for, or I am out that door."

"Theft, magical mischief, trespass, failure to Proxy in legal limits, destruction of property," Stotts intoned over the top of the cell.

Violet hadn't picked up yet. I hoped Kevin hung up on him.

"Then I want my phone call." Shame finally opened his eyes. He didn't look worried. Annoyed, yes.

Stotts' desk phone rang. He stared at it a second, then hung up his cell and squeaked over to answer the other phone.

"Stotts. Who?" Pause. "Interesting. Thank you." He hung up.

"You're both free to go." He took another drink of his coffee, watching us. "Don't leave town."

Okay, that was the fastest about-face ever. "Why are we free?"

And that was the dumbest thing I'd said all day. Don't argue with the nice policeman when he says you can go home, Beckstrom. But the fever, the night, the fight, everything was stacking up.

Shame didn't have any problem with the news. "Well, then. It's been lovely. Just. I'm sure I'll see you around, Detective." He was on his feet and walking toward the door.

I stood, feeling a little uncertain. Did I follow Shame or stay here and make sure Stotts didn't get Closed?

That was ridiculous. I couldn't babysit the policeman. I couldn't even protect him from the Authority if they really wanted to Close him. And unless I wanted to tell him all of their secrets so he could protect himself, I'd just have to hope I'd done enough to keep him safe.

"Who called?" I asked.

"Violet's lawyer. They're waiting for you outside." Stotts didn't stand. He didn't look any the worse for wear unless you counted the fingerprint burns on his neck.

"Where did you get the disk?" I asked.

"Found it out in St. Johns. Fully charged."

"That's strange," I said, and I meant it.

"Isn't it?"

I would have expected him to contact me to Hound it. But he hadn't. I felt like I'd somehow failed him. Like we were breaking up, choosing different teams, going our separate ways. "If you need a Hound, if you don't want me, you have the list and our contact information, right?"

"Yes."

"Davy's keeping an eye on the phones at the den."

"You're calling it the den now?"

I shrugged. "You can get hold of him anytime and he'll tell you who's available."

"That sounds like you're saying good-bye for good."

I tried to smile, didn't make it. "Of course not," I said. I walked across the room and out the door that Shame held open for me.

# Chapter Nineteen

Shame took the stairs like his shoes were on fire. I kept up, but was breathing hard by the time we made it to the lobby.

Shame kept walking.

"Shame, wait."

Wonders of wonders, he turned around. Stopped.

I huffed over to him.

"What's your hurry?"

"I hate police stations."

"From all that trouble you got into when you were a kid?"

He scowled. "No. You hate elevators. I hate cop shops."

"Allie?" A woman's voice called out. I knew that voice—Violet.

I looked back toward the regular offices and watched as she walked, slowly due to the girth of her belly, my way. On one side of her, looking like he was ready to catch her if she sneezed, was Kevin Cooper. Medium height, medium hair, medium everything, Kevin always faded into a crowd. If I didn't know him, I'd never guess he was a deadly good magic user. By the way he walked, quiet and respectful, and bodyguardish next to my dad's widow he just looked like an ordinary guy. He was not.

On the other side strode a happy-looking woman who

wasn't much taller than Violet. Her long dark hair was caught mid-escape from the clip that held it away from her face. She wore no makeup to disguise her clever brown eyes set in a round face. The bulky knee-length sweater over her business suit and skirt looked two sizes too large for her.

Melba Maide, Beckstrom Enterprises' highest-paid attorney. A tenacious litigator, she had a win-to-loss ratio that was bar none, and her jovial, even occasionally messy exterior hid piranhalike instincts. Behind her back when they were polite, they called her Sweet and Low, for how she clinched her arguments. In front of her back they always called her ma'am.

My dad had spoken highly of her. But then, he respected any woman who could bring him to his knees.

"Wow," Violet said. "Look at your hair."

I tucked my hair behind my ears. I hoped she was just talking about the streaks of white. "Hey." There. That brought my lame response quota up for the day. "How are you? What are you doing out of bed?"

"You were in trouble with the police. They were going to press charges. There is nothing that could keep me in bed."

Kevin shifted a little uncomfortably. I had a pretty good feeling he'd tried to do just that.

"You remember Melba?" Violet said.

I offered her my hand. "I do. Good to see you again." We shook.

"Nice to see you too, Allie. Although I prefer my socializing to happen before midnight." She laughed, a silly little giggle that somehow still felt genuine.

I couldn't help but smile, even though I knew the woman wouldn't think twice about carving my heart out and using it as a cup holder if I ever crossed her in a legal sort of way.

"Sorry about that. It was a misunderstanding. I was Hounding. Shame was with me. We ended up in the graveyard, and Detective Stotts got it in his head we were messing around with things."

Violet's eyebrows went up. "Theft, magical impropriety, illegal tapping, and Proxy don't sound like misunderstandings."

"Well, they were." I wanted to tell her more. That Stotts had a disk. That I'd told him she knew ghosts were attracted to it. That bad things were happening. But I couldn't say any of that with Melba around, because as far as I knew, Melba wasn't a part of the Authority.

I'd asked for a list of names once. They wouldn't give it to me. Afraid it would fall into the wrong hands. I didn't need it in my hands—I just wanted to at least read it once so I'd know when to keep my mouth shut.

I glanced at Kevin. He gave me an odd look. Like there was a spider crawling on my face, but he was too polite to mention it to me.

Okay, whatever.

"So do I need to fill out any paperwork? Go to any hearings?" I asked.

Melba shook her head, freeing a bobby pin that clattered on the floor. "You just need to go home, get some sleep, and stay away from the graveyard and people who get you into trouble." She chuckled again. "And if you are going to get into trouble, at least do something that's challenging. This almost wasn't worth leaving my bowl of ice cream for. Good night, Violet."

" 'Night, Melba. Thank you. Sorry to get you up so late."

"Oh, you know I'd pout if I couldn't come out and play. It's been fun. Stay out of trouble, Allie."

"I'll do my best."

Melba strode off, leaving a trail of bobby pins behind. She paused for a second to say something to Shame.

Whoa. Maybe she *was* a part of the Authority.

"So what really happened?" Violet asked.

"Not here," I said.

She glanced over at Shame. He was on his cell. I tried to catch what he was saying, but he was fumbling with putting a cigarette in his mouth, which was a perfect cover to keep me from both reading his lips and hearing his words.

Maybe Hayden? Maeve?

"How about we go out to my car?" Violet asked. "We'll take you home."

"Could you take me back out to the graveyard instead?"

"Allie, never return to the scene of crime," Violet chided.

"I'm not. Shame's car is there. I want to get it back for him."

"We can do that," Kevin said.

By the time we walked over to Shame, who was only a few feet away, he had hung up his phone and pocketed it.

"Give you a lift to your car," Kevin said.

"Thanks. You coming?" he asked me.

"Yes?"

"We're all going," Violet announced. She started off toward the doors at a purposeful waddle. She buttoned her coat—a nice heavy wool in lime green—and Kevin held the door open, letting her walk through.

I followed. Shame avoided eye contact and lagged behind. I didn't know why. He'd practically sprinted to get out of here before.

Violet's car was down a block and a half. Kevin strolled along like he wasn't paying particular attention to every shadow, rustle, and movement around us, except I knew he was. Shame, behind me, smoked. I just kept walking and wishing I didn't feel like hell. I should have asked Violet for an aspirin.

Kevin held the front door for Violet; Shame and I took the backseat. Shame left the door propped open, one boot out on the concrete, and sucked the flame out of the cig. He exhaled smoke in a thin stream, then put his foot in the car and shut the door.

He still looked like he was hurting. I wondered if he was feeling Terric's pain. They'd used magic together, Blood magic, Death magic. Maybe they were tied together even closer now.

Shame leaned his elbow on the doorframe, closed his eyes again, and rested his head in his hand. Kevin eased into traffic.

"Does it have something to do with Daniel?" Violet asked.

Since Shame wasn't talking, I did. "Not directly. It's about the disks. Stotts recovered one of the stolen disks."

"He called earlier today to tell me he found it in the St. Johns area," she said. "I was going to examine it tomorrow."

Okay, good. She knew that much.

"He had it with him in the graveyard." I said. "And I told him it attracts ghosts."

Kevin shot me a warning look in the rearview mirror.

"Why would you tell him such a thing?" she asked.

"Because it's true," I said holding eye contact with Kevin. He rolled his eyes and looked away.

From where I was sitting, I saw Violet in profile. She didn't look surprised, just resigned. "Is that what happened tonight? Ghosts?"

"Part of it. I told Stotts you knew about the disks attracting ghosts and he's going to ask you if that's true. I'd like you to say it is."

"Allie, you're not asking me to lie."

"I'm asking you to back me up on this one thing."

"Ghosts."

"Yes."

"I don't believe in ghosts. I'm a scientist."

"Okay, then it might not be ghosts, but there is something, maybe a magical interference, or an echo of spells clashing, or swamp gas or *something* that is very interested in the disks. And it can hurt. See?" I pushed my collar down to reveal the finger burns.

She flicked on the overhead light, and I moved so she could see without having to twist much.

"Those are from ghosts?"

"They're from whatever attacked Stotts and me back in the graveyard. If you think I'm lying, ask Stotts to let you see his burns."

She frowned. "Document this for me, please. With pictures of the burns. I haven't seen anything like that before."

It wasn't a promise that she would go with my ghost story, but at least she wouldn't completely brush it off. That was as good as I was going to get.

The truth was, the Veiled hadn't been interested in the disks before the wild-magic storm. I wondered if channeling the wild-magic had changed the disks somehow. Violet was the expert in the technologies. She might know.

"Did you work any kind of safeties into the disk? In case of overload or tampering?"

"They are still in the developmental stages. We never expected them to be outside the lab. But I have a redesign in mind that will be implemented in the next version. Ways to make sure only certified users can access the magic."

"Passwords?"

"Much more than that."

Kevin glanced at me in the mirror again. From that look I could tell he'd had some input on safety measures. Well, good. The Authority had done a pretty good job of keeping the most dangerous disciplines of magic out of people's hands. Hopefully he had used some of those techniques to put safeties on the disks.

"What about wild magic?" I asked.

"The disks aren't affected by it."

"Not even if they're directly hit?"

"Difficult to reproduce in a laboratory experiment, but let's assume a disk were . . . strapped to a storm rod that just happened to be hit by wild magic. . . . " She frowned. "I don't know. There is always, I suppose, a possibility that the disk could be reglyphed under strong enough force." She paused, the corner of her eyes tightening as she worked through the calculations. "The price to reglyph, to actually rewrite a disk would be . . . deadly. I suppose it's possible, but not at all practical. But if it were hit by a storm, maybe."

She shifted in her seat a little, pulling the seat belt into a better position. "If the conditions were right, wild magic might override the magic and glyphwork in the disk, and might re-create the paths of magic the disk holds. It's a sobering thought."

A disk had been changed or reglyphed to make Greyson half man, half beast. I could only assume people had died to pay that price. And Frank Gordon, the man we were pretty sure had turned Greyson into a Necromorph and had gotten me possessed by my dad, was dead now too.

Kevin drove through the graveyard. We weren't far from the gate when Stotts had found us. Shame's car was still there.

Shame opened his eyes, rubbed his face, dragging his hair out of the way. "This is it. Thanks to the both of you. I appreciate you bailing me out and going out of your way. Good night, Mr. Cooper, Mrs. Beckstrom." He got out, shut the door, and headed to his car.

Ditched me. He ditched me.

"Do you want us to take you home?" Violet asked. She had pivoted as much as her belly allowed. She glanced at Shame, then back at me, curious. Like she was trying to figure out what was really going on between Shame and me.

Welcome to the club.

"No, I think. Um, I think I need to—" I looked out,

watched Shame peer into the backseat of the car before he opened the driver's-side door.

"Tell me how I can help," she said.

My heart leaped at those words. I felt like I'd been holding up, holding tough for about a century and a half, dealing with all these life-or-death decisions, literally, alone. Zay wasn't talking to me much. Shame wasn't talking to me now either. I couldn't tell Nola or anyone else my troubles, because I'd be putting them at risk of being Closed no matter what I said. I was feeling pretty damn lost right about now. It wanted to tell her I just needed a couch for a night, a few hours of peace, a solid week of sleep.

I considered it for a moment, then went with logic. Where should I be right now? Back with the Authority, telling them about what had happened with the well. And with Stotts.

"I think I need to go check on Zay. Get some sleep and get rid of this headache. Could you take me to the inn over in Vancouver?"

"Of course," Violet said.

"It's late," Kevin said.

She frowned. "We're not going to call her a cab. We're taking her."

"Violet. You hired me to keep you safe."

"Safe doesn't mean smothered."

He didn't look at her, but didn't say anything either. Finally, he nodded. "That's true."

Wow. I was seriously impressed with his ability to not escalate this into a fight. Took a big man to swallow his pride. The steering wheel, however, looked like it was bending inward from his grip.

"We'll take you," Violet said. "It's not that far out of the way."

Actually, it was completely out of their way, and now I felt bad asking them for the ride.

My door flew open. Shame stood there.

"So are you coming or what?" he asked.

I looked at Violet. She frowned. Nodded. "That makes sense if you're comfortable going with him. I am a little tired."

Half of the tension drained out of Kevin and the steering wheel flexed back to round.

"Thanks," I said. "For everything. I'll call you soon. Take care of that baby, okay?"

Violet smiled. "Planning on it."

And then I was out of the car, in the cold air, and hoping Shame's heater was going full blast.

# Chapter Twenty

"Are you okay?" I asked as soon as Shame had started the car.

He sighed. "Let's not talk. I don't like you much right now."

"I know. I have a knack for pissing men off tonight."

"Stotts and me?"

"And Kevin and Zay."

"Zay? Did you talk to him? Did he wake up?"

I was an idiot. I'd been so wrapped up in everything else, I hadn't even told Shame his best friend had regained consciousness.

"He woke up."

"Was he talking? Did he know who you were?"

"Yes. Things were going fine. I was trying to fill him in on what had been going on, and then I told him I'd brought him back from death and he didn't want to talk anymore."

"He finally regains consciousness after being dead and you have a fight?"

"It wasn't a fight. He just needs some time. To think things through. To deal with what's happened." To get over the fact that I went into death and brought him back.

I rubbed at my forehead. My headache was behind my eyes, sinus pressure and a sore throat. I hoped the cold symptoms would pass soon.

"He would have done the same," I mumbled against my palms. "He would have gone into death after me."

"That's not what it's about," Shame said. "It's about love."

"I think it's about pride."

"No. When you hurt someone you care about, when you break them. . . . " He swallowed hard.

I waited. Finally, "You get angry?"

"You wonder if you can . . . care enough to find a way to let go of them. So you won't hurt them again. So you won't destroy them."

"That's called sacrifice," I said.

"That's called caring."

"How's that been working for you and Terric?"

"Jesus," he said with no heat. Then, "Not well, really. My life was miserable without him, and it's not so hot with him here either. At least you and Zay have the kind of thing that ends up with wedding rings attached to it. And you know, babies. Terric and me? Matching restraining orders. Maybe simultaneous murder charges."

I thought he was wrong about that. But him bringing up Zay and wedding rings and babies—things I hadn't even taken the time to think about—made me want to change the subject fast. "I would really love to change the subject," I said.

"Thank God. See the Blazers game the other night? Double overtime. I lost a fortune to Hayden. Speaking of, call him, won't you? Tell him I'm going to drop you off and we'll be there in about ten."

I dialed. "Where are you going?"

"To spring Terric."

"Shame, you can't march into a hospital and break him out without clearing it with the doctors."

He didn't say anything.

"Shame?" I said.

"Hello?" Hayden asked.

"Say hello to the nice man," Shame said.

I rolled my eyes. Bad idea. Headache. "This is Allie. Violet and her lawyer got Shame and me out. We're headed to the inn, but Shame's going to go check on Terric in the hospital. Tell him staging a prison break is a bad idea."

"Terric's already out. He's on his way here."

"Is he all right?"

"He says so. Dr. Fisher will look at him when he gets here. How long until you arrive?"

"About ten minutes."

"Good. Don't get arrested between now and then, hear?" He hung up.

"What did he say?" Shame asked.

"Terric's okay. He's been released from the hospital and will meet us at the inn."

"Hmm."

"Also, we are not to be apprehended by the law before we get there."

"Why do you think I'm driving?"

I leaned my head back and shut my eyes. Tried my best to relax, to meditate. Only ended up falling asleep, which was probably for the best anyway.

I snorted awake when Shame parked.

We were at the inn. I had the sleep-shakes. I was craving sleep something fierce and ten minutes of shut-eye hadn't done it for me. I needed sleep. Big squishy bunches of it. Soon.

The night was quiet with the kind of stillness that made you feel like everything was holding its breath for dawn. We walked up the front steps and wandered in, even though the porch light was off and the CLOSED sign hung in the window.

The wards were in full force, and I tasted the slick Earl Grey tea of Victor's handiwork as I stepped across the threshold.

Inside, lamps scattered among the tables cast lemon yellow circles of light throughout the main room. Victor, Hayden, Maeve sat at one table, talking quietly, coffee cups at their elbows and a map spread out between them.

Sunny and the three Georgia sisters were in the middle of a card game, and Joshua and Nik leaned chairs against the wall, feet propped on spare chairs, arms folded over their chests, catching some sleep. I didn't see the twins, or Dr. Fisher. Maeve looked up.

"Good, you're here." She motioned both Shame and me over. "Are you all right?"

"I'm good," I said. "Tired."

"Shame?"

"Fantastic. I'd like two of these kinds of days every week." He pulled out a spare chair and slouched down in it. "What's the news?"

Victor rubbed his hand over his hair and pushed back from the table. "Assuming you were able to cap the Winter well?"

Shame nodded. "We did. Terric did."

"Then we have one well capped, and so far, the other wells have not come under attack. We have closed over twenty gates tonight—"

Shame whistled softly.

Victor acknowledged that with a nod. "—and at this time are enjoying what appears to be an entire hour without either an arrest, a gate, the Hungers, the Veiled, or anything else happening."

No wonder everyone looked exhausted.

"We think there are more living Veiled on the streets than just Truance and the man you ran into."

I covered my yawn with one hand. "What about the networks? At the graveyard, the Veiled were drinking down the magic over the well. They could do that to the networked lines in the city, right?"

"Your father was very specific about how he created the wards and safeties built into the networked lines. He was aware of the Veiled, and Hungers, and other things that sometimes enter our world. The networks are guarded against them."

"He didn't put safeties in place to keep the dead from draining the disks," I said.

"How do you know?" Hayden asked.

"I asked Violet about it tonight. She said they never thought anyone would try to reglyph the disks. She's redesigning them so there are safeguards in the future. I think Kevin's helping her with that."

"That's good to know," Victor said. "I don't think the Veiled can drain the networks."

"They can drain the wells," I said. "Truance was at the well. She stabbed Terric."

Everyone looked at Shame. He crossed his arms over his chest and stared at his shoes.

"She used Blood magic on him, but Shame canceled the glyph before he was taken to the hospital."

Victor rubbed at his already bloodshot eyes. "What happened to Truance?"

"She disappeared."

"Unfortunate. If what Truance told you is true, the Veiled who have disks are looking for a way to recharge them. The wells make the perfect target. We're considering capping the other wells if necessary. I'd rather just take care of the Veiled and reclaim the disks before it comes to that."

"There's an approved way of taking care of the Veiled?" I asked around another yawn.

"Death magic is best."

I glanced at Shame. He'd used Death magic to kill that guy on the street. I didn't think he used Death magic in the graveyard. I was positive there was no way in hell I could drink someone down to dust. I didn't know how many of the others here could use Death magic. Maeve specialized in Blood magic, and most everyone else was a Closer—Faith magic.

"We doing this now?" Shame sounded as tired as I felt.

"Not until tomorrow, maybe even tomorrow night, if all goes well," Maeve said. "We need to rest. Sleep. Including you."

"Thought you'd never ask." He heaved up onto his feet. "Good night all. I assume someone will have a dangerous and daring plan in place by morning?"

"We're laying it out now," Victor said.

"Save a good part for me." He rolled his shoulders and shuffled across the room, aiming for the hall that led to the rooms above.

The outside door opened. Shame stopped. Turned.

Terric walked through the door. Carl and his twin sister, La, were right behind him. Terric paused, took in the people gathered, his gaze resting the longest on Shame.

Shame took a couple steps toward Terric, pure relief on his face.

Terric smiled slightly.

Shame smiled back.

Then Shame seemed to notice that everyone in the room was paying attention to the two of them. That connection, too tenuous to begin with, broke under the weight of scrutiny. He scowled and stalked away down the hall.

Terric's smile fell, and he suddenly looked tired and sick.

Shame had said sometimes you have to love someone enough to let go of them so you don't hurt them anymore.

I didn't think he understood how much he was hurting Terric by pushing him away.

"Are we going to do anything about the two of them?" Victor asked quietly.

"There isn't anything to do," Maeve said. "Shamus refuses to take the test to see if they are Soul Complements, and at the moment there aren't nearly enough of us to administer the test correctly."

"We could send Terric back to Seattle," Hayden said.

Maeve's mouth pressed into a thin line. Finally: "That has to be Terric's choice."

Terric walked the rest of the way into the room and, catching my gaze, headed my way. I met him halfway.

"How are you feeling?" I asked.

"Not great. You?"

"Could sleep a century away."

He glanced at the hallway Shame has disappeared down.

"He's worried about you," I said.

"I know."

"He's worried he's going to hurt you."

"I know."

"That's why he's pushing you away."

Terric shook his head. "Is that what he told you?"

"Yes."

"He's lying. It's not about me. It's about him. Shame isn't worried he's going to hurt me. He's terrified he might *like* me, and then he'll have to deal with what that says about him. He can be such a selfish ass." He took a breath that set him off in a spectacular coughing fit.

I put my hand on his elbow, and helped him over to a chair. Or rather we both managed to get him to a chair without falling down.

"Do you need water?" I asked.

He shook his head, still coughing. His eyes were

squeezed tight, tears at the corners, arm pressed against his ribs like he was trying to keep his guts in place.

Maeve appeared beside me. "Be easy, Terric." She gently brushed her fingers over his forehead, and his coughing eased, giving him time to breathe.

"I wish I knew how to do that," I said.

Maeve smiled over at me. "I'll show you someday."

"You going to be okay?" I asked Terric.

Dr. Fisher walked in from the kitchen area, and made a beeline straight for him.

"He'll be fine," Maeve said. "Get some sleep."

Terric nodded, and drank the water Sunny offered him. I stepped back to make room for the doctor. I figured he didn't need four women fussing over him.

"Nice work out there," I said. "You deserve a medal for what you did tonight."

Dr. Fisher was already drawing a Sight glyph—one of the medical versions that gave you a better look inside a body.

Terric winced a little. "Just doing my job. That's all," he croaked.

It was a lot more than his job. He had put himself in danger, dealt with debilitating pain to use Blood magic and Death magic—was probably still paying the price now—and been stabbed by a lunatic undead Veiled to keep me and Shame safe.

I slogged my way down the hall and up the stairs. I didn't have to sleep in the same room as Zay. There were a dozen other rooms on this level, more below, more above. But my feet, my heart, took me straight to his door.

Stupid feet.

I crept inside, not wanting to wake him. Not wanting to fight with him. Not wanting to make him worry. All I wanted was to pretend that we were okay. That he was alive and well, I was alive and well.

Zay wasn't in his bed. He was, however, in the bed I'd been in. Looked like he'd gotten there himself, too. The covers on the other bed were hanging down to the floor, and the machine he'd had hooked up to him was turned off, but not pushed against the wall or moved to some other storage place. He didn't have an IV or oxygen tube. He was on his side, the extra pillow dragged from the other bed and now stuffed under his head. He faced the door and was snoring lightly. He'd taken my shirt I'd left on the bed and held it against his heart.

For an infuriating man, he sure looked good sleeping.

I slid out of my shoes and socks and took off my coat. Used the bathroom and then walked back out into the room. Should I take his bed?

Everything in me didn't want to lie down where he had been so hurt, so close to death. I hoped he was on for some serious spooning. The bed almost wasn't wide enough for him.

I wanted to strip naked, but didn't know who would walk in, or how fast I might need to be ready in the morning. So I unbuttoned and unzipped my jeans and pulled my bra off without taking off his sweater. Then I crawled into bed behind Zay. I pressed my forehead against the hollow of his shoulder blades, one arm around his ribs.

He smelled so good.

His breathing paused. He inhaled deeply, his muscles relaxing even more. Touching him, holding him, made me feel like I was sinking into deep, warm water. Made me feel like I was finally where I belonged. Home. Before he could exhale, I was out.

## Chapter Twenty-one

I dreamed of sitting on the plush couch in my father's living room in the condo where I'd grown up.

"More coffee?" Dad asked.

Dad looked like he always looked—suit, tie, gray hair. But he was holding my red coffee carafe, the one Nola had given me. I loved that carafe.

I glanced at the cup in my hand. Empty. "Sure." I held out the cup.

"You're dreaming, you know," he said as a stream of mahogany-colored coffee filled the cup with that happy rising gurgle, the rich, deep, earthy scent hitting my nose.

"It's nice so far. That's not going to last, is it?"

He sat in the chair across from me. "I doubt it. But why not have a drink first?" His chair was close enough that if I wanted, I could touch him without having to scoot forward. He had a coffee cup now too, and took a drink.

I sipped. The coffee filled my mouth and burned warm and soft in my chest, soothing the hole where my magic used to be. It was delicious. Comforting. And nothing I'd ever expect from my dad.

"I'm having a hard time remembering all the reasons I'm angry at you," I said. "But I know I'm angry."

"It's been a complicated few months." He tugged at his

tie with one hand, loosening the knot there, then unbuttoned the first button at his collar.

"Since I can't seem to talk to you when you're awake, I thought this might be a good way for us to come to an . . . understanding."

That sounded bad. Dad's "understandings" always involved the other party capitulating to his desires. I drank coffee because I was pretty sure I'd be throwing whatever was left of it in his face in a minute.

"I have been reluctant to allow you to be aware of all the forces at work. Those who want magic, and why. But it is clear to me that our survival—both yours and mine—will be dictated by how well you and I can work together."

"So we're screwed?"

He smiled. Wow, I hadn't seen him smile in ages.

"No. There are always options. Careful thinking and careful actions see to that. But we are coming to an important crossroads. You remember we walked through death."

It wasn't a question, but still, it took me a minute. Then I did remember. Not clearly, but my dad was there and Stone and the monstrous Veiled. I had been looking for Zay. And I'd found him trapped by Mikhail.

"I remember."

"And you discovered that Mikhail and I, at this time, have complementary agendas."

"You mean you're on the same side of the war."

"Yes. But we have different motivations. I am seeking to put magic in the right hands."

"And to live forever," I said.

"Yes. And immortality." He said it like I'd reminded him he was wearing shoes. "To do so, I have made alliances."

"Mikhail. Who tried to kill us when Zay and I were testing. Who trapped Zayvion, and made me give my magic up to him and tried to kill Sedra. That Mikhail?"

"Mostly. He will have his revenge, Allie. Over those who betrayed him and sent him into death. I have no say in that."

"And you'll have your revenge too?"

He flashed me a hard smile. "There is a reason why we have similar agendas."

"So the same people who killed you killed him? That doesn't make any sense. James Hoskil was behind your death. And Greyson—but Greyson was a part of the Authority and James wasn't." My head hurt. I was having a hard time keeping my thinking on a linear path. Dreams could be so confusing. Or maybe it was just my life that was confusing.

"They were hands to the one who wanted us dead. Pawns. Both of them. That is all."

"Then who? Who wanted Mikhail dead and you dead? And why? And how do I know you're telling the truth anyway?"

"Even in your own mind, your own dreams, you doubt me?"

"We've been over that, but in case you need to hear it again—yes."

"Sedra killed Mikhail."

His words were like cold water. Cold, confusing water. Sedra was the head of the Authority. She made all the final decisions on magic and had stepped up as the head of the Authority after Mikhail's death. "I thought Dane Lannister shoved him through a gate because he was trying to kill her."

"That is what Sedra convinced Dane of. It's not true. Mikhail wasn't experimenting with dark magic, he was trying to join dark and light magic. He was trying to heal magic. Sedra killed him for it."

"Why?"

"Because he succeeded. On a very small level, within

Wards and Containments, he rejoined light and dark magic."

"How do you know?"

"I was there."

Okay. Even in my dream, I knew this was big. Important.

"And you never told anyone?"

"I did. They didn't believe me. Not even with a Truth spell." He smiled ruefully. "I am certain she is the one who sent Greyson to kill me."

For all that I did not like my dad, I was angry he had been killed. And right on top of that anger was my uncomfortable belief that he was the kind of man who might have done something that justified his murder.

"I was in her way. My technology was in her way, so she killed me. And now you are in her way."

"Well, she's been kidnapped, so I don't see how she can do anything to me. I think you might be worried about this because you're in my head. If I die, you die."

"That's a part of it, of course. But even if you . . . fell . . . I would find a way to see my agenda is accomplished."

And there it was. My pragmatic, coldhearted father's idea of love.

"Go to hell," I said without heat. "Get out of my dream. I want to wake up now."

"I don't want you harmed. Not because it would be inconvenient to me, but because you are my daughter and I have always cared about you."

It was as close to saying he loved me as I'd ever heard. And I still didn't buy it.

He threw his hands open and looked up at the vaulted ceiling. "Impossible. You are impossible."

"I want to wake up now," I said again.

"You need to trust me. I am asking, *asking* you to trust me. It is too difficult to draw upon magic. I am tired." It sounded like he had a hard time getting those words out of his throat. "I need you to stop fighting when I use magic through you. You could have been killed by Truance. And she isn't nearly the most dangerous enemy out there. The Veiled have bodies. They're the walking undead, and they're using my disks to do it. If they find a way to recharge the disks, they will tear the Authority, this city, and the world apart. And *they don't pay any price to use magic.* None. I need you to trust that when I use magic, I am doing it to keep you safe."

"Trust? If you want my trust you might want to try not lying to me, not trading away parts of my soul when it suits you. And not possessing me. This is over. As soon as I can find a way to get you out of my head, permanently, I am going to do so."

I watched as his expression closed down harder and harder until the man in front of me might well have been made out of steel. "You know your hatred won't stop me."

"My hatred doesn't have to stop you. *I'll* stop you. Cancel you. Cripple you. Send you back to death and make you stay there."

We glared at each other for what seemed a long time, and a million thoughts rushed through my head. Of Zayvion trapped in death, of saving Stotts, of Davy and Shame and Terric, and Violet. I'd been strong enough for all of them. I didn't know how I was going to stand up to my dad since he was, literally, a part of me. But I was plenty strong enough to find a way.

In dreams, we shared thoughts too easily. I know he had heard some of that. I ignored what he might be thinking. I did not want to be any closer to him than I already was.

He finally looked away, out the windows I knew faced the mountain. It was dark out, night in this dream. I didn't know what he saw there. "There is something I want to give you. A gift. Even if you will not give me your trust."

He stood. Walked toward the door that should lead to the kitchen. He opened the door.

And my mother stepped through.

Or rather, a memory of her. She wore jeans and a white T-shirt. Young, maybe in her twenties. I had forgotten how much red streaked her dark brown hair. I had forgotten the hazel-gray of her eyes. And then I was little again, laughing as she and I folded bright small pieces of paper into origami creatures.

"It's a crane," she said in a voice that meant love, safety, and the world to me. "See how the wings make it fly?" She helped me hold the front of the origami figure, and showed me how to gently pull the tail so the crane's wings moved.

"And if you fold a thousand of them, they will bring you peace, or a wish come true."

"That's going to take a long time," I said, looking at the stacks of paper peeking out from the pretty envelopes on the table.

"If it's something you really want, then it's worth giving up something to do it, right? This will just cost some time. Time is easy. All you have to do is start with one. What color? Pink? Yellow?"

"Red," I said, because it was her favorite color.

We found a red square with gold swirls on it. It wasn't easy remembering every fold, but Mom patiently helped me make each crease clean and straight.

"What are my girls up to tonight?" Dad asked.

He wore a black turtleneck and jeans, which seemed strange for a minute, until I remembered he always wore that on the weekend. In his hand was a wooden box the size of a shoe box, which he put down on the table. Across the lid, written in his clean, blocky print, was ALLISON ANGEL BECKSTROM'S BOX OF DREAMS.

He had made this for me, and it was my favorite keepsake holder.

"Cranes for wishes." I proudly held up the red crane.

"Very nice. Is that your first one?"

I nodded. "The next one is going to be blue." Because blue was his favorite color. "I'm going to make a thousand of them."

He was standing behind Mom's chair now, his hand on her shoulder, her hand over his. She always smiled more when he was here with us. I wondered if I should wish for him not to work so much and spend more time with Mom.

"One thousand and her wish comes true," Mom said.

"What are you going to wish for, Allison?"

I smiled. "If I tell you it won't come true."

"You never know." He took the seat next to Mom and selected a piece of paper with crushed flower petals worked into it. "I'm pretty good at making wishes come true."

Mom chuckled. "You are, indeed."

He made the first clean diagonal fold in the paper. Mom leaned over and kissed him on the corner of his mouth.

And then the dream was over.

"Wake up, Beckstrom."

I opened my eyes. The room was still dark, no morning light filtering in through the blinds. I'd been asleep, what? Minutes?

I pushed up and away from Zay. My right hand and the side of my chin were asleep from lying with my hand stuck under my face.

At the bottom of the bed stood Pike.

"Pike?"

"They're coming."

"Who?" I sat up the rest of the way and got out of bed,

looking for my bra and shoes, the last ribbons of the dream drifting away from me.

"The dead. They've found disks, and found a way to use them to be solid. Alive." He said the last word like it was one of his deepest desires.

"How many? How close?" The clock said it was four o'clock. I'd gotten about three hours of sleep. Didn't matter. When a ghost shows up and tells you you're about to get your ass kicked, it's time to be moving. At least my cold symptoms were gone.

"An army of dead. Seven solid dead lead it. I've never seen them, not when they were alive. But they're strong." He shook his head. "Strong enough that it's not easy to walk away. Away from them. And their promises."

"Why did you?" I turned my back to Pike so I could put on my bra. Yes, he was dead. Didn't mean he didn't have eyes.

"Because there isn't any promise that good, that's real. I might be dead. I'm not gullible."

I turned back around. "They're coming here? Do you know why?"

"There's disks here. Somewhere. And a well of magic." He looked toward the door like he could see through it. "They'll have them, Allie. Even if it means destroying every last room in this place, drinking down every last drop of magic, and killing every last person."

"Aren't you a cheery guy this morning? Any idea when they'll be here? Any idea how to stop them?"

He shook his head. "Time's a bitch from this perspective. I'm no help there."

"Weaknesses?" I found my shoes, shoved my feet into them. Where did I leave Zay's katana? Found it by the dresser.

He shook his head. "The solid ones are powered by the disks. They use magic like it doesn't hurt."

I frowned. That sounded familiar to me. Someone had recently told me that. A dream?

"So get rid of the disk, get rid of the undead magic user?" I said.

"Maybe. Something happens when they take those disks on. They become . . . more."

"How about a specific?" I was done dressing, and walked past Pike to get my coat. I passed near enough that I felt the icy chill of his presence. I didn't think I'd ever get used to that.

"Dead eyes see the world differently," he said. "See the magic running through it. For the most part. When those deaders take on a disk, it's like magic, all kinds of different magics, fill them up in a sort of chaotic way. Like a wild storm. It powers them."

"Are the different kinds of magic like darkness and light?"

"That's right. I hadn't thought of it that way."

Which he wouldn't have. The idea of dark magic wasn't known to the living except for members of the Authority. I glanced over at Zay. Wonders of wonders, he was still asleep. Even if he couldn't hear Pike, I wasn't exactly whispering.

"Anything else I should know?" I asked a little more quietly.

"That's it. Except one thing. I think you're possessed."

"Old news."

"Huh. Anyone I know?"

"My dad. It's a family issue I'm working on. I'll go tell the others about our visitors. Pike?"

He raised an eyebrow.

"Keep an eye on the Hounds for me, would you?"

That got half a smile out of him. "I'm retired, Beckstrom. That's your job now. This dog don't hunt and he sure as hell don't babysit no more."

"You'll never retire." I opened the door. "Even death can't keep you out of the good fight."

"Don't know if it's a good fight," he said. "But it's a fight."

I glanced over my shoulder. He was gone. I walked around to the front of the bed and drew my fingers across Zayvion's bare arm. "You stay here, Jones. We got this." I bent and kissed his lips. His mouth opened slightly and he sleepily kissed me back. He was deeply asleep, but still knew he was being kissed.

I pulled away and smiled. Warmth flushed down my chest, covering the cold lump where my magic used to be. It felt so good to know he was alive and not in a coma. I was proud of him for holding on. And I was pretty damn proud of myself too.

I draped the katana over my shoulder and strode to the door, still smiling. Time to get to work.

# Chapter Twenty-two

I didn't need to be a Hound to know where everyone was in the inn. But I wanted to first tell Maeve and Victor and Hayden what I knew. Down two flights of stairs, my fingertips brushing over the wood that had been shaped and smoothed by a hundred years of hands passing over it.

No one was in the main room. The cards had been put away, the tables arranged like they were waiting for breakfast, white tablecloths straight and clean, chairs gathered around. The only thing that showed it was not an average day was that by now the cooks and Maeve would normally be back in the kitchen, busy baking.

The front door remained locked, and I had the feeling Maeve had shut the place down for the day.

Smart.

I walked through the main room and into the hallway, through the kitchen, to the private stairs. Maeve's living quarters took nearly a third of the top of the building. She and her husband had lived here while running the restaurant, while raising Shamus, while guarding the well. I'd been to her "home" only once before, and had been struck by its simplicity, its warmth, and the very normal, nonmagical mementos that covered the walls and filled the shelves.

Plus, the framed pictures of Shame as a kid were adorable, and had given me months worth of fodder for teasing.

I stopped at the wooden door at the top of the stairs. There was a little bench on one side with a pair of shoes beneath it, and a hook for hats or coats or umbrellas on the other side. I knocked. Worried for a minute that no one would hear me, then heard footsteps approach.

The lock turned. The door opened. Hayden stood there, his hair stuck up on one side. He was shirtless, which showed off his build—muscled like an ox, not nearly as soft as I'd assumed, pale, except for the black hair covering his chest and running a thick line down his stomach to his jeans, which were unbuttoned.

"Want me to turn around so you can check out the bumper?"

Yes, I blushed. "The Veiled are coming."

That wiped the smirk off of his face.

"Tell me." He opened the door the rest of the way and I walked into Maeve's cozy living room. A rumpled blanket and pillow were on the couch and Hayden's boots were on the floor. Huh. So he and Maeve weren't sleeping together.

He walked down a hall, tapped on a door, opened it.

"Allie's here, says the Veiled are coming." Then he was back in the living room, stopping by a bookshelf filled with books and other interesting bits and pieces. "You wake anyone else?"

"Not yet."

"Don't bother." He picked out a stone that looked like a thunder egg and placed it in a niche in the shelf that was actually a notch in the wall.

I felt a wash of warmth brush past me like a summer breeze. I smelled roses.

Magic. Gentle, and sweet. I'd been dealing with so much pain and dark magic, I'd forgotten how clean and lovely magic could be.

"What was that?" I asked.

"Sets off a series of glyphs worked into the inn. Turns on

the lights in all the rooms occupied by a magic user. Lets them know we need everyone front and center."

"And you know this because . . . ?"

He strolled to the couch, sat, and started putting on his boots. "I've known Maeve and Hugh for a long time. Used to spend winters here, when I could. Had my hand in most of the remodeling and renovating they did back in the day."

Hugh was Shame's dad. Sometimes I forgot how much magic, at least the hidden ways of magic the Authority used, was held among a small circle of people.

"How do you know about the Veiled?" he asked.

"My friend Pike told me."

Hayden shrugged into his thermal undershirt and pulled a flannel shirt over that. "Do I know him?"

"Probably not. He's dead."

Hayden didn't miss a beat. "Which is why he knows about the Veiled."

"He used to be a Hound."

"That's right. I remember now. He say when they're going to hit and how many?"

Maeve walked into the room. She was still using a cane, her limp more prominent than the last time I'd seen her. But instead of a loose skirt, she wore brown leather pants tucked into over-the-knee boots, her daggers in the tops of her boots and at both hips. Ready for a fight.

"What's the situation?" she asked. "Talk while we walk."

I followed Hayden out the door. Maeve shut the door behind us and whispered something in a language that was not English—maybe Gaelic? I felt the Novocain tingle of a Ward flaring to life and locking down not only the door but this entire part of the floor.

"Pike," I said, "told me the Veiled are coming this way. Seven Veiled. Solid, using the disks. And an army of other Veiled."

"Did Pike know why they were coming here?"

"To get the rest of the disks."

Maeve's eyebrows lifted. "I see. Let's fill everyone in and prepare."

Hayden walked down the stairs, his height and bulk blocking my view. Maeve, though a little slower, kept up pretty well.

I hoped someone had a big old Veiled sucking device that would mow through them, reclaim the disks, and end this.

Everyone was gathered in the main room. Boots and coats and weapons. This group did not fool around when roused in the middle of the night.

Shame leaned against the wall on one side of the room, Terric the mirror opposite of him on the other side. Sunny straddled a chair backward, her chin resting on her arms crossed over the back of the chair. Nik sat at the same table with her, sitting with one foot hooked behind his chair, and twisted at the waist in a very unconscious, but undeniably sexy male model kind of way.

Joshua Romero was there too, and the Georgia sisters, all three of them, and the twins, Carl and La, but I didn't see Ethan Katz, who was my dad's accountant, or Paige Iuamoto, the Blood magic user, or Darla, who Shame said used Death magic. And I did not see Dane Lannister, who had been Sedra's bodyguard.

Add to that group Victor, who was just now arriving, straightening his sleeves as though daggers lay between his cuffs and wrists—which I knew they did—plus Maeve and Hayden and me, and we numbered fourteen.

Fourteen against whatever death could throw at us. Fourteen on short rations of sleep, health, and resources.

Sweet hells, we were doomed.

Still, Victor gave me a smile, something filled with more than a little relief. I thought it odd, considering the circumstances, but before I could go over and talk to him, Maeve spoke.

"Allie has an announcement," she said. "Please listen."

"My friend Pike was killed a few months ago. He showed up here this morning and told me the Veiled are coming this way. To get the disks, and take the well."

"There are protections in place on the inn," Maeve said, "defenses that will hold against known magical attacks. But the Veiled are not human any longer, and not alive in the strictest sense. We don't know how they're going to use magic, since we have never fought the Veiled. Both Shame and Allie have had encounters with the solid Veiled. Shame?"

He rubbed at his shoulder. "Ran into one on the street. A man. He came right at me, so it's clear they know members of the Authority, or maybe just strong magic users. I drained him, sucked the magic out of the disk in his neck." He licked his lips, gave a wolf's smile. "Through Death magic. I'd be lying if I said it was easy. The magic in the disk was hard to tap, hard to pull on. But he was solid flesh. Not quite living . . . " He looked off in a middle distance as if searching for words. "I couldn't kill him. But I could break his link to life, if that makes any sense."

"So cleaving spells?" Hayden asked.

Shame nodded. "Cleaving, drains, negates, End, if anyone wants a month of migraines. Death magic, if you can do it."

"Allie?" Maeve asked.

What could I say about Truance? "I saw Truance—the Veiled—in a chocolate shop. She didn't have a reflection, and when I cast Sight"—I traced the glyph so everyone could see which version I used—"she no longer looked like a woman, she looked like green fog. She attacked me. But I didn't fight her. My father did."

Everyone in the room suddenly looked a lot more awake.

"I know Jingo Jingo has been telling everyone that my dad is not in my mind, or that only pieces of his memory linger there, but Jingo Jingo was lying. My dad possessed me when Frank dug up his corpse. He's been in my head, at varying degrees of strength, ever since."

"How did your father fight her?" Victor asked. He didn't seem surprised, just acutely interested.

"First Truance did something with the mark on my left hand." I held up my hand. "The mark I got in death. It paralyzed me. I couldn't break her spell. She could see my father in me. She was talking to me as if he were the only one in my head."

Wow. This was quickly becoming one of my top five wish-someone-else-was-here-instead-of-me moments. Going over the event only made me angry, and ashamed that I couldn't control my own body, my own mind.

"So Dad pushed me into the back of my mind and took over my body. He cast magic, but I couldn't see what he was doing. I felt him pull magic through my right hand, then push it into a spell, and I felt my left hand go very cold. When I got control of my mind and body, the glyph had been drawn, my left hand was on fire, and I threw both at Truance. It hit her in the neck. She spoke a word, and disappeared. Using the disk, I think.

"She stabbed Terric in the graveyard. Shame didn't use Death magic." I paused to look over at him and he shook his head. "But when she was pinned, she disappeared again."

I didn't know what else to say, so I shut up.

"Well." Victor walked into the center of the room, taking the energy of all those gathered, putting it back on task. "We can assume Death magic is involved since the mark on your palm is from death. Not a condition I think any of us could imitate. We will need to concentrate on using cleaving spells. Are there any questions?"

"Proxy load?" Sunny asked.

Victor nodded. "We'll each carry our own price. If anyone falters, Shame has volunteered to Proxy."

I raised my eyebrows and looked over at Shame. He just shrugged.

Terric was looking at him too, angry, maybe more than that, afraid.

Shame ignored him. Maybe he did have a suicidal streak.

Victor went on. "The disks are locked and warded on the bottom level of the inn—the safest place within these walls. Until we find a way to destroy the disks, we will keep them out of the wrong hands just like any other kind of dangerous magic. We will keep them away from the Veiled."

"Maeve?" He stepped back, giving her the floor.

"We will take a blood oath. To protect each other, the disks, and the well." She drew a slender blade the length of her hand out of her belt. The silver blade glinted with beveled glass, and was shadowed with lead and steel. Glyphs were worked into the hilt, delicate as ebony spiderwebs etched into the glass blade. I knew it was a blood blade, because I carried Zayvion's with me.

Everyone in the room held out their left hands. I did the same. Maeve sang a song, something old and lilting. She had a beautiful alto, and her song carried magic I'd only ever imagined in my childhood dreams of fairies and lost kingdoms.

One by one she nicked the thumb of each magic user and with each taste of blood, the blade glowed a new metallic color. By the time she reached me, I thought the blade would be covered in blood, but instead a thick line of red filled the center channel of it, like the holding vial of a syringe, and the edge was bright and clean.

She sang a word that resonated in my bones, and pricked the tip of my thumb.

It didn't hurt. Exactly one drop of blood welled up and was drunk down by the blade.

But that one drop of blood created a tie, a bond between me and Maeve, me and the blade, me and every drop of blood within the weapon, every person in the room.

"Give me your word," Maeve said quietly.

"You have my word." The bond tightened and stretched in me, twisting into the magic that filled my bones, and anchoring there.

That was a hell of an oath spell. And a lot more elegant than a spit and a handshake. I had a good sense of everyone in the room. That was going to be handy in a fight.

She was still singing when she turned away from me, even though I thought I was the last to take the oath.

I looked up and saw a figure appear in the arched doorway at the far end of the room.

Tall, and oh-my-aching-heart handsome, Zayvion Jones paused, scanning the room for me. His gaze and soft smile touched me as if his hands were on my face, his lips against my mouth, kissing, holding. I swallowed and tasted pine and mint.

That man could do things to me.

He walked into the room, a little gingerly, as if he weren't quite steady on his feet. His ratty blue ski coat a little loose, his cheeks too hard an angle, too much bone at the arc, but still, he stood tall.

Shame sprang away from the wall and was on him in a second, first clasping his hand, then wrapping him in a hard hug before pulling away to really look at him.

Zay leaned forward and said something. I didn't hear it, not even with my good ears, and Shame whispered back. Maybe apologies or gratitude, before Maeve was there, singing softly, the blade in her hand.

Shame stepped to one side, grinning. Looking like his best friend had just waltzed off the battlefield of the dead and made it home alive.

Which he had.

Tired, thin, but radiating that calm strength, Zayvion held his left hand out for Maeve. With that movement, I could see the sword he had sheathed at his hip. Not his katana, which I had across my back, but another sword I'd seen him use a lot in sparring practice.

She nicked his thumb.

I felt the pulse of his blood join with my own, felt his words as my own as he swore his fealty to this battle, this war, this cause.

Oh, how I'd missed him.

And then Maeve's song was over, the vow was done, and the room erupted in happy, congratulatory voices as everyone gathered around Zayvion. They shook his hand, patted his shoulder, or simply stood there and smiled at him.

And it suddenly hit me. Guardian of the gates wasn't just the best at Closing. He wasn't just a magic user who could use all disciplines of magic, light and dark. He was their hope, the embodiment of what they hoped magic could be again someday. He was a knight, a hero, a protector, the walking representation of the Authority's ideal.

His near-death had done as much, or maybe more, to pull the Authority down than Jingo Jingo's betrayal, Sedra's kidnapping, Chase and Greyson's attack, or the wild storm.

Zayvion was more than just the guardian of the gates. He was the Authority's honor. He was their soul.

And he was my soul.

Terric strolled over to him. There were too many people in front of him to reach Zayvion, but as soon as Shame saw him, he motioned him over.

Zay's face lit up when he saw Terric, and they clasped hands. Shame leaned into Terric, unthinkingly, hand on his shoulder, Terric's hand on Shame's shoulder, both of them grinning like fools.

They had all been friends once. And right now, it looked

like they were all friends again. I'd like it to stay that way. With fewer near-death experiences.

"Aren't you going to go to him?" I hadn't even noticed Victor next to me. Made me wonder if Zay had learned the whole silent-on-his-feet thing from the man.

"Thought I'd let the crowd clear a little. Did you know he was awake?"

Victor smiled, but was still looking at Zay. It was the first really relaxed expression I'd seen out of him. He always seemed to handle everything with succinct grace and clear command. But beneath the Voice for Faith magic, and my teacher the Closer, was a kind man who had taken Zay under his wing, maybe even, in his way, taken me under his wing. The smile was nice, and made me wonder for the first time what Victor did on his own time when he wasn't trying to save the world from monsters and nightmares.

"I was upstairs checking on him when the Summon spell activated. You know the first thing he asked me?"

I shook my head.

"If you were okay."

"That's because I told him I was going out on the hunt with Shame and Terric. And he's not exactly happy I went into death for him either."

"I don't think that's what he was talking about." Victor mused. "He said he heard you talking in your sleep last night. Arguing with your father."

The dream. I remembered I'd dreamed something. Dad was in my dream asking a favor. A quick image of paper squares and a shoe box flashed behind my eyes. Someone else had been in the dream. Who?

Victor looked at me. "Is your father going to be a problem?" I knew what he was really asking. Did I want him to Close me. To Close my dad too, probably, though I didn't know how one would take a dead man's memories away.

But if anyone could do it, it would be this calm, capable man standing next to me.

"I won't let him get in the way."

Victor pursed his lips and nodded. "You're not alone, Allie. Not anymore. You are one of us. If you are hurt, we'll make sure the person hurting you winds up dead."

Correction: this calm, capable killer standing next to me.

He looked into my eyes, searching not for me but for my father. "And we will see to it that he stays dead. Permanently. No matter the cost. Tell your father that for me if you get the chance, won't you?"

My dad was dead silent. But I felt the slide of anger that was not mine waft through my mind.

"I think he heard you."

Zay looked up, his gaze a brush of heat across my cheeks, my chest. Sexy, hungry, that man made me want him.

"If you'll excuse me," I said. I didn't wait to hear if Victor answered.

I strolled across the room, my gaze locked on Zayvion. He smiled a slow, sweet grin that made me want to take his hand and lead him away from this fight. Preferably to someplace with a mattress, silk sheets, and a bottle of wine.

"Allie," he said once the crowd in front of him saw I was coming and cleared out of the way faster than night seeking shadows.

"Zay. Good to see you on your feet."

"Thank you. Good to see you on your feet too."

Was that a stab at me being hurt after saving him? Did he really want to get into a fight the first time I'd seen him standing since he took on Greyson and Chase? "Thank you." I tried to make it sound easy, nice. But I was running on too little sleep to pull off tactful. It came off a little cool.

"Allie—" He didn't get the chance to say anything else.

The room thrummed like a bass drum struck by a falling anvil. Magic flared, lifted, ran like water up the walls, windows, crawled across the ceiling, filling the glyphs—glyphs I had never seen nor sensed—throughout the room. The room darkened. Lights and glyphs took on a deep purple that made whites burn electric blue.

Like a well-practiced team, half the people in the room drew Sight spells, facing all four compass points. Half the people in the room drew their weapons, and traced glyphs for Block, Shield, or Impact but did not pour magic into them. Yet.

My left hand went cold.

"The Veiled are here," Victor said calmly, like he was reading a grocery list. "There are five—no, seven—solid Veiled. I recognize three: Truance Stimple, Frank Gordon, and Elijah Hemming."

"The blond woman is Lauren Brown," Hayden said.

"Anyone else?" Victor stepped back so others could look out the window.

Maeve shook her head. I took a quick glance out the glass.

Victor had a tendency to understate things. Have I mentioned that?

He was right: Truance and Frank Gordon, that twisted doctor who had tried to kill me and resurrect my father, were both striding our way from the access road. I guessed the thirtysomething blond bob in slacks and a black jacket was Lauren, whom Hayden recognized, and the dark-haired, short, thin man with the beard might be Elijah.

The others were a pin-stripped suit guy, a dark-haired woman, middle-aged, wearing a 1950s-style dress with heels and gloves. And behind her was a man who looked like he'd just stepped out of the early 1900s: bowler hat, vest, long jacket, and loose slacks on a scarecrow-thin frame. There was nothing old-timey or quaint about the hatred in his eyes.

I didn't recognize any of them except Truance and

Frank, both of whom had taken starring roles in my recent nightmares. And if Dad recognized the others he did not say anything.

Which was fine with me.

"No," I said, as the others had said.

Just to be sure, I cleared my mind, ignored my pounding heart, and set a Disbursement. Something that would hit me a week from now. I did not need pain in my way.

I cast Sight. All seven of the solid Veiled became people-shaped clouds of green light and magic. And surrounding them was an army of watercolor people. More Veiled, a lot more Veiled. Hundreds, with open mouths, and black holes where their eyes should be.

And behind them all was a tall, man-shaped shadow, the shadow who had followed me from death. And that, whatever it was, was our real enemy.

*No,* Dad whispered in my mind. Horrified.

I didn't like my dad, but I liked it even less when he was scared to death of something that was about to attack us.

*Daniel Beckstrom,* the thing out there said, its voice a scrape of metal and rock and pain grating through my mind. *Die.*

He tipped his head upward. If he'd had eyes, I would have sworn he was staring at me. He raised his hand, pointed at me. The mark on my left hand crackled with pain that shot up my arm and caught inside my head. I heard my dad scream.

Then the Veiled weren't standing anymore. They were running, fast. A mob, a swarm, a cloud of hungry, sharp fingers, teeth and claws, pouring toward the inn.

# Chapter Twenty-three

"Hold," Maeve said. I swear it sounded like she was standing next to me. The blood oath, carrying on our mingled blood and magic, allowed us to hear her. It was like wearing the disk cuffs, but focused on Maeve's strength and presence, filtered through her, clean and clear and very nice.

Dad had stopped screaming. I couldn't feel him at all. I swallowed hard, and tasted my own fear.

We held, spells at the ready, evenly divided at the compass points of the room. No chance the Veiled would politely line up and attack from the front door.

The Veiled hit like a heavy wind. I heard the old wood frame creak at the impact, the windows click and rattle. Dust sifted down from the rafters. The Veiled attached to the walls and feasted upon the magic in the building. As soon as they drew too hard on a Ward, they exploded into smoke and flames.

But there were more, thousands, to replace them. A flash of light, the sound of breaking glass, and the first Ward failed.

I shifted to the center of the room, behind one of the tables. I faced West, a Hold spell in my right hand, awaiting the magic to activate it. Zayvion's sword was strapped to my back. I wasn't ready to draw it yet.

I traced Sight with my left hand, which was cold, but not on fire yet, and poured magic up through my body and into the glyph. Being this close to the well made magic slick and easy to access. That was one thing going for us.

The world opened with wild streaks and luminescence of magic, held in each magic user's hands, burning like fire up the clean, tall white walls, across the ceiling, and lighting the wooden floor and windows in golden lacework.

Another flash of light and shattering sound as the Veiled chewed through another Ward. If enough Wards held long enough, it was possible that all the Veiled would be reduced to smoke before they breached our defenses.

"Now?" I asked.

"No," Maeve said. "Casting through the wards will cancel them."

Who came up with that defensive plan?

In front of me stood Victor, in front of him the table Terric and Shame and I had had breakfast at, was it only yesterday morning? We faced the windows. To our right stood Sunny, both blood blades drawn. She wore black tights, boots, and everything else denim: skirt, jacket, and cabbie hat that kept her dark hair out of her eyes.

One of the Georgia sisters stood behind Sunny, her staff glowing with sparks that swam like slender fish, up and down the length of the staff.

At the far end of the room, facing North, was Shame, sword at the ready, his back to me. The twins, Carl and La, stood behind him with curved scythes in their hands. At my back, I knew, was Hayden with that battle-ax and broadsword he carried, Zay, and another of the Georgia sisters. And at my left, facing South, was Terric, an ax in each hand, his back to Shame, Nik, who carried a blade a lot like Victor's, and the last Georgia sister. Maeve and Joshua stood in the center of us all. Someone was whistling. I think it was Nik.

Another Ward fell in a flash. And another.

The Georgia sisters lifted a Shield around the inside of the inn, an Illusion like the Shield they had used in St. Johns to keep the battle below the radar of the police, and more importantly, Stotts and his MERC crew. The Shield was a bubble that would keep the fight, noise, and magic inside.

The Shield closed and rang out like a deep drum. The Veiled were exploding into smoke, the wards failing faster, strobe-light flashes drumming against the windows.

I squinted against the light, and saw the shadow man draw a glyph. I didn't recognize it.

"What the hell is that thing?" Victor said. "It's drawing a gate. No," he said, "not a gate. It's the Rift. Shield!"

"Down!" Maeve said.

And even if I hadn't wanted to, her words in my blood, her Influence, made me drop to my knees.

Everyone in the room cast Shield and hit the floor. Good thing. The shadow man's spell sliced through the inn like a horizontal guillotine, a razor-sharp blade that would have taken off heads and torn through the torso of anyone still standing. Fast as a snake's tongue, the blade was gone. A second spell hit the inn like a bomb.

The explosion of Wards breaking was deafening, the light blinding, and the darkness it plunged the room into so deep that, if not for the blood oath spell, I wouldn't have known where any of us were. I had dropped Sight, so I could maintain Shield and keep Hold caught and ready in my right hand. My left hand hurt like a son of a bitch.

And the darkness robbed me of normal vision.

Shit.

A spark of violet flared up the side of the room—one of the Georgia sisters casting Light. The spell bloomed across the ceiling, caught like fire, and formed a lotus that spanned the ceiling, petals softly glowing lavender.

We were on our feet. Even though I was afraid, no one

else looked like this was anything more than a walk in the park.

No more watercolored people sucking at the Wards, though I didn't know why they weren't swarming the place.

Then I saw the seven solid, living Veiled, storming toward the inn.

Hello, nightmare.

Truance was in the lead, and right beside her was Dr. Frank Gordon. Frank looked exactly how I remembered him in life—crazy and vicious.

They blew open the door—what did you know, they did use the front door. Truance cast Block, Frank threw something that crawled, skittered, and pulled itself with dark, shadowy fingers up the walls to cut the lines and flow of magic in the inner Wards and glyphs.

Dark magic.

We threw everything we had at them.

The smell of machine oil and burned grass and scorched blackberries filled the air. Truance and Frank took one step, two, deflecting, absorbing our magic, and moved aside as the other solid Veiled joined them, spread out, shoulder to shoulder on either side of the door.

We couldn't break through their magic. Whatever they were using as a Shield absorbed our magic like a sponge in water.

Well, magic wasn't the only weapon we could use.

Zay's katana was in my hand. I cast Impact. Black flame wrapped my hand, poured down the blade, and fed the spell. It hurt. I didn't care. I ran forward and swung at their Shield, aiming for Frank's head.

The blade cleaved the Shield, cutting like I was dragging it through mud, the black flame so dark, it stung my eyes as it caught the Shield on fire.

I ducked. The Shield burst outward in big gooey drops of magic and black fire.

I was dizzy, my ears ringing, my left arm numb. I needed to stand up. I needed to cast a Block, a Shield.

A strong arm grabbed me around the waist and hauled me up onto my feet. Victor cast a Shield around us both and jogged with me toward the back of the room, the Shield moving with us just like the one my dad had cast in death.

My hearing cleared up, and I suddenly knew why we were beating a retreat.

The watercolor people rushed into the room, like a roaring gush of magic and hunger. I heard one of the Georgia sisters scream. Chanting and cursing filled the air as light and dark magic clashed, exploded, spells and glyphs howling as dark magic cleaved through the living world.

Victor pressed me up against the wall near the door to the hall. "Stay here."

He strode to the front line, his blade burning silver into the darkness, painting glyphs through the air as he destroyed Veiled after Veiled.

I shook my left arm until I could feel it again, looked for an opening, and took Sunny's right side. My left hand still licked with fire, but I didn't let the flame touch the blade. If I used the flame with magic again, it'd probably knock me out in midswing. I cut through the watercolor people, trying to hack a path to Frank.

Truance, Frank, and the others stood behind the watercolor people, and used magic like it had no end. They cast as if it cost them nothing, battering, bludgeoning, pressing us in a tighter circle, playing with us. The weapons in their hands radiated dark magic.

None of the seven spoke or even breathed. Disks shone eerie green at each of their throats as they pressed past defense after defense, breaking spells faster than we could throw them.

I cast Hold, Cleave, and Impact with my left and followed it up with the razor edge of Zay's sword. Still, I was pressed back, until there was almost no swinging room left.

I was not the only one struggling. Chants of spells were punctuated by curses and grunts of exertion as we fought to hold against the spells and Veiled pummeling us.

The watercolor people broke through, diving into blade and magic, hands grabbing, piercing, sucking, even as they were canceled, ended, killed. And every touch left a burning, bleeding mark behind, sucking away strength and stamina. My arms, shoulders, thighs were covered in burns.

Note to self: next time wear fireproof long johns.

I wondered why Shame didn't drink down their magic, but realized there was no chance of him getting through their defenses.

We were too close, too fatigued. Friendly fire crossed, collided, blew, sending fire to lick up one of the beams.

Something had to give.

"The hall!" Maeve's voice carried subtle Influence, enough to sink into my head without getting in the way of what I was doing. Damn, the woman was good.

"Go!" Victor said. He doubled his attack, magic and sword a dance of light and fire and steel. Hayden yelled—no spell that I could parse—just anger, and followed Victor, his broadsword taking the watercolor people down faster than they could rise. Blood and burns stood out on Hayden's face and Victor's hands. But none of us had so much as touched the seven Veiled.

With Victor and Hayden holding off the enemy, I ran for the hall. Zay, behind me, hesitated. Terric grabbed his arm and pushed him across the room.

"We follow orders. We get out alive." I could hear Terric through the blood in Maeve's spell.

Zay didn't argue. Once he made it to the hall, he turned and cast a glyph with his left hand over the palm of his right until a dark orb, burning like the Veiled's weapons, hovered there.

He heaved the orb at the Veiled. It exploded, and for the first time, I heard the Veiled scream.

A magic bomb! So someone did know how to make one of those. Boy had been holding out on me.

One of the Veiled fell, the dark-haired man, Elijah. He did not rise.

"What did you use?" I asked.

"Dark—" He had to take a breath. "—magic." He wiped his hand over his mouth. Casting that one spell had nearly wiped him out.

Zay was the only one I knew who could cast dark magic without going insane. And it looked like that would be the last dark spell he would be able to cast.

"Allie." Zay grabbed my hip and pulled me back. I don't know why I'd been just standing there staring out at the fight Victor and Hayden were losing.

"We need to help," I said.

"We are. We're closing down the room as they're working our way. Listen—about what I said. About you not knowing how to handle yourself—"

Really? In the middle of a battlefield was when he wanted to have a heart-to-heart about our relationship? "Don't want to talk about it right now."

Hayden and Victor gave ground, methodically running through spell variations that were astounding. They were now in the arched doorway to the hall.

"Nik," Victor shouted, "now!"

The pretty boy took three steps forward just as Victor and Hayden stepped back. Nik threw something out into the room that sounded like an entire building under demolition charges.

The Veiled screamed a second time. Another solid Veiled fell, Pinstripe Guy.

Music to my ears.

The room locked down like bulletproof glass had just been poured over the top of it.

"What was that?" I yelled, because the explosion had killed my ears.

"Lock," Shame yelled.

"Back," Maeve said. "Down the stairs. Now."

No Influence. We didn't need Influence. The solid Veiled, all five who were still standing, were no longer screaming. They were at the doorway, casting spells with staffs, swords, knives, and hands. Going through spells just as methodically as Victor and Hayden had gone through them, searching for the way to break the Lock that held them trapped in the room.

They had once been good magic users—no, great magic users. They knew as much as we knew about magic.

And they had the disks to fuel them and no price to pay.

Hells.

I ran for the stairs, even though it took everything I had to turn my back on them. Nik stayed at the doorway, moving back slowly in tandem with the twins, Carl and La, who sang, feeding magic to Nik as he fed it to the Lock spell, doing that liquid spell thing that Shame had done with his art Refreshing and shifting the glyph faster than they could try to take it down.

"Down the stairs," Maeve said again, and this time it was Hayden who thundered toward me and pushed my shoulder to get me moving.

We thumped down the stairs, as fast as we could, Maeve moving painfully slowly.

The floor opened up to one large space, walls lined with shelves and cabinets, files and desks and computers. I guessed this was the official business office of the restaurant. The stairs continued down to the bottom floor, where the well, and the disks, were stashed.

Hayden helped Maeve down the stairs while looking back over her shoulder to see when Nik and the twins were going to start down.

Zay glanced up the stairs, probably gauging if he could help in any way. There just wasn't room for more people on the stairs. He walked over to me. "About what I said. Earlier." He touched my arm and the reality of him, standing there, alive and mostly whole, hit like a lightning strike to my soul.

I wanted to lean into him, wrap around him, feel his touch, taste his lips, and never let go.

But, seriously, we were in the middle of a war here.

"Are you going to apologize?" I asked.

"Apologize for what?"

"For being mad at me pulling a reverse-Valkyrie and dragging you out of death?"

He scowled. So far he had not been burned by the Veiled. The ratty ski coat was doing a good job of keeping him safe.

"I won't apologize for being angry about that. You threw yourself into death."

"For you. To get you. To save you. I died for you."

"I don't want you to die for me. I want you to live for me. You broke your promise."

"What promise?"

"That you would never try to be the hero. Never put yourself in that kind of danger again."

I did vaguely remember promising him that. "When you died, all bets were off. We're in this together, and we'll both give every damn thing we've got to make sure we get out of it together."

Shame jogged over to us. "Later, lovelies. We have company."

Hayden and Maeve finally made it down the stairs.

Victor and Joshua chanted, a very Gregorian kind of sound, walking a circuit of the room and activating storage spells there.

Clever. Magic had been piped and captured in storage pockets where it could be accessed and used.

In case of emergency, break into chant.

I liked it.

"Defense," Maeve said. "We'll take them here. Pick them off one by one as they come down."

She was assuming they would break through the Lock.

The deep thump of a contained explosion made my molars ache, and then Nik and Carl and La were sprinting down the stairs.

"It's down, it's down," Nik said.

The Lock was broken.

"We protect the lower level. We protect the well. We protect the disks," Maeve said.

Other than us, what would keep them from just running down the stairs to the well? I glanced at the staircase. The stairs stopped here, on this floor. The wood flooring looking like one seamless piece.

They must have a hidden panel that closed off the stairs, or maybe Victor and Joshua's chant had triggered the inn's defense here. Nice.

Victor and Joshua completed their circuit of the room, completed the chant.

The walls hummed like a hundred cellos being plucked.

This floor was locked down. I didn't smell an Illusion, but then, I couldn't smell the very large Illusion the Georgia sisters were still maintaining over the inn. The sisters stood together, whispering a litany to hold their focus and Illusion, well protected and well behind the rest of us who surrounded the stairs.

"Zayvion," Victor said.

Zay looked up. Didn't let go of my arm.

"Go," I said. "Now's your chance to be the hero."

"Zayvion. Now," Victor said.

"Fuck." Zay leaned down, not much, since we were

nearly the same height. He pressed his mouth against mine, hard, needful, and a new heat filled me, licked fire across the cold emptiness inside me.

I opened my mouth, taking him in greedily, just as hard, my tongue, my teeth exploring, stroking, catching at him and telling him I didn't want to let go, didn't want him to let me go. Begging him to leave with me to someplace where I could touch him, savor his body, his heat, drag my fingers through his soul, until I knew, really knew, that he was alive and safe, and mine.

He pulled away. We were both breathing hard.

"This isn't over," he said.

"Damn straight it isn't. You still haven't apologized."

He smiled, and the fire in me flashed into an inferno. I leaned in for another kiss.

"Zayvion." Victor again.

And then Zayvion was gone. No longer just a man, my man. He would always be guardian of the gate, always belong to the Authority first.

A flash of jealousy fanned that fire in me. But I knew that was stupid. We all needed him to be the Authority's man right now.

"Can you Channel?" Victor asked him.

Zay took a deep breath, exhaled slowly. "Yes." He spread his feet shoulder width, and then placed his hands together in prayer in front of his chest. I felt his heartbeat jump, then settle into a strong meditative rhythm. He and I were bound by more than just a drop of blood in Maeve's dagger. We were Soul Complements.

I knew he was afraid. Worried. Exhausted. And I knew how determined he was to end this now.

With incredible finesse for someone who had just been dead, he pulled the magic out of the walls and created a pool of magic in the air in front of him, a strong, steady force ready to be accessed by any user in the room.

Talk about playing hero.

"Allie, I need you to be my eyes," Maeve said.

I strode over to her. She leaned heavily on her cane. Maintaining the blood oath must be costing her a huge price.

"How?" I asked.

"Cast Sight. Tell me when you see them."

I cleared my mind, set a Disbursement, and drew Sight. What I saw scared the crap out of me.

"Shadows are moving down the stairs. A lot like the watercolor people—no, they're spells. Maybe Death magic pouring down the stairs."

"Shame," Maeve said.

Shame and Terric moved forward, Terric cast Sight, canceled it, then cast another form of Sight until he finally saw what I saw.

"Got it." As soon as the words were out of his mouth, Shame was casting. Not dark magic like Zay wielded, but taking the magic Zayvion held in the glowing amorphous blob in front of him and spinning just a thin thread of it into Death magic, the transference of magic, of energy from one state to another.

Shame intoned a spell, his voice resonating in me. My left palm itched, burned, froze. The mark of death responded to Shame's words as if he were speaking to my soul. I had to fight to not go to him.

Great.

But the Death magic flooded toward him, and he negated the spells with the blade in his hand and opened his arms, drinking down the smoke and dregs.

Nice. Shame was bearing Proxy for this fight. I knew he could endure pain, but that hit of Death magic was bound to help ease the pain a little.

A green fog drifted at the edge of the ceiling. "They're coming down," I said. "The solid Veiled."

The first in line was Truance, bearing a curved sword that looked like a scimitar.

We hit her with everything we had.

She raised a Shield with her left hand, easily deflecting our magic. "You cannot stand in our way," she said. "There are more of us, so many more, who will fight to be alive again. Today, we will take the disks and the well. And we will gladly kill you, as you once killed us, to do it."

"Leave this world." Victor put so much Influence behind it, I dropped Sight and looked for the nearest exit.

*Allison,* my father said quietly, but clearly, inside my head. *Don't.* I don't know what he did, but I no longer felt the need to do as Victor said.

Still, I shuddered. I had almost zero resistance to Influence.

"You have lived your life," Victor continued, using magic to push against her Shield, to push against the others, so they could not move down the stairs. "Your deaths were justified by the Council of Voices of your time. It is the way of the Authority. It used to be a way you swore fealty to. Move on, Truance. Find peace in death, and let magic rest in our hands."

"The Authority broke magic, then used it for their petty games. But now the dead lay claim to what is rightfully ours. Magic. And life." Truance walked down the stairs, step by step, a smile on her face.

Just as her boot hit the floor, Hayden threw Fire at her, a burning twisted gout of flame-worked glyphs and spells that made me throw one arm over my face to ward off the heat. Fire wrapped a half circle in front of her, caught on her Shield, burning. She flicked her left hand, drawing the magic down into the sword she carried in her right.

She looked taller, younger. Stronger.

The spell, the magic in it, had made her stronger. Just like drinking magic made the watercolor people stronger.

Just like magic made the Hungers and other things that stepped through the gates of death stronger.

Shit.

Hayden realized what had happened too.

He canceled the spell, broke the flame into ragged edges that tore at Truance but could not quite reach her. She tugged at the collar of her coat, baring more of her throat, and drank the remaining magic into the disk like a smoker inhaling through a hole in the neck.

Frank, who had done nothing but smile his creepy smile, and the rest of the Veiled stood beside her. They lifted their hands and cast magic as one.

It is dangerous to cast magic with another magic user. It can kill you. It can kill everyone around you.

But apparently being dead with a disk stuck in your throat made group casting possible.

*Allison!* my dad yelled in my head.

He didn't have to yell. I felt it too.

An explosion rocked the inn. And I knew, without a doubt, that a gate into death had just opened over the well below us.

# Chapter Twenty-four

"Agate," I yelled.

Not that I had to. The room was filled with Closers. They all felt it too.

"Down!" Victor roared.

Victor and Joshua raised their hands to break the Illusion and barrier over the stairs.

*I'm sorry,* my dad said.

*No.* I opened my mouth to warn them, to tell them, to stop my dad.

But he picked me up and shoved me to the farthest corner of my head. Slick walls and darkness surrounded me. I slammed my fist into the walls, trying to break my own mind.

I yelled, screamed. Nothing.

Then I heard my own voice, oddly accented with my father's commanding cadence.

"I am Daniel Beckstrom," he said with my voice. "Do not let the barrier fall, Victor. Do not let them reach the well."

I couldn't see, couldn't tell what was going on.

Panicking about it wasn't going to do me a damn bit of good. I calmed my thoughts, closed my eyes, and recited my "Miss Mary Mack" song.

When I opened my eyes, I could see what my father

was seeing, though it was like I was standing at the back of a theater, watching what someone else watched on the screen.

I stood in front of Victor. Someone was behind me. I could only assume they had gotten hold of my wrists and were restraining me. It's the least of what I would have done.

"I can Close the gate," Dad was saying. I must have missed some of the conversation. "But you must let me cap the well without the capstone."

I didn't know who was fighting the Veiled while this little conversation was taking place. Lights flashed. I heard the electric crack of magic shattering a spell.

Okay, so maybe everyone who wasn't dealing with me, with Dad, was still fighting.

"You are no longer a part of the Authority, Daniel," Victor said. "You are as much an invader in our world as Truance and Frank. Leave us and return to death, or I will end you."

"When I was alive, I set traps on the inn that I can trigger. They will contain everything within these walls. Nothing living or dead, magical or otherwise, will be able to escape. The well, the Veiled, the gate, will be locked in. Secure."

Victor had a good poker face, but I could tell he believed Dad. He was weighing his options. Not how to win, but which of his enemies he should let become his conqueror.

"Why are you doing this to your daughter?"

It was not a question I expected from Victor.

I don't think my dad expected it either.

"It was my last option. I dislike being forced to make a snap decision. I never wanted to do this. Any of this. Although I had prepared for many outcomes."

"Why shouldn't we kill you now?" Zayvion asked, so close I knew it was he who held my wrists trapped so Dad couldn't cast magic.

"I know where Jingo Jingo is. And I know what he's using Sedra for."

Victor's eyes narrowed.

"And there is an enemy stronger than you or me loose in this world, my friend," Dad said. "I will do anything to stop him."

"Who?" Victor asked.

"Leander. He is the shadow man behind the undead Veiled. He's looking for Isabelle."

Holy shit.

Fear shadowed Victor's face. "Lock it down. We'll take care of the Veiled."

Victor looked over my shoulder. "Let her go," he said to Zayvion.

I couldn't feel my body, couldn't feel Zayvion touching me. I pushed at the walls surrounding me. Nothing budged. Trying to think calm thoughts when all I could picture was throttling my dad did not make using magic any easier either.

"What about the disks?" Zay asked.

Right. If we left the disks down by the open gate, a gate we could assume was allowing more of the Veiled through, we would be up to our asses in the un-living, disk-powered dead.

"Mr. Flynn should be able to help me retrieve those," Dad said. "He carries the crystal?"

Victor nodded once. "We used to be friends, Dan," he said, striding into the fray. "Don't make me regret that. Shame!"

Dad turned and I could see the battle.

We were not winning. There were still five Veiled standing, Truance, Frank, Pioneer Guy, the thirtysomething blond Lauren, and the 1950s woman. Two of them were holding the other disks from their fallen comrades in their hands.

And they were warping magic, sending it out in ways I'd never felt magic used. Dark, mutated. It reminded me of the Veiled in death. This was broken magic. Disks that had been broken on the anvil of the wild-magic storm and now were wielded by the undead.

Not a pretty combination.

Shame fell back from the line of magic users who stood equidistant around the room, containing the Veiled but unable to break their defenses. Victor spoke briefly to Shame, then took Shame's place.

Shame jogged over to me.

And stopped like someone had just slapped him in the face. "You must be Allie's dad."

"I am. We cannot let the Veiled get their hands on any more disks. And we can't break the barrier to physically retrieve the disks below. Do you know where they are kept?"

"I'm not going to tell you until you let Allie go."

"There is no time—"

"Then make it snappy." Shame returned my dad's gaze with a deadly nonchalance.

Options. It looked like my dad was running out of them.

"This could be our death," Dad said.

"That won't be anything new to you, will it?" Fearless, that boy, facing down my dad. Even from the back of my own brain, I could feel Dad's approval.

So unfair. When I faced down Dad he hated me for it. When some stranger did it, he got all warm and fuzzy. Bastard.

Dad took down the walls that surrounded me. I rushed out of that small dark space, letting anger cover up the screaming claustrophobia that had been eating at my sanity.

"You bastard," I said.

He ignored me. "Where are the disks?" he asked Shame.

"In the east safe."

I could feel the calculations go through his head, my head. Our head. Whatever.

"You carry the stone in your body." He wasn't asking Shame. "It shares many of the same properties as the disks. I am going to put my—Allison's—hand on your chest and charge it with magic."

"Then what?" he asked.

"Then I will cast you, body and soul, down to the lower level. I'll try to put you in front of the safe and leave enough magic in the stone for your return."

"Are you kidding?" I said. Yes, with my own mouth. Hey, what did you know? Dad really was sharing the body.

Shame grinned. "Hey, girl. Think he can do it?"

"Yes." I hated admitting it, but my dad really was that good.

Shame nodded. "Do it."

Dad put my hand—my left hand—on Shame's chest. I could feel the rush of cool flame fingering down into the crystal join with the hot flood of magic Dad pulled out of the room, and into my body, my bones.

Dark and light magic? Maybe. I was too close, too entranced to tell.

It felt good, felt right to give magic to Shame like this. It felt like this was how magic should always be used.

And from the expression of bliss on Shame's face, it was clear that this blend of magic did not hurt him.

Dad gathered more magic, pushed it through me until I was full, so achingly full, I didn't have room to breathe. Even the hollow space where my small magic had once held fast was stretched, filled, warm, heavy. It felt so right.

He spoke one word. Magic rushed out of me fast, too fast, taking the ache and pleasure with it and leaving me cold and empty. I cried out.

Shame disappeared.

Terric, across the room, yelled. Not in pain or pleasure, but in anger.

And everything seemed to slow. Dad filled half of my mind, more than that, filled me, touching me everywhere magic touched me. We were more one person than two, a reality that made me want to scream.

But he was very, very focused on Shame, on his heartbeat, which he felt through the blood bond Maeve had cast. On his body, and his magic, both of which he felt through the crystal that he fed a careful stream of magic into, giving just enough so the crystal would remain full, and not enough to burn Shame alive.

Great. I hadn't known that was a possible outcome. But freaking out about it right now would do none of us any good. So I chanted my mantra, staying calm, supportive. Not fighting my dad, nor the magic he wielded.

Trusting him. With me. With my magic.

It was the only thing I could think of doing to help Shame survive.

Someone screamed. I glanced at the fight—was able to move my head since Dad was focused on Shame breaking into the safe below us.

Nik was down, writhing on the floor. Hayden stood above him, fighting the Pioneer Man, but unable to stop long enough to do anything for Nik. Sunny was also down, a pale pile of limbs slumped against the wall.

The Veiled combined their magic and blasted a hole into the floor.

Everything went white—too white.

The room flooded with watercolor people.

"Out, out, out!" Hayden roared. He bent, picked up Nik like he was a child and put him in a fireman's hold as he headed for the stairs.

Joshua ran to Sunny, and pulled her up into his arms. She looked like a broken rag doll, blood smeared down the side of her pale face, fingertip burns everywhere, just like the rest of us.

"Move," Maeve said. "Everyone out!"

Everyone moved, ran for the stairs, hacked their way through the watercolor people who swarmed up the stairs in a tangled mob of holy-shit-we're-going-to-die.

Victor helped Maeve. She'd lost her cane in the fight, but wielded daggers and Blood magic.

Me? I stood there toward the back of the room. Thinking calm thoughts as the monsters reached the top of the stairs, pulled themselves up and out of the hole in the floor. I didn't know how I was going to get out of this. But I wasn't going to leave Shame behind.

Zayvion was suddenly beside me, casting Shield after Shield to keep the monsters at bay, each Shield weaker than the last.

"We have to go," he said.

"I'm not leaving Shame."

"How much longer?"

I didn't know. Dad had fallen into such a deep concentration, I couldn't reach him.

"I don't—" And then my mouth was no longer mine.

Dad spoke a word. Shame appeared in front of us, a heavy iron and glass box under his arm. Blood and burns covered his hands and much of his shirt.

The Veiled howled.

"Open it," Dad said.

Shame hesitated. Looked like he was going to pass out.

The monsters were closer. Much closer. Zay's Shields barely flashed up before they fell.

I touched the box, knew immediately what spell would break the seal. I cast a quick Unlock and the lid of the box flew open.

The disks inside pulsed with a palatable magic. Dark, rich, smelling like burned blackberries and too much sugar. I licked my lips and swallowed down the flavor of them.

The monsters in the room screamed.

My dad spoke another word.

The room seemed to press in half, closing in on me with sharp, complicated folds like the world had become an origami creation and I was nothing but colored paper.

And then we were outside. I hurt from head to toe, my skin fever-hot, a crippling headache stabbing down my spine. Black ashes, fine as feathers, fell from the sky to settle into a perfect circle around our feet. The oily tang and copper burn of spent magic, of spent disks, filled my nose.

Shame exhaled. "That. Was. Awesome." The box of disks in his hands was filled with smoke and slag. The disks were destroyed.

I tried to respond, but Dad had control of my body now, and I could not fight my way up through the pain to take over.

He walked over to the front of the inn, just as all the rest of the Authority ran out the door. Yes, they looked surprised to see Shame, Zay, and me already outside.

"Move," Dad said.

And they did.

I didn't know if he felt the same pain I felt—

—*Yes,* he said, *I do.*

Well, now I knew he could hear my thoughts. I wondered what he was doing with my body and as soon as I thought it, I knew we, I mean he, was going to trigger the traps and lock down everything that was in the inn.

I could still see through my eyes. The solid Veiled ran past the windows toward the door.

Dad lifted his hands above his—I mean my—head and sang a very soft song. At first I thought it was nonsense, but then I recognized the hush-a-bye song my mother used to sing to me when she tucked me into bed at night.

Magic coalesced out of the air over the inn, magic seeking magic, and joining in a beautiful lace knotwork that glimmered gray, silver, plum, in the predawn light.

Dad pulled my hands together, then apart, my left, marked with death, pointed at the sky, my right, marked with ribbons of color, pointed at the ground.

Magic pulled through me, easy as a thread through the eye of a needle. Magic from the ground, magic from the sky, caught, wove together, and locked down over the inn. Before the Veiled could reach the door, before the monsters could break free.

I expected an explosion, a deep thrum of closing, ending, the rattle of gears locking into place. But this spell might as well have been cast out of the roots and limbs of the trees that surrounded the inn, might as well have been worked into the soil and the rocks and the rain.

Seamless, natural. And yes, beautiful. I'd never seen magic used in such an organic fashion, as if it were indeed a natural part of the living world.

I didn't expect that kind of beauty, that kind of grace, from my father.

Then he was no longer at the front of my mind. He fell back, exhausted beyond endurance, nothing but smoke, a shadow.

Released from his control, I stumbled, fell to my knees, the damp gravel pricking my palms. I hurt like nobody's business. I sat there for a second or two.

Zay rested his hand on my shoulder. "Can you stand?"

I looked up at him. He didn't look much better than I felt. He was breathing through his mouth like he'd just run a marathon. Dark blood trailed down his temple, and fingerprint burns pocked his neck.

Yeah, I knew the feeling.

"Want me to carry you?" he asked.

Yes. No. Yes.

No. I told him I could stand on my two feet, and I would. No matter how tired and hurt I was. I didn't waste breath or strength answering him. I pushed myself up onto my feet. He held his hand out for me. I took it. There was no amount of pride that would save me from looking like a fool if I ended up falling flat on my face.

Even the low light of dawn made my eyes hurt. But Zayvion gathered me to him, and I wrapped my arms around that ratty coat of his, clutching the back of it in my fists so he couldn't disappear, fall away, go away again. I held him, alive and whole, against me and inhaled the pine scent of him, peppered by his sweat. He was too thin beneath those layers, thin enough that I could feel the tremble of exhaustion in his muscles.

Didn't we make a pair?

"I haven't seen that since Mikhail ran the show," Hayden said. "Very, very nice, Beckstrom. Not even a Hound would think there was anything magical going on here."

"The gate is Closed," Victor said with grudging admiration. "As you said it would be. So, too, the well."

"The Veiled?" Terric asked. "Is there a time limit on the disks? Will they simply run out of magic and stop living?"

"I don't know," I said, turning my face to the side so I wasn't talking into Zayvion's chest. "Dad sort of . . . blacked out or something."

"It won't matter," Victor said. "We won't let this sit that long. A day, maybe two. The Lock will hold until then; it's ingeniously fed from the latent magic in the river and soil. The Veiled are held in a stasis. A long sleep. It's very . . . poetic." There was that admiration again. "Maeve, is there still an Aversion set up at the top of the road?"

"It's underground, but we can trigger it," she said tiredly. "It should keep the curious away for a week at least. I can say the inn is undergoing inspections. I've already called the staff and told them they have a paid vacation for two weeks."

These people thought of everything. But then if you ran a business and practiced secret magic on the side, you'd pencil in some time for disaster planning.

The crunch of tires over gravel made me groan. I didn't know who was coming, hoped it wasn't Stotts, but figured there was no way I would get that lucky. We had just thrown a god-awful amount of magic around.

"Allie?" Victor said.

I pulled away from Zay, not too far, and squinted over at him.

Nik sat on the ground, his head in his hands, elbows propped on his knees. Whatever spell had caused him pain was gone now, but he was covered in blood and bruises and burns. Sunny didn't look much better, but the blood was wiped off her face, and she was conscious. None of us had come out of this unscathed. I'd never seen so many magic users look so exhausted, bloody, and bruised. I wondered where the doctor was. Wondered if anyone had called 911.

But the noise, the car—correction, cars—coming down the driveway, were not Stotts and his crew.

Four cars stopped. And out of the lead car stepped Davy Silvers.

"Heard you'd need a ride to someplace safe. We have food, beds, and Dr. Fisher standing by at the den."

Three other doors opened. Sid, Jamar, and Jack all stood next to their cars.

My Hounds. Come to the rescue.

None of the Authority stepped forward. I could tell Victor was weighing the options of the situation. We all still had our weapons out, and were clearly wounded from magic. Four Hounds meant four people to Close. I didn't know if all the Closers combined had enough energy to put themselves to that task.

Screw it. If there was one kind of person who knew how to keep their mouths shut, it was the Hounds. My Hounds, at least.

I tugged free from Zayvion. "I don't know about the rest of you, but I could use a cup of coffee. Davy, Jamar, Sid, Jack, I'll make introductions of all my friends once we get to the den, if that's okay. You will keep your mouths shut about all this, right?"

"About all what?" Jack asked. "I have room for four." He opened the back door of his car.

"I can take six," Jamar said.

That was all it took. We divided up into cars, Hounds helping the bloody, exhausted, dirty secret magic users into their cars.

Just as we turned around and headed back up the access road, I saw Pike, ghostly and pale, raise a hand in hello, or good-bye, before the sun crested the hills, and flooded the world with the gold, healing light of dawn.

# Chapter Twenty-five

We traveled in a loose caravan to the den, skulking off to lick our wounds while the morning sun gave a nod to spring.

Zay and Sunny and Joshua were in the backseat. None of us said anything, and Davy didn't ask anything. But once we reached the den, Get Mugged already bustling with traffic and energy, I looked over at him.

"Pike?" I asked.

"Yeah. Said you had a fight on your hands. Thought you might need our help. Sorry we got there too late."

"Only four of you came? Where's the love?" I said, trying, and failing, to make it sound like a joke.

Davy got it though. "We didn't think it'd take more than four Hounds to handle anything you could throw at us."

Joshua in the backseat chuckled. "I like your attitude. It's wrong," he said, his voice always more gentle than I expected. "But you have guts."

Davy glanced in his rearview mirror. "I don't think I'm the only one."

He parked. It didn't take long for us to shuffle into the elevators. Even I didn't walk the stairs, though Shame made faces at me while we rode the elevator.

And just like Davy said, the Hounds had outfitted the den to receive wounded, to hold meetings, and to sleep.

Every bunk was made and ready, the air smelled of garlic and bread and tomatoes, and I realized I was starving.

Casting magic, that much magic, made me hungry. But first, I wanted some meds to cut the pain.

"Dying of headache here," I said. "Anyone got pills?"

A chorus of rattling filled the room as every Hound pulled out a bottle of pain pills. I started laughing. Bad idea. It made my head hurt worse, but I couldn't stop.

Zayvion took my fingers and pulled me gently toward an open couch, and I sat. He flopped down next to me. Sweet hells, I had never been so tired. I leaned my head on the back of the couch and closed my eyes. Just for a minute.

I woke up when the doctor gave me a shot.

"What was that?" I asked.

"Same as I gave you earlier. Should take care of the headache. And anything else." I caught a quick glimpse of the needle she'd used. It was glyphed, and made of finely turned glass. I bet the needle itself was silver and some kind of spell was worked into the molecules of the drug.

The relief was almost instant. I was still sore, the burns on my arms, side of my neck, and chest still tender, and I knew my body was still enduring a lot of pain, but it was down somewhere around hurt instead of agony.

"That's so much better already. Thanks."

"I'll send you my bill." She stood, taking one of those old-fashioned black doctor bags with her as she moved across the room to talk with Victor, who sat with Maeve, Hayden, and Jamar on the other set of couches.

It was an odd mix in the room as the Hounds and the Authority felt each other out. I couldn't think of two more suspicious groups of people, but the general atmosphere was that of friends and business acquaintances getting together to catch up.

Jack had even started a card game with Joshua, Carl, La, and Bea, who caught me looking and gave me a smile.

The Georgia sisters were curled up on bunks against the far wall, their hair wet, like they'd had a chance to use the shower. Sunny was sitting on a stool in the kitchen, wearing one of Davy's old shirts and a pair of sweatpants, her hair wet and a hell of a bruise blooming against the milky white of her skin. She sipped from a mug, watching Davy make a grilled cheese sandwich like she'd just discovered someone she never wanted to look away from.

Shame and Terric were not in the poker game as I would have expected, but were both asleep on couches, one bruised, finger-burned arm over their eyes, one foot on the floor. They even both snored softly in the same rhythm. Shame had a blanket pulled over his hips and chest. It was amazing that none of the Hounds seemed curious about the crystal in his chest, or more likely, they just couldn't sense it.

The elevator pinged, and I glanced over.

Grant, the owner of Get Mugged, walked through the door, two coffee carriers in his hands and two bags filled with scones.

"Espresso, mocha, latte, and raspberry sweet-cream scones," he called out. "Help yourself, everyone." He plunked the goodies down on the counter in the kitchen, gave me a wag of his finger, and I raised my hand in a wan hello. He probably would have strolled on over to me in his cowboy boots if Davy and Sunny hadn't caught his attention and started a conversation with him.

No, I had no idea what to do with my nice, nosy, non-magical buddy being here among the Hounds and secret magic users, but hey, he brought coffee, and anyone who brought coffee, especially Get Mugged's coffee, was okay by me.

I knew there used to be Hounds who worked for the Authority. Back when Mikhail was the head, before he had died. I didn't think things were better with the two groups being separate. Yes, there was the whole secret-society stuff, but a lot of the Hounds had worked for Stotts, and never gone around telling people there was a secret police force that investigated magical crime. They could be trusted, if not with all the truth, certainly with some of the truth.

I thought of Grant as that kind of person too.

My mind chased the possibilities of Hounds and coffee shop owners and magic for a while and finally ended on Mikhail. And I remembered my dad had told me—maybe in a dream?—that Sedra had killed Mikhail. I wondered if the Authority knew that. I would ask about it, but not yet. Not here. Right now I wanted food and a shower, and some kind of assurance that the Veiled weren't going to break out of the Lock my dad had set.

Which meant I needed to talk to Victor, Maeve, or Hayden.

I took a deep breath, getting ready to stand.

"Where are you going?" Zay's eyes were closed, his long legs stretched out, heels resting on a footstool.

"Business. Coffee. Food. Shower. In that order."

He grunted but didn't move. Frankly, I didn't know how he was still awake. I stood, caught a glimpse of Grant playing cards. He had settled down next to Nik, and the two of them were laughing. He must have felt me looking at him. He glanced up, gave me a wink.

Huh. Maybe there was more than friendships being made today.

I walked over to Victor and Maeve. Everything hurt, even the bottoms of my feet, but nothing was broken, and hey, in the good-news department, I hadn't lost any memories after a major magic tussle.

Go, me. Maybe I was getting good at this secret magic thing.

"How's it going?" I asked. I wanted to sit, but the next time I sat, I wasn't going to get up for days.

"Good," Jamar said. "Want some privacy?"

Oh yeah, Hounds. They were perceptive like that.

"If you don't mind."

He smiled and pushed his glasses back on his nose. "Not a problem with me, bossman." He stood. "Pleasure meeting you all." He walked off and gave me an approving nod. I had no idea why.

"How are you doing, Allie?" Maeve asked.

"I'm okay, I think. Are we good?"

"The inn will stay closed," Maeve said. "The spell locking it down is . . . " She frowned. "Remarkable. Especially for who cast it. That kind of spell is a variation of Hold. When it was being used, many years ago, it was called Cherish. The magic is organic, much like the roots of a tree, made of both light and dark magic, and will cling and hold any organic thing in a state of stasis until the Cancel spell is worked. We have security in place to let us know if any outside, or inside, force tampers with it."

"There are some things we need to talk to you about," Victor said so quietly I almost couldn't hear him. I was positive the other Hounds couldn't hear him either. "Jingo, Sedra, Leander, and Isabelle. I'll want to talk to your father. But first we all need some rest." That, he said louder.

He was good at this.

"The gates?" I asked.

"That's the good news," Hayden said, surprising me that he too, could keep his voice below Hound notice. "There hasn't been a hint of a gate opening. We think the recent events put a plug in that for the time being."

I stood there nodding. We weren't out of the woods. There were a lot of unanswered questions about the solid Veiled, Jingo, Sedra, and how my dad knew that was Leander sending the Veiled to kill us. But for right now, this minute, we could rest.

I liked the sound of that.

"Are you staying? You're welcome to," I said. "I own the upper floor too, though there's only one mattress up there."

"No," Victor said. "We'll be going on our way. Each of us has . . . business to attend to."

"Maeve?" I asked. She lived at the inn. Her home had fallen victim to the fight. "You need a place to stay?"

"Don't worry about me. I have other property here in town, one with a lovely deep bathtub, a king-sized bed, and a change of clothes."

I looked at Hayden. He raised one eyebrow. Then smiled at Maeve. "King-sized bed, eh?"

"The couch is open," she said solemnly, even though she blushed. She was making the man court her proper-like. I highly approved.

"Looks like I'm set," he said to me. "How about you?"

I didn't know if he meant me and Zay, or me and Dad, or something else. "I'm going to take a shower, eat, and sleep. I'll keep my cell phone on, though, if you need me."

I started across the room slowly.

Victor spoke up. "Allie?"

I glanced at him.

"If you need us, for anything, never forget we are here for you. All of us. You have done amazing things to make this world a better place."

That was really sweet. And sincere. And if I didn't look away from his kind expression, I was just going to cry like a little girl.

"Wait until you see my encore," I said. Then I walked into the bathroom behind one of the only ceiling-to-floor privacy walls in the big, pleasantly crowded loft.

# Chapter Twenty-six

There were two showers in the room, spacious enough that I wasn't claustrophobic, and private enough that two people could shower and dress without seeing each other.

Where the rest of the den was sparsely decorated and leaned pretty heavily on the appeal of uneven brick walls, exposed pipes, and support beams, the bathroom was enclosed by honey-colored oak floors and basins tiled in deep green, lights set to be soothing rather than clinical among the brass, glass, and mirrors.

It was designed to be a place where a Hound could rest her weary bones.

And this was the first time I got to try it out. I tossed a towel over the shower door so I wouldn't have to search for one after my shower.

I took my time undressing, and lingered in the warm, wide fall of water. There was a bench along the shower wall, and I thought about adjusting the water and sitting there until I sucked down all the hot water in a three-mile radius, but I would probably just fall asleep and wake up when the water went cold.

I had the expected array of bruises and cuts, more burns than I remembered getting, but nothing was bleeding. That was something, right?

I heard someone enter the bathroom, which meant I had forgotten to lock the door. Smart, Beckstrom. "I'm taking a shower. Privacy, please."

The door shut. The person had not walked out.

"Don't make me hurt you," I said. "Because if you don't let me take my shower in peace, I will make you regret it."

"Speaking of regrets," Zayvion said. "I wish I would have gotten in here earlier."

I turned off the water and stood there dripping, trying to decide how I felt about him. How I felt about us.

"Well, you're too late. I'm perfectly capable of showering on my own."

Ouch. That sounded funny in my head, but came out too sharp.

I pulled the towel off the door, dried myself while trying to put my head and heart into some reasonable order. I loved the man. That had not changed.

But would it hurt him to thank me for all I'd given up for him?

I'd felt like a hollow shell since I relinquished my small magic into Mikhail's hands. There was a cold emptiness I could not fill. I didn't think I'd ever feel whole again. But I'd do it twice, if it meant Zay could live.

I opened the shower door.

"Hey, sexy," he said. He had a cup of coffee in one hand and a scone on a small plate in the other. "Thought you could use some coffee."

I smiled. "That was nice. Thanks." I took the cup, sipped, and sighed as the warmth trailed past the lump in my throat that threatened to make me cry.

I picked up the scone, took a bite, and put it back on the plate so I could carry it to the sink to set it down. I didn't want to let go of my coffee cup, so this required one-handed eating.

"Wait until you see my next trick," he said.

"Taming lions?"

"Too easy."

"Really?" I took another bite, washed it down with the coffee. "Tightrope?"

"Not dangerous enough."

I smiled again. "What, then?"

"This." He walked over to me, too thin in the black T-shirt and jeans. He licked his lips, and the look in those beautiful brown eyes made me hold my breath.

"I'm sorry," he said softly, taking my hand, scone and all, into his. "I'm sorry I said you couldn't handle yourself. That you didn't know enough. I was wrong. I'm still angry that you walked into death—death, Allie—what were you thinking?" He shook his head. "But thank you. Thank you for being my Valkyrie and saving me."

"Wow," I said. "Stuck the landing on that. Bruise your ego much?" Okay, maybe it was going to take me a couple minutes for his apology to really sink in.

"A little. Maybe a sprain. I can walk it off."

I pulled my hand out of his and put the remaining scone on the plate. I swallowed one last mouthful of coffee, then put the cup down too.

"I have a better idea." I untucked the towel wrapped around me, and let it fall to the floor.

"How about if you apologize again. Only this time naked, with me, in the shower, wet."

"Anything else?"

"And slow."

He grinned. "There's a room full of Hounds out there," he said. "They might hear us."

"I don't care who's out there. All I need, all I want, is you."

I wrapped my arms around him, sliding my hands up beneath his T-shirt, savoring the heat of his skin, the roll of his muscles as he shrugged out of his shirt. He pulled me against his body, the rhythm of his heart pounding in time with mine. Then he kissed me, gently, patiently, until the cold emptiness inside me began to fill with his warmth. He took his time to taste me, to touch me. Then we proved to each other, soul to soul, that we were inseparable, whole, and very much alive.

Read on for an exciting excerpt from
Devon Monk's next Allie Beckstrom novel,

***MAGIC ON THE HUNT***

Coming in April 2011 from Roc.

Zayvion stretched out on my bed. He lay on his side, elbow propped under his head, wide shoulders blocking most of the view of my door and apartment beyond. I faced him, covers tucked under my free arm.

We were not touching. We were not talking. We were at war.

"Two out of three?" Never go into battle without laying basic ground rules.

"Fair," he said.

Zay threw rock. I threw scissors. Damn.

"One," Zay said.

I threw paper. Zay threw rock.

"Mine." I looked into his eyes, brown and filled with that gold fire that came from using magic. And let me tell you, he'd been using it very nicely over the last three days since we'd sealed the undead magic users in Maeve's Inn. Three days we'd spent almost entirely in bed.

We both knew our rest would be short-lived. Victor had called last night and asked me to come down so he could talk to my dead dad, who was possessing my mind. He wanted to know what my dad knew about the solid Veiled sealed in the inn, and about Leander, who had followed me into this world through death's gate. I didn't want Victor digging in my head to talk to my dad about powerful undead magic users, but we were running out of time. Leander had tried to kill us all a couple days ago.

"Still with me?" Zayvion asked.

"Sorry. Tiebreaker?"

"Winning hand." He gave me a quick smile, then schooled his face into that impenetrable Zen mask.

"Think that's going to throw me?"

"What?"

"That Zen thing."

"What Zen thing?"

"You know what I'm talking about. It won't work. You are the easiest man in the world to read, Mr. Zayvion Jones."

One eyebrow quirked. "Bring it."

It was one of the most underrated survival skills in history—winning at rock, paper, scissors. Zay had thrown rock twice in a row. Would he stick with his game and throw it again? Or would he expect me to think he would and instead throw scissors to cut my paper?

I studied his eyes, his lips, his smile. Nothing.

We fist-pumped one, two, three.

I threw paper.

Zayvion Jones threw rock.

"Aha!" I crowed. "I win. I'd like my eggs scrambled, toast buttered, and coffee hot."

"You get a bowl of stale cereal."

"Oh, no. Hot breakfast was the deal."

"True." He pushed the covers down a little, getting his feet free. "What do you think about omelets?"

"I'm pro-omelet if there's cheese involved. If not, then I'm totally on scrambled's side."

"Maybe I'll make a nice, slow quiche." He leaned over me, forcing me to roll onto my back.

I made a face. "I don't like quiche."

"I can make you like quiche."

He kissed me, soft, easy. He moved down to my neck and the edge of my breast and kissed me there, his tongue catching my nipple.

"No, you can't," I gasped. Which was a lie. When he kissed me like that, I was pretty sure he could make me like anything.

"Tell me you want quiche."

"I want coffee."

"And quiche?"

"Omelets," I breathed.

He grinned. "Stubborn, stubborn, stubborn." He kissed me again.

Oh, baby. If he'd kept kissing me like that, I'd have eaten a dozen quiches.

He pulled back suddenly and sat.

"Wait. Where are you going?"

"Those omelets aren't going to cook themselves. Deal was hot breakfast." He mercilessly shucked out of the covers, pulling them off me in the process.

Cold air sent goose bumps over my bare legs and arms. "Oh, you are such a sore loser. Winner means I get to stay warm." I tugged the covers back over my shoulders.

"I'm not a sore loser. I let you win."

"You did not."

"Throwing rock three times in a row? Yes, I did. You make your eggs too runny."

"I cannot believe you are critiquing my kitchen skills in my own home."

"Not your skills. Just your eggs." He stood up. "Well, now. Since you're awake, how about winner sets the table?"

"Winner doesn't want a formal breakfast."

He strode out of the room wearing nothing but his boxers and the fine skin he'd been born with, though he grabbed a T-shirt from the dresser top.

"Not feeding it to you in bed," he called back, "again."

I smiled and pulled the covers over me, snuggling down. "Didn't want you to." Okay, that was a lie too. But he was right. It was probably time to start behaving like regular people instead of honeymooners.

I took a minute to stretch out and hog the bed all to myself. Zay's half was still warm and smelled of his cologne. I closed my eyes and savored the far-too-uncommon sensation of not hurting, not worrying, and not running for my life.

Things were good. Right here, right this minute. It felt good to be happy.

Yesterday, the higher members of the Authority—Victor, Maeve, and Hayden—had broken the magical lock on the inn my dad had left there. They had transported the undead magic users—Veiled who had used the disks my dad invented to reclaim bodies—to the secret prison the Authority used to deal with magic users who broke the law. Zay had been angry he hadn't been asked to help. Shame, the only one of us who they had asked go along, didn't want to talk about it afterward. He'd said they were still alive, but held in a prison they'd never break out of.

I was actually glad I hadn't had to face those people again. They had died once, and, as far as I was concerned, they had no right to be living again—especially when they had been bent on killing me and my friends.

The sizzle of bacon hitting the pan made me smile, and then the salt and maple of the bacon were joined by the rich, almost-chocolate scent of fresh-brewed coffee.

I knew I should get out of bed. If not to set the table, maybe to harass Zay while he cooked. But the bed felt too good to leave behind. Just five minutes more.

I woke to the sound of my front door opening.

We weren't expecting anyone. Maybe Shame had decided to drop in. I heard voices. Two. Zay and a man I couldn't quite place. My landlord?

I got out of bed and put my robe over my shorts and T-shirt. I strolled into the living room. Zay stood in the middle of the room, his back toward me, hands up and out to the side.

It was not my landlord who had walked into my apartment.

It was Dane Lannister, Sedra's bodyguard and a member of the Authority I hadn't seen since before we fought the Veiled. I'd last seen him during the wild magic storm when Jingo Jingo—my ex–death magic teacher and the current Authority betrayer—had kidnapped Sedra.

The gun in Dane's hand was new too.

He lifted the gun and aimed it at both of us.

"Don't move, don't cast magic, and don't make a sound, or I will kill you both."

Magic is fast. Bullets are faster. And neither Zay nor I was in any shape to dodge bullets.

I held very still, the thump of my own heartbeat in my ears so loud I almost couldn't hear him over the noise of it. How had he gotten in? I realized it wouldn't have been hard. Last I knew, last Zay knew, Dane was a good guy. One of the people in the Authority who was trying to make sure magic was safe for everyone. There was no reason to suspect he would be pointing a gun at us.

"We are going to do this quietly," he said. "Very quietly."

He stepped into the room and two other men I hadn't even seen followed behind him. I didn't know them, or at least I didn't think I knew them. They shut the door and it made no sound. Mute spells. They were using magic to make sure no one above or below us heard what was happening.

"I have business with you, Allison," he said. "Something I should have finished months ago. Don't—" he said to Zay, who had opened his mouth and inhaled. "Or I will shoot her between the eyes this time."

This time? My stomach twisted, and I wanted to vomit. I didn't know what other time he was talking about, but I had two bullet scars I didn't remember receiving. And even though I had no memory of him shooting me, my body, my adrenaline, made it clear he was responsible for at least one of my scars.

Zay did not move, did not twitch a muscle, did not cast magic, did not say a thing.

I tried to pick up the pieces of my brain, to think of what I could do to stop this so we didn't wind up dead. What weapons did I have? Magic. But I'd have to move to use it, and then I'd be dead.

I knew Zayvion was going over the possibilities too. I wasn't touching him, so I had no idea what he was thinking.

The two men strode across the room, silently, straight toward Zayvion. Without breaking stride, they both flicked their fingers, releasing a spell they'd been holding. I could hear more people behind us, maybe two, maybe four.

They'd used Illusions to give them time to spread out into the room. Illusions so well cast, I couldn't smell the magic they were using for it. There could have been an army of people in the room right now, with guns, knives, swords at our backs.

My skin crawled, and it was all I could do not to turn and look, but Dane's gun was unwavering. I could hear very soft footsteps on my carpet. I counted at least five people in the room. Two in front closing in fast on Zayvion, two behind doing the same, and Dane, still just on this side of the closed door, the barrel of his gun steady, finger on the trigger.

They hit Zayvion from behind. The Mute spell made sure I didn't hear what they hit him with. It might have been magic. It might have been a crowbar. He grunted and crumpled to the floor, unconscious.

"Eyes on me, Beckstrom."

I did as he said, trying to see what they were doing to Zayvion out of my peripheral vision. No luck.

"What do you want?" I asked.

I heard the ratchet of handcuffs opening, and then Zay was dragged to the far corner of my living room toward the radiator.

I chanced a look over my shoulder.

"Your attention, Allison," Dane said, "or I will shoot you. You don't have to be standing for what I want out of you."

Zay was bleeding, out cold. Five men, not four, were handcuffing, gagging, and blindfolding him. They all had guns too. I heard the meaty thump of a boot slamming into muscle. Probably ribs. I hoped it was just ribs.

I turned back to Dane. Furious. I didn't know how, but I was going to take him down.

"What the hell do you think you're doing? Do you even know what will happen to you when the Authority finds out about this?" Buying time, really. I didn't care what he thought was going to happen. I needed a minute to figure out what I could do to him and his five friends without hurting Zay. In theory, I could have called on enough magic to burn this place to the ground. I had enough magic at my fingertips, even without the small magic I'd sacrificed in death, to do it. But I'd have to pay just as big a price as the spell I cast, and then I'd be nothing but ashes and burned bones.

I didn't have any weapons—which scared the hell out of me, and that, in turn, only made me more angry.

I was good at angry.

He motioned with the gun. "Now that Zayvion is out of the way, you have two choices: do what I tell you to do or bleed."

If I lifted my hand to cast magic, I'd be on the ground bleeding. And I did not want to fall to the floor with six angry armed men in the room.

"All right," I said. "What do you want?"

*Dad?* I thought. I knew he was still there, still in my mind. But he had been silent for three days. Either he was too weak to help, or he was hiding from Dane. I didn't think Dane knew my dad was in my head.

No, he had to know. I'd been trying to convince everyone in the Authority my dad had been in my head for months now. Great.

"You are a problem," Dane said. "And the easiest way to get rid of a problem is to kill it. Simple, efficient, gone. A gun to the back of the head, a knife through the spine, magic to boil your blood, crush your skull, stop your heart. The kind of death we, Greyson and I, gave your father. The kind of death I will give you. But first, I want to know where Daniel is keeping Sedra."

Holy crap. I knew Greyson, along with James Hoskil, had been a part of my dad's murder, but I didn't know who else had been involved—had no idea Dane had been involved.

"My dad's dead," I said, anger steadying my voice. "He's not keeping Sedra anywhere. Jingo Jingo has her."

"A technicality. Jingo is working for your father. Carrying out what, I admit, is a very thorough plan to hold Sedra hostage and use her as a sacrifice to bring Mikhail back into power. I don't know what Daniel plans to get out of that. And I don't care. Tell me where she is."

"I don't know. Dad never told me his plans."

"Oh, he told you. You may not remember it." He paced toward me. "Daniel was paranoid about how much information any one person should be allowed to access. But not you. He told everything to you. You just don't remember."

He stopped. Not close enough for me to make a grab for his gun, but close enough I could smell the old vitamin stink of him. One sniff and a wash of fear rolled through me. I remembered that smell. That smell meant pain. Even though I was furious, a whimper filled my throat.

"The information, your father's information, is in your head," he said. "All I have to do is pull it out of you."

The men behind me were moving. I couldn't hear them, but I felt their footsteps, like a faint trembling beneath my bare feet, coming closer.

"Your father Closed you many times. Used you. He's been taking your memories away since the accident when you were five years old."

A high ringing started in my ears; my heartbeat thrummed behind it. I was breathing too fast. I didn't know if I was angry, panicked, or about to be sick. I didn't remember an accident. I didn't remember my dad Closing me.

That didn't mean those things hadn't happened.

He had to be lying. He had to be trying to knock me off my footing, to break me down so he could get me to tell him where Sedra was.

I didn't want to believe the bastard, but I knew—somehow I knew—every word was the truth.

His eyebrows lifted. "You didn't know, did you?" He shook his head. "He never even trusted you with that much. Isn't that sad? And now he's in there, isn't he? Filling up the holes in you he's been making for himself all these years. Taking up the room he's carved out in you."

"I told you I don't know where Sedra is," I said. "We're all looking for her. If you'd been here the last few weeks, you'd know that. Where have you been? Why haven't you been helping us look for her?"

"I know who my allies are." He lifted the gun slightly, aiming at my head. "Tell your father I want to talk to him."